Also by Nalini Singh

Guild Hunter Series
Angels' Blood
Archangel's Kiss

Psy-Changeling Series
Slave to Sensation
Visions of Heat
Caressed by Ice
Mine to Possess
Hostage to Pleasure
Branded by Fire
Blaze of Memory

Angels' Blood

NALINI SINGH

First published in Great Britain in 2010 by
Gollancz
An imprint of the Orion Publishing Group
Orion House, 5 Upper St Martin's Lane, London WC2H 9EA
An Hachette UK Company

A CIP catalogue record for this book is available
from the British Library

Printed in Great Britain by
Clays Ltd, St Ives plc

www.nalinisingh.com

www.orionbooks.co.uk

The Orion Publishing Group's policy is to use papers that are
natural, renewable and recyclable products and made from wood
grown in sustainable forests. The logging and manufacturing
processes are expected to conform to the environmental regulations
of the country of origin.

Angels' Blood

For the real Ashwini,
who is definitely not all kinds of crazy
(except when I drive her to it).
Best friends – and sisters –
don't come any better than this.

1

When Elena told people she was a vampire hunter, their first reaction was an inevitable gasp, followed by, "You go around sticking those sharp stakes in their evil putrid hearts?"

Okay, maybe the actual words varied but the feel was the same. It made her want to track down and exterminate the idiot fifteenth-century storyteller who'd made up that tale in the first place. Of course, the vampires had probably already taken care of it—after the first few of them ended up in whatever passed for an emergency room back then.

Elena didn't stake vampires. She tracked them, bagged them, and returned them to their masters—the angels. Some people called her kind bounty hunters, but according to her Guild card, she was "Licensed to Hunt Vampires & Assorted Others"—which made her a vampire hunter, with the attendant benefits, including hazard pay. That pay was very healthy. It had to be to compensate for the fact that hunters occasionally had their jugulars torn open.

Still, Elena decided she needed a pay raise after her calf muscle started protesting. She'd been stuck in a cramped corner of an alley in the Bronx for the past two hours, a too tall female with pale, almost white hair and silver eyes. The hair was a pain in the butt. According to her sometimes friend Ransom, she might as well wear a sign announcing her presence. Since dyes wouldn't work on it for longer than two minutes, Elena had a great collection of knit caps.

She was tempted to pull her current one down over her nose, but had a feeling that would only intensify the malodorous "ambience" of this dank piece of New York City. That led her to thinking about the virtues of nose plugs—

Something rustled behind her.

She swiveled . . . to come face-to-face with a stalking cat, its eyes reflecting silver in the darkness. Satisfied the animal was what it seemed, she returned her attention to the sidewalk, wondering if her eyes shone as freakily as that cat's. It was a good thing she'd inherited dark gold skin from her Moroccan grandmother or she'd have resembled a ghost.

"Where the hell are you?" she muttered, reaching down to rub at her calf. This vamp had led her on a merry chase—through his own sheer stupidity. He didn't know what he was doing, which made him a little hard to second-guess.

Ransom had once asked her if it bothered her to round up helpless vampires and drag their sorry asses back to a life of virtual slavery. He'd been laughing hysterically at the time. No, it didn't bother her. Just like it didn't bother him. The vamps chose that slavery—of a hundred years' duration—the instant they petitioned an angel to Make them almost-immortal. If they had stayed human, if they had gone to their graves in peace, then they wouldn't have found themselves bound by a contract signed in blood. And while the angels did take advantage of their position, a contract was a contract.

A flash of light in the street.

Bingo!

There was the target, chomping away on a cigar and boasting on his cell phone about how he was a Made man now and no prissy angel was going to tell him what to do. Even with several feet of distance between them, she could smell the sweat pooling under his armpits. The vampirism hadn't yet advanced enough to melt away the fat he wore like a spare coat, and he thought he could run out on a contract with an angel?

Idiot.

Walking out, she pulled off her knit cap and stuffed it in her back pocket. Her hair tumbled around her shoulders in a soft cloud, distinctive and bright. It wasn't a risk. Not tonight. She might have been well known by the locals, but this vampire had a distinct Australian accent. He'd recently arrived from Sydney—and his master wanted him back in that city, pronto.

"Got a light?"

The vampire jumped and dropped his phone. Elena barely stopped herself from rolling her eyes. He wasn't even fully formed—the canines he'd flashed in surprise were only baby teeth. No wonder his master was pissed. The bonehead had to have scuttled after not much more than a year or so of service.

"Sorry," she said with a smile as he retrieved the phone and weighed her up. She knew what he saw. A lone female with bimbo blonde hair, dressed in black leather jeans and a form-fitting long-sleeved top in the same color, no visible weapons.

Because he was young and stupid, the image made him relax. "Sure, sweet thang." He reached into his pocket for the lighter.

That was when Elena leaned forward, one hand sweeping behind her back and under her top. "Tut-tut. Mr. Ebose is very disappointed in you." She'd retrieved and locked the necklet into place before he processed the meaning of that huskily spoken censure. His eyes bulged red, but instead of screaming, he stood silently in place. A hunter's necklet had a way of freezing a man. Fear was a live thing skittering across his face.

She'd have felt sorry for him if she hadn't known that he'd torn out four human throats in the course of his escape. That was not acceptable. The angels protected their get but even they had limits—Mr. Ebose had authorized the use of any and all force necessary on this one.

Now, she let that knowledge bleed into the open, let the vampire see her willingness to hurt him. His face lost what color he'd managed to retain. She smiled. "Follow me."

He trotted behind her like an obedient puppy. Damn, but she loved the necklets. Her best friend, Sara, liked to shoot the targets with honest-to-god arrows—the arrowheads were doctored to contain the same control chip that made the necklets so effective. The instant it touched skin, the chip apparently emitted some kind of an electromagnetic field that temporarily short-circuited a vampire's neural processes, leaving the target open to suggestion. Elena didn't know the science of it all, but she knew the limits and advantages of her chosen method of capture.

Yeah, she did have to get closer to her targets than Sara, but conversely, there was no chance of missing and hitting an innocent bystander. Which Sara had once done. It had cost her half a year's pay to settle the lawsuit. Lips curving at the thought of how pissed her friend had been at not making the shot, Elena opened the passenger-side door of the car she'd parked nearby. "Inside."

The baby vamp squeezed in his girth with effort.

Making sure he was belted in, she called Mr. Ebose's head of security. "I've got him."

The voice at the other end instructed her to drop the package off at a private airstrip.

Unsurprised by the chosen location, she hung up and began driving. In silence. It would've been a bit redundant to try to make conversation, as the vamp had lost the ability to speak the instant she clamped him. The muting was a side effect of the neural straitjacket created by the necklet. Before the inception of the chip-embedded devices, vampire hunting had been something of a suicidal career choice, as even the babiest vamps had the ability to tear a human to pieces. Of course, according to the latest research, vampire hunters weren't quite human, but they were close enough.

Arriving at the airstrip, she cleared security and was directed onto the tarmac. The team charged with escorting the vampire back to Sydney was waiting beside a sleek private jet. Elena took the captured male to them and they immediately nodded at her to go on in. She had to stow the package personally, as they didn't have the license to handle him at this point in the journey. Clearly, Mr. Ebose had good lawyers. He wasn't taking any chances that could lead to him being brought up on charges by the Vampire Protection Authority.

Not that the VPA had ever managed to make cruelty allegations stick. All the angels had to do was display a couple of photos of humans with their throats torn out, and the jury was ready not only to acquit, but to give them a medal in the process.

Elena escorted the vamp up the steps and to the large open crate at the back of the passenger hold. "Inside."

He walked in then turned to face her, terror pouring off him in a wave that had already soaked through his shirt.

"Sorry, bud. You killed three women and one old man. That tilts the pity slate way over in the wrong direction." Slamming the door on him, she padlocked it. The necklet would go with him to Sydney, from there it'd be returned directly to the Guild, as per the agreed protocol with all chip-embedded devices. "He's ready to go, boys."

The head guard—all four had followed her inside—looked her up and down with eyes the startling shade of robin's eggs. "No injuries. Impressive." He handed over an envelope. "The transfer has been made to your Guild account, as agreed."

Elena checked the confirmation slip. Her eyebrows rose. "Mr. Ebose has been generous."

"A bonus for early and unharmed capture of the target. Mr. Ebose has plans for him. Old Jerry was his favorite secretary."

Elena winced. The problem with being basically immortal was that you could have a lot of things done to you and not die. She'd once seen a vampire who'd had every one of his limbs amputated . . . without anesthetic. By the time the Guild rescue squad liberated him from the clutches of the hate group that had kidnapped him, he'd been beyond reason or coherence. But there had been a video. That was how they knew the tortured man had remained conscious throughout. She bet the angels didn't show that video to the petitioners who came in their droves, hoping to be Made.

Then again, maybe they did.

The angels only Made about a thousand vamps a year. And from what Elena had seen, the hopeful outnumbered that by the *hundreds* of thousands. She had no idea why. As far as she was concerned, the cost of immortality was far too high. Better to live free and turn to dust when the time came than end up locked in a wooden box while you waited for your master to decide your fate.

Distaste an acrid film on her tongue, she slid both the confirmation slip and the envelope into a pants pocket. "Please thank Mr. Ebose for his generosity."

The bodyguard inclined his head and she glimpsed the edges of what she guessed to be a raven tattooed on his shaved head. He was too tall to see for sure but the others were shorter and all bore that unique mark.

"I see you're unattached." He glanced pointedly at the plain silver hoops in her ears. No married gold. No entangled amber. But she didn't make the mistake of assuming he wanted a date. The guards of the Wing Brotherhood practiced celibacy while on the job. Since the punishment for failure was the removal of a body part—Elena had never quite managed to discover which—she figured she wasn't temptation enough.

"Yes. I'm free workwise, too." She preferred to complete one job before lining up the next. There were always more vamps to chase down. "Mr. Ebose want me to track another renegade?"

"No. He has a friend who requires your services." The guard passed over a second envelope, this one sealed. "The appointment is for eight a.m. tomorrow. Please ensure you attend—it's been cleared with your Guild, the deposit paid."

If the Guild had signed off, that meant it was a legitimate hunt. "Sure. Where's the meet?"

"Manhattan."

Elena's soul went ice cold. For only one angel would that single word suffice as enough of a direction. Even the angels had a pecking order and she knew very well who was at the top. But, fast as it had swept over her, the fear passed. Mr. Ebose, while powerful, was hardly likely to know an archangel, one of the Cadre of Ten that decided who would be Made and who would do the Making.

"Is there a problem?"

Her head snapped up at the guard's quiet comment. "No, of course not." She made a show of checking her watch. "I better be going. Please give my regards to Mr. Ebose." With that, she exited the lush confines of the private jet and the pungent fear-stink of the cargo.

She'd never been able to figure out why so many morons got Made. Perhaps, she thought, they went in okay but turned into pricks after a few years of drinking blood. Who knew what the hell that stuff did to your brain. But that theory didn't explain her latest catch—he was two years old *max*.

Shrugging, she got into the car. And because she wanted to tear open the sealed envelope with her teeth, she waited until she was home in her beautiful nest of an apartment in lower Manhattan. Given how much time they spent chasing shit, most hunters tended to make their homes into havens. Elena was no exception.

Entering, she kicked off her boots and headed toward the luxurious bath and shower unit. Usually, she made a ritual out of washing off the grime and slathering on the creams and perfumes she collected. Ransom thought her girly tendencies the funniest thing ever, constantly teased her over them, but the last time he'd opened his big mouth, she'd got her own back by pointing out that his long black hair sure did look well conditioned.

However, tonight she had neither the patience nor the

inclination to pamper herself. Stripping, she made quick work of scrubbing away the reek of shit-scared vampire before slipping into a pair of cotton pajamas and running a brush through her hair as she put on some coffee. Soon as it was done, she took a full mug to the coffee table, set it down carefully on a coaster . . . then gave in to the demands of her rabid curiosity and tore open the envelope in one second flat.

The paper was thick, the watermark elegant . . . and the name at the bottom of the page terrifying enough to make her want to pack her bags and run. To the farthest, tiniest hole she could find.

Disbelieving, she ran her eyes over the page a second time. The words hadn't changed.

I would be pleased if you would join me for breakfast.
8 a.m.

Raphael

There was no address but she had no need of it. She looked up, able to see the light-filled column of the city's Archangel Tower from the huge plate-glass window that had made this apartment so ridiculously expensive . . . and attractive. Being able to sit and watch the angels take wing from the high balconies of the Tower was her guiltiest pleasure.

At night, they appeared as soft, dark shadows. But in the daytime, their wings shimmered bright in the sun, their movements incredibly graceful. They came and went throughout the day, but sometimes she saw them simply sitting, high up on those balconies, their legs hanging over the sides. The younger angels, she'd guessed, though youth was a relative term.

Even knowing that most of them were decades older than she was, the sight always made her smile. It was the one and only time she'd ever glimpsed them acting in a way that could be described as normal. Usually, they were coolly remote, so far from the common humdrum of humanity as to be beyond their understanding.

Tomorrow she, too, was going to be up there in that tower of light and glass. But it wasn't one of those younger maybe-approachable angels that she had to meet. No, tomorrow she was going to be sitting across from the archangel himself.

Raphael.

Elena bent over, sick to her stomach.

2

The first thing she did after recovering from the compulsion to throw up was call the Guild. "I need to speak to Sara," she told the receptionist.

"I'm sorry. The director has left the office."

Hanging up, Elena punched in the number to Sara's home line.

The other woman picked up after barely half a ring. "Now, how did I know I was going to hear from you today?"

Elena's hand clenched on the phone. "Sara, please tell me I'm having a delusion and you did not sign me up to work for an archangel."

"Er . . . um . . ." Sara Haziz, Guild Director for the entire U.S. of A., and all-around tough-ass, suddenly sounded more like a nervous teenage girl. "Hell, Ellie, it's not like I could say no."

"What would he have done—killed you?"

"Probably," Sara muttered. "His vampire lackey made it very clear that he wanted you. And that *he* is not used to being denied."

"You tried to say no?"

"I am your best friend. Gimme a little credit, here."

Slumping into the sofa cushions, Elena stared out at the Tower. "What's the job?

"I don't know." Sara began to make soft cooing sounds. "Don't worry—I'm not wasting my breath in a futile attempt to calm you down. The baby's awake. Aren't you, sweetie pie?" Kissing noises filled the air.

Elena still couldn't believe Sara had gone and tied the knot. And had a baby to boot. "How's Mini Me?" Sara had named her daughter Zoe Elena. Damn if Elena hadn't sniffled like a baby herself when she found out. "Hope she's giving you hell."

"She loves her mommy." More kissing noises. "And she said to tell you she's gonna Mini Me you after she grows a few more feet. She and Slayer are a crack team."

Elena laughed at the mention of the monster dog that lived to slobber on unsuspecting people. "Where's your beloved? I thought Deacon liked doing the baby stuff."

"He does." Sara's smile was apparent even through the telephone line and it made something inside Elena clench in the most vicious of ways. It wasn't that she begrudged Sara her happiness, or that she wanted Deacon. No, it was something far deeper, a sense of time slipping through her fingers.

Over the past year, it had become increasingly obvious that her friends were moving on to the next stages of their lives, while she remained in limbo, a twenty-eight-year-old vampire hunter with no strings, no attachments. Sara had put down her bow and arrow—except for the odd urgent hunt— and taken on the most critical desk job in the Guild. Her lethally skilled tracker of a husband had gone into the business of manufacturing hunter tools (and changing diapers), with a slow grin that all but shouted contentment. Hell, even Ransom had had the same bed partner for the past two months.

"Hey, Ellie, you gone to sleep?" Sara asked over the baby's happy squeals. "Having dreams about your archangel?"

"More like nightmares," she muttered, squinting as she

caught sight of an angel coming to land on the Tower roof. Her heart skipped a beat as his wings flared out to slow his descent. "You never finished telling me about Deacon. Why isn't he on baby duty?"

"He's gone to the store with Slayer to pick up some double-chocolate very-berry ice cream. I told him the cravings stick around for a while after birth."

Sara's delight in fooling her husband should have made Elena laugh, but she was too aware of the fear crawling up her spine. "Sara, did the vampire give you any hint of why he asked for me?"

"Sure. He said Raphael wanted the best."

"I'm the best," Elena muttered the next morning as she got out of the taxi in front of the magnificent creation that was Archangel Tower. "I'm the best."

"Hey, lady, you gonna pay me or just talk to yourself?"

"What? Oh." Pulling out a twenty-dollar note, she bent down and crushed it into the cabbie's hand. "Keep the change."

His scowl turned into a grin. "Thanks! What, you got a big hunt coming on?"

Elena didn't ask how he'd pegged her for a hunter. "No. But I do have a high chance of meeting a horrible death within the next few hours. Might as well do something good and up my shot at getting into heaven."

The cabbie thought she was a riot. He was still laughing as he drove off, leaving her standing on the very edge of the wide path that led up to the Tower entrance. The unusually bright morning sunlight glared off the white stone of the path, sharp enough to cut. Pulling off her shades from where she'd hung them—in the vee of her shirt—she placed them gratefully over her tired, sleep-deprived eyes. Now that she was no longer in danger of being blinded, she saw the shadows she'd missed earlier. Of course she'd known they were there—sight wasn't her primary sense when it came to vampires.

Several of them stood along the sides of the Tower but there were at least ten others hidden or walking around in the well-cared-for shrubbery outside. All were dressed in dark suits teamed with white shirts, their hair cut in the sleek, perfect lines patented by FBI agents. Black shades and discreet earpieces finished off the secret-agent effect.

But internal commentary aside, Elena knew these vampires were nothing like the one she'd tagged last night. These guys had been around a long time. Their intense scent—dark but not unpleasant—when added to the fact that they were guarding Archangel Tower, told her they were both smart and extremely dangerous. As she watched, two of them moved out of the shrubbery and into the path of direct sunlight.

Neither burst into flames.

Such a violent reaction to sunlight—another myth embraced by the moviemakers—would have made her job a heck of a lot easier. All she'd have had to do was wait until they went down for the count. But no, most vampires were perfectly capable of walking around twenty-four hours a day. The few that suffered from light sensitivity still didn't "die" when the sun came up. They simply found shade. "And you're procrastinating—soon you'll be composing an ode to the gardens," she muttered under her breath. "You're a professional. You're the best. You can do this."

Taking a deep breath and trying not to think about the angels she knew were flying overhead, she began walking toward the entrance. Nobody paid her any overt attention, but when she finally reached the door, the vampire on duty bowed his head in a small nod and opened it for her. "Straight through to the reception desk."

Elena blinked and removed her sunglasses. "Don't you want to check my ID?"

"You're expected."

The doorvamp's insidiously seductive scent—an unusual

trait thought to be an evolutionary adaptation against the hunters' tracking abilities—swirled around her in a sinister caress as she thanked him and walked through.

The air-conditioned lobby was a seemingly endless space dominated by deep gray marble shot through with discreet veins of gold. As an example of wealth, good taste, and subtle intimidation, it took first prize. She was suddenly very glad she'd traded in her usual jeans and T-shirt combo for a pair of tailored black pants and a crisp white shirt. She'd even tamed her slithery hair into a French twist and stuffed her feet into high heels.

Those heels hit the marble with sharp businesslike sounds as she crossed the lobby. As she walked, she noted everything around her, from the number of vampire guards, to the exquisite—though slightly odd—flower arrangements, to the fact that the receptionist was a very, very, very old vampire . . . with the face and body of a well-maintained thirty-year-old.

"Ms. Deveraux, I'm Suhani." The receptionist rose with a smile and walked out from behind her curving desk. It, too, was stone, but of a jet so well polished, it reflected everything with mirror perfection. "I'm so pleased to meet you."

Elena shook the woman's hand, sensing the flow of fresh blood, the beat of a racing heart. It was on the tip of her tongue to ask Suhani who it was that she'd breakfasted on—the blood was unusually potent—but she caught the impulse before it could get her into trouble. "Thank you."

Suhani smiled and, to Elena's eyes, it was a smile filled with old knowledge, with centuries of experience. "You must've made good time." She glanced at her watch. "It's only seven forty-five."

"The traffic was light." And she hadn't wanted to start this meeting out on the wrong foot. "Am I too early?"

"No. He's waiting for you." The smile faded, to be replaced by a slightly disappointed expression. "I thought you'd be . . . scarier."

"Don't tell me you watch *Hunter's Prey*?" The disgusted comment was out before she could stop it.

Suhani gave her a disconcertingly human grin. "Guilty, I'm afraid. The show is just so entertaining. And S. R. Stoker— the producer—is a former vampire hunter."

Yeah, and she was the Tooth Fairy. "Let me guess, you expected me to carry a big sword and have eyes that glow red?" Elena shook her head. "You're a vampire. You know none of that is true."

Suhani's expression slipped to reveal a cooler darkness. "You sound very certain of my vampirism. Most people never guess."

Elena decided now was not the time for a lesson in hunter biology. "I've had a lot of experience." She shrugged, as if it didn't matter. "Shall we go on up?"

Suhani was suddenly, and, it seemed, honestly, flustered. "Oh, I'm so sorry. I've kept you waiting. Please follow me."

"Don't worry. It was only a minute." And she was grateful for the chance it had given her to settle her thoughts. If this elegant but sensitive vampire could deal with Raphael, then so could she. "What's he like?"

Suhani's stride faltered for a second before she caught herself. "He is . . . an archangel." The awe in her voice was mixed with equal parts fear.

Elena's confidence took a nosedive. "Do you see him often?"

"No, why should I?" The receptionist gave her a puzzled smile. "He has no need to pass through the lobby. He can fly."

Elena could've slapped herself. "Right." She came to a standstill in front of the elevator doors. "Thank you."

"You're welcome." Suhani began to key in a security code on the touch screen mounted on a small plinth beside the elevator. "This car will take you straight up to the roof."

Elena paused. "The roof?"

"He'll meet you there."

Startled, but knowing a delay would gain her nothing, Elena entered the large, mirror-paneled car and turned to face Suhani. As the doors shut, she was uncomfortably reminded of the vampire she'd locked into a crate less than twelve hours ago. Now she knew what it felt like to be on the other side. If she hadn't been so certain she was under surveillance, she might have given in to the urge to drop her professional facade and start pacing like a crazy woman.

Or a rat stuck in a maze.

The elevator began to rise in a smooth movement that shrieked money. The glowing numerals on the LCD panel ticked over in a stomach-curdling sequence. She decided to stop counting after the car passed floor number seventy-five. Instead, she made use of the mirrors to ostensibly smooth down the twisted strap of her purse . . . while actually ensuring her weapons remained well hidden.

No one had ordered her to come in unarmed.

The elevator whispered to a smooth stop. The doors opened. Not giving herself a chance to hesitate, she headed out and into a small glass enclosure. It was immediately obvious that the glass cage was nothing more than the shell that housed the elevator. The roof lay beyond . . . and it had not even a token railing to stop an accidental plunge.

The archangel clearly didn't believe in putting his guests at ease.

But Elena wouldn't call him a bad host—a table set with croissants, coffee, and orange juice sat in solitary splendor in the middle of the wide open space. Another look and she saw that the roof wasn't bare concrete. It had been paved with dark gray tiles that glimmered silver under the sun's rays. The tiles were beautiful and unquestionably expensive. An extravagant waste, she thought, then realized that to a being with wings, a roof was assuredly not a useless space.

Raphael was nowhere to be seen.

Putting her hand on the doorknob, she pulled open the glass door and walked out. To her relief, the tiles proved to have a rough surface—the wind was soft right now but she knew that this high, it could turn cutting without warning, and heels weren't exactly stable at the best of times. She wondered if the tablecloth was bolted to the table. Otherwise, it would probably fly off and take the food with it sooner rather than later.

Then again, that might be a good thing. Nerves didn't make for easy digestion.

Leaving her purse on the table, she walked carefully to the nearest edge . . . and looked down. Exhilaration raced through her at the incredible view of angels flying in and out of the Tower. They seemed almost close enough to touch, the temptation of their powerful wings a siren song.

"Careful." The word was soft, the tone amused.

She didn't jump, having felt the push of wind engendered by his near-silent landing. "Would they catch me if I fell?" she asked, without looking his way.

"If they were in the mood for it." He came to stand beside her, his wings filling her peripheral vision. "You don't suffer from vertigo."

"Never have," she admitted, so terrified of the sheer power of him that she sounded absolutely normal. It was either that or start screaming. "I've never been up this high before."

"What do you think?"

She took a deep breath and a step backward before turning to face him. The impact hit her like a physical blow. He was . . . "Beautiful." Eyes of such pure undiluted blue it was as if some heavenly artist had crushed sapphires into his paints and then colored in the irises with the finest of brushes.

She was still reeling from the visual shock when a sudden wind swept across the rooftop, lifting up strands of his black hair. But black was too tame a word for it. It was so pure it held echoes of the night, vivid and passionate. Cut in careless layers that stopped at the nape of his neck, it bared the sharp angles of his face and made her fingers curl with the urge to stroke.

Yes, he was beautiful, but it was the beauty of a warrior or a conqueror. This man had power stamped on every inch of his skin, every piece of his flesh. And that was before she took in the exquisite perfection of his wings. The feathers were a soft white and appeared dusted with gold. But when she concentrated, she saw the truth—each individual filament of each individual feather bore a golden tip.

"Yes, it's beautiful up here," he said, breaking into her fascination.

She blinked, then felt her face color, having no idea of how much time had passed. "Yes."

His smile bore a hint of mockery, of male satisfaction . . . and of pure, lethal focus. "Let us have breakfast and talk."

Furious at having allowed herself to be blindsided by his physical beauty, she bit the inside of her cheek in reprimand. She wasn't going to fall into the same trap again. Raphael clearly knew how striking he was, *and* he knew the effect it had on unsuspecting mortals. Which made him an arrogant SOB she should have no trouble resisting.

Pulling out a chair, he waited. She halted a foot away, very conscious of his height and strength. She wasn't used to feeling small. Or weak. That he could cause her to experience either sensation—and without any apparent effort—made her angry enough to chance reprisal. "I'm not comfortable with anyone standing behind me."

A spark of surprise in those blue, blue eyes. "Shouldn't it be me who fears a knife in the back? You're the one carrying concealed weapons."

The fact that he'd guessed at her weapons meant nothing. A hunter was always armed. "The difference is, I'll die. You won't."

With a small, amused wave of his hand, he walked to the other side of the table, his wings brushing over the squeaky clean tiles to leave behind a shimmering trail of white gold. She was certain he'd done it on purpose. Angels didn't always shed angel dust. When they did, it was immediately collected up by mortals and vampires alike. The price for a speck of the bright stuff was more than that for a flawlessly cut diamond.

But if Raphael thought she was going to get down on her knees and scrabble, he had another think coming.

"You don't fear me," he said now.

She wasn't stupid enough to lie. "I'm petrified. But I figure you didn't make me come all this way just so you could push me off the roof."

His mouth curved, as if she'd said something funny. "Take a seat, Elena." Her name sounded different on his lips. A binding. As if by speaking it, he'd gained power over her. "Like you said, I have no plans to kill you. Not today."

She sat with the elevator cubicle at her back, aware of him waiting with old-world chivalry until she'd done so. His wings draped gracefully over the specially designed chair back as he followed suit. "How old are you?" she found herself asking before she could nip her curiosity in the bud.

He raised a perfectly arched eyebrow. "Do you have no sense of self-preservation?" It was a casual comment but she heard the steel beneath the surface.

Chill fingers trailed over her spine. "Some would say not—I *am* a vampire hunter."

Something dark and exquisitely dangerous moved in the crystalline depths of those eyes no human would ever have. "A born hunter, not a trained one."

"Yes."

"How many vampires have you captured or killed?"

"You know the number. It's why I'm sitting here."

Another gust of wind whipped across the roof, this one strong enough to rattle the cups and pull strands of hair from her twist. She didn't try to pin them back, keeping her full attention on the archangel instead. He was watching her in turn, much as a large beast of prey might watch the rabbit it was eyeing for dinner.

"Tell me about your abilities." It was nothing less than an order, his tone a blade that whispered warning. The archangel no longer found her entertaining.

Elena refused to look away, even as she dug her fingernails into her thighs to anchor herself. "I can scent vampires, differentiate one from the pack. That's it." A useless skill—unless one was a vampire hunter. It sort of made the term "career choice" an oxymoron.

"How old does the vampire have to be for you to sense his or her presence?"

It was an odd question and one she had to pause to consider. "Well, the youngest I've tracked was two months old. And he was the outer limits. Most vamps wait at least a year before trying anything funny."

"So you've never had any contact with a younger vampire?"

Elena had no idea where he was going with this line of questioning. "Contact, sure. But not as a hunter. You're an angel—you have to know they don't exactly function well the first month or so after being Made." It was that stage in their development that continued to fuel the myth about vampires being lifeless zombies given will.

They truly were creepy in the first few weeks. Eyes wide open but with nobody home, flesh pallid and wasted, movements uncoordinated. It was why the hate groups preferred to target new vamps. Most people found it far easier to mutilate and torture someone who looked like a walking corpse than someone who could be their best friend. Or brother-in-law, in Elena's case. "That young, they can't feed themselves, much less run away."

"Nevertheless, we will do a test." The archangel picked up the glass of juice beside his plate and took a drink. "Eat."

"I'm not hungry."

He put down the glass. "It's a blood insult to refuse an archangel's table."

Elena had never before heard the term, but if it involved blood, it couldn't be anything good. "I ate before coming here." A flat-out lie. She hadn't been able to keep down much more than water, and that with effort.

"Then drink." It was an instruction so absolute, she knew he expected instant obedience.

Something snapped inside her. "Or else?"

The wind stopped. Even the clouds seemed to freeze.

Death whispered in her ear.

3

Elena's instincts were screaming at her to grab the knife in her boot, do some damage, and get the hell out, but she forced herself to stay in place. The truth was, she wouldn't make it more than two feet before Raphael broke every single bone in her body.

It was exactly what he'd done to a vampire who'd thought to betray him.

That vampire had been found in the center of Times Square. He'd still been alive. And he'd still been trying to scream—"No! Raphael, no!" But his voice had been a rasp by then, his jaw hanging on by stringlike tendons, his flesh missing in places.

Elena—out of the country on a hunt—had seen the news footage after the event. She knew the vamp had lain there in agony for three hours before being picked up by a pair of angels. Everyone in New York, hell, everyone in the country, had known he was there, but no one had dared help him, not with Raphael's mark blazing on his forehead. The archangel had wanted the punishment witnessed, wanted to remind peo-

ple of who and what he was. It had worked. Now the mere mention of his name evoked visceral fear.

But Elena wouldn't crawl, not for anyone. It was a choice she'd made the night her father had told her to get on her knees and beg, and maybe, maybe, he'd accept her back into the family.

Elena hadn't spoken to her father in a decade.

"You should have a care," Raphael said into the unnatural silence.

She didn't collapse in relief—the air continued to hang heavy with the promise of menace. "I don't like to play games."

"Learn." He settled back in his chair. "You will live a very short life if you expect only honesty."

Sensing the danger had passed—for now—she unclenched her fingers with an effort of will. The force of the blood rushing back into them was painful in its extremity. "I didn't say I expected honesty. People lie. Vampires lie. Even—" She caught herself.

"Surely you're not going to practice discretion now?" The amusement was back but it was tempered with an edge that stroked like a razor across her skin.

She looked into that perfect face and knew she'd never met a more deadly being in her life. If she displeased him, Raphael would kill her as easily as she might swat a fly. She'd be smart to remember that, no matter how the knowledge infuriated her. "You said I had to do a test?"

His wings moved slightly at that instant, drawing her attention. They truly were beautiful and she couldn't help but covet them. To be able to fly . . . what an amazing gift.

Raphael's eyes shifted to look at something over her left shoulder. "Less a test than an experiment."

She didn't twist around, had no need to. "There's a vampire behind me."

"Are you sure?" His expression remained unchanged.

She fought the urge to turn. "Yes."

He nodded. "Look."

Wondering which was worse—having her back to an enigmatic and highly unpredictable archangel, or to an unknown vampire—she hesitated. In the end, her curiosity won out. There was a distinctly satisfied expression on Raphael's face and she wanted to know what had put it there.

Shifting, she turned sideways with her whole body, the position allowing her to keep Raphael in her peripheral vision. Then she looked at the *two* . . . creatures who stood behind her. "Jesus."

"You may go." Raphael's voice was a command that awakened abject terror in the eyes of the one who looked vaguely human. The other scuttled away like the animal it was.

She watched them leave through the glass door and swallowed. "How old was . . ." She couldn't call that thing a vampire. Neither had it been human.

"Erik was Made yesterday."

"I didn't know they could walk at that age." It was an attempt to sound professional though she was creeped out to her toes.

"He had a little help." Raphael's tone made it clear that that was all the answer she was going to get. "Bernal is . . . a fraction older."

She reached for the juice she'd rejected earlier and took a drink, trying to wash away the stink that had seeped into her pores. The older vamps didn't have that ick factor. They—except for the unusual ones like the doorvamp—simply smelled of vampire, like she smelled human. But the very young ones, they had a certain rotten-cabbage/putrid-flesh smell that she always had to scrub three times over to get rid of. It was why she'd begun collecting the body washes and perfumes. After her initial contact with one of the newly Made, she'd thought she'd never get the smell out of her head.

"I didn't think a hunter would be so disturbed at the sight of the just-Made." Raphael's face appeared oddly shadowed, until she realized he'd raised his wings slightly.

Wondering if that implied focus or anger, she put down the

glass. "I'm not, not really." True enough now that that first, instinctive flash of disgust had passed. "It's the smell—like a coating of fur on your tongue. No matter how hard you scrape, you can't get it off."

Open interest showed on his face. "The feeling is that intense?"

She shivered and looked around the table for something else to take the edge off. When he pushed a cut grapefruit in her direction, she dug into it with relish. "Uh-huh." The citrus fruit's acidic juices dampened the reek a little. At least enough that she could think.

"If I asked you to track Erik, could you?"

She shivered at the memory of those almost-dead/not-quite-alive eyes. No wonder people believed those stories about vampires being the walking dead. "No. I think he's too young."

"What about Bernal?"

"He's on the bottom floor of the building right now." The barely Made vampire's odor was so noxious, it permeated the building. "In the lobby."

Golden-tipped wings spread to shadow the table as Raphael put his hands together in a slow clap. "Well done, Elena. Well done."

She looked up from the grapefruit, belatedly aware she'd just proven how good she was when she should've flubbed it and gotten out of this, whatever "this" was. Shit. But at least he'd given her some idea of the job. "Do you want me to track a rogue?"

He rose from his chair in a sudden, liquid movement. "Wait a moment."

She watched, transfixed, as he walked to the edge of the roof. He was a being of such incredible splendor that simply seeing him move made her heart squeeze. It didn't matter that she knew it was a mirage, that he was as deadly as the filleting knife she carried strapped to her thigh. No one, not even she, could deny that Raphael the Archangel was a man made to be admired. To be worshipped.

That utterly *wrong* thought snapped her out of her dazed state. Pushing back her chair, she stared hard at his back. Had he been messing with her head? Right then, he turned and she met the agonizing blue of his eyes. For a second, she thought he was answering her question. Then he looked away . . . and walked off the roof.

She jumped up. Only to sit back down, blush reddening her cheeks, when he winged upward to meet an angel she hadn't seen until that moment. *Michaela*. The female equivalent of Raphael, her beauty so intense that Elena could feel the force of it even from this distance. She had the startling realization that she was looking on at a midair meeting between two archangels.

"Sara's never going to believe this." She forgot the stench of young vampire for the moment, her attention hijacked. She'd seen photos of Michaela, but they came nowhere close to the reality of her.

The other archangel had skin the color of the most exquisite, fine milk chocolate and a shining fall of hair that cascaded to her waist in a wild mass. Her body was quintessentially female, slender and curvy at the same time, her wings a delicate bronze that shimmered against the richness of her skin. Her face . . . "Wow." Even from this distance, Michaela's face was perfection given form. Elena fancied she could see her eyes—a bright, impossible green—but knew she had to be imagining it. They were too far away.

It made little difference. The female archangel had a face that would not only stop traffic, it would cause a few pileups in the process.

Elena frowned. Despite her appreciation for Michaela's looks, she was having no trouble thinking straight. Which meant the damn arrogant blue-eyed bastard *had* been fucking with her mind. He wanted her to worship him? They'd see about that.

No one, not even an archangel, was going to turn her into a puppet.

As if he'd heard her, Raphael said something to his fellow

archangel and winged back down to the roof. His landing was a lot more showy this time. She was sure he paused to display the pattern on the inside surface of his wings. It was as if a brush dipped in gold had started at the top edge of each wing and then stroked downward, fading to white as it neared the bottom. In spite of her fury, she had to face the truth: If the devil—or an archangel—came to her and offered her wings, she might just sell him her soul.

But the angels didn't Make other angels. They only made blood-drinking vampires. Where angels came from, no one knew. Elena guessed they were born to angelic parents, though, come to think of it, she'd never actually seen a baby angel.

Her thoughts derailed again as she watched the fluid grace of Raphael's walk, so seductive, so—

Rising to her feet, she sent her chair crashing to the tiles. "Get. Out. Of. My. Head!"

Raphael came to a standstill. "Do you intend to use that knife?" His words were ice. Blood scented the air, and she realized it was her own.

Looking down, she found her hand clenching on the blade of the knife she'd drawn instinctively from the sheath at her ankle. She'd never have made such a mistake. He was forcing her to hurt herself, showing her she was nothing but a toy for him to play with. Instead of fighting, she squeezed harder. "If you want me to do a job for you, fine. But I won't be manipulated."

His eyes flicked over the blood seeping from her fist. He didn't have to say anything.

"You might be able to control me," she said in response to the silent mockery on his face, "but if that would've gotten the job done, you'd have never gone through the farce of hiring me. You need me, Elena Deveraux, not one of your little vampire flunkies."

Her hand unclenched in a violent spasm as he made her release the blade. It fell to the ground with a thud cushioned to softness by the blood that had pooled below. She didn't move, didn't attempt to stem the flow.

And when Raphael walked to stand less than a foot from her, she stood her ground.

"So, you think you have me over a barrel?" The sky was a seamless blue but Elena felt storm winds whip her hair completely out of its coil.

"No." She let his scent—clean, bright, of the sea—settle over the lingering coat of vampire on her tongue. "I'm ready to walk away without a backward look, return the deposit you paid the Guild."

"That," he said, picking up a napkin and wrapping it around her hand, "is not an option."

Startled by the unexpected act, she closed her hand to help slow the bleeding. "Why not?"

"I want you to do this," he responded, as if that was reason enough. And for an archangel, it was.

"What's the job? Retrieval?"

"Yes."

Relief began to wash through her like the rain she could feel so close. But no, it was his scent, that fresh bite of water. "All I need to start with is something the vampire wore recently. If you have a general location, even better. If not, I'll get the Guild's computer geniuses on tracking public transport and bank records, et cetera, while I hunt on the ground." Her mind was already at work, considering and discarding options.

"You mistake me, Elena. It's not a vampire I want you to find."

That halted her in her tracks. "You're looking for a human? Well, I can do it but I really don't have any advantage over a good private investigator."

"Try again."

Not vampire. Not human. That left . . . "An angel?" she whispered. "No."

"No," he agreed and, once again, she felt the cool brush of relief. It lasted until he said, "An archangel."

Elena stared at him. "You're joking."

His cheekbones stood out starkly against the sun-kissed

smoothness of his skin. "No. The Cadre of Ten does not joke."

Her stomach curdled at the reference to the Cadre—if Raphael was any example of their lethal power, she never wanted to meet that august body. "Why are you tracking an archangel?"

"That, you do not need to know." His tone was final. "What you do need to know is that if you succeed in finding him, you'll be rewarded with more money than you can hope to spend in your lifetime."

Elena glanced at the bloodstained napkin. "And if I fail?"

"Don't fail, Elena." His eyes were mild but his smile, it spoke of things better not said aloud. "You intrigue me—I'd hate to have to punish you."

Her mind flashed to the image of that vampire in Times Square, that broken mess that had once been a person . . . Raphael's definition of punishment.

4

Elena sat in Central Park, staring at the ducks swimming around in a pond. She'd come here to try to get her head on straight but it didn't seem to be working. All she could think about was whether ducks had dreams.

She figured not. What would a duck dream about? Fresh bread, a nice flight to wherever the hell it was ducks went. *Flight.* Her breath caught in her throat as her mind flashed with snapshots of memory—beautiful gold-streaked wings, eyes full of power, the shine of angel dust. She rubbed the heels of her hands over her eyes in an effort to erase the images. It didn't work.

It was as though Raphael had implanted a damn subliminal suggestion in her head that kept spewing out pictures of the very things she didn't want to think about. She wouldn't put it past him but he hadn't had time to mess with her that deep. She'd taken off less than a minute after he'd told her not to fail. Oddly enough, he'd let her go.

The ducks were fighting now, quacking at each other and diving with their beaks. Jeez, even the ducks couldn't stay peaceful. How the hell was she supposed to think with all that racket? Sighing, she leaned back on the park bench and looked up at the clear spread of sky. It reminded her of Raphael's eyes.

She snorted.

The color was about as close to the agonizingly vivid hue of his eyes as a cubic zirconia was to a diamond. A pale imitation. Still, it was pretty. Maybe if she stared hard enough, she'd forget about the wings that haunted her vision. Like now. They spread over her line of sight, turning blue into white-gold.

Frowning, she tried to see past the illusion.

Perfect gold-tipped filaments came into focus. Her heart was a hunted rabbit in her chest, but she didn't have the energy to be startled. "You followed me."

"You seemed to need time alone."

"Could you put down the wing?" she asked politely. "You're blocking the view."

The wing folded away with a soft susurration she knew she'd never associate with anything other than wings. Raphael's wings. "Will you not look at me, Elena?"

"No." She continued to stare upward. "I look at you and things get confused."

A male chuckle, low, husky . . . and *inside* her mind. "Avoiding my gaze gains you nothing."

"Didn't think so," she said softly, anger a dark ember in her gut. "Is that how you get your kicks—forcing women to worship at your feet?"

Silence. Then the sound of wings unfurling and snapping shut. "You are using up your lives."

She chanced a look at him. He was standing at the water's edge, but his body was turned toward her, those eyes of impossible blue having shaded to midnight. "Hey, I'm going to die anyway." It tended to make a person cavalier. "You said so yourself—you can fuck me over with your mind anytime you please. I'm guessing that's the least of your little bag of tricks. Right?"

He gave a regal nod, strikingly beautiful in an opportune

ray of sunlight. A dark god. And she knew that thought was her own. Because the very thing that repelled her about Raphael also attracted her. *Power.* This was a man she couldn't take on and hope to win. A hotly feminine part of her appreciated that kind of strength, even as it infuriated her.

"So if you can do all that, what's this other guy capable of?" She turned away from the erotic seduction of his face and toward the ducks. "I'll be mincemeat before I get within a hundred feet."

"You'll be protected."

"I work alone."

"Not this time." His tone was pure steel. "Uram has a penchant for pain. The Marquis de Sade was a student of his."

Elena wasn't about to show him exactly how much that freaked her out. "So he's into kinky sex."

"That's one way to look at it." Somehow, he put blood and pain and horror into that single comment. The emotions wormed their way through her pores and wrapped around her throat, choking, cloying.

"Stop it," she snapped, eyes locked with his once more.

"Apologies." A slight curve of his lips. "You're more sensitive than I expected."

She didn't believe that for an instant. "Uram? Tell me about him." She didn't know much about the other archangel beyond the fact that he ruled a chunk of Europe.

"He's your prey." His face closed over, midnight eyes going near black, expression shifting to that of a Greek statue. Distant. Inscrutable. "That's all you need to know."

"I can't work like that." She stood but kept her distance. "I'm good because I get inside the target's head, predict where he'll be, what he'll do, who he'll contact."

"Rely on your inborn gift."

"Even if I could scent archangels"—which she couldn't—"it's not magic," she pointed out, frustrated. "I need a starting point. If you haven't got anything, I'll have to work it out from his personality, his patterns of behavior."

He walked toward her, closing the distance she wanted to

keep. "Uram's movements can't be predicted. Not yet. We must wait."

"For what?"

"Blood."

The single word chilled her from the inside out. "What did he do?"

Raphael lifted a finger, tracing it over her cheekbone. She flinched. Not because he was hurting her. The opposite. The places he touched . . . it was as if he had a direct line to the hottest, most feminine part of her. A single stroke and she was embarrassingly damp. But she refused to pull away, refused to give in.

"What," she repeated, "did he do?"

That finger passed over her jaw and whispered along the line of her neck, giving excruciating, unwanted pleasure. "Nothing you need to know. Nothing that will help you track him."

Raising her hand with effort, she pushed his off, knowing her success was very much a case of him indulging her. And that chafed. "Finished playing your sex games?" she asked point-blank.

His smile was less a shadow this time, those changeable eyes sliding from black to something closer to cobalt. Alive. Electric. "I wasn't doing anything to your mind, Elena. Not that time."

Oh, shit.

He'd lied. Obviously, he'd lied. Elena let out a sigh of relief and collapsed onto her sofa. She wasn't idiotic enough to be attracted to an archangel. That left door number two—that Raphael *had* been playing with her mind and telling her otherwise was simply some sort of a twisted way for him to mess with her.

The annoying little voice inside her head kept whispering that that kind of manipulation didn't mesh with what she knew of Raphael. On the roof, he'd made no secret of the fact that he'd been in her mind. Lying seemed beneath him. "Hah!" she said to the voice. "What I know about him isn't enough to fill a thimble—he's manipulated mortals for centuries. He's good at it." Not good. Expert.

And she was now in his hands.

Unless he'd changed his mind in the hours since she'd hauled ass from the duck pond. Her mood brightened. Reaching over to open up the laptop on the coffee table, she booted it up and used her wireless Internet connection to look up her Guild account. The transaction history showed one recent deposit.

"Too many zeros." She took a deep breath. Counted again. "Still too many."

So many that it made Mr. Ebose's substantial payment look like chump change.

Hands sweat-damp, she swallowed and scrolled down. The payment had come from "Archangel Tower: Manhattan." She'd known that. Obviously, she'd known that. But seeing it in black and white was a jolt to the system. The deal was done. She was now officially working for Raphael. And only Raphael.

Her Guild status had been changed from "Active" to "Contracted: Indefinite Period."

Closing the laptop, she stared out at the Tower. She couldn't believe she'd stood on top of that cloud-piercing building only that morning, couldn't believe she'd dared disagree with an archangel, but most of all, she couldn't believe what Raphael wanted her to do. Thousands of tiny little creatures skittered about in her stomach, inciting nausea, panic . . . and a strange, vibrant excitement. This was the kind of job that made legends out of hunters. Of course, to be a legend, you generally had to be dead.

The phone rang, blessedly ending that particular line of thought. "What?"

"Good day to you, too, sunshine," came Sara's cheerful voice.

Elena wasn't fooled. Her friend hadn't made it to the position of Guild Director by being Ms. Congeniality. Nerves of steel and a will like a bull terrier more like it. "I can't tell you anything," she said bluntly. "Don't even ask."

"Come on, Ellie. You know I can keep a secret."

"No. If I tell you, you die." Raphael had made that very clear before he'd let her leave Central Park.

Tell anyone—man, woman, or child—and we'll eliminate them. No exceptions.

Sara snorted. "Don't be melodramatic. I'm—"

"He knew you'd ask," she said, remembering what else the Archangel of New York had said to her in that deceptively easy tone. A naked blade sheathed in velvet, that was Raphael's voice.

"Oh?"

"If I tell you, he won't only take you and Deacon out, he'll do the same to Zoe."

The fury that crackled through the line was pure maternal protectiveness. "Bastard."

"Totally agree."

Sara seemed to be fuming too hard to speak for several long seconds. "The fact that he made that threat means this is big."

"You saw the deposit?"

"Hell, did I see the deposit! I thought the accountant had screwed up and deposited the whole thing into our account instead of just the Guild percentage." She blew out a breath. "Baby girl, that's some kind of cash."

"I don't want it." She was choking on the need to share the sheer incomprehensibility of the task with Sara, with that idiot Ransom, but she couldn't. "He's already cut me off from my best friends." Her hand fisted.

"Let him try," Sara said. "So you can't tell me the details. Big deal. I'll figure it out soon enough. I have some idea."

Excitement danced up Elena's spine. "You do?"

"Killer vampire?" She paused. "Okay, you can't answer but seriously, what else could it be?"

Elena slumped again.

"Remember that one that went rogue?"

"There's been more than one," she said lightly, even as her blood ran cold.

"About twenty years ago. We studied him in our Guild classes."

Not twenty, Elena thought, *eighteen*. "Slater Patalis." The name fell from her lips like a piece of nightmare, one she'd never shared with anyone, not even the best friend she trusted with everything else. "How many did he end up killing?" she asked—forced herself to ask—before Sara's antennae could start to twang.

"Official body count was fifty-two in the space of a month," came the grim response. "Unofficially, we think there were more." Something creaked and Elena could almost see Sara leaning back in that big leather executive chair she adored like a second child. "Now that I'm director, I have access to all sorts of supersecret stuff."

"Want to share?" She held on to the here and now, ignoring the screaming echoes of a past nothing could change.

"Hmmm, why not—you are my second in command in all but name."

"Ech." Elena stuck out her tongue. "No desk job for me, thank you."

Sara laughed softly. "You'll learn. Anyway, the official line on Slater was that he'd had a psych illness before he was Made, an illness he somehow managed to hide."

"Some kind of severe antisocial personality disorder." Until Sara's comment, Elena had thought she knew every disturbing detail of the life and crimes of the most infamous killer vampire in recent history. "Evidence of childhood abuse and mistreatment of animals. Classic serial killer profile."

"Too classic," Sara pointed out. "It's a load of crock. The Guild made it up after pressure from the Cadre of Ten."

For a second, Elena had the horrifying suspicion that Slater Patalis wasn't really dead, that the Cadre had saved him for some perverse reason of their own. But an instant later, sanity reasserted itself—not only had she seen the autopsy video, she'd snuck into the storage room and picked up the vial of Slater's preserved blood. Her senses had reacted.

Vampire, the blood had whispered, *vampire*. And when she'd uncorked the bottle, it had murmured to her in Slater's distinctive, hypnotic voice.

Come here, little hunter. Taste.

She bit down hard on her lower lip, drawing her own blood and banishing the memory of his. At least until the hour of nightmares. "You going to tell me the truth?" she asked Sara.

"Slater was normal when he went in as a Candidate," Sara said. "You know how fanatical the angels are about checking the short-listed applicants. He was scanned, analyzed, damn near split open with all the tests they did. The man was squeaky clean and healthy, in body and in mind."

"The rumors," Elena whispered, eyes wide, "we always thought they were urban legends but if what you're saying is true—"

"—it means there's one very bad side effect to being Made. A tiny, tiny, *tiny* minority of the Candidates have their brains scrambled beyond recovery. What comes out of the mess isn't always human."

It should've felt odd to call vampires human in any sense but Elena knew what Sara was talking about. Humanity, as a whole, included vampires. As Elena knew from her own family, vampires could mate with, and even reproduce with, humans. Conception was very difficult but not impossible, and though the children—all mortal—sometimes suffered from anemia and related disorders, they were otherwise normal. First rule of biology—if it can mate, it's probably the same species.

That rule couldn't be applied to those of Raphael's kind. Angels attracted groupies by the truckload—mostly vampires, though the occasional stunning human was allowed into the mix. But debauchery aside, Elena had never heard of a child coming from a mating between human and angel, or even vampire and angel. Perhaps, she thought, angels simply didn't sire children. Maybe they considered the vampires their children.

Blood instead of milk, immortality instead of love.

A mockery of a childhood. But then again, what did Elena know of childhood? "Sara—I'm going to need full access to the Guild's computers and files."

"No one but the director has full access." Sara's tone held a thread of the famous Haziz steel. "You promise me you'll think about the assistant director position and I'll give you access."

"That would be lying," Elena said. "I'd go crazy behind a desk."

"I thought that once upon a time, and I'm as happy as a clam."

"What do clams have to do with anything?" Elena muttered.

"Beats me. Say you'll consider it."

"There's a crucial difference between me and you, Ms. Director." She let her tone speak for her. "Choose an A.D. out of one of the other married hunters. Don't waste it on me."

A sigh. "The fact that you're single doesn't mean I want you out there in the line of fire. You're my best friend, my sister in all but blood."

Tears pricked at her eyes. "Ditto." After Elena's own family had disowned her, it had been Sara who'd picked up the pieces. Their bond was close to unbreakable. "You know as well as I do that I'm not made for safety. I was born to be what I am." A hunter. A tracker. A loner.

"Why do I bother arguing with you?" A shake of her head that Elena could almost see. "I'm coding you in now."

That was what Elena loved about the Guild. There was no messy paperwork—hunters chose their director, then trusted her to make the decisions. No meetings, no board. No fucking around.

"Thanks."

"Uh-huh." The sound of rapid typing. "A hint of warning—I

have a feeling certain high-security files are discreetly moni-
tored for access."

"By who?" But she knew the answer. "On what authority?"

"The same one that lets them hire out my people without
telling me what the hell is going on," Sara spat out. "I became
director so I could help keep hunters safe. Raphael is going to
learn that—"

"Don't!" Elena cried. "Please, Sara, don't approach him.
The only reason, the *only* reason I'm still alive is that he
needs me to do a job. Otherwise, you'd probably have spent a
lovely afternoon identifying my body"—or what remained of
it—"at the morgue."

"Jesus, Ellie. I took an oath to protect my hunters and I'm
not going to back off just because Raphael's one scary m—"

"Then do it for Zoe," Elena interrupted. "Do you want her
to grow up without a mom?"

"Bitch." Sara's tone was close to a growl. "If I didn't love
you so much, I'd have to come beat you up. Damn emotional
blackmail."

"Promise me, Sara." Her hand tightened painfully on the
receiver. "This hunt is going to be the hardest thing I've ever
done—don't make me worry about you, too. *Promise.*"

A long, long pause. "I promise I won't approach Raphael . . .
unless I think you're in lethal danger. That's all you're going
to get."

"That'll do." She'd just have to make sure Sara never discovered that the hunt itself equaled near-certain death. One
misstep and it would be bye-bye, Elena P. Deveraux.

Something beeped. "Got another call—probably Ash,"
Sara said.

Last Elena had heard, Ashwini a.k.a. Ash a.k.a. Ashblade,
was in bayou country on the hunt for a smooth-talking Cajun
vamp who had a habit of making enemies out of angels . . .
then playing cat and mouse with Ash. "She still down Louisi-
ana way?"

"No. The Cajun decided to 'tour' Europe." Sara snorted
inelegantly. "You know, one of these days, he's going to make

her really mad and find himself staked naked in public, honey-glazed and with a Bite Me sign around his neck."

"I want tickets." Hanging up to Sara's laughter, Elena rubbed her hands over her face and decided it was time to get to work. This hunt was going to go down no matter what—she might as well try to come out of it in one piece.

Untucking the white shirt, she changed her black pants for jeans and tied her hair up into a haphazard ponytail, then flipped open her computer a second time. Since she didn't like the idea of the Cadre looking over her shoulder—even if they were her employers—she pulled up an Internet browser and clicked through to a popular search engine rather than logging into the Guild's databases.

Then she typed in her query: *Uram*.

5

Raphael closed the door behind him and walked into the huge basement library hidden beneath the graceful beauty of a large cottage in Martha's Vineyard. A fire burned in the hearth, the only source of illumination other than the wall sconces, which created more shadows than light. There was a sense of age about this place, a quiet knowledge that it had been here far longer than the modern home above.

"It is done," he said, taking his seat in the semicircle of armchairs in front of the fire. It was too hot for him, but some of his brethren came from warmer climes and felt the promise of autumn in their bones.

"Tell us," Charisemnon said. "Tell us about the hunter."

Leaning back in his chair, Raphael glanced around at the others who sat with him. The Cadre of Ten was in session. But incomplete. "We'll need to replace Uram."

"Not yet. Not until after . . ." Michaela whispered, eyes tortured. "Is it really necessary to hunt him?"

Neha closed her hand on the other angel's shoulder. "You know we have no choice. He can't be left to indulge his new appetites. If the humans ever discover—" She shook her head, almond-shaped eyes full of dark knowledge. "They would fear us as monsters."

"They already do," Elijah said. "To hold power, we've all had to become a little bit the monster."

Raphael agreed. Elijah was one of the oldest among them. He'd ruled in one way or another for millennia, no sign of ennui in his eyes even now. Perhaps it was because Elijah had something the others didn't—a lover whose loyalty was unimpeachable. Elijah and Hannah had been together for over nine hundred years.

"But," Zhou Lijuan pointed out, "there is a difference between being feared, but looked upon with awe, and being totally abhorred."

Raphael wasn't so sure that line existed but Lijuan was an archangel cut from a different time. She held power in Asia through a matriarchal network that instilled respect for her in their children, and had been doing so for eons. If Elijah was old, then Lijuan was truly ancient—she'd become woven into the very fabric of her homeland, China, and of the lands around it. They told tales of Lijuan in whispered tones and looked upon her as a demigod. In comparison, Raphael had only ruled for five hundred years, a mere blink of time. But that could prove an asset.

Unlike Lijuan, Raphael hadn't ascended so high that he'd ceased to understand mortals. Even before his transformation from angel to archangel, he'd chosen the chaos of life over the elegant peace of his brethren. Now he lived in one of the world's busiest cities and, unbeknownst to its denizens, often watched them. As he'd watched Elena Deveraux today. "We have no need to debate secrecy," he said, cutting into Michaela's soft sobs. "No one can know of what Uram has become. It has been that way for as long as we've existed."

A slow round of nods. Even Michaela wiped away her tears and sat back, her eyes clear, her cheeks flushed. She was beautiful beyond compare. Even among angelkind, she'd always been the brightest of stars, never lacking for lovers or attention. Right then, her gaze met his and deep within them was a sensual question he chose not to answer. *So.* She didn't mourn Uram; she mourned herself. That fit far better with her personality.

"The hunter is female," she said a second later, her tone slightly edgy. "Is that why you chose her?"

"No." Raphael wondered if he'd have to warn Elena about this new threat. Michaela didn't like competition and she'd been Uram's lover for almost half a century, an incredible commitment for someone of her mercurial nature. "I chose her because she can scent what no one else can."

"Why, then, must we wait?" Titus asked, his soft tone at odds with the gleaming, muscular bulk of his body. He appeared a man carved from jet, as roughly hewn as the mountain stronghold he called home.

"Because," Raphael answered, "Uram has not crossed the final line."

A hush.

"You're certain?" Favashi asked, her words gentle. She was the youngest of them all, the most mortal in her thinking. Her heart and soul remained unscathed by the inexorable passage of time. "If he hasn't yet—"

"You hope too easily," Astaad interrupted in that harsh way of his. "He killed every one of his servants and retainers the night he left Europe."

"Why then did he not cross the line, do . . . what we must never do?" Favashi asked, unwilling to back down. That was why, despite her gentleness, she was the archangel who held sway over Persia. She bent, but Favashi did not break. Ever. "Surely he can be reclaimed?"

"No," Neha responded, as cool as Favashi was warm. In her homeland of India, snakes were worshipped as gods and Neha was worshipped as the Queen of Snakes. "I've made discreet inquiries with our doctors. It is too late. His blood is poison."

"Could they be mistaken?" Michaela asked, and perhaps there was a touch of caring in her tone.

"No." Neha's eyes shifted across the room. "I sent a sample to Elijah, too."

"I had Hannah look at it," Elijah said. "Neha is right. It's too late for Uram."

"He is an archangel—the hunter will not be able to kill him even if she finds him," Lijuan said, her shimmering white hair waving in a breeze that wasn't there. With age came powers so extraordinary that seeming "human" in any sense became close to impossible. Lijuan's eyes, too, were a strange pearl gray that existed nowhere on this earth. "One of us will have to see to that duty."

"You just want him dead because he threatened your power!" Michaela snapped.

Lijuan ignored her, as Raphael might a human. Lijuan had seen archangels come and go. Only she remained. Uram had been her closest contemporary. "Raphael?"

"The hunter is tasked with tracking Uram," he answered, recalling the terror in Elena's eyes when he'd told her of that task. "I'll execute him. Do I have the Cadre's agreement?"

One by one, they all said, "Aye." Even Michaela. She valued her life more than she valued Uram's. For they all knew that Uram was in New York because of Michaela. If he crossed the final line, it was his former lover who'd become his most desired target.

So it was done.

Raphael stayed in the room as the Cadre took their leave one by one. It was rare for the membership to gather in one place. They were powerful beyond measure, but it was better not to tempt the young ones. Some aspired to take their place through death. It was always the young who embraced such delusions. The older ones had gained the wisdom to know that to be an archangel was to surrender part of your soul.

Soon, only Elijah remained in the room, on the other side of the semicircle from Raphael. "Will you not go home to Hannah?"

Elijah's pure white wings shifted slightly as he stretched out his legs and leaned back in his chair. "She's with me wherever I go."

Raphael didn't know whether the other angel meant that literally. Some long-mated angelic pairs were rumored to share an effortless mental link, untrammeled by time or distance, but if they did, none ever talked about it. "Then you are indeed blessed."

"Yes." Elijah leaned forward, balancing his elbows on his knees. "How could this have happened with Uram? Why did no one see?"

Raphael realized the other man truly had no idea. "He wasn't mated and Michaela cares for no one but herself."

"Harsh." But he didn't refute the summation.

"You have Hannah to tell you if you're getting close to the edge. Uram was alone."

"There were servants, assistants, other angels."

"Uram was never merciful," Raphael said. "He rewarded any show of spine with torture. As a result, his castle was filled with those who hated him and those who feared him. It didn't matter to them if he lived or died."

Elijah looked up, his eyes clear, almost human. "There's a lesson for you there, Raphael."

"Now you are acting like my big brother."

Elijah laughed, the only archangel aside from Favashi who ever did such a thing and meant it. "No, I see in you a leader. With Uram gone, the Cadre of Ten has the potential to fragment—you know what happened the last time we splintered."

The Dark Age of man and angel, when vampires bathed in blood and the angels were too busy warring with each other to care. "Why me? I'm younger than you, than Lijuan."

"Lijuan is . . . no longer of this world." Frown lines creased his forehead. "She is, I think, the oldest angel in existence. She's gone beyond petty problems."

"This is no petty problem." But he understood Elijah's

meaning. Lijuan no longer looked upon this world. Her sight was focused somewhere far in the distance. "If not Lijuan, why not you? You're the most stable of us all."

Elijah fanned out his wings as he thought. "My rule in South America has never been challenged. It's true I have a steel hand with dissent, but," he said, shaking his head, "I have no desire for killing or blood. To hold the Cadre together, the leader must be more dangerous than any other."

"You call me brutal to my face," Raphael commented softly.

Elijah shrugged. "You inspire fear without Astaad's cruelty, or Michaela's capriciousness. It was why you clashed with Uram—you were too close to taking what was his. The leadership is already yours, whether you know it or not."

"And now Uram is being hunted." Raphael saw, in that vision, his future. To be tracked like an animal. By a woman with dawn-colored hair and eyes as silver as a cat's. "Go home to your Hannah, Elijah. I will do what has to be done." Draw blood, end the life of an immortal. But that, of course, was a misnomer. An archangel could die . . . but only at the hands of another archangel.

"Will you rest this night?" Elijah asked as they both stood.

"No. I must speak to the hunter." To Elena.

6

Elena finished her preliminary research on Uram and sat back, nausea a pulsing fist in her throat. Uram had ruled— and as far as the rest of the world knew, still ruled—parts of eastern Europe and all of neighboring Russia. Oh, just like America, those countries had their presidents and prime ministers, their parliaments and councils, but everyone knew that true power rested in the hands of the archangels. Government, business, art—there was nothing they didn't influence, either directly or indirectly.

Uram, it appeared, was a very hands-on sort of guy.

It had been the first story she'd found—a news article about the president of a tiny country that had once been part of the Soviet Union. The president, one Mr. Chernoff, had made the mistake of defying Uram publicly, calling for citizens to boycott the draconian archangel's businesses, as well as those of his "vampire children," and patronize those run by humans. Elena didn't agree with the president's rhetoric. Being humancentric was a kind of prejudice, too. What about all those poor vampires who were only out to make a living for their families? Most vampires didn't automatically gain power with the transformation—that took centuries. Some would always remain weak.

After reading the first few paragraphs of the article, which summarized President Chernoff's policies, she'd expected the story to end with a notice of his funeral arrangements. To her surprise, she'd discovered the president was alive . . . if you could call it that.

Soon after his inflammatory comments, Mr. Chernoff had suffered an unfortunate car accident—his driver had lost control of the wheel and crashed into an oncoming semi. That driver had walked away without a scratch, a feat labeled "miraculous." El presidente hadn't been so lucky. He'd had so many broken bones the doctors said he'd never regain full use of his limbs. His eye sockets had shattered *inward*, destroying his eyes. And his throat had been crushed just enough to ruin his vocal cords . . . but not to kill him.

He could no longer hold a pen or type.

He could no longer speak.

He could no longer see.

No one had dared enunciate it, but the message had come through loud and clear. Defy Uram and you would be silenced. The politician who'd stepped in to take Chernoff's place had pledged allegiance to Uram even before he took the oath of office.

Say what you would about Raphael, she found herself thinking, but at least he was no tyrant. She had no illusions about the fact that he ran North America with an iron fist, but he didn't meddle in inconsequential human affairs. A few years back, they'd even had a mayoral candidate who'd pledged to flout the archangel should he be elected. Raphael had let the campaign run, his only response a slight smile when some reporter dared approach him.

That smile, that hint that he found the whole situation ridiculous, had sunk the mayoral hopeful's chances as surely as the *Titanic*. The man had slunk off, never to be seen again. Raphael had achieved victory without drawing a single drop of blood. *And* he'd retained his powerful status in the eyes of the population.

"That doesn't make him good," she muttered, worried about the direction of her thoughts. Raphael might shine in comparison to Uram, but that wasn't saying much.

It was Raphael who'd threatened to harm little Zoe, no one else.

"Bastard," she muttered, repeating Sara's imprecation. That threat put him in the same league as Uram. The European archangel had reportedly once destroyed an entire school full of five-to-ten-year-olds after the villagers asked him to remove his pet vampire from their midst.

Elena would have frowned on such a request had the vamp not been taking blood forcibly. He'd violated several of the village females, left them broken. The villagers had turned to Uram for help. He'd replied by killing their children and stealing their women. That had been over three decades ago and none of those women had ever been seen again. The village no longer existed.

He was, without a doubt, a very bad man. And she was—

Something tapped on the plate-glass window.

Hand sliding down to retrieve the knife hidden under the coffee table, she glanced up. Her eyes locked with those of an archangel. Silhouetted against the glittering Manhattan skyline, he should've appeared diminished, but he was even more beautiful than in daylight. It was a measure of his control that he barely had to move his wings to maintain position—the sheer power of him buffeted her even through the glass.

She swallowed and stood. "That window doesn't open," she said, wondering if he could hear her.

He pointed upward. She felt her eyes widen. "The roof isn't—" But he was already gone.

"Damn it!" Angry at him for catching her unawares, for inciting this assuredly fatal edge of attraction, she slid the knife back, closed the laptop, and left the apartment.

It took her several minutes to get to the roof and push open

the door. "I'm not coming out there!" she called out when she
didn't see him. The top of her building had been designed
by some avant-garde architect who believed in form over
function—a series of uneven, jagged peaks spread out in front
of her. It was impossible to walk on them without sliding and
falling to your death. "No, thank you," she muttered, feeling
the wind whip her hair off her face as she waited with the
door partly open. "Raphael!"

Maybe, she thought, the architect hadn't been avant-garde
at all. Maybe he'd simply hated angels. That sounded good to
her about then. She might admire their wings, but she had no
misapprehensions about their inner goodness. "Inner goodness. Hah!" She snorted and suddenly he was landing in front
of her, his wings flooding her vision.

She backed up a step without meaning to and by the time
she recovered, he was inside and closing the door. Damn it,
she hated that he could make her react like a green recruit
tracking her first vamp. If it went on like this much longer,
she'd lose all respect for herself. "What?" she asked, folding
her arms.

"Is this how you welcome all your guests?" His mouth
held no hint of a smile, yet it was sensuality personified, lush
and ultimately seductive.

She took another step backward. "Stop it."

"What?" A hint of genuine confusion in those blue, blue
eyes.

"Nothing." *Get a grip, Elena.* "Why are you here?"

He stared at her for several long seconds. "I'd like to talk
to you about the hunt."

"So talk."

He looked around the confines of the landing no one ever
used. The metal stairs were rusted, the single lightbulb yellow
and on the verge of going out. *Flicker. Flicker.* A two-second
stretch. Then *flicker, flicker.* The pattern kept repeating, driving her half crazy. Raphael was obviously not impressed either. "Not here, Elena. Show me to your rooms."

She scowled at the order. "No. This is work—we'll go to Guild headquarters and use a meeting room."

"It matters little to me." A shrug that drew her attention to the breadth of his shoulders, the powerful arch of his wings. "I can fly there within minutes. It'll take you at least half an hour, perhaps longer—there has been an accident on the road leading to your Guild."

"An accident?" Her mind flooded with the gruesome details of the "accident" she'd just been reading about. "Sure you didn't arrange it?"

He gave her an amused look. "If I wished to, I could force you to do anything I wanted. Why would I go to the trouble of such maneuverings?"

The bald way he pointed out his power, and her lack of it, made her fingers itch for a blade.

"You shouldn't look at me in that fashion, Elena."

"Why?" she asked, prodded by some heretofore unknown suicidal streak. "Scared?"

He leaned a fraction closer. "My lovers have always been warrior women. Strength intrigues me."

She refused to let him play with her like this, even if her body disagreed. Vehemently. "Do knives intrigue you, too? Because touch me and I *will* cut you up. I don't care if you throw me off the nearest balcony."

He seemed to pause, as if thinking. "That is not how I would choose to punish you. It'd end far too quickly."

And she remembered that this was no human male she was parrying with. This was Raphael, the archangel who'd broken every single bone in a vampire's body to prove a point. "I won't let you into my home, Raphael." Into her haven.

A silence weighted with the crushing pressure of a hidden threat. She remained still, sensing she'd pushed him far enough tonight. And while she knew her worth, she also knew that to an archangel, she was, in the end, expendable.

His blue eyes filled with flames as power crackled through the air. She was an inch away from taking her chances and trying to outrun him in the narrow confines of the stairwell, when he spoke. "Then we'll go to your Guild."

She blinked in wary disbelief. "I'll follow you by car." Her ride was a Guild vehicle—like most hunters, she was out of the country so much that keeping her own wasn't worth the hassle.

"No." His hand closed over her wrist. "I don't wish to wait. We'll fly."

Her heart stopped. Literally. When it kicked back to life, she could barely speak. "What?" It was an undignified squeak.

But he was already opening the door, tugging her along.

She dragged her heels. "Wait!"

"We fly or we go to your home. Choose."

The arrogance of the command was breathtaking. As was the fury. The Archangel of New York did not like being told *no.* "I choose neither."

"Unacceptable." He pulled.

She resisted. She wanted to fly more than anything, but not in the arms of an archangel who might drop her in his current mood. "What's so urgent?"

"I won't drop you . . . not tonight." His face was so perfect it could've belonged to some ancient god, but there was no compassion in it. Then again, the gods had hardly been merciful. "Enough."

And suddenly she was on the roof, with no knowledge of having taken the steps from the landing. Rage flowed through her in a jagged wave of white lightning, but he wrapped his arms around her and rose before she could do much more than part her lips. Survival instincts kicked in. Hard. Locking her arms around his neck, she held on for dear life as his wings gained momentum and the roof fell away at dizzying speed.

Her hair whipped off her face, the wind bringing tears to her eyes. Then, as if he'd gained enough altitude, Raphael altered the angle of his flight, sheltering her against the wind. She wondered if he'd done it on purpose, then realized she was falling into the trap of trying to humanize him. He wasn't human. Not even close.

His wings filled her vision until she dared turn her head and look at the view. There wasn't much to see—he'd taken them above the cloud layer. Goose bumps broke out on every inch of her skin as the cold seeped into her bones. Her teeth threatened to chatter, but she had to speak, had to let the anger out before it carved a hole in her soul. "I told you," she gritted out, "not to mess with my mind."

He glanced down. "You're cold?"

"Give the man an award," she said, breath misting the air. "I'm not built for flight."

He dived without warning. Her stomach went into free fall even as wild exhilaration raced through her bloodstream. She was flying! It might not have been by choice, but she wasn't going to cut off her nose to spite her face. Holding on tightly, she absorbed every second of the experience, tucking away the sensory memories to savor later. It was then that she realized she had no reason to fear an accidental fall— Raphael's arms were like rock around her, unbreakable, immovable. She wondered if he even felt her weight. Angels were supposed to be far stronger than either humans or vampires.

"Is that better?" he asked, lips against her ear.

Startled at the warm timbre of his voice, she blinked and realized they were now skimming just above the high-rises. "Yes." She wouldn't thank him, she thought mutinously. It wasn't as if he'd asked her permission before launching them heavenward. "You didn't answer me."

"In my defense"—an amused comment—"it wasn't so much a question as a statement."

Her eyes narrowed. "Why do you continue to push into my mind?"

"It's more convenient than wasting time waiting while you talk yourself into something."

"It's a kind of rape."

Chill silence, so cold the goose bumps returned. "Be careful with your accusations."

"It's the truth," she persisted, though her stomach was shriveling into a terrified little ball. "I said no! And you went in anyway. What the hell else do you call it?"

"Humanity is nothing to us," he said. "Ants, easily crushed, easily replaced."

She shivered, and this time it was out of pure fear. "Then why allow us to live?"

"You amuse us occasionally. You have your uses."

"Food for your vampires," she said, disgusted at herself for having seen anything human in him. "What—you keep a prison full of 'snacks' for your pets?"

His arms squeezed, cutting off her breath. "There's no need. The snacks offer themselves up on silver platters. But you'd know that—your sister is married to a vampire, after all."

The implication couldn't have been clearer. He'd as much as called her sister, Beth, a vamp-whore. The derogatory term was used to describe those men and women who followed groups of vampires from place to place, offering their bodies as food in return for whatever fleeting pleasure the vampire deigned to give. Every vamp fed differently, hurt or pleasured differently. Some vamp-whores seemed determined to taste, and be tasted by, each and every one of them.

"Leave my sister out of this."

"Why?"

"She was with Harrison before he became a vampire. She's no whore."

He chuckled, but it was the coldest, most dangerous sound she'd ever heard. "I expected better from you, Elena. Doesn't your family call you an abomination? I thought you'd have sympathy for those who love vampires."

If she'd dared let go of his neck, she might just have clawed her nails down his face. "I won't discuss my family with you." Not with him, not with anyone.

You disgust me. Almost the last words her father had said to her.

Jeffrey Deveraux had never been able to understand how he could've birthed a "creature" like her, an "abomination" who refused to follow the dictates of her blue-blooded family and sell herself in marriage in order to expand the sprawling Deveraux empire. He'd told her to give up the vampire hunting, never listening, never *understanding* that to ask her to stifle her abilities was to ask her to kill something inside of her.

Go, then, go and roll around in the muck. Don't bother coming back.

"It must've been . . . interesting when your brother-in-law chose vampirism," Raphael said, ignoring her words. "Your father didn't disown either Beth or Harrison."

She swallowed, refusing to remember the pitiful hope she'd felt when Harrison was accepted back into the family fold. She'd wanted so desperately to believe that her father had changed, that he'd finally look at her with the same love he lavished on Beth and the two younger children he had with his second wife, Gwendolyn. His first wife, Marguerite, Beth and Elena's mother, was never spoken of. It was as if she hadn't existed.

"My father is none of your business," she said, voice harsh with withheld emotion. Jeffrey Deveraux hadn't changed. He hadn't even bothered to return her call—and she'd understood that Harrison had been allowed back because he was the scion of a major corporation that had deep ties with Deveraux Enterprises. Jeffrey had no use for a daughter who chose to indulge in her "disgraceful, inhuman" ability to scent vampires.

"What about your mother?" A dark whisper.

Something snapped. Letting go of his neck, she kicked out with her legs at the same time that she lifted her arms to do some damage to his oh-so-pretty face. It was a suicidal act, but if there was one topic on which Elena wasn't rational, it was her mother. That this archangel, this *immortal* who cared nothing for the firefly span of human life, dared use Marguerite Deveraux's ephemeral existence against Elena was unbearable. She wanted to hurt him in spite of the futility of the goal. "Don't you ever—"

He dropped her.

7

She screamed . . . and came to a hard landing on her butt, hands braced against the rough caress of expensive tile. "Ummph." Swearing inwardly at the bitten-off sound of surprise, she sat on the ground, trying to catch her breath. Raphael stood above her, a vision out of a painting of heaven and hell. Either. Both. She could see why her ancestors had seen in his kind the guardians of the gods, but she wasn't sure he wasn't a demon. "This isn't the Guild," she managed to say after much too long.

"I decided we would talk here." He held out a hand.

Ignoring it, she pushed herself to her feet, barely stifling the urge to rub at her bruised tailbone. "You always drop your passengers?" she muttered. "Not so graceful after all."

"You're the first human I've carried in centuries," he said, those blue eyes almost black in the darkness. "I'd forgotten how fragile you were. Your face is bleeding."

"What?" She lifted a hand to a tingling spot on her cheek. The cut was so thin she could hardly feel it. "How?"

"The wind, your hair." Turning, he began to walk toward

the glass enclosure. "Wipe it off unless you want to offer the Tower vampires a nightcap."

She rubbed it off using the sleeve of her shirt, then fisted her hands, looking daggers at his retreating back. "If you think I'm going to follow you around like a puppy . . ."

He glanced over his shoulder. "I could make you crawl, Elena." No trace of any humanity in his face, nothing but the glow of such power that she wanted to shade herself from it. It was an effort not to take a stumbling step backward. "Do you really want me to force you onto your hands and knees?"

At that second, she knew he'd do exactly that. Something she'd either said or done had finally pushed Raphael beyond his limits. If she wanted to survive this with her soul intact, she'd have to swallow her pride . . . or he'd break her. The realization burned going down and sat like a rock in her stomach. "No," she answered, knowing that if she ever had the chance, she'd stab a knife in his throat for the insult to her pride.

Raphael watched her for several long minutes, a cold standoff that turned her blood to ice. Around her burned a million city lights, but up on this roof, there was only darkness—except for the glow coming off him. She'd heard people whisper of this phenomenon but had never thought to witness it. Because when an angel glowed, he became a being of absolute power, power that was usually directed to kill or destroy. An angel glowed just before he tore you into a thousand pieces.

Elena stared back, unwilling—*unable*—to give in. She'd gone as far as she could. Anything else and she might as well crawl.

Get on your knees and beg, and maybe I'll reconsider.

She hadn't done it then. She wouldn't do it now. No matter the cost.

Right when she thought it was all over, Raphael turned and continued on to the elevator cage. The glow faded between one breath and the next. She followed, disgustingly aware of the sweat that had broken out along her spine, the sharp taste of fear on her tongue. But overlaying that was a deep, deep anger.

Raphael the Archangel was now the most hated person in her universe.

He held the door open for her. She walked through without saying a word. And when he came to stand beside her, his wings brushing her back, she stiffened and kept her eyes locked on the elevator doors. The car arrived a second later and she walked in. So did Raphael, his scent like sandpaper against her hunter-born senses.

Her knife hand was itching for a blade, almost painfully needy. She knew the feel of cold steel would center her but that sense of safety would be an illusion, one that might put her in even more danger.

I could make you crawl, Elena.

She clenched her teeth so hard her jaw protested. And when the elevator doors opened, she strode out without waiting for Raphael—only to come to an abrupt halt. Corporate decor sure had changed if this was considered business-appropriate. The carpet was a lush black, as were the gleaming walls. The sole pieces of furniture in her line of sight—a couple of small decorative tables—were also in the same exotically rich shade.

It shimmered with hidden color, with possibility.

Bloodred roses—arranged in crystal vases perched atop the small tables—provided a lush contrast. So did the long rectangular painting along one wall. She walked to it, mesmerized. A thousand shades of red in a fury that was somehow coolly logical, sensual in a way that spoke of blood and death.

Raphael's fingers on her shoulder. "Dmitri is talented."

"Don't touch me." The words dripped off her tongue like blades of ice. "Where are we?" She swiveled to face him, making a concerted effort *not* to go for a weapon.

Blue flames in his eyes but no violence. "On the vampire floor—they use this for . . . well, you'll see."

"Why do I need to? I know all there is to know about vampires."

A faint smile on his lips. "Then you won't be surprised." He offered her his arm. She refused to take it. His smile didn't falter. "Such rebelliousness. Where did you inherit it? Certainly not from your parents."

"One more word about my parents and I don't care if you break me into a million fucking pieces." Said through gritted teeth. "I'll cut out your heart and serve it to the street dogs for dinner."

He raised an eyebrow. "Are you sure I have a heart?" With that, he began to move down the corridor.

Not wanting to follow a step behind, she caught up so they walked side by side. "A physical one, probably," she said. "An emotional one? Not a chance."

"What does it take for you to truly fear?" He seemed genuinely curious.

Once again, it appeared she'd skated the thin edge of danger and come out alive. But it had been a close call—she wondered how forgiving Raphael would be after she completed the job and was no longer of use. She wasn't going to stick around to find out.

"I was born a hunter," she said, making a mental note to organize an escape hatch. Siberia sounded good. "Not many people know what that means, the inevitable consequences."

"Tell me." He pushed through a glass door and waited until she'd passed before closing it. "When did you realize you had the ability to scent vampires?"

"There was no realization." She shrugged. "I could always do it. It took me until I was about five to understand it was something different, abnormal." The word slipped out, her father's word. She felt her mouth thin. "I thought everyone could do it."

"As a young angel might think everyone can fly."

Curiosity spiked out of the anger. "Yes." So there were child angels. But where? "I knew our neighbor was a vampire before anyone else did. I accidentally ratted him out one day."

She still felt bad about that, though she'd only been a child at the time. "He was trying to pass as human."

Raphael's face settled into lines of displeasure. "It would've been better had he given the chance to someone else. Why accept the gift of immortality if you wish to be human?"

"I gotta agree with that one." She shrugged. "Mr. Benson was forced to move out after a neighborhood uproar."

"Not a tolerant place, your childhood home."

"No." And her father had been at the head of that intolerance. How it had humiliated him that his daughter was one of the monsters. "A few years later, I felt Slater Patalis brush by as he murdered his way across the country." Her heart froze in her chest, chilled by the secret horror connected to that name.

"One of our few mistakes."

Not really a mistake, she thought, not if he'd been normal going in. But she couldn't say that without betraying Sara. "So you see, I'm used to fear. I grew up knowing the bogeyman lurked outside."

"You lie to me, Elena." He stopped in front of a solid black door. "But I will let it pass. You'll soon tell me the truth of why you dance with death so eagerly."

She wondered if he had Ariel and Mirabelle's names in his files, if he knew the truth of the tragedy that had destroyed her mother and turned her father into a stranger. "You know what they say about being overconfident."

"Exactly." A small nod. "So tonight, I'll show you why those you call whores seek their vampire lovers."

"Nothing you do or say will convince me to change my mind." She scowled. "They're little more than drug addicts."

"Such obstinance," he murmured, and pushed open the door.

Whispered sounds, laughter, the tinkle of glass. It flowed out like an invitation. Raphael's eyes dared her to step inside. Fool that she was, she accepted the challenge and—slipping a knife from an arm sheath into her palm—walked in, piercingly aware of the archangel at her back, the naked vulnerability of her spine . . . until her mouth dropped open in shock.

The vampires were having a cocktail party.

She blinked, taking in the muted, romantic lighting, the plush couches, the hors d'oeuvres accompanied by slender flutes of champagne. The food was clearly for the human guests, male and female, who stood talking, laughing, and flirting with their vampire hosts. Dinner suits lay snugly over lithely muscled shoulders, while cocktail dresses ran the gamut from long and slinky to short and sexy, the overriding themes black and red, with the occasional daring splash of white.

Conversation stopped the second they saw her. Then their eyes flicked behind her and she almost *heard* the collective sigh of relief—the hunter was on the archangel's leash. Stifling the childish urge to show them different, she slid the knife discreetly back up into the sheath.

None too soon, too, because a vampire was walking toward her, glass of wine in hand. At least she hoped it was wine—the dark red liquid could as easily have been blood. "Hello, Elena." The words were said in a beautiful, deep voice but it was his scent that was truly intoxicating—rich and dark and luscious.

"Doorvamp," she whispered, throat husky. It was only when she found herself pressed against the living heat of Raphael that she realized she'd backed away from the clawing beauty of the invisible caress.

"My name is Dmitri." He smiled, displaying a row of sparkling white teeth, not a fang in sight. An old vamp, an experienced vamp. "Come, dance with me."

Heat uncurled between her legs, an involuntary reaction to Dmitri's scent, a scent that held a very special—and highly erotic—allure for the hunter-born. "Stop it or I swear I'll make you a eunuch."

He looked down at the blade now pressing against his zipper. When he raised his head, his expression was more than a fraction annoyed. "If you're not here to play, why come at all?" The scent dissipated, as if he'd drawn it into himself. "This is a place of safety and enjoyment. Take your weapons elsewhere."

Flushing, she got rid of the knife. It was obvious she'd just committed a major faux pas. "Raphael."

The archangel curled his hand around her upper arm. "Elena is here to learn. She doesn't understand the fascination you hold for humans."

Dmitri raised an eyebrow. "I'd be happy to show you."

"Not tonight, Dmitri."

"As you wish, sire." Giving a small nod, Dmitri walked away . . . but only after wrapping a tendril of scent around her as a parting shot.

His slow smile said he could scent her response, knew she was weak-kneed with it. But the effect faded with every step he took, until she no longer craved the sensual pain of his touch—Dmitri's scent was as much a tool of mind control as Raphael's abilities. But for the first time, she began to understand why some hunters became sexually—even romantically—intertwined with the very creatures they hunted.

Of course, they didn't hunt the ones like Dmitri. "He's old enough to have repaid the hundred-year debt several times over." Not to mention his considerable personal power—she'd never met any vampire with that much sheer magnetism. "Why does he stay with you?"

Raphael's hand was a brand on her upper arm, burning through the material of her shirt to stain her skin. "He requires constant challenge. Working for me gives him the opportunity to fulfill his needs."

"In more ways than one," she murmured, watching as Dmitri went to a small, curvy blonde and put his hand on her waist. She looked up, enraptured. Not surprising, given that Dmitri was wet-dream beautiful—silky black hair, dark, dark eyes, skin that spoke of the Mediterranean rather than cold Slavic climes.

"I'm no procurer." Raphael was openly amused. "The vampires in this room have no need of such services. Look around, who do you see?"

She frowned, about to snap back a sharp rejoinder, when

her eyes widened. There, in that corner, that leggy brunette . . .
"No way." She squinted. "That's Sarita Monaghan, the super-
model."

"Keep going."

Her eyes drifted back to Dmitri's curvy blonde. "I've seen
her somewhere, too. A TV show?"

"Yes."

Thrown off balance, she continued to scan the room. There
was a famous rugged-jawed news anchor, happily ensconced
on a couch with a striking flame-haired vampire. A little to
their left sat a powerhouse New York couple, majority share-
holders in a Fortune 500 company. Beautiful people. Smart
people.

"They're here by choice?" But she knew the answer. There
was no hint of desperation in any of the eyes that met hers,
none of the glassiness of will stolen. Instead, it was flirtation,
enjoyment, and sex that filled the air. Definitely sex. The languid heat of it dripped off the walls.

"Do you feel it, Elena?" Closing his free hand over her
other arm, he held her to his chest, his lips brushing her ear as
he bent down to speak. "This is the drug they crave; this is
their addiction. Pleasure."

"Not the same," she said, standing her ground. "The
vamp-whores are nothing more than camp followers."

"The only thing that separates them from this crowd is
wealth and beauty."

It stung her to realize he was right. "Fine, I take it back.
Vampires and their groupies are all nice, healthy folks." She
couldn't believe what she was seeing—the TV anchor was
sliding his hand up the split in his date's skirt, oblivious to
anyone else.

He chuckled. "No, they aren't nice. But they aren't evil, either."

"I never said that," she retorted, eyes fixated on the excruciating pleasure on the anchor's face as he stroked the redhead's pale, pale skin. "I know they're just people. My point
was that—" She swallowed as another woman moaned, her

vampire lover's mouth hovering a teasing inch above the pulse in her neck, a hot whisper that promised ecstasy.

"Your point?" He grazed his mouth over her own pulse.

She jerked, wondering how the hell she'd ended up in an archangel's arms—a man she'd been planning to knife in the heart. "I don't like how the vampires use their abilities to enslave humans."

"But what if the humans want to be enslaved? Do you see anyone complaining?"

No. All she could see were the lush brushstrokes of sensual play, an erotic mix of male and female, vampire and human. "Did you bring me to a damn orgy?"

He chuckled again, and this time, the sound was warm, liquid, like melted caramel over her skin. "Sometimes they cross a few lines but this is what it seems. A party where partners may be found."

His hands slid up and down her arms, his breath ruffling the curling hairs at her temple. For a fleeting second, she wavered. What would it feel like to lean back, to let Rapha— *Oh, Jesus.* What was happening to her? "I've seen enough. Let's go." She struggled in his hold.

He tightened it, his wings coming around to cut off her view of the room, his chest hot and hard at her back. "Are you sure?" His lips whispered over skin so sensitized, she had to fight the urge to shiver. "I have not taken a human lover for eons. But you taste . . . intriguing."

8

Human lover.

The words unlocked her from the prison of sensory delight the Archangel of New York had spun with cool control. She was a toy to him, nothing more. After he was done, she'd be discarded like all unwanted toys. Used up. Forgotten. "Find someone else to amuse yourself with. I'm not in the market." She pulled away, and this time, he let her go.

Wary, she spun around to face him. She expected anger, perhaps fury, at being denied, but Raphael's face was a mask, watchful, unbreakable. She wondered if he'd been playing with her all along. Why the hell would an archangel take a human lover when he had a harem of stunning vampire beauties to pick from?

Say what you would about the dietary requirements, vampirism sure did do great things for the skin and body. Any vampire over five decades old was svelte, with flawless skin. Their allure, too, grew with each passing year—though the intrinsic force of it depended on the individual. Elena had met very old vampires who remained more prey than predator, but the truly powerful ones . . .

Some, like Dmitri, were good at hiding their strength, their incredible charisma, until they wanted to use it. Others had gone too far along the timeline and leaked power almost continuously. But even the weak ones, the ones who'd never be anything close to what Dmitri was now, were stunningly beautiful.

"I get the lesson," she said when he remained silent. "I should be more tolerant of other people's sexual practices."

"An interesting way to put it." He finally lowered his wings, folding them neatly behind his back. "But you've only glimpsed the tip of the iceberg."

She wondered if the TV anchor had his fingers in the vamp's panties by now. "I've seen enough." Her face grew hot at the sense that all sorts of erotic things were going on behind her back.

"A prude, Elena? I thought hunters were free with their affections."

"None of your damn business," she muttered. "We either leave or I accept Dmitri's offer."

"You think that matters to me?"

"Sure." She met his eyes, forced herself to hold her ground. "Once that vamp sinks his fangs into me, I won't be able to walk *or* work."

"I've never heard a man's cock described as a fang before," he murmured. "I'll have to share your estimation of his skills with Dmitri."

Elena knew her blush was burning up her cheeks but she refused to let him win this verbal skirmish. "Fang, cock, what's the difference? It's all sexual to a vampire."

"But not to an angel. My cock serves a highly specific purpose."

Lust—sharp, dangerous, unbidden—squeezed her chest so tight she could barely breathe. Her blush receded as all the heat in her body shifted. To low, damp places. "I'm sure it does," she said sweetly, standing firm even as her body betrayed her. "Servicing all those vampire groupies must get tiring."

His eyes narrowed. "Your mouth could get you into more trouble than you can handle." Except he was looking at that same mouth with anything but censure. He was looking at it as if he wanted it wrapped around him.

"No way in hell," she croaked out past the thickening in her blood.

He didn't pretend not to understand her out-of-the-blue comment. "Then I shall make sure we are very much in heaven when it happens." Eyes darkly indigo with challenge, he turned to open the door.

She stalked out—after sneaking a last, guilty look at the festivities. Dmitri was staring straight at her, his lips brushing the milk-and-cream skin of the blonde's arched neck, his hand lying perilously close to the soft rise of her breasts. As the door closed, she saw his fangs flash bright. Her stomach twisted in a vicious shock of hunger.

"Would you go to his bed sweetly?" Raphael asked against her ear, his voice an unsheathed blade. "Would you whimper and beg?"

Elena swallowed. "Hell, no. He's like double-frosted chocolate mud cake. It looks good, you want to eat the whole thing, but in reality it's too sickly sweet." Dmitri's sensual nature was suffocating, heavy, a blanket that repelled even as it attracted.

"If he is cake, what am I?" Cruel, sensual lips against her cheek, her jaw.

"Poison," she whispered. "Beautiful, seductive poison."

Behind her, Raphael went so still she was reminded of the calm before a storm. But when the storm hit, it was delivered in a silky smooth voice that shoved deep inside her, laying her bare. "Yet I think you would rather drown in poison than gorge on cake." His hands closed over her hips.

Lust in her throat, brutal and demanding. "But then, we both know about my self-destructive streak." Stepping away, she put her back to the wall and faced him, willing her body to stop readying itself for a penetration she'd never allow. "I have no desire to be your chew-toy."

The lines of his face might've been starkly masculine, but at that instant, his lips were pure temptation, soft, bitable, sensual in a way only a man's mouth could be. "If I were to splay you out on my desk and thrust my fingers into you right now, I think I'd find different."

Her thighs clenched as need spasmed through her. The image of those long powerful fingers thrusting in and out of her as she lay helpless was suddenly the only thing she could see. Closing her eyes just made it worse so she flicked them open to stare fixedly at the black shimmer of the opposite wall. "I don't know what kind of kinky shit goes on in this building, but I don't want any part of it."

He laughed, the sound full of dark, male knowledge. "Perhaps you've led a more sheltered life than I'd believed if you think of that as kinky."

It was a taunt that dared her to respond. She fought the urge. So what if she wasn't as openly sexual as some of the other hunters? So what if the testosterone gang had named her the Vestal Virgin after she turned them down one after the other. She wasn't, in fact, a virgin, but if it would keep her safe from Raphael's erotic games, she'd play along. "I'd like to stay sheltered, thank you very much. Can we please have this meeting before I fall asleep?"

"My bed is very comfortable."

She could've slapped herself for giving him that opening, especially when her brain began to supply her with visions of him in bed, wings stretched out, thighs bare, co— She gritted her teeth. "What did you want to tell me?"

His eyes gleamed, but all he said was, "Come." He began to stride back to the elevator.

Running, she caught up, irritated at the way he expected her to obey. Like she was a puppy. However, for once, she kept her mouth shut. She wanted to get as far away as possible from the vampire floor with its reek of sex, pleasure, and addiction.

The elevator ride was short, and this time when she exited, it was into a classy setup. Cool white was the overriding theme, with elegant accents of white gold. But when Raphael ushered her into his office, she found that his desk was a huge black chunk of polished volcanic stone.

If I were to splay you out on my desk and thrust my fingers into you right now, I think I'd find different.

She cut off the thought before it could crawl into her mind again, remaining on the far side of the desk as Raphael circled it to stand by the glass, his gaze on the city lights and, beyond them, the dark spill of the Hudson.

"Uram is in the state of New York."

"What?" Startled but pleased by the abrupt shift into work mode, she raised her hands to fix the mess the wind had made of her hair, pulling it back into a tight ponytail. "That makes our job stupid-easy. All I have to do is alert the hunter network to be on the lookout for an angel with dark gray wings."

"You've done your homework."

"His pattern is as distinctive as yours," she said. "Almost like a gypsy moth's."

"You will not alert anyone."

She set her jaw, any lingering hint of desire dying a quick death. "How am I supposed to do my job if you cut me off from the very things I need to do it effectively?"

"Those things will be useless to you in this hunt."

"Oh, come on!" she yelled at his back. "He's a big fricking angel with one-of-a-kind wings. People will notice him. And could you face me when we're talking?"

He turned, his eyes blue flame. Power licked off him in waves she could almost feel. "Uram won't stand out. Just like I don't."

She frowned. "What are you talking about— Oh, fuck." He wasn't there anymore. She knew he had to be there but he was no longer visible to her sight. Swallowing, she walked to his last known position, and reached out.

To touch warm, male skin.

A ghostly hand closed over her wrist when she would've pulled back. Then one of her fingers was sucked into the mouth she'd stared at earlier, the hot-wet heat a violent provocation to the renewed pulse between her thighs. That was when she realized she couldn't see that part of her finger. "Stop it!" Wrenching away, she stumbled back against the desk.

Raphael appeared as a mirage, then solidified. "I was proving a point." He shifted to stand in front of her, blocking her in.

"You usually suck on people to prove a point?" Her fingers curled. "What the hell was that?"

"Glamour," he answered, tracing the shape of her mouth with his eyes. "It allows us to move hidden among the masses. It's part of what makes an archangel out of an angel."

"How long can you hold it?" She tried not to wonder what he was thinking when he looked at her that way, tried to remember that he'd threatened Sara's baby and her own life. But it was hard with him so close, so touchable. He looked almost human. Darkly, sexually human.

"I can hold it as long as it takes," he whispered and she had no doubt it was a double entendre. "Uram is older than I am. His power is greater. All he'd need to do is—" He cut himself off so abruptly, she knew he'd almost revealed too much. "At full power, he can hold the glamour close to indefinitely. Even weakened, he can still maintain it for most of the day, going to ground during the night hours."

"We're hunting the Invisible Man?" She leaned farther back, until she was almost sitting on the desk.

His hands were on the gleaming surface on either side of her hips without her knowing how he'd gotten so close. "That's why we need your sense of smell."

"I scent vampires," she said, frustrated, "not angels. I can't scent you."

He brushed off the detail as if it meant nothing. "We must wait."

"Wait for what?"

"For the right time." His wings rose, blocking out the view, draping them in night. "And while we wait, I'll indulge my need to see if you taste as tart as you sound."

The sensual web snapped. Not giving him warning, she

used her agility to slide backward and off the other side of the desk, scattering paper as she went. "I told you," she gasped, heart thudding at the narrow escape, "I don't want to be your snack, your chew-toy, your fuck-buddy. Find a vampire to sink your fang into." She strode out of the room and down the hall without waiting for an answer.

Somewhat to her amazement, no one stopped her. When she reached the ground floor, she found a taxi waiting—for her. She was about to tell the driver to get lost when she realized she had no money. Since she had no desire to walk home in the creeping chill of midnight, she got into the backseat. "Get me the hell out of here."

"Of course." The driver's voice was smooth. Too smooth.

She glanced up to meet his gaze in the mirror. "Vamps drive taxis now?"

He smiled but couldn't pull off Dmitri's effortless charm . . . and he definitely couldn't pull off the dangerous sensuality of the archangel who seemed determined to turn their "relationship"—hah!—sexual.

It'd be a cold day in Lucifer's personal kingdom before that happened. Sex was not on the menu. And neither was Elena.

9

Raphael watched the taxi pull away, surprised she'd taken it. Elena was proving the most unpredictable of all those under his command. Of course, she'd argue with that description, he thought, amused in the way only a lethally powerful immortal could be.

The door opened behind him. "Sire?"

"Dmitri, you are to stay away from the hunter."

"If the sire so wishes." A pause. "I could reduce her to begging. She would no longer disobey your orders."

"I don't want her to beg." Raphael was surprised to find that to be true. "She'll be more effective with her spirit intact."

"And after?" Dmitri's voice was full of sensual anticipation. "May I have her after the hunt? She . . . draws me."

"No. After the hunt, she's mine." Any begging Elena would be doing would fall on his ears alone.

10

He was going to kill her.

Elena sat bolt upright in her beautiful artwork of a bed. The headboard was a one-of-a-kind design of the most delicately formed metal, while the white-on-white sheets and puffy comforters were embroidered with tiny, tiny flowers. To the right of her bed were sliding French doors that led out onto a small private balcony she'd turned into a miniature garden. And beyond that lay the view of Archangel Tower.

Inside, the walls were papered in a heavy cream design with accents of blue and silver that echoed the deep blue carpet. The curtains on the French doors were gauzy and white, though there was a heavier set of brocade curtains she usually kept tied back. Huge sunflowers bloomed against the white porcelain of the large Chinese vase in the opposite corner of the room, bringing the sunshine inside.

She'd been given that vase by a grateful Chinese angel after she tracked down one of his wayward charges. The young vampire—having barely completed her Contract—had decided she didn't need angelic protection anymore. Elena had found her huddling terrified in a sex shop that catered to a very weird set of clientele. The job had taken her into the bowels of the Shanghai underworld, but the vase was a piece of light, unblemished by time. The whole room was a haven, one she'd spent months getting just right.

But right then, she could've been sitting on a dirt floor in a hovel somewhere south of Beijing. Her eyes were open but all she saw was a frozen image of that vampire in Times Square, the one not a single fucking person had dared help. She knew she wouldn't end up that way, not if Raphael wanted the whole thing swept under the rug, but she was most certainly dead.

He'd told her about glamour.

As far as she was aware, no hunter, no *human*, knew about that particular little piece of archangelic power. It was akin to seeing the face of your kidnapper—no matter what he says after that point, you know you're done for.

"No. Fucking. Way." Clenching her hands on her beautiful Egyptian cotton comforter, she narrowed her eyes and considered her options.

Option 1: Attempt to back out.

Probable result: Death after painful torture.

Option 2: Do the job and hope.

Probable result: Death but probably no torture (good).

Option 3: Get Raphael to give her an oath not to kill her.

Probable result: Oaths were serious business so she'd live. But he'd still be able to torture her until she went insane.

"So think of a better oath," she muttered to herself. "No death, no torture, definitely no turning me into a vampire." She bit her lower lip and wondered if the oath could be extended to her friends and family. Family. Yeah, right. They hated her guts. But she didn't want them ripped open while she was forced to watch.

Blood hitting tile.

Drip.

Drip.

Drip.

A whistling, gurgling plea.

Looking up to find Mirabelle still alive.

The monster smiled. "Come here, little hunter. Taste."

Drip.

Drip.

A wet, tearing sound, thick, obscene, out of a nightmare.

Elena shoved off the comforter and swung her legs over the side of the bed, face ice-cold. That particular memory had the ability to destroy any and all warmth in her soul. Sitting there with her head in her hands, she stared down at the deep blue of carpet and tried to zone out. It was the only way to escape when the memories found a hole in her defenses and snuck inside, their talons as grasping and as venomous as that of—

Something smacked to ground on the balcony.

The gun she kept under her pillow was in her hand and pointed toward the French doors before she even realized she'd moved. Her hand was steady, her body flushed with adrenaline. Scanning the balcony through the gauzy curtains, she saw no one, but only a very stupid hunter would lower her guard that easily. Elena wasn't stupid. She got up, unmindful of the fact that all she wore was a white tank top and mint green panties cut to mimic tiny shorts, the sides slit halfway up and decorated with pretty pink ribbon.

Gaze focused outside, she used her free hand to push the gauzy curtains aside, one at a time. The balcony came into full view. No pissed-off vampire stood there. The fuckers couldn't fly but she'd once seen three of them scale a high-rise building like a pack of four-legged spiders. That bunch had done it as a joke, but if they could do it, so could others.

She double-checked.

No vampire. No angel, either.

Her arm was starting to ache a little from holding the gun in position but she didn't breathe a sigh of relief. Instead, she started scanning the edges of the balcony—she had a lot of plants out there, including creepers that hung down from the curved "roof" she'd had added—but she made damn sure nothing ever blocked her view of the balcony rim. If someone was clinging out there, she'd be able to see their fingertips.

More importantly, any intruder would've left streaks on the gel she sprayed out there every week. The stuff was made specially for hunters and cost an arm, a leg, *and* a kidney, but it was a highly effective way to detect intrusion. When inactive, it blended into any surface, but once touched by either vampire, human, or angel, it turned a vivid, unmissable red.

The gel was undisturbed and her senses didn't detect vampire.

Relaxing only slightly, she shot a quick look downward. Her eyebrows rose. A plastic message tube lay next to her lush red begonias. She scowled. The begonia stalks were easily breakable. If whoever had dropped this had so much as bruised the plants she'd babied to blooming health despite the cool kiss of summer's end, there'd be hell to pay. Finally convinced the area was secure, she lowered the gun and clicked open the door.

The breeze brought her the vibrant living pulse of the city but nothing else.

Even then, she was very, very careful as she edged out her body and rolled the tube toward her using her foot. She'd almost gotten it inside when she saw the feather drifting down to land gently on a curling fern. Kicking the tube inside, she lifted her gun and pointed it to the balcony roof—the guy who'd built it for her had told her she was crazy to block even part of the view, but he'd obviously never thought of danger coming from above.

Sure, she'd lost some visibility, but no one could ambush her from above without warning—though obviously she was getting too reliant on that shield if she'd missed her uninvited guest. That wouldn't happen again.

"This ammo goes through stone, much less the fake stuff you're sitting on," she called out. "Get the hell off there before you break it!"

The flap of wings sounded immediately. A second later,

a flushed angelic face peered at her upside down. Her eyes rounded. She hadn't known angels could do that. "You the delivery boy? Straighten up—you're giving me vertigo."

The angel nodded then righted himself. He looked like one of those mythical cherubs the Renaissance artists had liked to paint, his face round and sweet, his hair all golden curls. "Sorry! I never saw a hunter before. I was curious." His eyes went huge as his gaze drifted south. His wings had already been beating fast as he tried to keep position, but now they went hyper.

"Eyes up or I'll shoot a hole in your wing."

His head snapped up, cheeks red. He dipped slightly to the left before righting himself. "Sorry! Sorry! I just got out of the Refuge. I—" He gulped. "I wasn't supposed to tell you that! Please don't tell Raphael."

Since the angel looked like he was about to cry, Elena nodded. "Relax, kid. And next time you have a delivery, come to the front door."

He winced. "Raphael said I had to do it this way."

Elena sighed and waved at him. "Shoo. I'll take care of Raphael."

The young angel looked terrified. "No, it's okay. Please don't. He might . . . hurt you." The last two words were less than whispers.

"No, he won't." Elena was going to make the archangel swear an oath. Though she had no idea how. "Now go—Dmitri gets jealous."

The boy paled and took off so fast she barely saw him. Well now, that was interesting. As far as anyone knew, angels controlled vampires. But what if power was much more fluid? It was something she'd have to consider.

Later.

After she'd made Raphael promise not to kill, maim, or torture her.

Locking the doors after checking on and watering her precious begonias—the yellow one was blooming like full summer wasn't a month past, which put a smile on her face—she pulled the curtains shut and slid the gun back under the pillow. Only then did she pick up the message tube and unscrew it.

The phone rang.

She considered ignoring it. Her curiosity was killing her. But a quick glance at the caller ID showed it was Sara. "Hey. What's up, Ms. Director?"

"I was going to ask you the same question. I had a really weird report last night."

Elena bit her lip. "From who?"

"Ransom."

"Figures," she muttered. The other hunter had the strangest hobby, considering his fascination with guns and weaponry. The fact that they lived in a major metropolitan city full of light pollution didn't seem to faze him. "He was stargazing, wasn't he?"

Sara blew out a breath. "With his super-duper high-powered gee-whiz telescope. And he told me you were, um, flying?" The last word was an incredulous question.

"I'll have to thank Ransom for calling me a star."

"I don't believe this," Sara whispered. "Oh, my— You were up there? Flying?"

"Yep."

"With an angel?"

"Archangel."

Pure silence for several long seconds. Then, "Holy shit."

"Uh-huh." She started unscrewing the lid again.

"What are you doing? I can hear you breathing."

Elena grinned. "You're such a nosy friend."

"It's in the best-friend rule book. Spill while I try to get over my shock."

"I had a delivery by angel a few minutes ago."

"What is it?"

"I'm just trying to . . ." Her voice trailed off as she succeeded in removing the lid. Fingers trembling, she stared at the contents of the tube, a tube that was lined several times over with cushioning material. She had a feeling baby-angel had been meant to make his drop with far more care. "Oh."

"Ellie? You're killing me."

Heart in her throat, she extracted the exquisitely crafted sculpture with careful fingers. "He sent me a rose."

A disappointed snort came through the telephone line. "I know you don't date much, sweet pea, but you can get those for five bucks at the corner store."

"It's made of crystal." Even as she spoke, light reflected off the rose in a distinctive fashion and her mouth fell open. "No way."

"No way, what?"

Disbelieving, she opened a nearby drawer, found a high-tensile cut-through-anything blade she didn't use much because the weighting was slightly off, and tried to gently scratch a tiny part of the stalk. The knife made no impact. But when she tried it in reverse, the rose scratched the blade's "scratch-proof" surface. "Oh, shit."

"Ellie, I swear I'm going to beat you to a pulp if you don't tell me what's going on. What is it? A mutant blood-sucking rose?"

Biting back a laugh, she stared at the indescribably lovely thing in her hand. "It's not crystal."

"Cubic zirconia?" Sara asked dryly. "Oh, wait, plastic."

"Diamond."

Absolute silence.

A cough.

"Could you please repeat that word?"

Elena held up the rose to catch the light. "Diamond. Flawless, one piece."

"That's impossible. Do you know how big it would have to be to carve out a rose? Is it microscopic?"

"Width of my palm."

"Impossible, like I said. Diamonds aren't carved. Really, it's impossible." Except Sara sounded a little breathless. "The man sent you a diamond rose?"

"He's not a man," Elena said, trying to stop the quintessentially female part of her from reacting in sheer delight at the wonder of the gift. "He's an archangel. A very dangerous archangel."

"Who's either besotted with you or tips his employees really well."

Elena laughed again. "Nah, he just wants to get in my pants." She waited until Sara had stopped choking on the other end to continue. "I said no last night. I don't think the archangel likes the word 'no.'"

"Ellie, my darling, please tell me you're messing with me." Sara's tone was a plea. "If the archangel wants you, he *will* have you. And—" She cut herself off.

"It's okay, Sara," Elena said softly. "If he takes me, he'll break me." Archangels weren't human, weren't close to human. When they were done with their pleasures, they cared nothing for their toys. "Which is why he'll never have me."

"How do you plan to ensure he doesn't come after you later?"

"I'm going to make him swear an oath."

Sara made a hmming sound. "Okay, I have the files up. Angels take oaths seriously. As in dead seriously. But you have to word it exactly right. And it's give-and-take. He'll want his pound of flesh. In your case, probably literally."

Elena shivered, the idea no longer wholly unappealing. And it wasn't the diamond. It was the eroticism of the night before. Dark, stroked with badness, but also the most potent sexual flirtation she'd ever experienced. Her body had sung for him and he'd barely touched her. What would happen if he drove himself inside of her, hot and hard . . . and again?

Her cheeks flushed, her thighs pressed together, and her heart was suddenly a drumbeat in her mouth. "I'll return the rose." It was extraordinary, a remarkable creation, but she couldn't keep it.

Sara misunderstood. "That won't be enough. You have to have something to bargain with."

"Leave that up to me." Elena tried to sound confident when the truth was, she had no idea of how she was going to bargain with an archangel.

He'll want his pound of flesh.

Her mind hiccuped without warning, and Sara's words mixed with the reawakened memory of Mirabelle's violated body. Her soul chilled. What if Raphael's price was something worse than death?

11

She put the message tube on Raphael's desk. "I can't accept this."

He lifted a finger, keeping his back to her as he stood by the windows, phone to his ear. It seemed odd to see an archangel with such a modern device, but her reaction made no logical sense—they were masters of technology, no matter that they looked like something out of fairy tale and legend.

How much truth was in those legends, no one knew. For all that angels had been part of mankind's history since the earliest cave paintings, they remained shrouded in mystery. Since man, as always, hated a vacuum, those of her kind had spun a thousand myths to explain the existence of angelkind. Some called them the scions of the gods, others saw them as simply a more advanced species. Only one thing was certain—they were the rulers of the world, and they knew it.

Now His Highness kept talking in a low murmur. Irritated, she started prowling around the room. The deep shelves on the side wall caught her attention. Made of a wood that was either a true ebony or had been treated to appear that way, they displayed treasure after treasure.

An ancient Japanese mask of an *oni*, a demon. But this one held an edge of mischief, as if it had been made for a children's festival. The artwork was precise, the colors brilliant, though she felt the age of it like a heavy weight in her bones. On the shelf next to it sat a single feather.

It was an extraordinary color—a deep, pure blue. She'd heard rumors of a blue-winged angel in the city over the past couple of months, but surely those rumors couldn't be true? "Natural or synthetic?" she whispered almost to herself.

"Oh, very much natural," came Raphael's smooth voice. "Illium was most distressed at being stripped of his prized feathers."

She turned, lines marring her forehead. "Why did you damage someone so beautiful? Jealous?"

Something sparked in his eyes, hot and certainly lethal if let out. "You would have little interest in Illium. He likes his women submissive."

"So? Why take his feathers?"

"He needed to be punished." Raphael shrugged, walking to stand less than a foot from her. "It was being grounded that really hurt him—the feathers grew back within a year."

"A blink of time."

The danger level seemed to lessen at her sarcasm. "For an angel, yes."

"So, were his new feathers like before?" She told herself to stop staring into those eyes, that no matter what he said, such contact had to make it easier for him to invade her mind. But she couldn't look away, not even when those flames turned into what looked like tiny whirling blades. "Were they?" she repeated, her voice rough with sudden hunger.

"No," he responded, reaching out to trace the shell of her ear. "They grew back even more beautiful. Blue edged with silver."

Elena laughed at the scowl in his voice. "That's the color scheme of my bedroom."

Naked heat sizzled between them. Powerful. Vibrant. His eyes still locked with hers, Raphael trailed his finger down her jaw to her neck. "Are you sure you don't want to invite me in?"

He was so utterly beautiful.

But male, very male.

Just one taste.

It was the darkness in her, the small core conceived on a blood-soaked kitchen floor the day she lost her childhood.

Drip.

Drip.

Drip.

"Come here, little hunter. Taste."

"No." She jerked away, palms damp with a thin sheen of fear. "I just came to return the rose and ask you if you had any more information about Uram's whereabouts."

Raphael lowered his hand, his face contemplative when she would've expected fury at being denied. "I'm good at vanquishing nightmares."

She stiffened. "And creating them. You left that vampire out in Times Square for hours." *Stop, Elena,* her mind ordered. *For God's sake, stop! You have to make him give you an oath of safety*—but her mouth wouldn't listen. "You tortured him!"

"Yes." Not even a tinge of remorse.

She waited. "That's it? That's all you have to say?"

"Did you expect guilt?" His expression stilled, became cold as frost. "I'm not human, Elena. Those I rule are not human. Your laws don't apply."

She clenched her hands painfully hard. "The laws of common decency, of conscience?"

"Call it what you will but remember this"—he leaned in, speaking in an icy whisper that cut across her skin with whiplash cruelty—"if I fall, if I *fail*, the vampires go completely free, and New York drowns in the blood of innocents."

Drip.

Drip.

Drip.

She reeled under the impact of those brutal images. One a

memory. One a possible future. "Vampires aren't all evil. Only a small percentage of them ever lose control, same as the human population."

His hand cupped her cheek. "But they're not human, are they?"

She remained silent.

His hand was hot, his voice glacial. "Answer me, Elena." The arrogance he displayed was breathtaking, but what made it worse was that he had every right to it. The power of him . . . it was beyond staggering.

"No," she admitted. "Bloodlust-ridden vampires kill with a viciousness that's unique—and they never stop. The death toll has the potential to reach thousands."

"So you see, iron control is necessary." He came even closer, until the fronts of their bodies touched and his hand slid down to her waist. She could no longer see his face without tilting back her head. It seemed like too much effort at that moment. All she wanted was to melt. Melt and take him with her, so he could do erotic, luscious things to her aching body.

"Enough of vampires," he said, his lips on the shell of her ear.

"Yes," she whispered, her hands stroking up his arms. "Yes."

He kissed his way down past her ear, along her jaw, before answering. "Yes."

Ecstasy laced her bloodstream, a biting pleasure she had no desire to resist. She wanted to peel off his clothing and find out if an archangel really was built like a man, to lick his skin, mark him with her nails, to ride him, possess him . . . be possessed by him. Nothing else mattered.

His lips touched hers and she moaned. The hands on her hips tightened as he lifted her without apparent effort and began to kiss her in earnest. Fire traveled through the raw eroticism of the openmouthed kiss to curl her toes, coming to pool in the vee between her thighs. "Hot," she whispered when he let her breathe. "Too hot."

Ice silvered the air and it was a cool mist that surrounded her, seeping into her pores in a stroke of possession. "Better?" He kissed her again before she could answer, his tongue inside her, his body hard and perfect and—

Nothing else mattered.

The words were wrong. The thoughts were wrong.

Sara mattered.

Beth mattered.

She mattered.

Raphael's lips traveled down her neck and to the flesh exposed by the open buttons of her shirt. "Beautiful."

I have not taken a human lover in eons. But you taste . . . intriguing.

She was a plaything.

To be toyed with and discarded.

Raphael could control her mind.

Giving a scream of pure rage, she kicked off him hard enough to send herself sprawling. The shock of pain as her tailbone connected with the floor snapped the final tendrils of a desire so visceral, so addictive, it made a fool out of her even now. "You bastard! Is rape what turns you on?"

For a single fleeting second, she thought she saw shock shadow his expression, but then that familiar arrogance looked back at her. "It was worth a try." He shrugged. "You can't say you didn't enjoy it."

She was so mad she didn't stop to think, to consider why she'd come here. Giving another scream, she rushed him. To her surprise, she got in a few good licks before he grabbed her arms and forced her against a wall.

His wings spread out to block her view of the room and it wasn't until he growled, "Leave us!" that she realized someone else had entered.

"Yes, sire."

Vampire. Dmitri.

And she'd been so fucking disoriented, so filled with manufactured lust turned into rage, that she hadn't heard him enter. "I'm going to kill you!" Her sense of violation had her humiliatingly close to tears. She should've expected such tactics from Raphael but she hadn't. Which made her an A-grade moron. "Let me go!"

He looked down at her, the blue of his eyes suddenly dark—as if a storm had rolled in. "No. In this state, you'll force me to hurt you."

For a second her heart kicked. *He cared.* She screamed again. "Get out of my head!"

"I am not in your head, Guild Hunter."

The use of the formal title was a verbal slap, one that brought her back to her senses. Instead of responding with the blood-fury boiling inside her, she took several deep breaths and tried to go to that calm place in her mind, the same place she went to whenever the memories of Ariel— No, she couldn't return there. Why wouldn't the past leave her alone today?

Another deep breath.

The scent of the sea, cool, crisp, powerful.

Raphael.

She opened her eyes. "I'm fine."

He waited several long seconds before releasing her. "Go. We'll discuss this later."

Her hand itched to go for a weapon but she simply turned on her heel and walked out. She had no intention of dying—not until she'd carved out Raphael's lying eyes and thrown them in the deepest, dirtiest cesspool she could find.

As soon as he heard the elevator doors close, Raphael called down to security. "Don't lose her. Ensure she stays safe."

"Yes, sire," was Dmitri's response, but Raphael heard the edge of disbelief.

He hung up without responding to the unasked question. Why had he allowed the hunter to live after she attacked him?

Is rape what turns you on?

His mouth tightened, his knuckles whitening as he fisted his hands. He'd done and been accused of many things through the ages. But never had he taken a woman against her will. *Never.* He hadn't done so today either.

But something had happened.

It was why he'd allowed her to assault him—she'd needed to vent her rage, and his disgust with himself was such that he'd welcomed the blows. There were some taboos that should never be broken. That he'd crossed a bright line he'd laid down centuries ago made him wonder about his own mental state. He knew his bloodstream was clear—he'd been tested yesterday—so this wasn't a result of the toxin putrefying his mind, sending his powers out of control.

Which left him with the unknown.

He swore in a low, ancient language long dead. He couldn't ask Neha, the Queen of Poisons. She'd see a weakness and immediately move to strike. None of the Cadre who might know the answer could be trusted in this except for Lijuan and Elijah. Lijuan had no interest in petty power. She'd gone too far, changed into something not wholly of this world. Elijah, Raphael wasn't sure about, but the other male was the scholar among them.

The problem was, Lijuan eschewed modern conveniences like the phone. She lived in a mountain compound hidden deep within China. He'd either have to fly to her or . . . His fist tightened even further. He couldn't leave his city while Uram roamed. Which left only one real choice.

As he turned to stride out, his eye fell on the message tube Elena had left behind. Destiny's Rose was an ancient treasure, one he'd earned as a young angel in the service of an archangel of ages long past. Legend said that it had been created by the combined power of the first Cadre. Raphael didn't know the truth of that, but it was undeniably priceless. He'd given it to Elena for reasons he didn't entirely understand. But she would have it. It bore her name now.

Grabbing the tube, he headed up to the penthouse and,

specifically, to the room of pure black in the dead center. The human covens would see that room as evil. They saw darkness as evil. But sometimes, darkness was nothing more than a tool, neither good nor evil.

It was the soul of the man using the tool that changed things. Raphael's hand clenched on the message tube. For the first time in centuries, he wasn't sure who he was. Not good. He'd never been that. But neither had he been evil . . . until today.

Poison

They were fools, all of them. They thought he was going to die.

He laughed, despite the pain that sliced through his eyes and into his body, agony that threatened to turn his bowels to water, his bones to so much pulp. He laughed until it was the only sound in the universe, the only truth.

Oh, no, he wasn't going to die. He was going to survive this trial they called poison. A lie. An effort to consolidate their own power. Not only was he going to survive, he was going to come out of it a god. And when he was done, the Cadre of Ten would tremble and the earth run dark with rivers of blood.

Rich, nourishing, sensual . . . blood.

12

Elena walked out the Tower door and kept going, ignoring the taxi standing by. An incandescent anger, richer, deeper, more deadly than anything she'd ever before felt, fired through her nerve endings, causing pain but also keeping her alive, keeping her going.

The bastard, the goddamn bastard!

Tears pricked. She refused to let them rise. To do that would be to admit that she'd expected something more from Raphael, something *human*.

Catching a familiar scent, she spun on her heel, knife in hand. "Go home, vamp." Her voice was molten fury.

Dmitri gave a courtly bow. "Be that I could do as my lady asks. Unfortunately"—he straightened, his shades reflecting her own angry image back at her—"I have other orders."

"Do you always do as your master commands?"

His lips thinned. "I stay with Raphael out of loyalty."

"Yeah, right. Like a little puppy dog." She dug in her claws, in the mood to draw blood. "Do you sit up and beg when he asks, too?"

Dmitri was suddenly in front of her, having moved so fast

he was gripping her knife hand before she could draw breath. "Don't push me, hunter. I'm the head of Raphael's security force. If it were up to me, you'd be strung up in chains, screaming as your flesh was flayed off your bones."

The erotic scent of him made the image even more barbaric. "Didn't Raphael tell you to stop the scent games?" She dropped a knife down from her arm sheath and into the palm of her weaker hand. Weaker, not weak. All hunters could fight with both hands.

"That was last night." He bent closer, the planes of his face exquisitely drawn, the curve of his lips touched with a hint of cruelty. "Today, he's probably extremely pissed with you. He won't mind if I take a discreet bite." A hint of fang as he flashed her on purpose.

"Right here on the street?" she asked, looking up at the line of his throat, vividly conscious of the push of his erection.

He didn't bother to glance around. "We're near Archangel Tower. The streets belong to us."

"But"—she smiled—"I. Fucking. Don't!" Slashing out with her knife, she carved a line across his throat.

Blood sprayed in an arterial rush but she'd already dodged out of the way. Dmitri grabbed at his neck and fell to his knees, his shades falling away to display eyes blazing fire. She read her death in those eyes.

"Don't be a baby," she murmured, wiping the knife on the grass and sliding it back into the sheath. "We both know a vamp your age will recover within the next ten minutes." A violent wave of vampire scent crashed into her senses. "And here come your flunkies to help you out. Nice talking to you, Dmitri darling."

"Bitch." It was a wet gurgle.

"Thanks."

He actually smiled, hard, lethal, scary as hell. "I like bitches." The words were already clearer, his healing progressing at a faster pace than she would've believed.

But it was the dark hunger in his tone that got to her. Damn kinky vampire had actually liked the knife. *Shit*. Turning her back to him, she ran. The second he healed, he'd come after her. And right now, she was worried less about being killed than about being seduced out of her fucking mind.

Dmitri might make her ache with need, but she didn't want him when he wasn't around to dose her with that scent of his. It was a compulsion, that scent, far stronger than any other she'd ever heard of. But that was hardly surprising given who he called sire.

Raphael had taken her between one breath and the next. She'd thought she'd learned to detect him, to pick up the odd sense of disconnection between mind and self that had accompanied his earlier attempts. But this time, there had been nothing. One second she was worrying about vampire serial killers, the next she was crawling all over him, trying to suck his tongue down her throat. If she hadn't snapped out of it, she was pretty sure she'd have been sucking other things, too.

Her face flushed.

Not in anger, though that was there. In desire. In heat. She might not want Dmitri when he was out of range, but she wanted the archangel. That made her a candidate for the asylum, but under no circumstances did it excuse what he'd done.

An instant later, she passed out of the restricted Tower zone to hit busy city streets, but instead of slowing down, she pushed herself even harder. Reaching into her pocket as she ran, she pulled out a cell phone and pressed in an emergency code. "I need a retrieval," she gasped as soon as someone answered. "Sending location." She pressed a button, activating the special GPS widget—it would transmit her location to the Guild computers until she switched it off. Because she couldn't stay in one place. The second she did, the game was over.

She kept an eye out for a taxi, but, of course, there were none in sight.

Two minutes later, tendrils of hunger snaked around her, searching, caressing. A sumptuous warmth bloomed in the pit of her stomach. Shoving a fist against that body part, she took in another gasp of air and made a hard left. High-class department stores zipped by, followed by the Zombie Den—the hangout of choice for the vamps and their whores.

Images of the erotic scenes she'd witnessed last night filled her head.

Opulent.

Sensual.

Seductive.

Not whores, addicts. And the worst thing was, she couldn't blame them. If Raphael ever got her in bed—not a chance since she was going to cut off his balls the first opportunity she got—she'd probably crave him to the end of her days. Infuriated, she pumped up her arms and swerved around a kid on a skateboard.

"Where's the vamp?" the kid called out, jumping off his board in excitement. "Dude . . ."

Oh, fuck! She glanced over her shoulder and saw Dmitri gaining on her. The blood on his shirt was a scarlet flower but his neck was fine, his pretty face wiped clean. Snapping back her head, she darted into traffic, crossing the road to the blaring of horns, curses, and several excited screams. A tourist started snapping photos. Great. He'd probably get a shot of her being vampire-bit right before Dmitri turned her into a begging, crawling thing concerned with sex alone.

Her gun was suddenly in her hand. Knives were her weapon of choice, but if she was going to stop the son of a bitch before he got to her, she'd have to shoot him in the heart. There was a very slight chance she might actually kill him that way, and if she did, she'd be brought up on charges. Unless, of course, she could prove harmful intent. She could see it now.

"See, Your Honor, he was going to fuck me silly, make me like it."

Yeah, that would fly. With her luck, she'd end up with some old fogey of a judge who thought like her father—that women were pawns, spreading their legs their only talent.

Fury boiled through her in a second violent wave. She was about to turn, her finger already on the trigger, when a motorcycle screeched to a stop in front of her. It was pure black, as were the rider's clothes and helmet. But there was a discreet gold *G* on the gas tank.

Switching direction, she jumped onto the back and held on for dear life.

Dmitri's hand brushed her shoulder as the motorcycle peeled away. She turned to find him standing at the curb, watching her go. He blew her a kiss.

Raphael closed the door to the black-on-black room. For a second, he stood in the utter lack of light and considered what he was about to do.

Lijuan was totally removed from humanity.

What had happened between him and Elena had been very human, very real.

He set his jaw, knowing he had no other choice. Not with Caliane for a mother. If this was the beginning of some kind of a degeneration . . .

Walking instinctively to the center of the room, he focused his angelic abilities to a shining beam deep within. Like the glamour, this was something only an archangel could do. But unlike the glamour, it demanded a far heavier price. For the twelve hours after he did this, he would be Quiet, ruled by a part of his brain that had never known mercy and never would.

It was why he rarely used this form of communication. In the aftermath, he became something far closer to the monster that lurked in his heart, in the hearts of all archangels. Power was a drug and it didn't only corrupt, it destroyed. It was during one of these Quiet periods that he'd punished the vampire who had ended up in Times Square.

The punishment had been nonnegotiable. But the Quietness in him had changed the timbre of it to something close to evil. Now, Raphael made sure not to schedule anything that could turn destructive during these periods. The problem was, once he went cold, he saw things in a different light and could very well change his mind.

But this had to be done.

Centered, ready, he spread out his wings to their fullest extent. The tips just barely touched the edges of the room and he could taste the blackness of the walls in his throat. Most humans and vampires believed that angel wings weren't sensitive except at the arched line above the shoulders. They were wrong. Some quirk of angelic biology meant that an angel was fully conscious of any impact on his wings, whether it be in the center or at the very edge of his primaries.

Now he soaked in the blackness as if it were power. It wasn't. The power came from within him, but the lack of stimulation—a kind of sensory deprivation—amped up his awareness of that power to excruciating levels. First it was a hum in his blood, then a symphony, then a thundering crescendo that filled every one of his veins, stretching his tendons to breaking point and lighting him up from within. It was at that instant—before an internal implosion that could leave him stunned for hours—that he raised his hands and threw power at the wall in front of him.

It buckled, then liquefied into a churning pool that reflected nothing in its ebony depths. Quickly, before the power could grow restless and seek to shove itself back into his body, he directed it into a searching pattern set to Lijuan. The ability to communicate over vast distances came from the same root as their mental gifts, but unlike those mental gifts, it was so potent it required a vessel to contain it. The walls within this room provided the most efficient of those vessels, but he could use other objects and surfaces if pushed.

If he'd tried this sending—to the other side of the world—using only his mind, he'd probably have shattered parts of his brain and destroyed this building in the process. In front of him, the swirling slowed, then stopped completely. The liquid smoothed over to black glass. Within was a familiar face and only the face. The searching was very specific—it would show him nothing but Lijuan.

"Raphael," she said, her surprise open. "You chance the use of this much power while Uram is in your state?"

"It was necessary. I'll be back to full strength by the time he devolves to the next stage."

A slow nod. "Yes, he hasn't crossed the final line, has he?"

"We'll know when he does." The whole world would know. Everyone would hear the screams. "I need to ask you a question."

Her eyes were fathomless when she looked at him, so pale the iris was almost indistinguishable from the white of the eye. "There is a monster inside us all, Raphael. Some will survive, others will break. You have not yet broken."

"I lost control of my mind," he told her, not questioning how she knew what she did. Lijuan was more ghost than human, a shadow who moved seamlessly between worlds the rest of them never glimpsed.

"It is evolution," she whispered, a smile that was not a smile creasing her face. "Without change, we would turn to dust."

He didn't know if she was talking about him or herself. "If I keep losing control, then I'm useless as archangel," he said. "The toxin—"

"This has nothing to do with the Scourge." She waved a hand and he saw wrinkles. She was the only angel who showed even such small marks of age and she seemed to revel in them. "What you are experiencing is something else entirely."

"What?" He wondered if she was lying, drawing out the conversation in order to weaken him. It wouldn't be the first time two archangels had worked in concert to topple a third. "Or do you know nothing and play at being a goddess?"

Frost in those blind eyes, flickers of emotion so *other* as to be nothing known. "I am a goddess. I hold life and death in my hand." Her hair flew back in that ghostly wind she alone could generate. "I can destroy thousands with a thought."

"Death does not a goddess make or Neha would be beside

you at this moment." The Queen of Snakes, of Poisons, left a trail of bodies in her wake. No one disagreed with Neha. To do so was to die.

Lijuan shrugged, an oddly human gesture. "She is a foolish child. Death is only half the equation. A goddess must not merely take life . . . she must give it."

He looked at her, felt the insidious beauty of her words, and knew what he'd only before suspected—she'd gained a new power, a power whispered of but never believed. "You can make the dead walk?" Not alive, they would not be alive. But they would walk, they would talk, and they would not rot.

Her only response was a smile. "We are talking about you, Raphael. Are you not afraid I'll use your problem to destroy you?"

"I think you have little interest in New York."

She laughed, a cool sound that whispered of the grave and sunshine in one. "You are a clever one. Far cleverer than the others. Here's what you need to know—you did not lose control."

"I forced a woman to want me." His tone was vicious. "It may be nothing to Charisemnon, but it is to me." The other archangel held power over most of North Africa. If he saw a woman he wanted, he simply took her. "What is that if not a total loss of control?"

"There were two people in that room."

For an instant, he didn't understand. Then he did and it made his blood turn to ice. "She has the ability to influence me?" He hadn't been under any creature's control since escaping Isis's tender mercies ten centuries ago.

"Would you kill her if she does?"

He'd killed Isis—it had been the only way to break free of the powerful angel bent on keeping him prisoner. He'd killed others, too. "Yes," he answered, but part of him was no longer so sure.

Is rape what turns you on?

The impact of those words still reverberated in the endless

night he called a soul. His eyes flicked over Lijuan's face. "If she was controlling me, it wasn't conscious." Otherwise, she wouldn't have accused him of rape.

"Are you sure?"

He stared at her, in no mood to play games.

It made her smile widen. "Yes, you are a smart one. No, your little hunter does not have the power to bend an archangel to her whims. Are you surprised I know who it was?"

"You have spies in my Tower, like you have spies everywhere."

"And do you have spies in my home?" she asked, her tone a razor.

He threw up a shield, reflecting back her cutting power. "What do you think?"

"I think you're far stronger than the others realize." Calculation filled her gaze, even as she dropped into less formal speech.

Raphael would've cursed himself for having made a mistake except that he knew this was part of Lijuan's modus operandi. To speak with her, you had to be, if not an equal, at least strong enough to make things interesting. "If you weren't a woman, I'd say you have a need to prove whose cock is bigger."

She actually giggled but the sound was somehow . . . off. "Oh, that I'd found you when I was still interested in such things." She waved a hand. "You would've made a fine lover." Her lips turned sensuous, some faded remembrance lighting sparks in the winter chill of her eyes. "Have you ever danced with an angel in flight?"

Memory hit Raphael like a body blow. Yes, he had danced. But it had not been in pleasure. However, he said nothing, simply watched, listened, knowing he was her audience.

"I had a lover once who actually made me feel human." She blinked. "Extraordinary, isn't it?"

He considered what kind of a young angel Zhou Lijuan might've been and found he didn't like the answer. "Is he with you still?" he asked for form's sake.

"I had him killed—an archangel can never be human." Her face shifted, becoming less and less of this world, a caricature of angelic features, paper-thin skin over bone glowing from within. "There are some humans—one among half a billion perhaps—who make us something other than what we are. The barriers fall, the fires ignite, and the minds merge."

He stayed absolutely silent.

"You must kill her." Her pupils had expanded to devour the irises, her eyes black flame, her face a burning skeletal mask. "Unless and until you do, you can never be certain when the barriers will fall again."

"What happens if I don't kill her?"

"Then she will kill you. She will make you mortal."

13

Ransom stopped the motorcycle in the bowels of Guild HQ. Pulling off his helmet, he hung it on the right handlebar. "My, but you lead an interesting life, Elieanora."

She rubbed her cheek against the braid hanging down his back, too happy with him to tell him to stop using that stupid name. Not only was it not her name—okay, maybe on her birth certificate—it made her sound about a hundred years old. According to Ransom, she'd been drunk the night she confessed her secret shame. She thought it was more likely he'd hacked into some database and stolen the intel.

Reaching back, he patted her thigh. "Am I going to get lucky tonight?"

"You wish." Grinning, she slapped away his hand and got off the bike.

His too-handsome-to-live face bore a wide grin. "It was worth a try." With high cheekbones and rich copper-gold skin inherited from his Cherokee ancestors, not to mention green eyes from Ireland—via a short sojourn in an Australian penal colony—he was pretty enough to lick up like ice cream.

It was almost a pity they were just friends. Almost. "The night I sleep with you, you'll cry like a baby."

His eyes widened as he unzipped his leather jacket. "I know you're into knives, but in bed? Isn't that taking it a little far?"

Leaning in, she put her hands on his shoulders. "The instant we have sex, we stop being friends. Tear-time, honey pie." It was a relief to be doing something as normal as bantering with Ransom.

He wrapped an arm around her waist. "You don't know what you're missing."

"I'll survive." She knew full well he didn't really want to mess up their friendship. And the second sex intruded, that's exactly what would happen—Ransom didn't deal well with intimacy. He might not be sleeping with Elena, but she bet she knew him a hell of a lot better than his girlfriend did. "And I won't even tell Nyree you were hitting on me."

Shadows moved across his face. "She left me."

"Well, that's a new one. It's usually you doing the cutting and running."

"She said I had commitment issues." He squeezed her waist in emphasis. "Where the hell does she get that from?"

"Er, Ransom"—she patted his cheek—"your longest relationship, not counting me or Sara, was with Nyree and that was what, eight weeks?"

He scowled. "Who the fuck needs commitment? We had good times. I can find another piece of ass the second I walk into a bar."

Despite all the problems in her own life—certain-death job, kinky vampire, superpowerful archangel—she felt her attention switch completely. "Wow, hell froze over while I wasn't looking. You care about her."

He dropped his arm. "I let her leave *stuff* at my place. Girly shit."

Which, she assumed, was as good as a marriage certificate to him. "And?"

"And what?"

Sensing that line of questioning would get her nowhere, she changed gears. "That's your plan—to go out and find an easy lay?"

"You're the morality police now?"

The shrug made her muscles protest, threatening to remind her of how she'd overstretched them in the first place. "Hey, none of my business if you and Nyree decide to find new bed partners."

His skin turned white over bone. "She lets any other fucker lay a hand on her, he'll be singing soprano the rest of his miserable life."

"Maybe you should let Nyree know." Elena decided that was about the limit of the advice she was capable of right then. It was time to return to the nightmare of her life. "Now get your cute butt up off there. We need to powwow with Sara."

"She's on her way," he told her, sprawling back on the bike with an easy grace that made most women drool. "When you called for a retrieval, she told me to haul ass and to make sure you stayed hidden until she knew what was going on."

Elena remembered what Sara had implied about spies in the Guild. Raphael's spies. Her hands fisted. "I hate men."

Ransom sat back up, face absolutely expressionless. "What happened?"

And she knew that if she told him, he'd be ready to go archangel hunting with her. She called him her sometimes-friend because they tended to fight half the time, but when push came to shove, Ransom would stand at her back. But this was a private war. "Personal stuff," she answered, just as the elevator doors opened to reveal Sara.

She strode out, a petite woman with skin the rich, melting color of cinnamon coffee and huge brown eyes set off by dark hair cut in thick, straight bangs and twisted up off her neck. Her tailored burgundy suit and white lace camisole screamed executive, but she had her feet perched on what looked like five-inch high heels. "You smell like you've been running a marathon," was her greeting to Elena. "And you"—a glance at Ransom—"look like a reject from a biker show."

"Hey!" Ransom took offense. "I'll have you know I'm a certified biker dude."

Sara ignored him to fix Elena with a gimlet eye. "Ellie, my darling, please explain to me why the office has been flooded with calls about, and I quote"—she crooked her fingers in the air—"a vicious vampire on the loose, a crazy knife-wielding maniac, and oh, this one's my favorite—an assassin carrying a gun!"

"I can explain."

Sara folded her arms and tapped one fashionably clad foot. "Explain why you flashed not only a knife but a gun? I hope to God you didn't actually use either of them without authorization because if the VPA gets ahold of it, we're screwed."

Elena rubbed the back of her neck. "Exigent circumstances. He was trying to make me his bed buddy. I declined. He gave chase."

Ransom choked back what sounded suspiciously like a laugh. "Why did you say no? It's been a dry spell of what, forever?"

She threw him a dirty look before returning her gaze to Sara. "You know I'd never have considered using the gun otherwise."

Sara held up a hand. "How, exactly, did you 'decline' his offer?"

"By slitting his throat."

The silence in the garage was broken only by the sound of water drip-dripping somewhere in the distance. Sara just stared. So did Ransom. Then the idiot male started laughing hysterically. He laughed so hard he fell off the bike and onto the scarred concrete of the garage floor. Even that didn't stop him.

Elena would've kicked him, except he'd probably use the chance to pull her down with him. "Shut up before I do the same to you."

He tried to stop laughing. Failed. "Jesus, Ellie. You are awe-some!"

"What you are," Sara muttered, "is a magnet for trouble."

"I—" Elena started to defend herself.

Sara held up her hand again and started counting off on her fingers. "Because of you, I have messages on my phone from the governor *and* the freaking President of the United States of America." Down went one finger. "Because of you, half of New York now thinks there's a wild vampire on the loose." Another finger. "Because of you, I got three more gray hairs!"

Elena grinned at the last. "I love you, too."

Shaking her head, Sara finally bridged the distance between them and hugged her with ferocious strength. After this many years of friendship, they had the height thing figured out. Elena bent, Sara tiptoed, and they met in the middle. Breaking apart, they looked at each other. "Are you in trouble, Ellie?"

Elena bit her lower lip and glanced from Ransom's suddenly sober face to Sara's. "Sort of. Raphael and I had a slight . . . disagreement." She wasn't sure why she wasn't serving him up on a platter. Maybe it was because she was terrified of what he'd do to her friends—hunters or not, they were no match for an archangel. Or maybe it was something far more dangerous. "And Dmitri apparently thinks that makes me fair game."

"The vampire?" Sara clarified. "Raphael's security chief?"

"Yep." She shoved a hand through her hair. "You guys are not going to believe this—when I cut his throat, he got off on it. He thinks I'm the hottest thing since blood on a stick."

"There's no such thing as blood on a stick." Of course, that was Ransom.

"Exactly!" She threw up her hands. "I'm not into weird vampire shit either!"

"Okay, this isn't as bad as I thought," Sara muttered. "Do you think he'll lay a complaint with the VPA?"

Elena thought back to the air kiss. "No. He's having too much fun."

"Good for the Guild, not so good for you." Sara tapped her foot again. "Right, you'll go to ground in the Cellars until you can contact Raphael and get him to rein in Dmitri. In the meantime, Ransom will deal with lover boy—"

"No," Elena interrupted.

Ransom stood, brushing off the seat of his pants. "You don't think I can handle him?" There was an edge to his tone.

"Don't be so male," she snapped. "He has the scent thing happening." And Ransom was hunter-born. Not as strong as Elena, but strong enough to be vulnerable.

Another silence. Sara glanced from Elena to Ransom. "Okay, new plan, I'll get Hilda to deal with Mr. Vamp if he turns up."

Hilda was human. She could also bench-press a car and was one of the few individuals immune to any and all vampiric powers.

"Fuck." Ransom turned and gave them his back as he spit out a string of curses that would've stripped the paint off the walls had they actually been painted to begin with. "Since I'm useless here, I'm going to get drunk."

Elena put a hand on the stiff muscle of his shoulder. "You're not useless. You're a hunky bite of sex and I'm not sure if Dmitri swings both ways. Cut me some slack for wanting to protect my friend. You'd do the same if the tables were turned."

"You're not the one who got scent-ambushed and woke up naked with bites all over his fucking body."

She hadn't actually expected him to bring up the incident. He never had before. Maybe this Nyree was even better for him than she'd thought. "True," she murmured. "Yeah, it's better you don't go to Nyree in this mood. You might hurt her. Go get drunk."

He hissed out a breath.

"She's probably out anyway." Elena mouthed "shut up" at

Sara when it looked like her best friend was going to inter-
vene. "Since she's mad at you, she probably took some time
off—what did you say she did?"

"Librarian."

Ransom was dating a *librarian*? "I bet she took the chance
to put on a sexy little—"

Ransom moved so fast she barely managed to jump out of
the way as he peeled out of the garage. She dusted off her
hands. "My work here is done." And good thing, too, because
she hadn't been sure where she was going with the sexily
dressed librarian.

"He serious about her?" Sara's tone was astonished. "As
in, he wants her for more than boinking?"

"Yep." She put her thumbs in the belt loops of her jeans
and rocked back. "I don't like the Cellars."

"Tough titties." Sara was pure Guild Director at that moment. "I'm not losing my best hunter—and don't you dare tell
Ransom I said that—to a lust-crazed vampire. Get in the elevator."

Elena got in with Sara, then pulled off the panel that hid
an auxiliary keypad. Inputting the code to the secret hide-
away that existed in some form in every Guild building, she
replaced the panel. "Is it true that in L.A. they've got the
hidey-holes in the elevator shaft?"

Sara nodded. "Small cubbies—connected, but way too
cramped. Ours is better."

The doors opened to reveal a subterranean network so old,
it dated to the time of the first American Guild—that history
was part of the reason why New York functioned as the per-
manent home of the Guild Director, and consequently, as HQ
for the entire United States Guild.

"Ours might be better," Elena said, stepping out, "but I bet
they don't have to dodge carnivorous bugs with a taste for human flesh." The building supports in front of her were massive, but only dirt lay beneath as far as the eye could see. Even
if someone unauthorized did make it down here, they'd probably give up long before they discovered the truth.

"Badass vampire hunters eat bugs for breakfast." Light words, but Sara's expression was serious. "You good? I have to get upstairs to initiate damage control."

Elena nodded, then put out a hand to stop the doors closing. "You said you had a message from the president?" It was an attempt to temper the icy tendril of fear that twisted into her mind without warning as a primal part of her reacted to something she didn't yet understand.

Sara nodded. "He saw the news footage—wanted to know if he should be worrying about a wave of bloodlust-crazed vampires."

"Nervous guy."

Sara responded with a snort. "Do you realize exactly how *many* vamps were chasing you? Just stay under and make up with Raphael—I can't believe I'm saying that—as soon as possible."

As the doors closed, plunging Elena into pitch blackness, she wasn't sure if she ever wanted to speak to Raphael again. She'd thought— The truth was, she didn't know what she'd thought. Her hand flinched involuntarily as her body remembered how Raphael had forced her to hurt herself. From that to lusting after him in less than twenty-four hours. Her mouth tightened. Maybe the bastard had been messing with her mind from the start, letting her believe she was free when all the time, he was making her dance to his tune.

"Which makes him an archangel and me an idiot," she said, walking ten paces left and feeling her way down to the base of the column there. A few minutes later, she unearthed—literally—the stash of weatherproof torches. After making sure hers worked, she spent several more minutes reburying the hoard for the next hunter, then began to make her way through the concrete, metal, and earth jungle.

It took her ten minutes to reach the doorway to the Cellars. It looked like some junkie's idea of a door, all twisted up, graffitied, and shot full of holes. But she knew that that door was backed up by eight inches of pure steel. Shining the torch on what appeared to be a long-broken keypad, she coded in.

Welcome, Elena.

The message flashed across the tiny screen a second before a retinal scanner slid out of the slot. She dutifully put her eye to it and two minutes later, she was inside. But that only meant she'd passed the first hurdle. This shelter was designed to hold even if a hunter was forced or coerced into bringing an enemy inside.

Standing in the seemingly solid steel cubicle, she waited until Vivek cleared her through the second set of doors. She was scanned by several lasers the second she stepped out. All her weapons were noted, as was the lack of any biological or chemical weapon.

"*Barev*, Elena."

The words came out of hidden speakers. "*Barev*, Vivek. How's the weather in Armenia these days?" The Cellar Manager liked languages. Over time, it had become a game to guess the origin of the greetings he used.

"Cloudy, with a three percent chance of rain."

Grinning, she headed down the main corridor. "So, what evil plans have you got for me today, O Great Knower of All Things?"

Vivek laughed, safe in the small, bomb-proof, flood-proof, earthquake-proof, probably end-of-the-world-proof room at the center of the Cellars. "Scrabble."

"Bring it on. You still owe me three hundred bucks."

"That's because you cheated." There was a slight pettiness to his tone but that was Vivek. He lived down here twenty-four/seven out of choice.

Up there, I'm nothing, a burden. Down here, I'm king.

She couldn't argue with him. Vivek controlled everything in the Cellars. "Give me a few minutes to shower." Raphael wasn't a vampire, but the rawly masculine essence of him was burned into her brain, her skin, her very pores. She wanted him gone!

14

"How did you lose her?" Raphael stared at Dmitri, impassive.

"She cut my throat."

Raphael looked at the vampire's clean shirt, his damp hair. "It occurred soon after she left if you've had time to clean up."

"Yes. She didn't want an escort home."

"Did you provoke the attack?" he asked calmly, because the answer mattered nothing to him, except as a test of Dmitri's loyalty.

"I wanted to taste her."

Raphael struck out without warning, slamming Dmitri to the floor with a broken jaw. "I told you she was off-limits. Are you challenging my authority?"

The vampire stood, waiting for his jaw to heal enough that he could speak. "You fought."

"Yes, but I didn't rescind my order."

A bow of Dmitri's head. "My apologies, sire. I did not realize her blood was yours." Disappointment in his eyes, but no hint of rebellion. "I'm surprised you only broke my jaw."

With the dazzling clarity of absolute Quiet, Raphael could see that Dmitri was sincere. "I need you functional. We have work to do."

"I can track her."

That was a secret no mortal knew. Vampires like Dmitri, the ones who gained the ability to entrance hunters with the seduction of scent, could also sometimes turn the tables on their foes. "That's not necessary." This was his hunt—he knew where she'd go. If he was wrong, he knew who to ask. They would answer.

"What would you like me to do?" Dmitri asked, his voice almost normal. He was old enough that most injuries—especially those that involved little to no loss of blood—healed relatively quickly.

"Get me the Guild Director's home address, as well as that of Ransom Winterwolf."

15

Elena made the word "hide" then waited as Vivek thought. "Anytime this century, V."

"Patience." He sat with absolute stillness, but it was no act of self-discipline. Vivek had lost all feeling below the shoulders in an accident as a child. If he hadn't, he'd have been hunter-born. Instead, aside from his considerable duties as Cellar Manager, he functioned as the Guild's eyes and ears in a connected world, his high-tech wheelchair built for wireless capability—he often knew what people were saying about the Guild before the words even passed their lips.

Now, he murmured something under his breath and on the computer board, the letters shifted to make HOME. "What next, Ellie?" It was clear he wasn't talking about the game.

She tapped her fingers on her thigh. "I need to talk to Sara."

"You're under blackout orders."

"Then you talk to her—tell her she's in danger. Everyone knows she's the one person certain to know my location." And it wasn't Dmitri she was worried about.

Vivek used a vocal command to open the door through

which she'd entered. "Go. I'll make the call then let you back in."

She wasn't in the mood for his childishness. "I'm not going to steal your damn codes!"

"Go or I don't move."

Shoving away from the computer console, she strode out. "Hurry up." The door snapped shut behind her.

Sliding down to sit with her back against it, she didn't stop to consider that Ransom might also be in danger. She wasn't used to thinking of him as vulnerable. She wouldn't have worried so much about Sara either, before the baby. Not only could Sara take care of herself, but her husband, Deacon, was a lethal son of a bitch. But God, Zoe was so little.

The door slid open behind her. "Sara wants to talk to you." Vivek sounded peevish.

She walked in to find him sulking in the blackout booth, which meant Sara didn't want him listening in. Elena winced. When Vivek sulked, life in the Cellars got very uncomfortable—bone-melting temperature changes, odd smells in the air, food that tasted like sawdust. Once, she'd had to spend a whole torturous month down here after Vivek had had a fight with Sara. Talk about a shit storm. But Vivek's moods were nothing, not when Sara's life was on the line.

Elena picked up the old-fashioned phone. It was so old it was hackerproof. "Sara, you need to get down here with your family."

"The Guild Director doesn't turn tail and hide." Sara's tone was hard, revealing the steel backbone that had given her the strength to hold her position in a profession overrun with testosterone.

"Don't be an idiot!" Elena clenched her hand hard enough that her nails left half-moon crescents on her palms. "Dmitri isn't some baby vamp. He's Raphael's head of security!"

"And that's something else we need to discuss—just how big a 'disagreement' did you and Raphael have?"

Her soul chilled. "Why?"

"Because I came back to my office to find a new message waiting—he's looking for you, Ellie."

"I'll talk—"

"You're going nowhere near him," Sara snapped. "You didn't hear the message. If a naked blade could speak, that's what it would sound like."

Elena cursed under her breath. What the hell had happened between her leaving the Tower and the message? He'd let her go without a fight. So why was he hunting her now? "Are you sure he's that angry?"

"Angry isn't the word I'd use. Lethal would fit better." There was real concern in Sara's voice. "What did you do to piss off an archangel?"

Loyalty warred with the inexplicable need she had to keep what had happened in the office, private. "I hit him."

A long, indrawn breath. "You *hit* an archangel?"

She recalled the sense of danger that had blasted off him like heat radiation. "It was his own fault, so if he stops to think about it, he'll calm down."

"Archangels aren't exactly good at saying sorry." Sarcasm dripped from every syllable. "It doesn't matter what he did, you'll have to grovel or he'll grind you to dust."

"I won't grovel." Not for anyone. "You know that."

"Of course I know that, you moron. I was making a point."

"The point being that I'm dead meat." Because she wouldn't apologize to that bastard. Not even to save her own life.

"Pretty much."

"That proves *my* point."

"Which is?"

"That you need to get Zoe and Deacon to a safe house. If Raphael's gunning for me, he'll come after you and yours to get my location." She paused, swallowed bile. Her life was one thing, but . . . "I won't let my pride put your family in danger. I'll call him and—"

"Shut up." Quiet words. Furious words. "I'll get Zoe out of the city. Deacon and I can look after ourselves."

"Sara, I'm sorry."

"You really fucking think I'd let you barter your soul so easily?" She hung up.

Elena felt like shit, but knew her best friend would forgive her. And Sara angry meant Sara in action. About to return the receiver to the cradle, she hesitated. A swift glance showed that Vivek had pointedly turned his back to her. Taking the chance, she pressed the cutoff button, then quickly dialed an outside line. "Hurry up," she muttered under her breath as the phone rang and rang on the other end.

"Beth Deveraux-Ling speaking."

At the sound of that familiar voice, moisture threatened to film Elena's vision. She cut it off with the ruthless ease of practice. "Beth, it's Elena."

"Why do you keep using that name?" Beth asked and Elena could almost see her frown. "You know Daddy prefers you use your full name, or Nell if you must shorten it."

"Beth, I don't have time for this. Is Harrison there?"

"Harry doesn't like talking to you." Her voice lowered. "I don't even know why I do—you turned my husband over to an angel."

"You know why," Elena reminded her. "If I hadn't brought him in, the next hunter would've had orders to execute him. Angels don't like losing their property."

"He's not property!" Beth sounded close to tears.

Elena rubbed at her temples with her fingers. "Please, Bethie, get Harrison. This is important." Her sister was high-strung at the best of times, and quite incredibly spoiled to boot. "He'll want to know."

A stubborn pause before Beth finally folded. Elena waited for several seconds, eyes trained on Vivek's back. He'd know she'd made an outside call the second he exited the cubicle but she had to do this. And there was no danger to the Guild— even if someone traced the call, it was set up to come back to a dummy account.

"Elena?"

She snapped to attention. "Harry, look, I need—"

"You need to listen," Harry interrupted.

"I don't have time for your—"

"I'm trying to help you." It was a sharp reproof. "I don't know why—maybe I don't want to be known as the brother-in-law of the hunter who was found spitted on a stick in Times Square! I can't believe you managed to insult someone of Dmitri's stature."

Elena froze. "You know?"

"Of course I know. Dmitri's the most senior vampire in the area and I report directly to him unless my master wants a face-to-face." His voice turned bitter. "I've been having quite a lot of chats with Andreas since you ended my hope of escape."

"Damn it, Harry, you signed a contract. In blood!"

"I wouldn't expect you to understand family loyalty," he said, slicing right through her heart. "But I suspect your life is important to you."

"I called to warn you," she gritted out, refusing to let her twerp of a brother-in-law hurt her. "You might be a vampire, but Beth is mortal."

"Not for long. We've petitioned for her to be Made."

Elena's soul went ice-cold. "You are not dragging her into that world. Does she have any idea of what she's signing on for or did you tell her it was all roses and fairy tales?"

"Oh, believe me, Elieanora, we know it's not perfection but it is immortality. And not that you'd have any comprehension of the concept, but I love Beth—I don't want to spend eternity without her."

That halted Elena, because, all his faults aside, Harrison Ling did actually seem to love his wife. "Look, Harry, we can fight about this later—hide from Dmitri until this blows over."

"Why should I hide?"

"He'll try to get my location out of you."

"He already asked and I told him I didn't have a clue," Harry replied. "Since he appears to know precisely how *close* you are to your family, he believed me."

"Just like that." Elena frowned. "No strong-arm tactics?"

"Of course not. We're civilized beings."

Elena's mind rebutted that with a memory of Dmitri's smile as his neck spurted blood. "Fine," she muttered. "As long as you're safe."

"Where are you?"

Every one of her instincts screamed in warning. "You don't need to know."

"Turn yourself in," he urged. "That's what I meant about your life—if you give yourself up, Dmitri might be swayed toward leniency. It'd also make our life easier if I brought you to him. Beth agrees with me."

That was all she was to him and Beth, Elena thought, refusing to consider the crushing hurt in her chest—a convenient way to curry favor. "Since when did you become Dmitri's pimp, Harry?"

The sharp hiss of an indrawn breath. "Fine, get yourself killed. Did I mention that Dmitri's looking for you on behalf of his sire?"

"What?"

"Word is that Raphael's gone cold."

Elena didn't know what that meant, but Harry's tone made it clear it wasn't anything good. "Thanks for the warning."

"It's more than you gave me."

Vivek began to bring his chair around.

"Gotta go." She hung up in the nick of time.

Exiting the blackout booth, Vivek headed immediately to his computers. She expected an explosion when he detected the unauthorized call, but he just sighed and shook his head before turning his chair to face her. "Why do you even bother, Ellie?"

That shook her, far more than anything else he could've done. Her legs folded and she collapsed into a chair. "They're family."

"They rejected you because you didn't fit the mold." His mouth twisted. "Believe me, I know all about that."

"I know, Vivek." His family had institutionalized him

after the accident. "But I can't leave Beth vulnerable when there's a chance I can protect her."

"You know she'd hang you out to dry if it ever came to it?" His tone was as bitter as darkest coffee. "She's married to a vampire—he comes first."

Elena couldn't disagree, not with Harrison's words still ringing in her ears. Her family wanted to turn her in to a high-level vampire. Forget about what that vampire—and more importantly, his sire—might do to her. "That's who they are," she whispered, "but that's not who I am."

"Why not?" Vivek shifted his chair back around to face the computer. "Why bother? It's not like they'll ever love you."

Elena had no answer to that, so she left. But the words burrowed into her skull, and dug in. Painful. Clawing.

"Hey, Ellie!"

She jerked up her head to see another hunter lounging in the doorway to one of the sleep rooms. Tall, slender, with long, straight black hair and snapping brown eyes, Ashwini was one hell of a tracker. She was also all kinds of crazy. Which was why Elena liked her. "Hey, yourself," she said, glad for the chance to get her mind off things, if only for a few minutes. "I thought you were in Europe."

"Was. Got back a couple of days ago."

"You were already in the country when you called Sara?" God, had that been only yesterday?

Ashwini nodded. "Hunt took an unexpected turn."

"Yeah?" she said, forcing her thoughts back to the here and now.

"Damn Cajun."

"Uh-oh."

"I finally get within a block of him and all of a sudden, he's come to an 'understanding' with the angel who put out the track." Her eyes narrowed. "One of these days, I'm going to turn him into gator-bait."

Elena grinned. "Then where would the rest of us get our entertainment?"

"Fuck you." Said with a grin before she yawned, lifted up her arms, and stretched, sinuous as a cat. "I like sleeping down here."

"What, you like the ambience?" She rolled her eyes. "How was Europe anyway?"

"Sucked. I was in Uram's territory."

Elena's nape pricked. This wasn't coincidence—Ash was a little bit spooky in her prescience. "How's the situation there?"

The other hunter shrugged, the movement lithe and unconsciously graceful. According to the Guild rumor mill, she'd been a trained dancer with a prestigious company before deciding to take up hunting. Ransom had once asked her to perform. It had taken two weeks for his black eyes to fade.

"Uram's fallen off the grid," she now said. "The locals are scared of their own shadows—they think he's spying on them."

Elena caught the glint in the other hunter's eye. "But you don't think so?"

"Something's hinky. No one's seen his assistant, Robert Syles, for a while either. And Bobby likes the TV cameras." Ashwini shrugged. "My guess is that they're doing some hunting of their own. Maybe angels. We'll hear about it soon enough." Another yawn.

"You'd better get back to sleep."

"Nah, I'm all recharged now. But I do have to shower—got to head out again in an hour." She turned. "Oh, hey, El, one other thing I picked up—seems like they found more than a few decapitated bodies around the time Uram went AWOL. It looks like the poor buggers were his servants. Must've been some temper tantrum. Lucky we don't have to hunt these bastards."

Elena nodded, feeling weak. "Yeah, lucky."

16

Raphael stood outside the nondescript little house in a suburb of New Jersey, silently applauding the Guild Director's cleverness. The woman had left her beautifully restored brownstone for this little wooden house surrounded by a hundred other such houses. Her home looked utterly ordinary except that he knew it was a fortress. He also knew that the director and her husband, both extremely experienced hunters, were taking turns at keeping an eye out for vampires, weapons close at hand.

Of course, to shoot, they had to see. And he was simply not there to their senses—he'd wrapped the glamour around himself the second he dived off the balcony of his penthouse suite and into the fading light of Manhattan, his power almost completely restored. True darkness had fallen during his flight and now he looked through windows that shimmered gold.

Light. Warmth. Illusion.

The seemingly ordinary surburban yard in front of him was set with sensors, likely connected to booby traps that could be set off from inside the house. Raphael guessed there was a basement leading to a hidden exit—no hunter would ever allow her family to be trapped.

If he hadn't been in the Quiet, he might've been impressed. The security was brilliant, would hold perfectly well against a high-level vampire, though probably not Dmitri. He was far too experienced. But even Dmitri would have had to dodge the weapons. Raphael, on the other hand, didn't even have to step foot inside the house.

But you should, a primeval, reptilian part of his mind whispered, *you should teach them a lesson, teach them that no one stands against an archangel and comes out the winner.*

He considered the instruction with the chill reason of his current emotional state and disregarded it. The Guild Director was intelligent and good at her job. It made no sense for Raphael to kill her—such an action would throw the Guild into chaos, during which a considerable number of dissatisfied vampires would try to escape from their masters. Some might even succeed because the hunters would be too broken up by the death of their director to be effective. Humans were so weak.

None of yours will escape, that voice whispered again, a voice he only ever heard during the Quiet. *They wouldn't dare. Nobody disobeys you, not after we made an example out of Germaine.*

Germaine was now somewhere in Texas, but the vampire had never forgotten his hours in Times Square and he never would. They were branded into his memories, pain such as no one should survive. Raphael remembered taking care of Germaine during another time of Quiet. After the Quiet, he recalled that he'd been dissatisfied with what he'd done. Accessing his memories, he found that he'd felt . . . remorse. He'd gone too far.

What a ridiculous idea. What a ridiculous emotion. He was an archangel. Germaine had dared attempt a betrayal.

His punishment had been just. As would the Guild Director's be if she stood in Raphael's way.

Kill her child, the voice murmured. *Kill her child in front of her. In front of Elena.*

17

An alarm blared next to Elena's bed, jerking her out of a fitful sleep. Already fully dressed, she got up and started running. Vivek was waiting for her, his door open. "Hurry! On the phone! Sara!"

Vaulting over his wheelchair when it got in her way, she picked up the receiver. "Sara?" Fear was a vile taste on her tongue, sharp and pungent.

"Run, Ellie," Sara whispered and there were tears in her voice. "Run!"

Ice turned her limbs useless. She stood there. "Zoe?"

"She's fine," Sara sobbed. "She wasn't here. Oh, God, Ellie. He knows where you are."

Not for a moment did Elena think Sara was talking about Dmitri. No vampire, however powerful, would reduce her friend to this. "How? What did he do to you?" Her fingers clenched on a knife handle and only then did she realize she'd drawn it.

"How?" Hysterical laughter cut off midstream. "I told him."

The shock immobilized her. "Sara?" If Sara had betrayed her, then she had nothing left.

"Oh, Ellie, he flew to the window and looked at me, told me to open it. I didn't even hesitate!" It was almost a scream. "Then he just asked me where you were and I answered. I answered! Why, Ellie? Why would I answer?"

Elena's breath rushed out of her. Trembling with relief, she put out a hand to brace herself against Vivek's computer panel. "It's okay, Sara."

"It's not fucking okay! I ratted out my best friend! Don't you dare tell me it's okay!"

"Mind control," Elena said before Sara could really get into her tirade. "He plays with us like toys." He'd certainly played with her—her body, her emotions. "There was nothing you could've done."

"But I'm immune," Sara said. "I'm Guild Director partly because I have a natural immunity to vampire tricks, like Hilda."

"He's not a vampire," Elena reminded her distraught friend. "He's an archangel."

A deep, shaky indrawn breath. "Ellie, there was something seriously wrong with him tonight."

Elena frowned. "What do you mean? Did he do anything . . . evil?" She had to force out the word. Some stupid, deluded part of her didn't want to believe that Raphael could be evil.

"No—he didn't even mention Zoe or threaten her in any way. But then he didn't need to, did he? He could twist my mind like a pretzel."

"If it's any consolation," she said, remembering Erik's animal stare, Bernal's terrified compliance, "he can apparently do that to vampires as well."

A sniff. "Well, at least the bloodsuckers don't have anything on me. You have to get the hell out. He's on his way to you now and in his current mood, he might just destroy the Guild to get to you. He knows all the codes—I gave them to him." Another short scream. "Okay, I'm calm now. I told Vivek to change the codes but I don't think that'll stop Raphael. He wants you."

"I'm outa here. And I'll leave a message making sure he knows I'm in the wind so he doesn't come after Vivek."

"Go to the Blue safe house."

Blue was an unmarked delivery truck that would blend seamlessly into traffic, effectively disappearing the driver. "I will," Elena lied. "Thanks."

"What the hell for?" Sara spit out. "But I can give you this—he wasn't acting normal. I've spoken to him on the phone and you know how good I am with voices. It was different— flat, toneless . . . cold. Not angry, not anything, just *cold*."

Why did everyone keep using that word? Raphael was many things, but he'd never struck her as cold. However, she didn't have time to ask for details. "I'm heading out now. I'll check in when I can. And don't worry—no matter what, he won't kill me. He needs me to finish the job." She hung up before Sara could realize there were worse things than death. Some of them involved screaming and screaming and screaming until your voice broke.

"New codes." A piece of paper rested in the printer tray. "Use them to get out—I'll change them again the instant you exit the elevator."

She nodded. "Thanks, Vivek."

"Wait." He zipped his chair off to a small locker in the corner. She didn't know what he did, but the locker suddenly swung up. "Take that."

Elena picked up the small, sleek gun. "Won't do much good against an archangel but thanks anyway."

"Don't shoot his body," he told her. "Those rounds are meant to shred an angel's wings."

No! The idea of destroying the incredible beauty of those wings caused an almost physical pain in her heart. "They grow back, heal," she forced herself to say.

"Takes time. And we've been keeping records—it takes an angel longer to heal his wings than anything else. It'll cripple him long enough that you can get out of a tight spot. Unless . . ." Fear spiked his tone. "I heard what you said about mind control. If he can do that from a distance, I don't know if anything will help."

She tucked the gun into the back of her pants after making

sure the safety was on. "He's not controlling me now, so there's a limit to his abilities." At least she hoped so. "I don't think he'll come down once he knows I'm gone but you need to be safe. Has Ashwini left?"

"Yes, and nobody else was down here." His eyes were scared but resolute. "I'll lock up behind you, then bunk down." He nodded at the entrance to the secret room hidden behind a wall. He could survive in there for days. "Be safe, Ellie. We need to finish our game."

Bending, she gave him an impulsive hug. "I'll beat your skinny ass when I come back." Now it was time to keep herself alive . . . and whole. Because there were lots of body parts a hunter didn't need in order to successfully track prey.

Raphael stood in front of the elevator he'd been told would transport him to the Cellars. But it appeared he had no need to go down below. His quarry had been flushed out.

The message was pinned to the side of the elevator doors, held up by a nail that had been driven in with enough force that concrete dust littered the ground.

You want to play, angel boy? Then let's play. Find me.

It was a challenge, clear and simple. A foolish thing for the hunter to do. In the Quiet, he couldn't be enraged, but he understood strategy very well. She wanted to draw him away from the Guild and her friends.

He considered that. That primeval part of him whispered, *Will you let her lead you around on a leash? She insults you.*

He ripped the note off the wall. "Angel boy," he read out loud, crumpling the paper in his hand. Yes, she needed to learn some respect. When he found her, she was going to beg for mercy.

I don't want her to beg.

The echo of his own words stopped him for several long seconds. He remembered that he was intrigued by the hunter's fire, that she relieved the boredom of centuries. Even in the Quiet, he understood the decision not to harm her. To prematurely break a new toy, one that promised such pleasure, was a foolish act. But there were ways to ensure respect without fully destroying the object of his search.

The Guild could wait. First, he had to teach Elena Deveraux not to play games with an archangel.

Elena drove to the Blue safe house through the streets with grim purpose. She wasn't going to hide—that would simply lead to more problems for those she cared about. She had every certainty that Raphael would go after them one by one until he found her. So she did the only thing she could to keep them all safe.

She went home.

And waited, gun in hand.

Raphael stood outside an apartment building, and even in the Quiet, he knew that he was dangerous. If Elena was inside those walls, then blood would spill. There was no room for flexibility in his mind. This was one place where he would not accept or permit her presence.

Wrapping the glamour around himself once more, he entered the apartment through the front door, breaking the dual deadlocks without effort.

Voices from the other room. Male and female.

"Come on, baby, just—"

"I'm through listening to you!"

"I admit I was an idio—"

"A giant, pigheaded imbecile would be more like it."

"Fuck this!"

The sound of rustling, then jagged breaths. Hot, deeply sexual.

Raphael entered the bedroom and pinned Ransom to the

wall with a single hand around his throat before the hunter could say a word. But Ransom reacted fast, snapping out with his legs and screaming, "Get out, Nyree! Run, baby!"

Nyree?

Something hit Raphael's back. He looked over his shoulder to find a small, curvy female pelting him with whatever object came to hand. When her fingers closed around a heavy paperweight, he flicked a finger and sent her to sleep. She collapsed slowly into the sofa.

The hunter stilled. "If you've hurt her, I don't care what I have to do—I will find a way to kill you."

"You can't," he responded, but let the man go. "She's sleeping, nothing more. It'll allow for an easier conversation."

Ransom's knife hand was suddenly slashing toward Raphael's wings. He actually grazed the feathers before Raphael locked his mind, forcing him to drop the blade. Sweat broke out on the other man's brow as he fought the compulsion.

"Interesting. You're very strong." Raphael considered this. He could kill the man, but then the Guild would lose one of its finest hunters. "It's not in my best interest to kill you. Don't try to attack me and you'll live."

"Fuck you," Ransom said, attempting to move forward. "I won't tell you where Ellie is."

"Yes, you will." He focused his abilities without remorse, without anything but cold purpose. "Where is she?"

Ransom smiled. "I don't know."

Raphael stared at the other man, knowing it to be the truth—no one could lie under compulsion. There were rumors of humans who had some kind of immunity to angelic powers, as a number of them had to vampiric ones, but Raphael had never met one—not in the fifteen centuries of his existence. "Where would she hide if she was trying to protect her friends?" he asked instead.

He could see Ransom fighting not to answer, but the compulsion won. "She wouldn't hide."

Raphael thought that over. "No, she wouldn't, would she?"

He walked to the front door. "Your lady will wake in a few minutes."

Ransom coughed as Raphael set his mind free. "I owe you a punch to the jaw. Maybe a black eye or six, too."

"You're welcome to collect," Raphael said, seeing in this hunter another possible diversion from the jaded edge of immortality. "I won't even punish you if you succeed."

The hunter, now crouching by his woman, raised an eyebrow. "Sure you'll be around for me to hunt? Ellie's probably waiting, carving knife in hand."

"I may indulge my toys," Raphael said, "but only so far."

"What the fuck did she do, anyway?" Ransom asked and Raphael saw the delaying gesture for what it was—the hunter was trying to give his friend as much time as he could.

You must kill her.

Lijuan's voice was a cool whisper in his mind, as pitiless as the winds of Quiet. "That is between me and Elena," he said. "You'd do well to stay out of this war."

Ransom's face turned stony. "I don't know how angels do it, but out here, we stick by our friends. She calls, I'll answer."

"And you'll die," Raphael replied. "I don't share that which is mine."

According to Elena's watch, she'd been sitting on her sofa staring out at the Tower for close to an hour. Maybe her choice of location wasn't as obvious as she'd thought. She frowned and tugged at the T-shirt she'd changed into after her arrival. That was when her cell phone rang. Pulse rocketing as she recognized the personalized ring tone, she pulled it out and put it to her ear. "Ransom? Oh, my God, he got to you!"

"Calm down," Ransom replied. "I'm fine."

"Your voice sounds a little husky."

"He's a strong motherfu— Sorry, babe."

Elena frowned. "Huh?"

"Nyree," he explained. "She thinks I swear too much. Of

course, she just swore a blue streak when she woke up from the nap your boyfriend put her in during our conversation."

"Did he hurt you?"

"I'm insulted—I can handle myself."

Relief washed through her. "Yeah, yeah. So?"

"So the big, bad, and able-to-mind-control angel thinks you're his. As in 'I don't share my woman.' "

Elena swallowed. "You're messing with me."

A bark of laughter. "Hell, no. This is way too interesting as it is."

"Oh, Jesus." She bent over and stared at the carpet, trying to think. Yes, she'd kissed him. And yes, he'd been sending out some strong vibes—vibes she'd responded to despite herself—but all that was de rigueur for the powerful angels and vampires. Sex was just a game. It meant nothing. "Maybe he was saying that to put me on edge." That would make more sense.

"Oh, no, babe. This was for real." His voice became serious. "The man wants you—but I'm not sure if he wants to fuck you or kill you."

Rising from her bent-over position, Elena stared out at the window in front of her. Her stomach nose-dived. "Ah, Ransom? I have to go."

Silence. Then: "He found you."

Her eyes on the wide spread of white gold as Raphael hovered effortlessly outside, she closed the phone and put it very carefully on the small table next to the sofa. "I'm not letting you in," she whispered, though there was no way he could hear her.

I can get in anytime I please.

She froze at the crystal clarity of his tone. "I told you—no fucking with my head!"

Why?

The chill of that single word got through to her as nothing else could have. Sara had been right—there was something different about Raphael tonight. And it was very, very bad for her. "What's wrong with you?"

Nothing. I am Quiet.

"What the hell does that mean?" She inched her hand toward the gun at her back, never moving her eyes off his face as he watched her through the glass. "And why are your eyes so . . . cold?" That word again.

He stretched out his wings even farther, fully displaying the gold and white pattern on the underside. So beautiful it threatened to distract. "Clever," she said, focusing deliberately on his face. "Trying to manipulate me without using your mind."

You were right when you said I need you fully functional. Too much mind control and I could bend your mental pathways permanently.

"Bullshit," she muttered, having almost reached her gun. "You can hold me for a while but the second you stop exercising active control, I'm free."

Are you sure?

Oddly enough, though he was scaring the bejesus out of her right then, she didn't feel as vulnerable to the threat of compulsion as she usually did. When he was being his normal arrogant, lethal-as-hell self, there was a pulse of sexual attraction between them that scrambled her usual defenses.

But this man—this cold, cold man with death in his eyes . . . Her hand closed on the butt of the gun.

18

"You know what," she said, fighting to keep her expression calm, "the only thing I'm sure about right this second is that you're acting out of it."

Is that why you have a gun?

Her hand froze on the weapon, the beads of sweat on her spine turning to ice. "What gun?"

His hair whipped off his face as if caught in a driving wind, but he kept his position without any apparent effort. His face was so pure in its beauty that her heart kicked a beat. It was as if he'd been carved by the most masterful of artisans, the lines of his face clean and quintessentially male. Without a doubt, he was the most beautiful man she had ever seen.

Or perhaps, I am simply that to you.

She flinched, snapping out of the fascination. And this time, she knew he hadn't been messing with her mind—that thought had been her own stupidity at work. "Simply what?" she asked, just to keep him talking.

Beautiful.

She snorted. "Believe me, angel boy, you turn female heads wherever you go."

Most women see cruelty in me, too much for beauty.

Caught short by that apparently honest assessment, she found herself staring at him with new eyes. Yes, there was cruelty in him. He wasn't pretty, wasn't handsome, wasn't anything so tame. He was dangerous and strong, the epitome of what appealed to her hunter senses. All her life, she'd been too strong, too fast, too unfeminine for human men. They liked her, but after a while, most claimed she made them feel emasculated.

She'd never let on how much that hurt, but it did, it hurt a hell of a lot. Maybe she wasn't a tiny doll like Beth, but she was very definitely female. And she appreciated the male of the species, most especially this male. "You're capable of cruelty," she agreed quietly, "perhaps even horror, but you haven't crossed over into evil."

Haven't I?

Her palm lay sweaty on the gun. "No."

You sound very certain. And yet you accused me of rape this morning.

Her temper spiked. Ignoring the warning cry of her own common sense, she pulled out and held the gun openly at her side. "This morning, you tried to take by force something I might've given you freely had you waited."

A long pause filled only with the sound of her adrenaline-spiked breaths. She wondered what he heard out there, in the velvet darkness of the night, with the streets so far below.

Such honesty.

"I said 'might.' And buddy, your chances went down the drain the instant you pulled that stunt. I won't be manipulated into sex." Not even by a sex-god of an archangel.

He seemed to be thinking that over. His eyes met hers through the glass. He shrugged. *Sex is fairly pointless anyway.*

That made her blink. It didn't fit at all with the darkly sensual man who'd devoured her like his favorite candy that very morning. "Are you alright?" she asked, wondering if he was on some sort of angelic drug.

His response was to blow out the plate-glass window between them. It happened so fast, she barely had time to throw up her arm to shield her eyes. One second the window was there, the next, it was lying in several neat pieces on her carpet. Not a sliver had touched her. When she dropped her arm, she found herself looking out at a huge square of darkness, the wind sliding into her apartment on smooth, silky wings.

Raphael was nowhere to be seen.

Scared, but not for herself, she looked down at the gun in her hand. With trembling fingers, she clicked on the safety again. She'd fired in instinctive self-defense, aiming not for Raphael's face, but for his wings as Vivek had advised. An angel without wings . . .

"Oh, God." Stepping carefully over the large shards of glass—eight perfect triangular pieces—she made her way to the edge and glanced down.

A whisper of wind from *behind* her. "Definitely no problems with vertigo."

She might've fallen had he not had his hands securely on her hips. "You bastard! You scared me to death!" Twisting, she tried to get away.

He held her still, wrapping both arms around her waist. "Behave, Elena."

The oddness of his tone clanged a serious alarm bell in her head. She couldn't help but think of her earlier thoughts—there were a lot of things worse than death. "Are you planning to drop me?"

"You just told yourself that I won't kill you, that I'm more likely to torture you."

Something snapped. "Get. Out. Of. My. Head!" Squeezing her eyes shut, she shoved outward with every ounce of willpower she possessed. It was a stupid, human reaction, but she *was* human in every way that mattered.

Behind her, Raphael sucked in a breath. Startled, she intensified her attempts to block him, even as the spiraling emptiness of a deadly fall spread out in front of her. Elena didn't look away—she'd rather face death than have her mind invaded, for what was that if not another form of crawling? But she damn well wasn't going to go without a fight. She switched the way she held the gun. This time, she *would* purposefully aim for his wings.

"Well, well," Raphael said against her ear. "It seems the hunter-born have another skill."

Her head was starting to ache. But she kept up the pressure, hoping her brain would learn to do this automatically after a while. Of course, that wasn't going to be an issue if she didn't get away from Raphael. It was becoming clearer by the second that whatever was wrong with him it was very, very dangerous for her. "Why are you here, doing this? Is it because I cut Dmitri?"

"He was under orders not to touch you."

Tired of leaning away, she relaxed into him, her head against his chest. He took her weight with ease. "What did you do to him?"

"His jaw will have healed completely by now."

The night darkness was so close, the lights from the other buildings so bright, it felt as if she was standing on the edge of the world. But it wasn't the emptiness in front of her that was the real threat. "Does violence excite you?"

"No."

"Hurting me," she pushed, "making me bleed, that gets Dmitri off. Same for you?"

"No."

"Then why the fuck are you holding me here?"

"Because I can."

And she knew that in this mood, he really might break her.

So she shot him. No warning, no second chances. She simply aimed blindly behind her and shot. The second his arms loosened, she sent herself sideways. She could've as easily fallen, but she trusted her reflexes and they didn't let her down.

She landed on the huge shards of plate glass. They held, but she cut the side of her face and the palms of both hands as she clutched at the glass to keep from sliding off and out into the pitch-black of the night. The instant she had any leverage, she used one of her more acrobatic moves to flip over the glass and to a crouching position on the carpet.

Shoving the hair out of her eyes, she looked toward Raphael. He lay crumpled on the glass, propped up against the table where she'd put her phone what felt like hours ago. He was staring down at his wing, and when she followed his gaze, what she saw made her sick.

The gun had done what Vivek had promised. It had almost destroyed the bottom half of one wing. What Vivek hadn't told her was that when an angel's wings got hurt, he bled. And he bled dark red. It dripped onto the glass, sliding across the clean surface to sink into her carpet. Shaking, she got up. "It'll heal," she whispered, trying to convince herself. If she'd crippled him—"You're immortal. It'll heal."

He looked up, a dazed incomprehension in those incredible, unreal blue eyes. "Why did you shoot me?"

"You were torturing me with fear—probably would've ended up throwing me off the ledge a few times and catching me again, just to hear me scream."

"What?" He frowned, shook his head as if trying to clear it, then looked at the open space where her window used to be. "Yes, you're right."

That wasn't the answer she'd expected. "You were there—why do you sound like you can't believe it?"

His eyes met hers again. "In the Quiet, I'm . . . changed."

"What's the Quiet?"

He didn't answer.

"Do you go there a lot?"

His lips tightened. "No."

"So, are you normal now?" Even as she asked, she was running into the kitchen for towels. When she came out, it was to find him in the same position. "Why won't it stop bleeding?" Her voice rose as panic took hold.

He watched her try to stem the flow without success. "I don't know."

She glanced at the gun she'd left on the other side of the

room. Maybe it was stupid to remain here, but she knew this Raphael as she hadn't the other. Whatever the Quiet was, it had turned him into the worst kind of a monster. But was she any better? That gun, the damage it had done . . . Grabbing her phone, she called the Cellars, her fingers slick with Raphael's blood. In front of her, his blue eyes seemed to dim, his head dropping back. "Come on," she said, cupping his cheek with fingers stained red. "Stay awake, Archangel. Don't go into shock."

"I'm an angel," he murmured, his voice slurred. "Shock is for mortals."

Someone picked up the phone. "Vivek?"

"Elena, you're alive!"

"Damn it, Vivek, what the hell was in those bullets?"

"I told you."

"Has it been tested?"

"Yeah. It's been used in the field a few times—gives you maybe twenty minutes to half an hour at most. Angels begin to heal the instant after the bullet hits."

She glanced down at Raphael's shattered wing. "It's not healing. It's getting worse by the minute."

"That's impossible."

She hung up since he clearly knew nothing. "Come on, Raphael! What do I do?"

"Call Dmitri." His color was fading to gray, a pale death mask that struck terror into her heart.

Guilt and fear for him choking a knot in her throat, she dialed Archangel Tower and was immediately put through to Dmitri. "Get to my apartment," she ordered.

"That's not—"

"I've done something to Raphael. He's bleeding and it's not clotting."

A blink of silence. "He's immortal."

"His blood is red, same as mine."

"I'll kill you in tiny, tiny bites if you've harmed him." He hung up.

"Dmitri's on his way," she told Raphael, as the cell phone

slid out of her bloody hand. "I don't think he thinks very highly of me."

"He is loyal." His hair fell over his forehead, making him look absurdly boyish.

Another spurt of blood hit her leg, hot and rich. "Why the hell aren't you healing?"

A moment of brightness in those glassy blue eyes. "You've made me a little mortal."

Those were his last words before lapsing into unconsciousness—probably nothing but the shock speaking, she realized. She was still by his side when Dmitri and several other vampires arrived. They simply broke down the door instead of bothering to knock.

"Hold the hunter." Dmitri ignored her as his lackeys dragged her away from Raphael.

She would've struggled but she knew it was pointless. There were too many of them and she had no chip-embedded weapons on her. Bearing unique serial numbers and with each and every use tracked by the VPA and Guild both, the devices were issued only for hunts, or when a hunter's life was in demonstrable danger from a vampiric threat. The official line was that it was to stop hunters from becoming dangerously overconfident, but they all knew it was because the powerful vamps didn't like the idea of being vulnerable to any old hunter with a grudge. Right now, she didn't care. "Help him!"

Dmitri threw her a glance filled with pure malice. "Be quiet. The sole reason you're not dead is because Raphael will enjoy doing the task himself." Lifting a hand, he spoke into some kind of a transmitter snapped around his wrist. "Enter."

Two large angelic males suddenly appeared in the open wall that had been her window, a stretcher held between them. The shock on their faces when they saw Raphael told her this was worse than bad. Her stomach shriveled in on itself, but the angels recovered quickly, following Dmitri's instructions to put Raphael on the stretcher and fly him to the Tower.

One of the angels—a redhead, balked. "Wouldn't it be better to take him straight home?"

"The healer and medics are about to reach the Tower," Dmitri responded.

Nodding, the angel picked up the front of the stretcher as his partner followed suit on the other end. "See you there."

Elena wasn't exactly sure about the power dynamics in the room. The hierarchy of the world was supposed to go archangel-angel-vampire-human, in that order. But Dmitri was clearly running the show here—and unlike with the baby angel who'd made the drop at her apartment, these angels were old and powerful.

Now, with Raphael gone, Dmitri's attention shifted to her. As he walked closer, she cursed the stupid policy on chip-embedded weapons. Without them, she was as vulnerable as a child.

And Dmitri looked ready to tear her apart with his bare hands.

Walking until he stood only inches from her, he gripped her chin, his hands bloody, his gaze black with a heart of flame.

She gasped. "Your eyes—" There was a spiking circle of red where the pupil should've been, a spreading stain with bladelike edges. "What the hell?"

His hand tightened. Then he leaned closer. She froze. If he tried to take blood, she knew she wouldn't be able to remain quiet—instinct would take over and she'd try to go for her weapons. It wasn't something she could stop. But Dmitri surprised her again. His lips brushed her ear instead of her neck. "I'm going to watch him break you. And then I'll lick up your blood for dessert."

Fear—raw and brutal—bloomed in the pit of her stomach, but she faced him with studied nonchalance. "How's your neck?"

His fingers tightened hard enough that she knew she was going to have bruises. "In my time, women knew their place."

She didn't ask, wouldn't fall for that trick.

But it turned out Dmitri didn't need her cooperation. "Flat on their back, legs spread."

She narrowed her eyes. "Raphael hasn't rescinded his hands-off policy, so I'd watch it if I were you."

He laughed and the sound was a razor slicing over her skin. His fingers gentled, cupped her cheek, and he came even closer, until she was pressed between muscled vampire flesh. But it was only Dmitri she truly "saw"—his lethal rage, his eyes . . . his scent. It wrapped around her like the most obscenely luscious of coats, tasting of fur and diamonds and sex. "I hope he keeps you alive for a long, long time." His tongue flicked over the thudding beat of her pulse. "I hope he invites me to play."

19

An hour later, Elena tugged at the restraints locking her arms to the chair. All she succeeded in doing was tightening the ropes around her ankles. *Hog-tied.* She was hog-tied! Her arms had been wrenched behind her back and tied, then the rope run down to wrap securely around one ankle, before crossing over to her other ankle. The final touch had been to take the rope back up to her wrists and around her waist to the back. She was effectively chained to a heavy chair that she had no hope of tipping over.

"I can smell blood, Elena," Dmitri drawled, walking back into the room. "Are you trying to flirt?"

She glared at him, recalling exactly how much fun he'd had divesting her of her weapons. He hadn't been crass. No, he'd been sensuality personified, that damn drugging scent of his snaking through her body like the most potent aphrodisiac on the planet. She'd still managed to get in some kicks—before being bound, having her cuts disinfected, and parked in what looked like a small sitting room somewhere in the higher levels of the Tower. "How's Raphael?"

Dmitri came to stand in front of her, having taken off his

charcoal suit jacket and dark red tie to reveal a crisp white shirt. The top few buttons were open, exposing a delicious triangle of bronze skin. Not a tan, she thought. He was clearly from somewhere with a hotter sun, somewhere exotic and— "Stop it!" Now that she was concentrating, she could distinguish the faint scent he was stroking over every inch of her skin.

He smiled and there was a promise of pain in that smile. "I wasn't focusing anything on you."

"Liar."

"I confess." He came even closer, bending down to brace his hands on the arms of the chair. "You're very sensitive to my scent." He closed his eyes, drew in a deep breath. "Even sweaty and bloody, you have a unique scent of your own. It makes me want to take a big, greedy bite."

"Not in this lifetime," she said, voice husky with the strength of will it was taking to resist his slow seduction.

She'd misjudged Dmitri because he didn't leak power like the other old ones she'd met, which meant he was in a class of his own . . . and probably more than capable of throwing off the effects of a control chip.

That was a secret hunters had died to protect—because sometimes, a vampire's second-long disorientation, his belief that he'd been tagged and immobilized, was all you had. In that second, you could escape or do actual damage. "Why are you fixated on me?" she asked bluntly, burying her knowledge of the chip's fatal flaw. As far as she knew, only angels could read minds—and they had no reason to sabotage the effectiveness of a hunter's most powerful weapon—but she wasn't taking any chances. "You're so fucking sexy"—damn it, it was true—"you've got to have women throwing themselves at you. Why me?"

"I told you—you make things interesting." His lips curved but the bloody spikes in his eyes reminded her he wasn't exactly happy with her right then. "You'll live, you know."

"I will?"

"At least until you complete the job." He stared at her.

She stared back. Dmitri very likely knew every detail of the job, but if he didn't, she wasn't going to spill the beans and dig her grave even deeper. "You can't imagine how much pleasure that gives me."

"What do you know about pleasure, Guild Hunter?" His tone turned blade sharp, his skin almost glowing from within.

Her throat dried up as she realized she'd been wrong again. Dmitri wasn't only powerful, he was *powerful*. So old that now he wasn't concealing it, the age of him made her bones ache. "I know that what you promise as pleasure will lead inexorably to pain."

He blinked, his lashes incongruously long. "But with a master of the art, all pain is pleasure."

Shivers raked up her spine, brushed across her nipples. "No, thanks."

"The decision is no longer up to you." He rose to his full height. "Are you hungry?"

Startled by the pragmatic question, she shook off the drugging aftereffects of his scent, and took a moment to think. "I'm starving."

"Then you'll be fed."

Scowling at the way he'd phrased that, she said nothing as he disappeared out the door, only to return several minutes later with a covered plate. When he removed the lid, she found herself looking at what appeared to be a dinner of grilled fish in some kind of white sauce, teamed with lightly sautéed vegetables and baby potatoes. Her mouth watered. "Thanks."

"You're welcome." He grabbed another chair and moved it opposite her without effort, though it was the twin of the one she sat in, unable even to tilt. "What would you like first?"

She set her jaw. "I am not letting you feed me."

He speared a piece of carrot. "The men who accompanied me to your apartment—do you know who they were?"

She kept her mouth shut, not trusting him not to shove food at her while her guard was down.

"Members of the Seven," he said, answering his own question. "Those vampires and angels who protect Raphael with no thought to our own advancement."

Curiosity was a flame inside her, enough for her to speak. "Why?"

"That's for us to know." He ate the carrot with every appearance of enjoyment. While vampires couldn't gain sustenance from such food, she knew they could digest a certain amount without problem. It was why most low-level vamps were able to pass for human. "What you need to know is that we'll get rid of anything, and *anyone*, who poses a threat to him, even if it means we forfeit our own lives."

"And that's supposed to make me feel happy about you shoving a fork in my direction?"

He scooped up a piece of the fish, making sure to coat it with the sauce, which looked tauntingly delicious. "Until Raphael wakes, I'm constrained against hurting you. He gave me a direct order not to. The others aren't subject to such orders. I hand them this fork and walk out that door, and you'll understand a whole new meaning to the word 'pain.'"

She blew out a breath. "Free my hands at least—you know I can't hurt you without weapons."

"I do that, you're dead." He lifted the fork toward her mouth. "You're alive right now because I'm keeping the others from you. If they think you can manipulate me . . ."

She didn't trust him an inch. But she was starving and she was a hunter—she knew a hunger strike would achieve nothing while weakening her. She opened her mouth. The fish was as delicious as it looked. But she held it in her mouth for almost a minute, tasting carefully. Only when she was satisfied it was clean, did she swallow. "No narcotics?"

"Unnecessary. It's not like you can fly." He fed her a bite of potato. "And Raphael will want to see you as soon as he wakes."

"His wings?"

Dmitri raised an eyebrow. "You sound like you care."

She couldn't see any point in lying. "I do. I only meant to

get away from him—he was acting really weird." She ate. "I mean, he's immortal. It should've just given me enough time to get a head start."

"True." He fed her another forkful, sliding out the tines more slowly than was warranted. When she narrowed her eyes, he gave her that cool, dangerous smile that never reached his eyes. "Which is why you've just gone from hunter to the number one threat to angels."

"Oh, please." She shook her head when he offered her broccoli. Smiling, he ate it, then fed her a forkful of peas instead. She ate, thought it over. "That kind of a gun's been used before." It couldn't be a secret, not if it had been fired against angels.

"Yes. We know of it. It causes temporary damage." He shrugged. "The archangels apparently find it a fair weapon, given that humans have few other ways to combat angels who get too pushy."

"Maybe it was a bad angle," she murmured. "Did I hit a major artery or something?" She knew all about vampire biology, but angels were another matter altogether. "Enough," she said when he offered her another bite.

He put down the fork. "You'll have to ask Raphael those questions—if you still have your tongue, of course." Getting up, he disappeared a second time, returning with a bottle of water.

After drinking and managing not to dribble, she looked at him again. Still darkly sexy, still an inch away from ripping out her throat. "Thanks."

His answer was to lay one finger against the pulse in her neck. "So strong, rich and sweetly potent. I look forward to my own dinner—too bad it's not you."

Then he was gone.

Elena watched the door with absolute focus as she began twisting in her chair, determined to get out of the ropes. Dmitri was protecting her against the others right now, but who knew how long that would last.

The only problem was, the ropes had been tied by an apparent master.

But with a master of the art, all pain is pleasure.

Bondage, that figured. Dmitri probably liked to tie his women up in all sorts of interesting positions. Her face flushed. She didn't want him—not when he wasn't throwing out that damn scent like a lure. But she melted the instant he turned on that talent of his.

She didn't like melting against her own will.

Not even for an archangel.

Her jaw clenched at the memory of what had taken place in Raphael's office. Now that she'd shot him, she felt a bit better about the whole incident. Like she'd evened the score. Of course, he probably took a dimmer view of the whole affair. He'd only tried to get her in bed—and try as she might to convince herself otherwise, she'd enjoyed the seduction . . . at least until it got to the mind-control part. In return, she might've crippled him.

Dear God, she'd destroyed half his wing.

Her eyes smarted and she realized she was horrifically close to tears. Blinking rapidly, she banished the unwelcome emotion. Hunters didn't cry. Not even for an archangel. But—what if he didn't recover?

Her guilt twisted into a heavy knot in her stomach, getting tighter and hotter and more destructive with every passing second. She had to get to him, see for herself how he was doing. "No hope in hell," she muttered, knowing that if she'd been in Dmitri's position, she'd have done the exact same thing in isolating the possible threat.

Arms straining and calf muscles aching, she gave up trying to undo the bonds and relaxed into the chair. She wasn't going to be able to sleep but she could try to rest enough that when Raphael woke and the showdown began, she'd be ready. But just as her muscles began to loosen, she remembered the gaping hole in her apartment wall. "Dmitri!"

He appeared a minute later and, from the look on his face,

he was in no way pleased. "You called, my lady?" Had the words been any sharper, they would've drawn blood.

Blood.

Was she *trying* to get herself killed? "I interrupted your . . . dinner. I'm sorry."

He smiled, revealing no hint of the fangs she knew were there. "Are you offering yourself in reparation?"

"I want to know about my apartment—the wall, did you close it off?"

"Why should we?" He shrugged and turned away. "It's only a human dwelling."

"You piece of—"

He snapped around, face different, lethal, unearthly. "I'm hungry, Elena. Don't make me break my word to Raphael."

"You wouldn't."

"Push me and I will. I'll get punished, but you'll still be dead." Then he was gone.

Leaving her alone with a racing heartbeat and a lancing pain in her heart. Her home, her haven, her damn nest was being destroyed right this second by the wind, dust, and rain if the heavens opened. It made her want to curl up and bawl her eyes out.

It wasn't the individual things in the apartment that she worried about, it was the place itself. Home. She hadn't had one for a very long time—after her father had thrown her out, she'd been forced to bunk permanently at Guild Academy. There was nothing wrong with the facility, but it wasn't *home*. Then she and Sara had finished their training and shared an apartment for a while. That had been a home, a welcome one, but it hadn't been hers. But the apartment, it was hers in every way.

A single tear streaked down her face. "I'm sorry," she said, telling herself she was talking to her ruined home. But the truth was, she was speaking to an archangel. "I never meant to hurt you."

A cool sea breeze in her mind. *Then why were you carrying a gun?*

20

Elena went utterly quiet, much as she imagined a small mouse might in front of a very big, very bad cat with large teeth. "Raphael?" she whispered, though she knew that fresh, clean, rainy scent as well as her own. And that was something that made no sense at all—how could he have a scent inside her head?

Go to sleep, Elena. Your thinking is keeping me awake.

She took a deep breath. "How are you—the injury?"

Are you bound?

"Yes." She waited for an answer to her own question.

Good. I wouldn't want you disappearing before we had a chance to talk about your penchant for weaponry.

Then the sense of him was gone from her head. She whispered his name again, but knew he was no longer listening. Her guilt soon morphed into anger. The bastard—he could've had her released, but he'd left her tied up. Her wrists were sore, her back hurt from the damn chair, and—"And he's got a right to be pissed." Raphael had terrified her on that ledge tonight, but he hadn't actually harmed her. Meanwhile, she'd shot him. If the man was furious, he had reason. That didn't mean she had to like it.

And there was still the matter of his compelling her to have sex.

Humiliating as it was, she'd told him the truth tonight—if he'd only waited, it was highly likely she'd have crawled all over him voluntarily at the first opportunity.

Her cheeks burned. She was going to have *Idiot* tattooed on her forehead as soon as she got out of here. From the start she'd told herself to be wary, to never forget that she was nothing but a throwaway source of entertainment for Raphael. Apparently that didn't matter to her hormones.

The archangel made her burn.

The worst thing was, she couldn't blame the fascination on lust alone. Raphael was far too intriguing a male for anything that simple. But tonight, tonight he hadn't been right. Or maybe, another part of her whispered, he *had* been—what if the stranger she'd shot had been the real Raphael . . . the Archangel of New York, a creature capable of torturing another being until that person was nothing but a screaming, destroyed piece of monstrous art.

Raphael's eyes were closed, but he wasn't truly asleep. He was in a semiconscious coma, a condition for which humans or vampires had no equivalent. The angels knew it as *an-shara*, a state of being that could be achieved only by those who had lived longer than half a millennium, and that allowed both reason and deep rest at the same time. Now, the conscious part of him was absorbed in knitting the wound Elena had made with her little gun, while the rest of him slept. A useful state. But not one that could be brought on by choice.

Anshara only came to pass when an angel had been badly injured. That had happened rarely in the last eight hundred years of Raphael's existence. When he'd been young and inexperienced, he'd damaged himself—or been damaged—a few times.

Images of dancing in the sky before his wings tangled, and he plummeted to earth with the certain understanding that his blood would paint a red carpet across the meadow floor.

Ancient memories. Of the boy he'd been.

Broken arms, broken legs, blood spilling out of a shattered mouth.

And her. Standing over him, crooning. "Shh, my darling. Shh."

Sheer terror racing through his bloodstream, his heart heavy with the knowledge that he was helpless to stop her . . . his mother, his greatest nightmare.

Black haired and blue eyed, she'd been the feminine image from which he'd been cast. But she'd been old by then, so very old, not in appearance but in the mind, in the soul. And unlike Lijuan, she hadn't evolved. She'd . . . devolved.

In the present, he could see his wing knitting together filament by filament but it wasn't enough to keep the memories at bay. During *anshara*, the mind disgorged things long locked away, covering the soul in a layer of opaqueness no mortal could hope to understand. These were the memories of a hundred different mortal lifetimes. He was old, so old . . . but no, he wasn't ancient. These memories weren't all his. Some were those of his race, the secret repository of all their knowledge, hidden inside the minds of their children.

Caliane's memories rose to the surface.

And he was looking down at his bleeding and broken body from a crouching position, watching his/her hand stroke his hair off his face. "It hurts now but it had to be done."

The boy on the ground couldn't speak, drowning in his own blood.

"You will not die, Raphael. You cannot die. You are immortal." Leaning down to press a cool kiss against the bloody ruin of the boy's cheek. "You are the son of two archangels."

The boy's miraculously undamaged eyes filled with betrayal. His father was dead. Immortals could die.

Sadness shifted through Caliane. "He had to die, my love. If he had not, hell would have reigned on earth."

The boy's eyes grew darker, more accusing. Caliane sighed, then smiled. "And so must I—that is why you came to kill me, is it not?" Soft, delighted laughter. "You can't kill me, my sweet Raphael. Only another of the Cadre of Ten can destroy an archangel. And they will never find me."

A shocking transition into his own mind, his own memories. Because he had none of Caliane's after that—she'd made the memory transfer as he lay so badly injured he hadn't even been able to crawl for months. Nor had he been able to lift his eyes to watch her take flight. Instead, his last memory of his mother was of the sight of her bare feet stepping lightly across the verdant green of the meadow, a trail of angel dust sparkling in her wake.

"Mother," he tried to say.

"Shh, my darling. Shh." Then a gust of wind blew dirt into his eyes.

When he blinked awake, Caliane was gone.

And he was looking into the face of a vampire.

Bloodborn

He fed.

His parched bones swelled, filled with life.

But he needed more.

So much more.

This was the ecstasy the others had been trying to keep from him while bloating themselves with power. Now they would pay the price. Blood dripped from his canines as he screamed a challenge that shattered window glass on every building within a mile radius.

It was time.

21

Dmitri's expression held pure relief. "Sire?"

"What time is it?" he asked, his voice strong. *Anshara* had done its work. But he'd have to pay the price it demanded soon.

"Dawn," Dmitri answered in the old way. "Light is just touching the horizon."

Raphael got out of bed and flexed his wing. "The hunter?"

"Bound in another room."

The wing was back to normal except for one thing. He looked down at the inner pattern. The smooth brushstrokes of gold had been interrupted at the point where Elena's bullet had torn through. Now the bottom half of that wing bore a unique pattern in gold on white—an explosion from a central point. He smiled. So, he would carry the mark of Elena's burst of violence.

"Sire?" Dmitri's voice was questioning as he noted the smile.

Raphael continued to look down at the wing, at the mark caused by the Quiet. It would serve as a useful reminder. "Did you hurt her, Dmitri?" He glanced at his second, noting the disheveled hair, the wrinkled clothing.

"No." The vampire's lips curved upward in a feral smile. "I thought you'd enjoy that pleasure."

Raphael touched Elena's mind. She was asleep, exhausted from a night spent attempting to break her bonds. "This is a battle between me and the hunter. No one else will interfere. Take care the others know that."

Dmitri couldn't hide his surprise. "You won't punish her? Why?"

Raphael answered to no one, but Dmitri had been with him longer than any other. "Because I took the first shot. And she is mortal."

The vampire's expression remained unconvinced. "I like Elena, but if she escapes punishment, others might question your power."

"Make sure they understand that Elena occupies a very special place in the scheme of things. Anyone else who dares challenge me will soon wish I'd shown them the same mercy I showed Germaine."

Dmitri's face paled. "May I ask one question?"

He waited in silent permission.

"Why were you so badly injured?" Dmitri pulled out a gun he'd had tucked into the small of his back. "I checked the bullet she used—it should've only caused minor damage, given her a head start of ten minutes at most."

Then she will kill you. She will make you mortal.

"I needed to be injured," he responded obliquely. "It was the answer to a question."

Dmitri looked frustrated. "Can it happen again?"

"I'll make sure it doesn't." He took pity on the leader of his Seven. "Do not worry, Dmitri—you won't have to watch the city shudder under the rule of another archangel. Not for another eternity."

"I've seen what they can do." The vampire's eyes swirled with the rivers of memory. "I was under Neha's tender mercies for a hundred years. Why didn't you stop me when I rebelled against your authority?"

"You were two hundred years old," Raphael pointed out, heading toward the bathroom. "Old enough to choose."

Dmitri snorted. "Old enough to be cocky with no real knowledge to back it up. A damn pup with delusions of grandeur." A pause. "Have you never wondered—if I'm a spy?"

"If I had, you'd be dead."

Dmitri smiled and there was a loyalty in his eyes that surprised Raphael each time he saw it. The vampire was incredibly powerful, could've set up a stronghold of his own, but he chose to give his life over to an archangel. "Now I will ask you a question, Dmitri."

"Sire."

"Why do you think I intend to spare Elena's life?"

"You need her to track Uram," Dmitri responded. "And . . . there is something about her that fascinates you. Not much fascinates an immortal."

"Feeling the stirrings of ennui?"

"I see its edge on the horizon—how do you fight it?"

Raphael wasn't sure he had been fighting it. "As you say, very little fascinates an immortal."

"Ah." Dmitri's smile turned sexual in the way of vampires. "So you must savor that which fascinates."

Elena woke when her bladder protested. It was a good thing hunters were trained to restrain their natural urges in such circumstances—some hunts involved hours upon hours of immobile watchfulness. Still, it wasn't comfortable.

I will send Dmitri.

Her face went so hot, it felt like she had third-degree burns. "Do you always spy on people?" It was tempting, but she didn't try to use that headache-inducing shield thing she seemed to have developed. Better to save that for when he was really messing with her.

No. Most people aren't very interesting.

The arrogance of the answer was stunning . . . and welcome. This was the archangel she knew. "I'm not letting that vampire escort me to the bathroom. He'll probably try to bite me."

Wait for me, then.

That just made her want to scream. "Get him to untie me. I can hardly make a daring escape with you up and around."

I don't think Dmitri trusts you with your hands and feet unbound.

She was about to tell him exactly what she thought of that when the door opened to admit the vampire in question. He looked like he'd been up all night, his shirt rumpled, his previously neat hair messy. It only made him look lusciously sexy. "Do vampires sleep?"

He gave her a startled look. "You're a vampire hunter. Don't you know?"

"I mean I know you sleep, but do you really need it?" She stayed very still as he went behind her. "Dmitri?"

Cool fingers brushing her hair out of the way to bare her nape. Knuckles running along skin. "We can go without sleep for longer than humans, but yes, we need it."

"Stop that," she muttered when he continued to stroke her with his knuckles. "I'm not in the mood."

"That sounds promising." His breath whispered against her nape, a dangerous place for a vampire with cool hands. It meant he hadn't fed. "What can I do to get you in the mood?"

"Untie me and let me use the bathroom."

He chuckled and then she felt a tug on her wrists. The bonds fell magically away. "How the hell?"

"I learned rope bondage from a true adept," he murmured, playing with strands of her hair as she released herself from the ropes.

She would've snapped at him to stop it but he wasn't hurting her and now that Raphael was awake, she had a feeling it wasn't Dmitri who posed the real danger. "Bathroom?" She jumped to her feet as soon as the ropes were undone, then moaned. "My muscles. Why the hell did you have to tie me up so hard?" She threw him an evil look.

"Maybe I was getting my own back." He rubbed a hand across his throat.

"I thought you liked pain."

A dark smile, filled with whispers of badness that would hurt oh so good. "But you didn't stay to play."

She sniffed the air suspiciously. No scent. He was just being his usual self. And gorgeous as he was, he didn't make her stupid with lust. Maybe a touch affected, but what woman wouldn't be? "For the last time, where's the—" She followed the direction of his raised hand toward a small door. "Thanks."

Once inside, she frowned and tried to use that "shield" that might turn out to be nothing but her imagination running wild. There was no way she wanted Raphael in her head at that moment. Ten minutes later, she'd used the facilities, washed her face, brushed her teeth using one of the disposable toothbrushes under the sink, and combed her hair using the dinky disposable brush. There was even a small white hair-tie included in the pack, which she used to pull her hair up into a ponytail, her own hair-tie having being lost God only knew when.

Looking in the mirror, she decided she'd do. The thin cuts on her face were barely noticeable and though her palms were a little tender, they wouldn't limit her range of movement. As for clothes—her fatigue-green T-shirt looked okay and her black cargo pants weren't too badly wrinkled. It was as good an outfit to die in as any. Not that she was going to make it easy for the archangel. That thought in mind, she quickly disassembled one of the disposable razors, intending to get to the blade.

"Fuck!"

"Did you find the razors, Elena?" came Dmitri's voice from the other side. "You wound me with your estimation of my IQ."

She threw the plastic in the trash. That vampire had somehow managed to remove the blade without destroying the razor as a whole. "Very funny." Opening the door, she walked out.

Dmitri stood on the opposite side of the room, his hand on the doorknob. "Raphael wants to see you." Gone was any hint of friendliness.

"I'm ready."

That seemed to amuse him. "Are you?"

"How about a knife at least?" she bargained. "Make it a fair fight?"

He opened the door. "If it comes down to it, there will be no fight. But for some reason, I don't think Raphael plans to kill you."

That's what Elena was afraid of. "Where are we going?"

"To the roof."

Elena tried to remain calm as they made their way to the elevators and shot up. But there was no way she could forget the last time she'd gone up to the roof. Her hand clenched, remembering the ruthless ease with which Raphael had illustrated his control over her. Why the hell did she keep forgetting the reality of his nature?

Even as she thought that, she kept her mind tightly focused, thinking "closed" thoughts.

The doors opened to reveal the glass cage atop the roof . . . and déjà vu smashed into her full force. A table set with a white tablecloth, croissants, grapefruit, juice, and coffee sat in solitary splendor on that beautiful roof. The only difference was, this time, Raphael stood with his back to her on the farthest edge.

Forgetting all about Dmitri, she stepped out of the elevator and headed toward the exit. The elevator doors closed behind her, but she was barely aware of its—and Dmitri's—departure, her focus on the wings of an archangel she'd last seen bleeding out on her apartment floor. "Raphael," she said as soon as she exited the glass cage.

He turned slightly and she took it as an invitation to go to him—she had to see for herself that the damage had been healed. His wings appeared perfect from a distance and it was only as she got closer that she saw the startling change. "It's as if you grew the pattern of the gunshot."

He raised the wing so she could see the full scope of it. "I thought it was isolated to the underside, but it's both."

She stood, stunned. It was a scar but it was the most amazing scar she'd ever seen. "You do realize this makes your wings even more unique." Even more inhuman in their beauty.

The wing lowered. "Are you saying you shot me as a cosmetic procedure?"

She could gauge nothing from the tone of his voice. Wary, she walked to stand beside him—but with several feet of distance between them.

He spoke again before she could, his eyes on her face. "You're hurt."

"Just surface cuts." She showed him her palms. "They hardly even sting."

"You were lucky."

"Yeah." The glass had been thick, less sharp than if she'd broken a dish. "So?"

His eyes shaded in that incredible way, until they were close to black. "Things have changed. There's no more time for play."

"You call threatening to throw me to my death, play?"

"I didn't threaten you, Elena."

She narrowed her eyes. "You were holding me over a very dark, very open space."

His hair lifted off his face as the wind pushed inward. "But you survived. And I just spent a considerable amount of energy patching myself up."

"Sorry." She folded her arms, scowling, defensive. "What's the punishment?"

"Will you take it meekly?" His wings stretched out behind him, spreading to cover the space behind her as well.

"Not a chance," she muttered. "I haven't forgotten what triggered this whole incident."

"It doesn't excite me to take an unwilling woman."

Caught by surprise, she dropped her arms. "Are you saying you didn't do it on purpose?"

"It doesn't matter. What does matter is that you did enough damage that I need to . . . refuel."

A hint of unease crawled up her spine. "What's that supposed to mean? Do you need rest?"

"No. I need an infusion of energy."

"Like a vampire needs blood?"

"If you like."

She frowned. "I didn't know angels needed that sort of thing."

"It happens rarely." Folding back his wings, he came closer. "It takes a lot for the well to run this close to dry."

He was right next to her now and she didn't know how that had happened. No, that was lying to herself. He was close because she'd let him get close. "You scared me last night."

Those dark, dark blue eyes reflected open surprise. "Do I not scare you usually?"

"Not like that." She couldn't help it, she reached out a hand to touch his wing before her neurons shrieked a warning and she wrenched it back. *No one* touched an angel's wings without permission. "Sorry."

He spread out the "scarred" wing. "Do you need to convince yourself that it's real, not an illusion?"

Not caring that it amused him, she ran her fingers over the part of the wing she'd destroyed. The sensation was . . . "So soft," she murmured, and yet she could feel considerable muscle and strength behind it. The warm vitality of it was a living pulse that beckoned her to continue stroking. When she lifted away her hands, reluctant to stop but knowing she had to, the tips of her fingers glittered. "Angel dust."

"Taste it."

She looked up, vividly conscious of the wings closing around her. "Taste?"

"Why do you think humans pay a fortune for it?"

"I thought it was a status thing—you know, look at my vial

of angel dust, it's bigger than yours." She stared at the brilliant sparkles coating the tips of her fingers. "It tastes good?"

"Some call it a drug."

She froze with her index finger close to her lips. "As in befuddle my mind?"

"No, it has no narcotic or other effect on the brain. It's simply the taste."

She met those beautiful, dangerous eyes and knew he could tempt her into hell itself. "Maybe this is your revenge?" Flicking out her tongue, she took a careful taste.

Ambrosia.

A shudder vibrated through her body, her toes curled, and she almost purred. "Wow, orgasm on a stick." And a good orgasm at that. "You go around shedding this stuff?" A tendril of jealousy snaked its way up her body. She crushed it, telling herself she was going to add *Big* in front of her *Idiot* tattoo. "Guess it's a power trip to see mortals scrambling for it."

His lips curved. "Oh, this is a special blend for you." Taking one of the fingers she hadn't licked, he rubbed it along her lips. "What we usually shed is apparently comparable to the most delicious of chocolates or the finest of wines. Decadent, rich, and very expensive."

She told herself she wasn't going to lick the glitter off her lips. "And this blend?" The taste was inside her mouth without her having any knowledge of taking it in. And Raphael was incredibly close, his wings creating a white gold wall around them, his hands strong and warm on her hips. "What's so special about it?"

"This blend," he murmured, bending his head, "is about sex."

She put her hands on his chest but it wasn't a protest. After the blood, the fear, she needed to touch him, to know this glorious creature existed. "Another form of mind control?"

He shook his head, his mouth a hairbreadth from hers. "It is only fair."

"Fair?" She flicked her tongue along his lower lip. It made his hands clench on her hips.

"If I licked you between your thighs, your taste would have the same aphrodisiac effect on me."

22

No woman on the planet could've resisted the sexual heat of Raphael at that moment. "Is this your idea of refueling?" she murmured, biting down softly on his lower lip.

His arms slid around her. "Sex and power have always been connected." And then he kissed her.

Her feet lifted up on tiptoe as she tried to get closer. His arms crushed her to his chest, his wings blocking out the world as she gripped his shirt and tried not to drown under the overload of pleasure. That erotic, aphrodisiac angel dust seemed to be sinking into her pores through every inch of exposed skin, snaking through her body to collect in the hot, aching place between her thighs, the excess flowing through her body in a rush of liquid heat. Her breasts ached, her lips craved him.

"How's the power generation going?" she gasped when he let her up for air.

His eyes were still as dark but sparks of electric blue glittered in the depths. "Exquisitely."

Her reply was lost in the fury of his next kiss. Under her hands, his chest was hard, sculptured, hot. She wanted to shape, to taste, to pet. Stroking up, she found the collar of his shirt, and slid one hand inside to lie against his shoulder. His reaction was to grip her bottom with one hand and raise her so the hard ridge of his erection pressed against the vee of her thighs.

There was nothing removed or angelic about him at that moment. He was pure sexy, gorgeous male. And strong, so beautifully strong it made her feel feminine to the core. For the first time in her life, she didn't have to hold back her hunter strength. That was a little-known fact about hunters who were born, not trained. They were stronger than an ordinary human, more likely to survive an encounter with a pissed-off vamp.

"Good," was Raphael's only reaction when she wrapped both legs around his waist. He continued to hold her as if she weighed nothing and it was almost as erotic as the way his hand shaped her, strong and confident.

"You kiss pretty well for a guy with wings," she murmured into the intimacy of his mouth. The truth was, he was threatening to blow off the top of her head.

"And your mouth is going to get you into trouble yet again." He shoved a hand up under her T-shirt, spreading those strong fingers against her spine, igniting a shock of pleasure. "Feeling coerced?"

"Extremely." But he'd been telling the truth about the angel dust—it tasted like pure sex but didn't seem to be affecting her mind . . . at least no more than could be accounted for by the lust racing through her system.

He shifted his hold at that moment, continuing to support her with one hand under her butt, while the other snaked around her body to cup her breast. Electricity arced through her. "You don't waste time," she said, breaking the kiss to suck in a breath.

"Mortals don't live long." He pinched her nipple through her bra. "I have to take advantage of you while I can."

"Not funny. Oh—" She pushed into his hands, wondering at herself. She'd never, not once, fallen for the vampires she so often came in contact with. More than one hunter had—hell, the old ones were not only pretty, they were smart and knew exactly how to please a lover. Dmitri was the perfect example.

Yet Elena had resisted, knowing that, for all their appeal, they were, in the end, almost-immortals who saw her as nothing more than a fleeting diversion. And she'd fought too hard for her right to live to value it so cheaply. But here she was, wrapped around an archangel. "How long do you play with your toys?"

He cupped her breast. "As long as they amuse me."

The answer should have dampened the heat between them but those eyes of his, they were furious with sex, with hunger, with passion such as she'd never before known. "I have no intention of amusing you."

He molded her sensitive flesh. "Then this will blow over very fast." His tone said otherwise. "Now open your mouth."

She did just that—to tell him not to give her orders. But he took advantage, sweeping in to entangle her senses in a wash of male hunger and the exotic, erotic taste of angel dust. She dug her fingers into his back, glorying in the heavy muscle under her touch. His lips left hers to trail down her neck—he grazed her with his teeth, leaving marks. "I would like very much to fuck you, Elena."

She sucked in a cool breath of air, then buried her face against his neck, vividly conscious of his hand on her breast. "Such a romantic proposal."

His wings brushed her back as he closed them even tighter around her. "Would you prefer flowery words, paeans to your beauty?"

She laughed, licked at his skin, taking the savage, quintessentially masculine scent of him deep inside. The idea of Raphael serenading her was preposterous. "No, honesty works for me." Especially when that honesty was coated in pure sexual fire, a dark heat focused solely on her.

"Good." He began to move.

"Stop." She wiggled, surprising him into letting her go.

The second her feet touched the ground, she pushed off his chest . . . then had to use him to balance herself when her legs wobbled.

He put one hand on her waist to steady her. "I never took you for a tease."

"I'm also not a pushover." She wiped the back of her hand across her lips. It came away sparkling with fine glitter, making her wonder about the rest of her face. "I just spent the night tied up in a chair, buddy."

"You're saying we're even?" He folded back his wings.

The sudden space made her realize how close she was to the edge of the roof. Taking a few wary steps forward, she nodded. "You disagree?"

Eyes the color of the deepest oceans gleamed. "Whether I do or not, it's good you stopped us. We have something to discuss."

"What?"

"It'll soon be time to earn your paycheck."

Fear and exhilaration burst through her veins. "You have a bead on Uram?"

"In a sense." His face was suddenly very ascetic, all traces of sensuality smoothing away to reveal the bone structure no mortal man would ever possess. "We'll eat first. Then we will speak of blood."

"I don't want to eat."

"You will." His tone was absolute. "I won't be accused of mistreating my hunter."

"Change that pronoun," she said. "I'm not yours."

"Really?" His lips curved slightly and it wasn't amusement. "Yet you have my mark driven into your skin."

She brushed at the backs of her hands. The damn glittery stuff stuck. "It'll wash off."

"Perhaps."

"You better hope it does—a glow-in-the-dark hunter won't exactly blend in."

A very male appraisal gleamed in those eyes. "I could lick it off you."

The embers low in her body flamed up, melting her from the inside out. "No, thanks." *Yes, please,* her body murmured. "I need to shower anyway."

The austere expression on his face shifted to pure sensuality between one heartbeat and the next. "I'll wash your back."

"An archangel deigning to wash a hunter's back?" She raised an eyebrow.

"There would be a price, of course."

"Of course."

His head tilted up without warning. "It seems we'll have to postpone that discussion."

She turned her head in the same direction, but could see nothing except a painfully bright sky. "Who's up there this time?"

"No one you need to concern yourself about." The arrogance was back full force. Then he snapped out his wings and the air rushed out of her.

Someone so beautiful shouldn't exist, she thought. It was impossible.

I'm only beautiful to you, Elena.

She didn't tell him to get out of her head this time. She kicked him out.

He blinked, his face otherwise expressionless. "I thought I'd imagined that little trick of yours."

"Guess not." Her elation had her grinning so hard her face felt like it might crack. Damn, if she could really do this . . . But then logic reasserted itself. Doing this gave her one hell of a headache, so she had to stop being stupid and keep it in reserve for when she really, desperately needed it. "Logic sucks."

Raphael's lips curved but this time, the smile held an edge of cruelty, a reminder that the man she'd kissed was also the Archangel of New York, also the man who'd held her over a mortal fall and whispered of death in her ear. "Eat," he said now. "I'll return to join you."

Again, that sense of déjà vu hit her as he simply stepped

back off the roof. She stood in place this time, though her stomach went into free fall. But then there he was, winging his way upward, the wind of his flight whipping air across her face. It was tempting to keep watching after him, but she turned away, well aware she was walking a very thin line.

Raphael wanted her, but that was something separate from his duties as the Archangel of New York, a fact she'd do well to remember—even if she survived Uram, she'd still likely be marked for death. The simple fact was that she knew too much. And she wasn't even close to getting Raphael to swear an oath. Damn. Striding over to the breakfast table, she hesitated. Back to the elevator shaft or to the wide-open sky?

In the end, she chose the elevator shaft. She could probably handle anything that came out of the elevator, but she knew damn well she couldn't survive an archangel. The first thing she did was grab the knife beside her plate and slide it into her boot. It was only sharp enough to cut bacon but it could do some damage if necessary. Then she ate. Food was fuel and she needed to be fully charged if she was going to go hunting. Adrenaline thumped through her, laced with the icy bite of fear—but that just amped up her excitement.

She was hunter-born—this was what she was made for.

There was a sound at her back, a whisper of awareness along her hunter senses. "Sneaking around, Dmitri?" She'd scented him the instant he stepped out of the elevator.

"Where's Raphael?"

Surprised at his curt tone, she watched as he moved around to stand beside the table. Gone were any and all hints of elegant sexuality, everything that normally sugarcoated the truth of what he was. She looked into that handsome face and knew he'd seen kings fall and empires rise. Dmitri had held a sword once upon a time, she thought, certain he had far more in common with some ruthless age of blood and death than the civilization hinted at by his perfect stone gray suit. "He's in a meeting," she said, pointing up.

Dmitri didn't follow her gesture as most humans would

have, continuing to stare at her with an intensity that would've scared many, that probably should have scared her. "What?" she asked.

"What do you see, Guild Hunter?" His voice was deep, whispering of things better left unwitnessed, horrors caged in the depths of the night.

"You, sword in hand," she said honestly.

Dmitri's face remained calm, unrevealing. "I still dance with steel. You're welcome to watch."

She paused in the act of taking a small croissant from the bread basket. "Has Raphael rescinded his hands-off policy?" She'd simply assumed not. Stupid, stupid.

"No." The breeze ruffled his hair but the strands settled back into perfect lines as soon as it had passed. "However, since you're going to be dead soon, I want to taste you before it's too late."

"Thanks for the vote of confidence." She bit into the croissant with a snarl. It was one thing to think that herself, quite another to hear it from someone else's lips. "But I suggest you stick to your pretty blondes. Hunter blood's too sharp for your palate."

"The blondes come too easily to my embrace."

"Are you using weird vampire powers on women?"

He laughed and it was more echo than sound, holding none of the heat she'd come to associate with him. This one spoke of thousands of yesterdays, an eternity of tomorrows. "If seduction is a power, then yes. I've had centuries to perfect what a mortal man must accomplish in a few paltry years."

She remembered the ecstasy on the blonde's face, the sensual hunger on Dmitri's. But he hadn't been looking at the blonde. "Have you ever loved?"

The air seemed to stop moving as the vampire by the table watched her without blinking. "I see why you intrigue Raphael. You have little sense of your own mortality." His eyes turned from human to pure obsidian in the blink of an eye. No whites, no irises, nothing but pure, unrelieved black.

She barely stopped herself from reaching for the knife in

her boot. He'd likely decapitate her before she so much as touched metal. "Neat trick. Do you juggle as well?"

A pause filled with death, then Dmitri laughed. "Ah, Elena. I do believe I'll be sorry to see you dead."

She relaxed, sensing the change in his mood even before his eyes returned to normal. "Nice to know. Maybe you can name one of your kids after me."

"We can't have children, you know that." His tone was matter-of-fact. "Only the just-Made can."

"My job mostly involves tracking the under-hundred crowd—I don't come into a lot of contact with that many really old vamps. Not enough to have long conversations with, anyway," she told him, finishing off her orange juice. "What do you consider just-Made?"

"Two hundred years or so." He shrugged, the gesture very human. "I've heard of no conceptions or impregnations after that point."

Two hundred years.

Twice her lifetime. And Dmitri spoke of it as if it were nothing. So, how old was he? And how old was the man he called sire? "Does it sadden you? Knowing you'll never have children?"

A shadow passed over his face. "I didn't say I'd never been a father."

Raphael's return saved her from choking on the foot in her mouth. Somehow she knew to look up, to see the fantasy of his wings backlit to glowing life by the sun. "Beautiful." A whisper.

"So, he has enthralled you."

She forced herself to look away and toward Dmitri. "Jealous?"

"No. I have no need for Raphael's leavings."

She narrowed her eyes, but he wasn't done.

"You can hardly sit in judgment on those who prefer vampire lovers now." A curl of scent snaked around her, insidious in its seduction. "Not when you wear Raphael's colors in your skin."

She'd forgotten about the damn dust. Raising her hand, she rubbed at her face. Her fingers came back shimmering white gold. The temptation to bring those fingers to her lips and lick was so strong, she had to force her hands down to clutch at her thighs. The dust left streaks against the black material, glittering trails of accusation. Dmitri was right—she'd well and truly fallen.

But that didn't mean she was going to offer herself up to this vampire, no matter the sex and sin taste of him. "Stop, or I'll extract your canines while you sleep," she said under her breath. "I mean it, Dmitri."

The scent twisted around her body, infiltrating her very veins. "So sensitive, Elena, so exquisitely sensitive. You must've been exposed to our beauty very young." There was anger in his tone then, as if the idea repulsed him. "Who?" He vanished the tendril of scent.

Drip.

Drip.

Drip.

Come here, little hunter. Taste.

Her stomach revolted. She'd forgotten *his* scent, buried the memory of the shameful rush of heat between her legs, the incomprehension in her child's mind. "He's dead," she whispered, eyes on Raphael as he landed on the edge and began walking toward her.

"Did you kill him?"

"Would you hurt me if I had?"

"No. I may be a monster," he said, his voice strangely gentle, "but I'm not a monster who preys on children."

They both went silent as Raphael approached. Terror kicked in her chest as she truly saw him—he was glowing, bathed in that white-hot overflow of energy that promised death. She pushed back her chair, stood.

But she left the knife in her boot. No need to antagonize him if the rage wasn't directed at her. "Raphael," she said as he came to stand on the other side of the table.

His eyes were blue flame when he looked at her, but it was Dmitri he focused on. "Where are the bodies?"

"Brooklyn. There were—"

"Seven," Raphael interrupted. "Michaela received their hearts special-delivery this morning."

23

"Uram?" Elena asked, trying not to think about the stomach-churning "delivery" Raphael had just described. "Is he—"

"Later." Raphael cut her off with a slice of his hand. "First we'll go to the site and see if you can track him."

"He's an archangel. I scent vampires," she pointed out for what felt like the millionth time, but neither archangel nor vampire was listening.

"I've organized transport," Dmitri said and she had the sense that more information was being communicated than the words she could hear.

Raphael shook his head. "I'll take her. The longer we wait, the more the scent will dissipate." He held out his hand. "Come, Elena."

She didn't argue, her curiosity rabid. "Let's go."

And that was how she found herself tucked against Raphael's chest as he flew her to an abandoned warehouse in an unfamiliar part of Brooklyn. She ended up squeezing her eyes shut for most of the journey because Raphael was doing that invisible thing again, and this time he'd extended it to cover her. It made her nauseated to not be able to see herself.

"Do you sense him?" he asked moments after he landed on a patch of dirt with a few struggling clumps of grass and helped her get to her feet.

She took a deep breath and was hit with an influx of smell. "Too many vamps. It'll make it harder to separate out the scents." She couldn't see a single vampire, couldn't see any living creature at all, but she knew they were there—though this wasn't a place anyone would want to end up.

The chain-link fence on either side was ragged with holes, the buildings scrawled over with graffiti, the grass scraggly underfoot. There was a pervading sense of disuse, but over-laying that was the odor of rotting garbage . . . and something even more foul. She swallowed bile. "Alright. Show me."

He nodded at the warehouse in front of her. "Inside."

The large warehouse door slid up, though he'd spoken in a low tone. She wondered if he could speak to all his vampires mind-to-mind. But she didn't ask that, couldn't. Because the scent of garbage, of disuse, was suddenly wiped out by stomach-churning foulness.

Blood.

Death.

The sickening miasma of bodily fluids left to stew in an airless space.

The urge to gag tore at her throat. "Never thought I'd say this, but I wish Dmitri was here." She'd welcome his seduc-tive scent at this point. A wash of clean, fresh, rain scent hit her on the heels of that thought. She drew it in, then shook her head. "No. I can't afford to miss the cues. But thank you." Then she stopped hesitating and walked into the hor-ror.

The warehouse was huge, the only light coming in through narrow windows high up on the walls. Her brain couldn't un-derstand the piercing clarity of that light until she felt the crunch of glass underfoot. "The windows are all broken."

Raphael didn't reply, moving behind her like a midnight shadow.

She crunched her way through the glass and onto a patch of clear concrete. Deciding to focus, she stood in place, widened her senses, searched.

Drip.

Drip.

Drip.

No, she thought, teeth gritted, this was no time to lose it.

Drip.

Drip.

Drip.

She shook her head but that sound—the soft, wet splash of blood hitting a hard surface—didn't disappear. "The dripping," she said, realizing the sound wasn't in her head. Horror choked off her breath but she made herself move forward, through the gloom and toward the very end of the cavernous space.

The nightmare came into sight slowly.

At first, Elena couldn't make sense of it, couldn't figure out what it was that she was seeing. Everything was in the wrong place. It was as if some sculptor had gotten his pieces mixed up, stuck them into place while blindfolded. That leg, the bone, it had been driven through a woman's sternum, her torso ending in a bloody stump. And that one, she had beautiful blue eyes but they were in the wrong place, staring out at Elena from the gaping maw of her neck.

Drip.

Drip.

Drip.

The blood, it was everywhere. She glanced down in fresh horror, terrified she was standing in it. Her relief was crushing when she saw the rivulets were sluggish, easy to avoid. But the bodies continued to drip, hanging from a tangle of rope like the most macabre of puzzles. Now that she'd looked down, she didn't want to look back up.

"Elena." The rustle of Raphael's wings.

"A minute," she whispered, her voice raw.

"You don't need to look," he told her. "Just follow the scent."

"I need an example of his scent before I can go anywhere," she reminded him. "What he gave Michaela—"

"Michaela destroyed the package. She was in hysterics. Do what you can here. We'll visit her afterward."

Nodding, she swallowed. "Tell your vampires to vacate the area around the warehouse—at least a hundred yards in every direction." There was too much sensory input, as if the sheer amount of blood was amplifying everything, even her own hunter abilities.

"It's being done."

"If any of them are like Dmitri, they need to get out completely."

"There are none. Do you wish to scent those who came inside, for elimination purposes?"

It was a good idea but she knew that if she turned her back on this madness, she'd never return. "Did any of them spend a lot of time near the bodies?"

A pause. "Illium took on the task of determining if any had survived."

"It's obvious they're dead."

"The ones on the floor—their fate wasn't immediately clear."

She'd been so horrified by the hanging bodies that she hadn't paid attention to the pile below. Or perhaps she hadn't wanted to see, to know. Now she did and wished she hadn't. Unlike the nightmare above, these bodies looked as if they were sleeping, one on top of another. "Were they arranged like that?"

"Yes." A new voice.

She didn't turn, guessing it to be Illium. "Are your wings blue?" she asked, coating her pity and sorrow in a casing of dark humor. These three girls below, they were so young, their bodies smooth, uncharted by age.

"Yes," Illium said. "But my cock isn't, in case you were wondering."

She almost laughed. "Thank you." That comment had snapped through the nightmare, allowing her to think. "Your scent won't interfere with my senses." Her nose was ten times better than that of most humans, but when it came to tracking, she was a bloodhound attuned only to vampire. Or that was her normality. This . . .

The sound of footsteps retreating. She waited until she heard the door close. "You took his feathers and he remains with you?" Her eyes traced the bodies. A symphony of unbroken, tangled limbs and curved spines, unmarked but for the gray chill of death.

"Others would have taken his wings."

An angel without wings. It made her remember how she'd shot Raphael. "Why are they so washed out?" Their race was immaterial. Chalk white, dull mahogany, it mattered little. All three girls in the pile were pale in a way that screamed— "Vampire. A vampire fed from them. Drained them." She went to step forward, halted. "The M.E. hasn't been here. I can't touch them."

"Do what you must. Ours are the only eyes that'll see this."

She swallowed. "And their families?"

"Would you leave them with this image of suffering?" A cold blade of anger in every word. "Or a story of a sudden plane crash or car accident in which the body was destroyed beyond recognition?"

Drip.
Drip.
Drip.

Deluged with blood and death on every side, her brain struggled to fight the memories of old horrors, things no amount of time would wipe away. "He didn't drain the others. Just these three."

"The others were for play."

And somehow, she knew the evil that had butchered the ones above had done so in front of the living girls, shoving terror through them, feeding on their fear. She stepped nearer the drained girls, having skirted the dripping nightmare above.

Going down on her haunches, she moved long black hair away from a slender neck. "In cases where a human dies, I usually get the strongest scent impression at the point where blood was taken," she said, talking to drown out the pervading, endless sound of blood hitting concrete. "Oh, Jesus."

Raphael was suddenly on the other side of the bodies, his wings flared out in a way that struck her as odd . . . until she realized he was attempting to keep them out of the blood. He hadn't been wholly successful. A bright red splash marked the tip of one wing. She looked away, forcing her gaze back down to the shredded neck of the girl who'd looked so peaceful from a distance. "This wasn't a feed," she said. "It's like he tore out her neck." Remembering Michaela's "delivery," her eyes dipped. The girl's heart, too, was gone, ripped out of her chest.

"A feed would've been too slow," Raphael said, continuing to keep his wings off the floor. "He must've been starving by this point. He needed a bigger hole than the fangs provide."

The clinical description actually helped calm her. "Let's see if I can pick up his scent." Tightening every muscle in her body, she leaned close to the dead girl's neck and breathed deep.

Cinnamon and apples.
Soft, sweet, body cream.
Blood.
Skin.
A jagged lash of acid. Sharp. A scent with bite. Interesting. Full of layers. Pungent but not putrid.

That was what always amazed her. When vampires went bad, they didn't magically gain an evil scent. They smelled the same as they always had. If Dmitri went bad, he'd retain his allure, his seductive chocolate cake and frosting and sex with all the toppings kind of smell. "I have it, I think." But she had to confirm.

Standing, she waited until Raphael had risen before gritting her teeth and stepping below the abattoir hanging from the ceiling. She took every step with slow deliberation, knowing she might just run screaming from this warehouse if touched by even a single drop of cold blood.

Drip.

A splash by her foot. Close, too close.

"Far enough," she whispered and then went absolutely still, sorting through the scent layers once more. It was harder here, much harder. Terror had a scent, too—sweat and urine and tears and darker fluids—and it overlaid everything in this area. Like a thick perfume that had been sprayed with wild abandon, cloaking anything more subtle.

She dug down, but the terror was a choking grip around her throat, a hand clamped over her mouth, stopping her from sensing anything else. "How long ago did they die?"

"We estimate two to three hours, perhaps less."

Her head jerked up. "You found the location so soon?"

"He made a lot of noise toward the end." A tone so glacial, she barely heard Raphael in it, and yet it was chill with rage, not like when he'd been Quiet. "A neighborhood vampire called Dmitri after coming to investigate."

"You told me this morning I'd be earning my paycheck. You expected this?"

"I knew only that Uram had to be reaching a critical point." His eyes moved over the nightmare. "This . . . no, I did not expect this."

She didn't think anyone could have—it was something that simply shouldn't exist. And yet it did. "The vampire—what will happen to him?"

"I'll take his memories, make sure he remembers nothing." Said without the least apology.

She wondered if that was what he planned for her, but this wasn't the time to ask. Instead, she set her shoulders and dug deeper. Nothing. "There's too much fear here. I'll have to go with what I got from the body." Stepping away with as much care as she'd entered, she tried not to think about what hung above.

Drip.

A drop of blood splashed off the shiny black of her boot.

Her gorge rose. Turning, she ran, not caring if it betrayed weakness. The damn door had been pulled down behind them and now refused to open. Her hand slid off the hot metal. She was at screaming point when it shifted a fraction. She fell to her stomach and squeezed out into the dead earth of the yard.

The sun shone bright overhead as she stood bent over, retching. She was aware of Raphael coming to stand beside her, his wings spreading out to shade her from the sun. She waved him down. She craved the heat—her soul was cold, so icy cold.

She didn't know how long she stood there bent in half, but when she rose, it was to the awareness of being watched. The vampires she'd sent from the warehouse? Illium? Watching the hunter lose her breakfast.

Her mouth tasted disgusting as she used the edge of her T-shirt to wipe at her lips. She wasn't the least bit embarrassed. To see that and not be affected . . . it would've made her a monster akin to the killer who'd anointed her in blood before she'd even been old enough to date.

"Tell me why," she said, voice husky.

"Later." A command. "Search for him."

He was right, of course. The scent would fade if she didn't hurry. Not replying, she kicked some loose dirt over her recently lost breakfast and began to jog slowly around the warehouse, attempting to pick up Uram's exit point. Most vampires used doors but you could never tell. And this killer had wings.

A sharp bite of acid.

She halted, finding herself in front of a small side entrance. From the outside, it looked normal, but when she tugged it open, she found the inside covered with bloody handprints. Too small to have been made by a man of Uram's size. She followed the line of sight . . . and saw the hanging shadows deep in the warehouse.

She slammed the door shut. "He let them run, let them think they had a chance to escape."

Raphael stayed silent as she zigzagged out from the doorway.

"Nothing," she said. "His scent is there because one of the girls managed to get out and he had to retrieve her." She bent down to stare at the brown grass. "Dried blood," she said, swallowing past the raw flesh of her throat. "Poor kid actually managed to crawl this far." She frowned. "There's too much blood."

Beside her, Raphael went very still. "You're right. There's a trail leading away from the door."

She knew his eyesight was keener than hers. Like raptors, angels could reputedly see the tiniest of details even during flight. "It can't be Uram's," she murmured. "I'd have scented it." She followed Raphael as he walked the trail—she could no longer see anything past the first few feet. "Did he drag a body out here, maybe?" They were at the chain-link fence. She went down, examined the small hole at the bottom. "There's blood on the edges of the metal." Excitement slammed into her, a two-fisted punch.

"I'll have to fly across."

As he winged over, Elena found another hole to push through. The blood was more obvious on the other side—there was no grass to hide it, just hard-packed dirt. Her excitement turned into an almost painful hope. "Someone crawled through that hole." Rising to her feet, she found herself staring at the closed door of a small shed. It looked like it might once have been a guard station for the abandoned parking lot behind it.

There was blood on the door.

"Wait here," Raphael ordered.

She gripped the closest part of him—his wing. "No."

The look he shot her was not friendly. "Elena—"

"If we have a survivor, seeing an angel is going to freak her out." She let go of his wing. "I'll check first. She's probably dead, but just in case . . ."

"She lives." An absolute statement. "Go. Get her. We can't waste time."

"A life is not a waste of time." Her hand fisted hard enough that she knew she'd have crescent-shaped marks in the flesh of her palms.

"Uram will kill thousands if we don't stop him. And he'll get more and more depraved with each kill."

Snapshots of the mutilated bodies inside the warehouse cascaded through her mind. "I'll hurry." Reaching the guard station, she took a deep breath. "I'm a hunter," she said loudly. "I'm human." Then she pulled open the door, making sure to stay out of the line of fire in case the person inside had a weapon.

Pure silence.

Using the utmost care, she looked around and . . . into the face of a small woman with darkly slanted eyes. The woman was naked but for the rust red stain of blood, her arms gripping her raised knees as she rocked soundlessly, blind to anything but the terrors of her mind.

24

"My name is Elena," she said softly, wondering if the woman even knew she was there. "You're safe now."

No response.

Backing out, she looked to Raphael. "She needs medical attention."

"Illium will take her to our healer." He came closer but the woman started whimpering at the first glimpse of his wings, her muscles locking so tight Elena knew they'd have to break her bones to release them.

"No." She stood to block the view. "It needs to be one of the vampires. No wings."

His mouth was a flat line, whether in anger or impatience, she couldn't tell. But he didn't seize control of the woman's mind. "I've asked Dmitri to come. He'll take care of her."

Her heart froze. "As in kill her?"

"Perhaps she would welcome mercy."

"You're not God, to make that decision."

Raphael's face was a study in silence. "No harm will come to her while you are gone."

She read between the lines. "And when I return?"

"Then I will decide if she dies or lives." Eyes of blue fire. "She might be infected, Elena. We must test her. If she is, she has to die."

"Infected?" She frowned, then shook her head. "I know—later."

"Yes. Time is passing." His head angled slightly to the left. "Dmitri comes, but he can't approach until he poses no danger to the scent trail. Leave the woman—the leader of my Seven has a weakness for innocents caught in violence."

Elena nodded at the oblique reassurance, and bent down. "Dmitri is going to help you. Please go with him."

The woman didn't stop rocking but she was no longer making that keening sound and her body wasn't so tense. Praying that Dmitri would be able to get her out without harming her, she made her way back under the chain link and to the other side.

"Can you check the roof—see if there's any sign he took off from there?" As Raphael nodded and flew up, she circled her way around the building. She finally found Uram's exit point on the right side of the warehouse, a few feet from a gaping hole in the chain link.

Aware of Raphael following overhead, she made her way through the hole to the grassy wilderness of the neighboring lot. Blood coated the tips of the grass, as if Uram had run his hand along the top. She found a feather—a brilliant, silvery gray that shimmered with flecks of amber. Its delicate beauty was an insult, a mockery of the blood and suffering she'd seen inside the warehouse. Fighting the urge to crush it, she held it to her nose, drawing in the richness of Uram's true scent. That bite of acid but other things, too. An edge of metal, a dark blade. Blood refined, she thought. Acid and blood and something else, something that spoke of . . . sunlight. She shivered, shoved the feather into her pocket, then carried on.

The scent simply ended in the middle of the lot. "Shit." She put her hands on her hips and blew out a breath, waving Raphael down. He landed in a feat of pure grace.

"Uram took flight."

"Yes," she said. "I never had that problem with vampires—that's how I can track them. I can't track a being who can fly!" It made her blood boil. She wanted to make the monster pay for the bright young lives he'd stolen. "Dmitri?"

"I've told him to approach. And angels don't always fly," Raphael said. "You're the only one who has any chance of finding his scent on the streets." He paused. "We'll return, so you can bathe and gather your things." He glanced at his wing, distaste open on his face. "I must also clean off the blood."

She blushed at the reminder of how ripe she had to be by now. "Why do I need to gather my things?"

"This hunt won't be long, but it will be intense."

"He'll keep killing," she guessed, fists tight. "Leaving a trail."

"Yes." Raphael's anger was tightly controlled, but the sheer force of it almost cut her skin. "You need to stay close to me or one of my angels so that you can be flown out immediately after we discover a fresh kill."

She realized he wasn't giving her a choice. "I suppose if I say no you'll just make me?"

A moment where the only sounds were those of the grass rustling and the whispers of wings at her back as other angels landed—to begin cleanup, she guessed.

"Uram must be stopped." Raphael's face was quiet, expressionless . . . and all the more dangerous for it. "Would you not say that goal excuses any and all means used?"

"No." But her mind filled with an endless slideshow of images—of a woman with her mouth full of organs that should've remained inside her body, another whose head had been impaled on her arm, a third who stared sightlessly out of empty eye sockets. "I'll cooperate."

"Come." He held out an arm.

She went closer. "Sorry if I stink." Her cheeks heated.

His arms closed around her. "You smell of angel dust." With that, he lifted off—and turned them invisible.

She closed her eyes. "I'm never going to get used to that."

"I thought you liked flying."

"Not that." She held on harder, hoping she'd laced her boots up tight. She wouldn't want to accidentally brain someone. "The being-invisible thing."

"The glamour does take some getting used to."

"You aren't born with it?" She fought a shiver as they rose higher.

"No. It's a gift that comes with age."

She bit her tongue at the question that wanted out.

"Learning discretion, Elena?" A tinge of amusement dulled the fury she could sense just beneath his skin.

"I—I—" When her teeth began to chatter, she decided to hell with discretion, and pretty much crawled onto him, wrapping her legs around his waist. He was so deliciously warm. "I'm trying to limit the reasons for which you might have to kill me."

He changed his hold to accommodate her. "Why should I kill you when I can wipe your mind?"

"I don't want to lose my memories." Even the bad ones, they were what made her who she was. Now, today, she was a different Elena to the one who'd never known what it was to kiss an archangel. "Don't make me forget."

"Will you trade your life to keep your memories?" A soft question.

She thought that over. "Yes," she said quietly. "I would rather die as Elena, than live as a shadow."

"We're almost to your apartment."

Forcing open her eyes, she turned to look at her home. The blown-out window had been covered by some sort of clear plastic, but whoever had done it hadn't bothered to anchor it in anything but a cursory fashion. One side was down, flapping in the wind. Her eyes watered. She told herself it was caused by the rush of air cutting over her face.

Raphael flew to that corner and had her tug at the plastic until enough of it was free that she could squeeze inside. Once she was in, she made a wider hole and he walked in, snapping his wings closed behind him. The wind whistled into the apartment as she stood there taking in the mess and feeling her heart break.

The glass was still where it had been when Raphael had shattered the window. So was the blood. Raphael's blood. Her own where she'd cut herself. But a massive wind had come through the living room at some stage, throwing her bookshelf to the floor and breaking the twin to the vase in her bedroom. Papers littered the carpet and the walls were streaked in a way that said there'd been a small squall, a flash of rain that had destroyed what wasn't already broken. The carpet felt damp, the air musty.

At least the door had been fixed enough that it shut. She wondered if it had been boarded over from the outside, nails pounded into the beautiful wood.

"Wait," she said, scooping up her—thankfully—still functional cell phone. "I'll get an overnight bag." With that, she walked over the glass and carpet toward her bedroom, back ramrod straight. "Do I have time to shower here?"

"Yes."

She didn't give him time to change his mind, heading into the bedroom to grab a towel and some underwear.

"I don't like the color scheme."

She paused with her hand on a pair of plain cotton panties. "I told you to wait."

He strolled in, went to her French doors, and pushed them open. "You like flowers."

"Raphael, leave." Her hand trembled she was clenching it so hard.

He looked over his shoulder, a lethal chill in his eyes. "You'd cause a fight over my curiosity?"

"This is my home. I didn't invite you in, not when you blew out the window and destroyed my living room, and not today." She stood her ground, seconds from a breakdown. "You will respect that, or I swear to God, I'll shoot you again."

He stepped out onto the balcony. "I'll wait here. Is that acceptable?"

Surprised he'd bothered to ask, she considered it. "Fine. But I'm closing the doors."

He didn't say anything as she closed the French doors and then, for good measure, pulled the heavy brocade curtains. The last thing she saw was the back of a pair of wings shot through with gold. The beauty of him hit her afresh each time, but today, she was too splintered inside to appreciate it. God, it *hurt*. Rubbing a fist over her heart, she walked into the bathroom and turned the shower to scalding.

It was tempting to take her time, to pamper herself, but those girls deserved better. So she made quick work of it, washing her hair with her favorite shampoo and using an antibacterial soap on her body. The angel dust did wash off . . . mostly. Odd glints kept hitting her as she got out of the shower, towel-dried her hair and body, then stepped into a pair of black cotton panties, a black bra, fresh cargo pants, again in black, and a dark blue T-shirt. It wasn't yet cold enough for long sleeves during the day, but she made a note to pack a windbreaker.

Socks and boots went on next, before she picked up a hairbrush. Running it quickly through her hair, she tugged the wet mass back into a tight ponytail and spent the next few minutes stocking up on weapons from her secret stash. Feeling clean and well armed at least, even if she couldn't expunge the sickening images of slaughter from her mind, she threw some things in an overnight bag, then pushed back the curtains. Raphael was nowhere to be seen.

Her hand crept toward her gun and she had it in hand before she opened the door. The message was written boldly on the gel she used to coat the balcony wall. *The car is waiting below.* Which meant, she realized, that her front door wasn't boarded up. A small mercy.

Shoving the gun back under her T-shirt, she locked the doors and grabbed the overnight bag. She was about to walk out when she remembered she'd been out of touch since hanging up on Ransom the night before. Picking up the landline, she called Sara. "I'm alive and that's all I can say."

"Ellie, what the hell is going on? I've got reports of angels flying all over the city, of missing girls but no bodies, and—"

"I can't talk about it."

"Shit, it's true. Killer vampire."

Elena didn't say anything, figuring it was better to let the rumor circulate. She'd never lied to Sara and she wasn't about to start now. Even doing it by implication went against the grain.

"Hon, you need a pullout? We have places no angel knows about."

Elena trusted the Guild but she couldn't run from this. It was personal now. Those girls . . . "No. I need to finish this." Uram had to be stopped.

"You know I'm here for you."

She swallowed the knot in her throat. "I'll call you when I can. Tell Ransom for me, and don't worry."

"I'm your best friend. It's my job to worry. Check under your pillow before you leave."

Ending the call, she took a steadying breath and did as directed. Her lips curved—Sara had left her a present. Fortified, she walked out into the ruin of her living room. Raphael had apparently put the plastic back in place, but she knew it wouldn't last. It didn't matter. The room was too damaged for anything less than a major overhaul. But she would put it back the way it had been.

She knew how to rebuild.

I have no desire to house an abomination under my roof.

Her stuff in boxes on the street, thrown out with the garbage in the aftermath of that final, brutal fight with her father. She'd walked out. Jeffrey had punished her for it by erasing her from his life. Amazingly, it had been Beth who'd called her, Beth who'd helped her salvage what the rain and snow hadn't destroyed. None of the treasures of her childhood had survived—those, Jeffrey had thrown onto a backyard fire and burned beyond recognition.

A single tear escaped her control. She dashed it away before it could touch her cheek. "I'll fix it." It was a promise to herself. And she would replace that glass with a solid wall. She didn't want to see the angels anymore.

Even as she thought that, she knew it for a lie.

Raphael was in her blood, a deadly, addictive drug. But that didn't mean she'd make it easy for him when the time came to bury the Cadre's secrets. "First you'll have to catch me, angel boy." Adrenaline turned her grim smile into a challenge.

25

The car was idling at the curb, a sleek black panther with a vampire leaning against its gleaming paint. Another old one, she realized at once. He was wearing sunglasses with a black-on-black suit, his chocolate-dark hair cut like some GQ model's, but his lips . . . they were dangerous. Bitable. Sensual. "I've been told not to hurt you." He opened the back door.

She dumped her bag inside, frowning inwardly at the odd familiarity of his scent. "Promising start."

He took off the sunglasses and she got the full impact of his eyes. Bright green and slitted like a snake's. "Boo."

She didn't jump—because she was too stupefied by what she was seeing. "Fancy contact lenses don't scare me."

His pupils contracted. *Oh. Wow.* "I was Made by Neha."

"The Queen of Poisons?"

"The Queen of Snakes." Smile slow and definitely unfriendly, he put the sunglasses back on and stood aside to let her enter the car.

She did so only because of his first words to her. So long as Raphael had this one on a leash, they'd get along fine. The second that leash slipped, she had a feeling she'd need every one of the weapons strapped to her body. "What's your name?" she asked as her "driver" got in.

"To you—Death."

"Very funny." She stared at the back of his neck. "Why do you want to kill me?"

"I'm a member of the Seven."

She suddenly realized why she recognized his scent— he'd been in her apartment the night she shot Raphael. He was the one who'd held her with her arms pinned behind her back. No wonder he wanted to gut her. "Look, Raphael and I have sorted things out. Not your problem."

"We protect Raphael from threats even he might not yet see."

"Great." She blew out a breath. "But . . . did you go inside the warehouse?"

The temperature dropped. "Yes."

"Killing me is not the priority," she said softly, but she was no longer speaking to him. "Where are you taking me?"

"To Raphael."

She watched the streets pass by and realized they were heading out of Manhattan and toward the George Washington Bridge. "How long have you been with Raphael?"

"You ask a lot of questions for a dead woman."

"What can I say? I prefer to die well-informed."

A short distance over the bridge and she might as well have been in Vermont. Trees dominated the skyline, veiling the expensive homes that lined this particular stretch, most of them with clifftop outlooks and ridiculous buffers of land. She'd heard rumors the driveways were longer than some roads, and the fact that she couldn't glimpse a single house from the car tended to support that theory.

The driver turned in front of a pair of ornate metal gates and pressed something on the dash. The gates opened soundlessly, belying their apparent age. Elena sucked in a breath as they headed into the corridor of trees. This area was marked on maps as the Fort Lee / Palisades region, but even non–New

Yorkers called it the Angel Enclave. Elena didn't know anyone who'd ever been beyond the gates that guarded each magnificent property. Angels were very private when it came to
their homes.

The driveway *was* long. It was only as they turned that she
caught sight of the large house at the end. Painted an elegant
white, it had obviously been built for a being with wings—open
balconies ringed the second and third floors. The roof was
sloped, but not so much that an angel couldn't land.

Huge windows took up most of the wall space, and though
she couldn't fully see it, it appeared as if the left-hand side
might feature a stunning creation of stained glass. But even
that wasn't the true glory—crawling up along the sides of the
house were what looked like a hundred rosebushes, all amazingly still in full bloom. "It looks like something out of a fairy
tale." The dark and dangerous kind.

The driver almost choked on his laughter. "Do you expect
fairies inside?" He brought the car to a halt.

"I'm hunter-born, vampire. I never believed in fairies."
Stepping out, she closed the door. "You coming in?"

"No." He leaned back against the hood, arms folded, mir-
rored sunglasses reflecting back her own image. "I'll wait
here—unless you plan to start screaming. Then I want a ring-
side seat."

"First Dmitri and now you." She shook her head. "Is pain
really what floats the boat of all the old vamps?"

Another smile, this one with a deliberate hint of fang.
"Come into my parlor, little hunter, and I'll show you."

Come here, little hunter. Taste.

Cold slivered through her, chasing away the sun's warmth.
Not responding to the vampire's provocation, she grabbed her
bag and strode to the front door, able to hear the murmur of
the Hudson in the background. She wondered if the house had
a water view, or if the trees blocked it. Probably didn't matter
to a being who could fly up for a good vantage point.

The door opened before she got there. This time, the vamp

was of the ordinary variety. Experienced but not old, not like the driver and Dmitri. "If you'd please follow me," he said.

She blinked at the plummy British tone. "You sound like a butler."

"I am a butler, madam."

Elena didn't know what she'd been expecting, but a butler was not it. She followed in silence as he led her through a wash of brilliant colors—sunshine coming in through the stained glass she'd guessed at—to a pair of carved wooden doors. "The sire awaits you in the library. Would you care for a cup of coffee or tea?"

"Wow, I want a butler, too." She bit her lower lip. "Would it be too much trouble to ask for a snack? I'm starving." Throwing up was hell on a girl's appetite.

The butler's expression didn't change, but she could've sworn he was amused. "Preparations have been made for a cold lunch. It'll be served in the library."

"Then some coffee would be great. Thanks."

"Of course, madam." He went to open the library doors. "I can take your bag to your room if you wish."

"Then I wish." Still musing over the idea of having met a real live butler, she handed the bag to him and walked inside. Raphael was standing by the huge windows on the right-hand side, backlit by sunshine. His wings glittered gold and white and it was such an arresting sight that she almost missed the second person in the room.

The woman stood by the mantel, wings of bronze, eyes too green to be mortal, and skin of such a beautiful dusky shade it was as if gold had been pounded into bronze and then mixed with cream. Her hair was a curly mass of brown and gold that reached the curve of her butt. A butt displayed very nicely in the catsuit currently painted over her body. A shimmery bronze, the garment zipped up the front and left her arms bare. Right now, it was unzipped just enough to hint at the perfect globes of her breasts.

"So, this is the hunter you find so fascinating." The voice

was smooth whiskey, honey and cream, sensual and full of venom.

Elena shrugged. "I'd say it's more a case of finding me useful."

The female archangel raised an eyebrow. "Didn't anybody ever teach you not to interrupt your betters?" Astonishment in every word.

"Why, yes, they did." She let her tone say the rest.

The archangel flicked out a hand and that was when Raphael spoke. "Michaela."

Michaela dropped her hand. "You allow the human too much freedom."

"Be that as it may, the Guild Hunter is under my protection for the duration of the hunt."

Michaela's smile was sweet poison. "Pity Uram is so creative, otherwise I would've enjoyed teaching you your place."

"I'm not the one he's courting with gifts of human hearts."

That wiped the smile off Michaela's face. She straightened, her skin beginning to glow. "I look forward to eating your heart when it's delivered."

"Enough." Raphael was suddenly in front of Elena, blocking her from Michaela's rage.

She wasn't stupid enough to repudiate the gesture. She stayed behind him quite happily, using the time to rearrange her weapons to maximum advantage. Including the small gun she'd found hidden under her pillow. It was identical to the one Vivek had given her. Sara was the real angel, she thought as she moved that gun from an ankle holster to one of the side pockets of her cargos, from where she could fire without having to take it out.

That done, she focused on Raphael's wings. Up close, they were impossibly perfect, impossibly brilliant. She couldn't help but stroke her finger down the part closest to her. Some things were worth the dance with danger.

"We don't need her." Michaela's voice dripped power.

"Yes, we do." Raphael's tone shifted, became an icy flame. "Calm down before you overstep the rules of Guesthood."

Elena wondered what those rules were even as she realized that Raphael had never spoken to her in that tone. Oh, he'd used some pretty harsh stuff, but not this one. Maybe it was reserved for other archangels. If so, they were welcome to it. She had no desire to face him down in that kind of a mood.

"You'd make an enemy out of me over a human?" The word "human" might as well have been "rodent."

"Uram is an archangel in the grip of a killing lust." Raphael's tone hadn't changed—she could almost glimpse the ice particles in the air. "I have no desire to see the world descend into another Dark Age because of your constant need to be the center of attention."

"You think to compare us?" A snide laugh. "Kings have fought and died for me. She is nothing, a man in women's clothing."

Elena was really, really starting to hate Michaela.

"Then why are you wasting our time?"

A short silence, then the unmistakable sound of wings settling. "Release your pet hunter. I'll wait to deal with her after."

"Great." Elena walked out from behind Raphael. "Join the queue."

Michaela folded her arms across her front, plumping up her breasts. "Do tell. It might be entertaining to see who gets to you first."

"Excuse me if entertaining you isn't at the top of my agenda." Oh, she could be brave now, when she knew Raphael needed her. After . . . well, she had so many other problems, it didn't seem worth the effort to mollify a pissy archangel.

Raphael curved his hand over her hip. Michaela's eyes zeroed in on the touch, the green heated with a spark of unhidden fury. Well, well, wasn't Ms. Angel a fast mover? According to several of the articles she'd found that first night, Michaela and Uram had been hot and heavy for years. But here her lover wasn't yet in his grave and the female archangel had already picked out a replacement.

"Elena,' " Raphael said, and she understood it was a command to behave. "We need to discuss certain aspects of the hunt."

Deciding she was too curious about Uram's descent into vampirehood to waste time antagonizing Michaela, she zipped her lips and waited.

Someone knocked at that moment and a second later, Jeeves entered with a gleaming silver tea and coffee setup, his minions pushing along a cart filled with food, which they placed on a beautiful wooden table by the windows.

"Will that be all, sire?"

"Yes, Montgomery. Make sure we're not disturbed unless it's one of the Seven."

With a nod, Montgomery left, closing the door behind himself. Elena went to the table and chose the only viable seat—at the head, with a bookshelf at her back. Michaela took the other end while Raphael remained standing. Elena wondered if Michaela was waiting to be served. Snorting inwardly at the idea, she poured her own coffee—and, because she was feeling generous, and okay, maybe because she wanted to irritate Michaela—Raphael's as well. Then she put down the carafe.

"So," she said, "tell me what I need to know to hunt this son of a bitch."

Michaela actually hissed. "You'll speak of him with respect. He is an ancient, so old your puny human mind can't imagine all that he's seen and done."

"Did you see what we found in that warehouse?" She put down the coffee, suddenly sick to her stomach. Those images were burned into her brain. Like the ones of that vampire who'd been tortured by the hate group, they would never leave. "He might be an ancient, but he's no longer anything close to sane. Seriously fucked up would be a better description."

Michaela swiped out a hand, sending her table setting crashing to the floor. "I won't help a human hunt him down like a rabid dog."

"You agreed." Raphael's knife blade of a voice. "Do you recant your vote?"

Tears shimmered in those green eyes. "I loved him."

Elena might've believed the stunning archangel had she not caught that earlier flash of fury. This woman loved nothing and no one but herself.

"Enough to die for him?" Raphael asked with smooth cruelty. "Now he sends you his victims' hearts. After he sates the first surge of bloodlust, it'll be your heart he desires."

Michaela wiped away a tear, making a show of coming to grips with herself. Most men would've fallen for her act hook, line, and sinker. "You're right," she whispered. "Forgive my emotional nature." A deep breath that pushed up her breasts to full advantage. "Perhaps I should return to Europe."

Elena knew from her research that Michaela held power over most of central Europe, though it was unclear where her boundary ended and Uram's began.

"No." The single word was resolute. "It's clear he followed you here—if you move, so will he. We may not be able to catch his trail again until it's too late."

"He's right," Elena said, wondering why Raphael hadn't shared Uram's fixation with Michaela earlier. Her guess was that it had something to do with the murders—perhaps a hunter could only track an archangel after he killed? But archangels killed many people. "We have a scent now and if he's circling around you, we have a general idea of where to look for him. I need to know the outline of that area—the places where you spend most of your time."

"I'll provide it," Raphael said. "I want you to listen to Michaela's story of how she received his offering and tell us how far Uram has devolved."

Elena looked at him, squinting against the brightness at his back. "How would I know?"

"You've hunted vampires who've devolved."

"Yes, but Uram is no vamp." She really wanted to know why and how in hell an archangel had gone so wrong. Her earlier anger at being told to run this blind rose anew.

"For the purpose of this hunt," Raphael said, steel in his tone, "he is. Michaela."

The female archangel leaned back in her chair. "I woke to the sound of something tapping against my window. I assumed it to be a trapped bird and got up to release it."

The image should've been incongruous with Michaela's selfish beauty, but there was a powerful sense of truth in her words. Perhaps, to be "human" in her eyes, you had to have wings.

"But," the archangel continued, "when I reached the window, I found no bird. As I was about to turn away, my eye fell on the lawn and I noticed a lump sitting in the center. I thought it was an animal that had crawled there to die." No shudder of distaste, rather a sense of sadness. Again, it felt true.

Animals obviously ranked higher in Michaela's worldview than humans. Having seen some of the things humans were capable of, Elena couldn't disagree.

Michaela took a deep breath. "I opened the balcony doors and asked one of the guards below to check on it. As you know, the lump turned out to be a burlap sack filled with seven human hearts." A pause. "My guards tell me they were still warm."

26

Elena's stomach didn't roil this time. She'd expected as much. "This kind of stuff—taking trophies, taunting people, or in your case, giving gifts—is behavior similar to what you see in vampires after the bloodlust first takes control. At this point, they're more animal than human."

"We knew that, hunter." Michaela made the last word an insult, wiping out any warmth Elena might've felt over the archangel's attitude toward nonhumans.

"Then I can't give you more." She was out of her depth and it was no use pretending otherwise. No hunter in known history had tracked an archangel. "But I will tell you one thing— Uram is far bolder than any vampire. He was there tapping on your window." She saw Michaela shiver, couldn't blame her for being creeped out. "If he carries on at this speed, he'll leave the animal stage behind and start thinking with high-level calculation within the week."

"So soon?" Raphael asked.

She nodded. "Most devolved vamps' first kills are messy, as this was. But it was secret, too. He knew he'd be caught if he didn't hide it."

Raphael nodded. "And vampires in the grip of bloodlust don't think that clearly."

"Over sixty percent are caught locked in bloodthrall at the site of their first kill." A state between lust and stupefaction, it made the vampires insensate to everything around them. Elena had once walked right up to one—he hadn't moved even when she neckleted him, a beatific smile on his face, his hands still buried in his victim's chest. "I have a feeling," she continued, shaking off the memory, "that Uram never went into bloodthrall. If he had, the hearts wouldn't have been warm."

"That is . . . unexpected," Raphael said. "Bloodthrall would have slowed him down."

"But even the worst vampiric killer doesn't slaughter every night," Elena began. "There should be a lull. He's fed the lust—he's bloated with power, with—"

"You forget—he's not a true vampire." Raphael's frame came into view as he shifted slightly. "He won't stop. For now, it seems he hunts at night and during the early morning, so we have the daylight hours to regroup. If he devolves as fast as you predict, then he'll start to hunt in daylight, too."

Elena's eyes widened. "You're saying he's always in bloodlust."

"Yes."

"Dear God." That made Uram a monster beyond comprehension.

The scrape of a chair, the sound muffled by the carpet but still somehow harsh.

Elena looked up to find Michaela on her feet.

"I can't sit here and listen to you speak of Uram this way. You have no comprehension of what it is to lose someone you've known half a millennium." Her eyes met Elena's and at that second, Elena believed her.

"No," she said. "I'm sorry."

Michaela flicked off the sympathy. "I don't need a mortal's pity. Raphael, I would speak with you."

"I'll escort you out."

As they left the room, their wings occasionally brushing, Elena felt a surge of jealousy so strong her hand was on her gun before she realized it. The touch of cold metal against warm skin was what brought her back. Gritting her teeth, she turned and attacked the sandwiches with relish.

By the time Raphael returned, she was no longer starving, which was probably why she didn't stab a fork through his eye when she saw the brush of bronze angel dust on his wing. "Is that like a cat marking its territory?"

Raphael followed her gaze, flaring out the affected wing. "Michaela isn't used to being denied." Picking up a fancy cloth serviette, he came to her. "Wipe it off."

The urge to rebel against the command smashed up against her need to rub that bitch's mark off his wing. Stupid possessiveness won. "Turn around."

He did so in graceful silence. Standing, she dampened the cloth with water before touching it to his wing. She was very careful not to get any of the sticky stuff on herself, but her caution appeared to have been unnecessary. "It's coming off easy. Not like the one you dusted me with." Even now, the light caught on stray flecks embedded in her skin, flecks she was sure Michaela had seen.

"I told you—yours was a special blend."

Something warm and melty spread through her body. "Marking me, angel boy?"

"I prefer to do that with my cock."

Shocked by the rush of wet heat between her thighs, she put the napkin on the table. "All gone."

He flexed his wings, then turned. "You truly are an enigma. So fearless in hunting vampires, so prudish in your sexual tastes."

"I'm not fearless. I'm scared shitless," she said. "And as for the rest—being an enigma is good, right? After all, you only play with your toys as long as they amuse you." She didn't know how it had happened, but she found herself backed up against the table, with Raphael blocking her in.

When he lifted her to the table itself, she didn't protest.

She even spread her thighs to accommodate him. Part of her was still cold. What she'd seen in that warehouse had brought too much to the surface. That sound, that dripping, it was a never-ending drumbeat in her head. She wanted to forget. And Raphael—dangerous, seductive, lethal Raphael—was far better than any drug. "No dust," she murmured as he slid his hands up her thighs to grab her hips. "I don't have time to wash it off."

But he didn't kiss her. "Tell me about your nightmares, Elena."

She froze. "Spying again?" She was human—she kept forgetting he had no respect for the boundaries of her mind.

His eyes turned chrome blue. "I have no need to. You don't have sex in your eyes. You have death."

She wanted to shove him away, but part of her—the cold part—liked the heat of his touch, was excited by that veiled hint of menace. No other man had ever come close to handling everything she was.

So she satisfied her urge to kick at him by leaning back, palms down on the table. It was a good thing they weren't near the food, otherwise, her hair would've been in the coffee. "So," she said, "you're an expert in reading women?"

"I've been alive a long time."

She felt her eyes narrow. "Have you and Her Royal Bitchiness ever fucked?"

He squeezed her hips. "Be careful, Elena. I can't always be around to protect you."

"Is that a yes?" She could imagine them mating in flight, a blinding—a goddamn beautiful—image of white gold and bronze.

"No. I've never taken Michaela up on her offer."

"Why not? She's hot—tits and ass are all men ever see."

"I prefer lips." He bent and bit down a fraction too hard on her lower lip before raising his head. "And yours are quite succulent."

Michaela's, she thought on a crashing wave of pleasure,

were nicely shaped but thin. But— "I'm not buying." She didn't change her position. "Who the hell cares about lips?"

"If you were on your knees with your lips wrapped around my cock, I would care a great deal."

The image made tiny inner muscles tighten in damp readiness. "How come guys always think of women going down on them? How about the other way around?"

Cobalt lightning, hands sliding down, thumbs rubbing along the inner crease of each thigh. "Take off your pants."

Her stomach clenched. "We have a killer to discuss."

"But you want to forget."

"You haven't answered my question." Breathless words, her body so hungry.

"I choose not to sleep with Michaela because I have no liking for black widows. Her poisonous whispers probably helped drive Uram to this."

She sat up, gripping his forearms. "This? What *is* this?"

His thumbs continued to move, touching the very edge of exquisitely sensitive flesh that ached for a harder, deeper caress. "You don't need to know."

A flash of fury overlaid the lust. "I can't work blind."

"Treat him as a vampire, the most dangerous vampire in the known universe." One of his thumbs pressed against her clitoris. "Now, take off your pants."

She fought to draw in air. "Fat chance. Tell me about Uram."

He pushed closer, his wings brushing her knees. Then, to her disappointment, he moved one of his hands . . . only to thrust it up under her T-shirt.

Her heart ricocheted around her chest as he cupped her breast, but she forced out the words. "Why can I scent him now when I couldn't before?"

Raphael slid his hand off her breast, back over her thigh and to her knee. The other hand he slid below her own arm to place palm down behind her, his biceps brushing her breast. "Because"—he lifted her leg, hooking it around his waist as he pulled her forward—"he drew first blood." Their lower bodies came into direct contact and she couldn't help it. She moaned.

"But," she said through the haze, "I wasn't able to scent Erik, the just-Made vamp."

"I misled you at the time, Elena. Both Bernal and Erik were Made around the same time—but Bernal was allowed to feed, while Erik wasn't, not until after the test."

That Raphael had been able to curb the bloodhunger of one of the just-Made was another example of his sheer power, but Erik wasn't the one she wanted to talk about. "Why? Why did Uram turn vampire?"

"He's still an archangel." Rocking her against him, he shoved up her T-shirt, bent his head, and bit her nipple through her bra.

She jerked, pulling at his hair. "Stop that." But he was sucking now and oh, damn, it felt good. Like he'd be the best sex she'd ever imagined, much less had. "Raphael."

He raised his head. "I'll give you a choice."

She pushed her T-shirt back into place, feeling way too vulnerable. Her nipple ached in the most sexual way. "Yeah?"

"Either I splay you out on the table and drive my cock into you, or—"

"—or?" She wanted to snuggle up to him, taste the tendons in his neck.

"Or, I splay you out on the table and lick you to your pleasure, then drive into you."

"Gee." She was having trouble thinking past the needy pulse between her legs. "I choose option *c*."

He settled her back against his erection with the arm around her back. "There is no option *c*."

Oh, to hell with it. She leaned in and grazed that beautiful throat with her teeth. A girl had to live. His arm tightened as she sucked, as she tasted. Then he said, "Does option *c* involve you sucking on other parts of my anatomy?"

Damn, but the archangel could be sexy when he wasn't in

a killing frame of mind. Giving a last, regretful lick, she pushed away. "I'm not fucking you, not until you tell me the truth about Uram."

Something dark crawled across his face. "Sexual blackmail, Elena?"

She snorted. "You treat me like a pet. Go fetch the bad archangel/vampire/whatever the fuck he is, Ellie, but don't you dare ask me why. It'd be too much for your little human head." Dropping the saccharine-sweet tone, she glared. "I don't sleep with men who think I'm a brainless twit."

That lethal darkness turned to amusement but she was aware she was skating a razor-thin edge. Raphael was indulging her for reasons of his own. The archangel who'd forced her to close her hand over a knife blade was also Raphael and she'd do well to remember that—no matter how badly she lusted after him.

"The more you know," he said, "the bigger a liability you become."

"I already know too much." She held her ground. "This isn't about protecting me—it's about protecting the archangels."

"To trust a mortal is the ultimate in foolishness. It's what cost Illium his feathers."

Oh, he knew exactly how to get to her. "I'm not just a mortal. I'm Elena Deveraux, Guild Hunter and the woman you pulled into this shit. The least you can do is tell me why."

"No." A flat declaration made by the Archangel of New York. "Nothing you say will sway me. No mortal can know. Not even the one I want to fuck."

The cold place had filled with lust. Now it filled with pure fury. "That puts me in my place, doesn't it?"

The bastard kissed her. She was so mad, she bit him hard enough to draw blood. Raphael pulled back, lip already beginning to swell. "We are no longer even, Elena. You're now in debt."

"You can deduct it from my slow and painful death." She dropped her leg from his waist. "It's time to talk murder."

He leaned in, caging her with his arms. "You're holding a knife again."

She clenched her hand around the handle. "You drive me to violence." Sliding the knife back into her boot, she folded her arms and tried not to think about how good he smelled. "What did you do with the survivor?"

"Dmitri has taken her to our healers, our doctors."

"Because she might be infected. With what?"

"Uram's madness."

She was so shocked at getting a straight answer that it took her close to a minute to respond. "That's not possible. Madness isn't catching."

"Uram's brand may be."

Christ. "But she's human."

Raphael's eyes flamed cobalt. "She was. Now the doctors will tell us what she's become." He paused. "We know she ingested some of Uram's blood—it could've been by accident but more likely, he made her feed from him."

She didn't give in to pity. That woman—girl, really—had survived a monster intent on destroying everything she was. She deserved a fucking medal for courage, not pity. "If she is infected, will you kill her?"

"Yes."

Elena wanted to hate him for that, but she couldn't. "Four years ago," she found herself saying, "there was a rash of killings on the banks of the Mississippi. Young boys strangled; their eyes removed."

"A human."

"Yes. A hunter." Bill James had been her friend once upon a time, her trainer before that. "We—me, Ransom, and Sara— had to find and execute him." Hunters always took care of their own.

A cool whisper of a breeze as Raphael unfurled his wings and curled them back in. "So many nightmares in your head."

"They make me who I am."

"Did you kill this hunter?"

"Yes." It had come down to the two of them. "Sara was

badly injured, Ransom too far away, and Bill was about to kill a terrified young boy. So I stabbed him through the heart." No time to get her gun, so much blood everywhere, the look of betrayal in Bill's eyes as his heart pulsed one last time, a chaos of memory. Now she looked up into another pair of eyes. "If that girl's become a monster, she needs to die."

"Am I a monster, Elena?"

She looked into that perfect face and saw the echoes of cruelty, of time. "Not yet," she whispered. "But you could be."

His jaw was a harsh line. "It's a symptom of age—cruelty."

It hurt her to know that the humanity in Raphael—buried deep, but there—might one day cease to exist. Yet at the same time, she couldn't help but be glad for his immortality. Someone this magnificent shouldn't die. "Tell me about the Quiet."

His wings extended to their full width. "We must go to Michaela's home and see if you can pick up a scent—there's a good chance he spent hours watching her before today."

She blew out a frustrated breath. "Fine. We flying?" Her heart hitched—she was becoming used to being carried in Raphael's arms, the sound of his wings steady and powerful.

"No," he said, lips curving as if he'd read her excitement. "Michaela's American home is next door."

"Convenient." For sneaking into Raphael's bed.

He finally moved enough that she could hop down. "Michaela has been many things through the centuries—scholar, courtesan, muse—but she's never been a warrior."

My lovers have always been warrior women.

She wondered how many of those women had been as foolish as her—foolish enough to walk into his arms knowing that if push came to shove, the archangel would end her life with a single, final thought. "It's time for this warrior to earn her keep."

Bloodlust

He was sluggish, sated, the blood heavy in his gut.

He'd overindulged, but what glorious overindulgence it had been.

Dipping his fingers into the bowl of blood he'd saved from the cattle he'd butchered, he brought them to his mouth and licked.

Flat. Lifeless.

Disappointed, he smashed the bowl to the floor, spreading a dark red stain on the white carpet. But there was still the beauty above. He looked up, even as the dull heaviness in his limbs began to lighten, turning into a slow kind of anticipation.

Now he knew—the blood had to be fresh.

Next time, he'd take it straight from their beating hearts. His eyes grew red with violent hunger. Yes, next time, he wouldn't kill . . . he'd keep.

27

Elena wasn't the least surprised when Michaela's mansion turned out to be a place of beauty and grace. The archangel might be a two-faced bitch, but she hadn't earned her reputation as the muse of artists across the ages by accident.

"This was where we found the . . . gift," the vampire guard told her, pointing to a patch of bloodstained grass.

The bite of acid was sharp here despite the other vampire's presence. Either Uram had mingled some of his own blood with the hearts, or he'd landed on the lawn itself. Talk about brazen . . . and creepy. The hairs on the back of her neck rose. "Can you move out of the immediate area?"

He gave a short nod but didn't take a step. "I was hunted once."

Elena looked up to where she could see Raphael and Michaela talking on a high balcony overlooking the lawn, and wondered if either angel would mind if she simply coldcocked the idiot at her side—she didn't have time to deal with this kind of shit. "Can't have been too bad if you're still here."

"My mistress flayed the skin off my back and made it into a purse."

She wondered how well that info would go down with the faction who ascribed heavenly origins to the angels. "Yet you serve her even now." It sounded like something the bitch goddess would do.

The vampire smiled, showed teeth. "It was a very nice purse." Then he finally walked away. She'd have to watch her back around that one, she thought. Whatever else Michaela had done to him over the centuries, he was no longer all there.

"Immortality has way too many drawbacks," she muttered, adding the possibility of becoming a purse to her mental list. Her eye fell on the bloody grass again. Kneeling, she confirmed the scent, then began walking out in ever-increasing circles.

Uram's scent blanketed the area. The archangel had most certainly touched down, standing there cloaked in glamour while Michaela's guards remained clueless. Elena would've worried about running into him, but the scent, while pervasive, wasn't as strong as it would've been had he been in the immediate vicinity. That made her wonder—were other archangels able to sense their brethren through the glamour?

If not, no wonder Michaela was spooked.

Unsurprisingly, the scent was particularly intense near the edge of the lawn. Looking up, Elena found herself with a direct line of sight into the bank of windows on the third floor. Michaela's bedroom was smack in the middle.

If this had been an ordinary hunt, Elena would've been grinning ear to ear by now. With this recent a trail, she could've run her prey to ground by sundown. But vampires didn't fly. Still, she thought, eyes narrowed, now she knew Uram's Achilles' heel. His compulsion toward Michaela would constrict the breadth of his hunting grounds. She glanced up again, her mind pure, focused hunter. She needed the map of Michaela's movements that Raphael had promised to get.

Raphael was aware of Elena moving farther and farther away as she performed a methodical search. He kept his eye out for Riker, Michaela's favorite guard. Riker did whatever Michaela told him to—it would make no difference to the vampire that Elena was under Raphael's protection . . . though he probably should've killed her the second he recovered from the shooting. Because if Lijuan was right, then Elena was his fatal weakness.

Death was a concept he hadn't considered in centuries. But Elena had made him a little bit mortal. As she was. She'd die if Riker tore out her throat. And Michaela was capricious enough to have given such an order. She knew Raphael wouldn't start a war over a mortal.

Destiny's Rose.

An image of the ancient treasure danced in his head. In all his centuries of existence, he'd never once considered giving it away. Until Elena. His mortal. Perhaps he'd fight Michaela over her after all. "You have safeguards in place?"

"Of course."

Those safeguards were obviously not enough—the entire Cadre had expected Uram to come for her, and yet she'd been caught unprepared. "Do you need more men? You're far from home."

"No." Pride dripped from the single word as she strode to the edge of the balcony and stared down, following Elena's progress. "If your hunter has the scent, it means he was watching me long enough to have left a discernible imprint."

Raphael could have asked Elena to confirm, but after the incident that had led to the Quiet, he was making an attempt to stay out of her head. A sign of the weakness Lijuan had warned of—an attack of human scruples? Perhaps. But Raphael had never liked what he became in the Quiet. And this time . . . it had been a fraction too close to Caliane's madness. "You're still as you were?" he asked, burying that ancient memory.

Michaela's skin tightened, the sharp lines of her bones almost cutting through her skin. "I'm an archangel without glamour, yes."

"Unfortunate."

She laughed, a low sound designed to make men think

of sex. The first time he'd seen Michaela, she'd had her mouth on the cock of the archangel who'd ruled ancient Byzantium. Her eyes had met his as she drove the archangel to his little death and Raphael had known she would one day rule. Two decades later, the Archangel of Byzantium was dead.

His eyes picked out Elena as she entered the wooded area that divided his property from Michaela's. "Have you spoken to Lijuan about it?" he asked, even as he watched Elena purse her lips in concentration. Her mouth was lush, seductive. He was very interested in having it all over his body. But like all warrior women, she'd have to be tamed to his hand.

"She talks in riddles," Michaela spit out, "has no explanation for why the glamour eludes me."

Under normal circumstances, that lack wouldn't be much of a concern—Michaela had other skills, some known, some not, but no one could doubt her status as archangel. However, in this one situation, she was at a lethal disadvantage, because along with glamour came an immunity to it. Raphael couldn't hide from Uram but the Angel of Blood couldn't hide from him either. "Call Riker back."

"Why?"

"You can't see Uram, but Elena can scent him."

Michaela's next words were dismissive. "Riker is watching her, nothing more. And there are other hunters if he loses control." A pause. "She's human, Raphael. She knows nothing of the pleasures I could show you."

Raphael flared out his wings in preparation for flight. "I would have thought Charisemnon would appeal. He was your lover once."

Green eyes met his as he went to the very edge of a balcony made for angels—no railing, nothing to prevent a deadly fall. "But you I've never tasted. I can do things that will make eternity an erotic dream."

"The trouble is, your lovers seem to have very short life spans." He flew down, across the yard, and over the wooded area.

Riker was standing a few feet from Elena, his smile full of menace.

Far from appearing frightened, Elena was flicking a knife through her fingers, her stance that of someone trained in hand-to-hand combat. As she opened her mouth as if to speak, Raphael flew down to land behind Riker, one hand on the vampire's shoulder, the other on his back.

"This is my territory," he said. "Your mistress is a guest." That was all the warning he gave before he thrust his hand through Riker's clothing, flesh, and muscle to grip his panicked heart. A second later, that heart was in Raphael's hand and Riker was twitching facedown on the ground.

"Why?"

He looked up to meet Elena's horrified gaze over the continued pulse of Riker's vampire heart. "There are boundaries. It's better for mortals and immortals alike if those boundaries are not crossed."

Her grip on the knife was white-knuckled. "So you killed him?"

Raphael dropped the heart to the ground and looked at his bloody hand, wondering if Uram had taken his victims' hearts the same way. "He's not dead."

"I—" She swallowed as he approached, took a step back. "I know they can heal a hell of a lot of damage but completely removing the heart?"

"You fear me again." He hadn't seen that look on her face since that first meeting on the roof.

"You just ripped a vampire's heart out with your bare hand." Her voice echoed with shock. "So yes, I fear you."

He looked down at the blood coating his skin. "I wouldn't do this to you, Elena."

"You saying my death will be short and sweet?"

"Perhaps instead of killing you," he said, "I'll make you my slave instead."

"I hope to hell that's your twisted idea of a joke." Biting words, but she put away the knife. "We might as well head back so you can wash off the blood. I've lost the trail any-way."

"He flew?"

"I'm guessing, yes." She folded her arms, nodded toward Michaela's house. "You get the map of her movements?"

"It'll be delivered within the next hour." As they walked, he wondered why a mortal's opinion of him mattered. "Do you plan to walk those streets and see if you can sense him?"

"Yes." She strode forward with determined steps. "If he's as fixated as you guys think—and hell, he *is* wooing her with bloody hearts—he won't go far from her."

"No, he won't." The bloodborn *always* killed another angel before devolving completely. In most cases, it was the angel who had been closest to them—a macabre sacrament, as if they were cutting away everything they'd once been.

Elena nodded. "Then we might be able to beard him in his lair while he's sluggish from the amount of blood he took. Unless that's different with you lot?" She glanced at him, her eyes sliding to his bloody hand and forearm before she sucked in a breath and looked away.

"From what we know," he said, hand curling into a fist, "the bloodborn—"

"Bloodborn?" She scowled. "You have a name for whatever it is Uram's become? That means it's not an isolated incident."

"The bloodborn," he said, ignoring her implied question, "are affected as the vampires are by overindulgence. He'll be lazy, sleepy, vulnerable."

Elena's fury at his refusal to answer her question was un-hidden, but whatever it was that she might've said was lost as her cell phone rang. Pulling it out of a pocket, she flipped it open. "Yes." Her eyes turned chaotic. "What?" A pause. "I—" For the first time, he saw her look unsure. "Yes. I'll be there." She closed the phone. "I need to take off for a while. I'll be back by the time Michaela delivers her map."

"Where?" he asked, disliking the expression on her face.

A hard glance. "None of your damn business."

He should've been angry. Part of him, the part with over a thousand years of accumulated arrogance, was. But the rest of him was intrigued. "A taste of my own medicine?"

She shrugged, her mouth pinched.

"Your father."

Her shoulders tightened. "What, you can listen in to conversations now?"

"Even archangels can't do that." Not always true, but true in this case since he'd vowed not to eavesdrop on her mind. "But I did my research."

"Good for you." If words could cut, he'd have been shredded.

He looked down at his bloody fist and wondered if she saw him as a monster now. "Jeffrey Deveraux is the only human being you seem unable to handle."

"Like I said, it's none of your business." Her jaw was clenched so tight, she had to be in pain.

"Are you sure?"

Raphael's question repeated over and over in Elena's head as she strode up the steps to the tony brownstone her father maintained as his private office. There was another office high up in a tower of steel and glass, but this was where the real wheeling and dealing went on. It was also a place you entered only by invitation.

Elena had never set foot across the threshold.

Now she stopped in front of the closed door, her eye falling on the discreet metal plaque to the left.

DEVERAUX ENTERPRISES, EST. 1701

The Deveraux family could trace their roots back so many years, Elena sometimes thought they must've kept records even while crawling out of the primordial ooze. Her lips tightened. Pity the other side of her familial ledger wasn't so established. An orphaned immigrant raised in foster homes on the outskirts of Paris, Marguerite had had no family history to speak of—nothing beyond the vague memory of her mother's Moroccan origins. But she'd been beautiful, her skin gold, her hair close to pure white.

And her hands . . . gifted hands, hands that wove magic.

Elena had never been able to understand why her parents had married. Most likely, she never would. The parent who might have told her was dead and the one who remained seemed to have forgotten he'd once had a wife named Marguerite, a woman who spoke with an accent and laughed loud enough to banish any silence.

She wondered if her father ever thought about Ariel and Mirabelle, or if he'd erased them from his world, too.

Ari's eyes staring into hers as she screamed. Belle's blood on the kitchen tiles. Her bare foot sliding on the liquid, the jarring hardness of the floor as she fell. Warm wetness against her palm.

A hand clutching a still-beating heart.

She shook her head in a harsh negative, trying to wipe away the mishmash of nauseating images. What Raphael had done . . . it had been another reminder that he wasn't human, wasn't anything close to human. But the Archangel of New York wasn't the monster she'd come to face.

Raising her hand, she pressed the buzzer and looked up at the discreet security camera most execs probably never made. The door opened a second later. It wasn't Jeffrey on the other side. Elena hadn't expected it to be. Her father was much too important a man to open the door for his eldest living child. Even when he hadn't seen that child for ten cold years.

"Ms. Deveraux?" A perfunctory smile from the small brunette. "Please come in."

Elena stepped inside, taking in the woman's ghost-pale skin against the sedate navy color of her well-cut suit. She was every inch the executive assistant, the lone touches of flamboyance coming from the glittering diamond on her right middle finger, and the high mandarin collar of her jacket. Elena drew in a deep breath, felt her lips curve.

The woman's spine went stiff. "I'm Geraldine, Mr. Deveraux's personal assistant."

"Elena." She shook the woman's hand, noted the cool temperature. "I'd suggest you get yourself a prescription for iron."

Geraldine's calm expression flickered only slightly. "I'll take that under advisement.'

"You do that." Elena wondered if her father had any idea of his assistant's extracurricular pursuits. "My father?"

"Please follow me." A hesitation. "He doesn't know." Not a plea, almost an angry declaration made in clipped private-school vowels.

"Hey, what you do in your own time is nobody's business but yours." Elena shrugged, mind filling with the image of Dmitri bending over that blonde's neck. Of the hunger in his eyes after she cut his throat. "I just hope it's worth it."

The other woman gave a soft, intimate smile before leading Elena down the hall. "Oh, it is. It's better than anything you could imagine."

Elena doubted that, not when she kept flashing back to Raphael's hand on her breast, powerful, possessive, more than a little dangerous. Too bad she couldn't forget that same hand shoving through a man's rib cage to tear out his heart.

Geraldine halted in front of a closed wooden door. She gave a quiet knock and drew back. "Please go in. Your father is waiting for you."

"Thank you." She put her hand on the doorknob.

28

Jeffrey Deveraux stood by the fireplace, hands in the pockets of a pin-striped suit she guessed had been tailored to his tall frame. Marguerite had been a bare five feet tall. It was Jeffrey who'd given Elena her height. He was six feet four without shoes—not that her father was ever anything less than perfectly put together.

Pale gray eyes met hers with the cold watchfulness of a hawk or a wolf. His face was all sharp lines and angles, his hair brushed back from a severe widow's peak. Most men would've had gray in their hair by now. Jeffrey had gone straight from aristocratic gold to pure white. It suited him, throwing his features into sharper relief.

"Elieanora." He finished polishing his spectacles and slid them back on, the thin rectangular frames as effective as ten-inch-thick walls.

"Jeffrey."

His mouth tightened. "Don't be childish. I'm your father."

She shrugged, shifting into an unconsciously aggressive posture. "You wanted me. Here I am." The words came out angry. Ten years of independence and the second she entered her father's presence, she reverted to teenager who'd spent a lifetime begging for his love and been kicked in the guts for her efforts.

"I'm disappointed," he said, unmoved. "I'd hoped you'd picked up some social graces from the company you've been keeping."

She frowned. "My company is the same as always. You'll have seen Sara, the Guild Director, at various events, and Ransom—"

"What your *hunter*"—said with a grimace of distaste—"friends do is of no interest to me."

"I didn't think so." Why the fuck had she come to heel at his command? Her only excuse was shock. "So why did you bring them up?"

"I was referring to the angels."

She blinked, then wondered why she was surprised. Jeffrey had a finger in every major pie in the city, not all of them strictly legal. Though of course, he'd flay her alive if she dared imply he was anything other than lily-white. "You'd be surprised at what they consider acceptable." Raphael's pitiless justice, Michaela's hungry sexuality, Uram's butchery, none of it would fit with her father's perception of the angels.

He waved off her words as if they didn't matter. "I need to talk to you about your inheritance."

Elena's fist clenched. "You mean the trust my *mother* set up for me." She could've starved on the streets and Jeffrey wouldn't have given a damn.

Skin pulled taut over Jeffrey's cheekbones. "I suppose genetics do tell."

She was one step away from calling him a bastard but ironically, it was her mother's voice that held her back. Marguerite had brought her up to respect her father. Elena couldn't do that, but she could respect her mother's memory. "Thank God," she said, letting him take the insult as he would.

Swiveling, Jeffrey walked to the desk set below the

windows on the other side of the room, his steps silent on the deep claret of the Persian carpet. "The trust matured on your twenty-fifth birthday."

"A bit late, aren't you?"

He picked up an envelope. "A letter was sent to you by the solicitors."

Elena recalled throwing the unopened piece of mail in the trash. She'd figured it for yet another attempt at coercing her into selling out the shares she'd inherited in the family firm—through her paternal grandfather, a man who'd actually seemed to love her. "They did a real knock-up job of following up."

"Don't try to pass off your own laziness on others." Walking back, he shoved the envelope into her hand. "The money's been deposited in an interest-bearing account under your name. The details are all there."

She didn't look down. "Why the personal touch?"

Pale gray eyes narrowed behind the spectacles. "Distasteful as I find your choice of occupation—"

"It's not a choice," she said coldly. "*Remember?*"

Silence that warned her to never again bring up that bloody day.

"As I was saying, regretful as your profession is, it does bring you into contact with some powerful people."

Her stomach soured. What the hell had she expected? She knew she meant nothing to her father. Still she'd come. Instead of lashing out as she might've done as a teenager, she kept her mouth shut, wanting to know exactly what it was he expected of her.

"You're in a position to help the family." A steely-eyed gaze. "Something you've never cared to do."

Her hand clenched on the envelope. "I'm only a hunter," she said, turning his words back on him. "What makes you think they treat me any better than you do?"

He didn't flinch. "I've been told you're spending considerable time with Raphael, that he may be open to suggestions that come from you."

She told herself he wasn't implying what she thought he was implying. Shaking inside, she met his eyes. "You'd whore out your own daughter?"

No change in his expression. "No. But if she's already doing it herself, I see no reason not to take advantage."

She felt herself go sheet white. Without a word, she turned, opened the door, and walked out. It slammed shut behind her. A second later, she heard something smash, the discordant splintering of crystal against brick. She halted, stunned at the thought that she'd evoked any kind of a response from the always controlled Jeffrey Deveraux.

"Ms. Deveraux?" Geraldine came running around the corner. "I heard . . ." Her voice trailed off uncertainly.

"I'd suggest you make yourself scarce for the next little while," Elena said, snapping out of her frozen state and heading toward the door. Jeffrey had probably lost it because she'd dared defy him, unlike the rest of his band of sycophants. It had had nothing to do with the fact that he'd called his daughter a whore to her face. "And, Gerry"—she turned at the door—"don't ever let him find out."

The assistant gave a jerky nod.

Elena had never been so grateful to be out in the noise of the city as she was that day. Not giving the door a backward look, she walked down the steps and away from the man who'd contributed his sperm to her creation. Her hand clenched again and she remembered the envelope. Forcing herself to calm down enough that she could think, she slit it open and pulled out the letter. This was her mother's legacy to her and she refused to let Jeffrey cheapen it.

The amount of money was small in the scheme of things—Marguerite's estate had been split equally between her two living daughters, and consisted of the money she'd made from the sale of her one-of-a-kind quilts. She'd never needed to use any of it because Jeffrey had insisted on giving her a huge allowance.

Masculine laughter, strong hands throwing her into the air.

Elena staggered under the impact of the memory, then

brushed it aside—it was nothing more than wishful thinking. Her father had always been a stern disciplinarian who didn't know how to forgive. But, she was forced to admit, he *had* felt something for his Parisian wife—there had been that huge allowance, gifts of jewels on every occasion. Where had all those treasures gone? To Beth?

Elena didn't particularly care about their monetary value, but she would've liked to have just one thing that had once belonged to her mother. All she knew was that she'd come home one summer from boarding school and found every trace of Marguerite, Mirabelle, and Ariel gone from the house—including the quilt Elena had treasured since her fifth birthday. It was as if she'd imagined her mother, her older sisters.

Someone smashed into her shoulder. "Hey, lady! Get out of the fucking way!" The lanky student turned to give her the finger.

She returned the gesture automatically, glad he'd broken her paralysis. A quick glance at her watch confirmed she still had some breathing room. Deciding to take care of things then and there, she made her way to the bank branch specified in the letter. Luckily, it was fairly close. She'd completed the paperwork and was rising to leave when the bank manager said, "Would you like to see the contents of the safe-deposit box, Ms. Deveraux?"

She stared into his puffy face, the probable result of too much good food and not enough exercise. "A safe-deposit box?"

He nodded, straightening his tie. "Yes."

"Don't I need a key and"—she frowned—"my signature on the access card?" She knew that only because she'd had to look it up during a particularly complicated hunt.

"Normally, yes." He straightened his tie for the second time. "Yours is a somewhat unusual situation."

Translation: her father had pulled any number of strings for God alone knew what reasons of his own. "All right."

Five minutes later, she'd had her signature witnessed and

was handed a key. "If you'll follow me to the vault—we use a dual-step system here. I have the key to the vault; you have the one to the box itself." The bank manager turned and led her through the hushed confines of the solid old building and through to the back.

The safe-deposit boxes were hidden behind several electronic doors that appeared incongruous in the belly of the historic structure.

Elena.

She knew she hadn't imagined that dark whisper in her head. "Get out."

The man she was following gave her a startled look over his shoulder. She pretended to be engrossed in her nails.

You're late.

Narrowing her eyes, she gritted her teeth and wondered if it was worth the headache to keep him out of her head.

A car will meet you when you exit the bank.

She halted, stared at the back of the manager's jacket, able to smell his fear. "Who exactly did you call a few minutes ago?"

When he glanced at her, his eyes were panicked, a rabbit's. "No one, Ms. Deveraux."

She gave him a cold smile that made it clear he'd pissed her off well and good. "Show me the box."

Clearly surprised by the reprieve, he did as ordered. She waited until he'd placed the long, metal box on a viewing table before waving him off. He was nothing, an ant in Raphael's army. Alone, she stared at the opposite wall. "Raphael?"

Nothing.

Lips pressed tightly together, she unlocked the box and took off the lid, expecting . . . she didn't know what she was expecting, but it wasn't what she found. Jewelry boxes, letters bound with ribbon, photos, a receipt for a small storage locker. On top of it all was a black leather notebook, the edges embossed gold. She reached out her finger, touched, then drew back and slammed the box closed. She couldn't do this. Not today. Calling the bank manager back after she'd relocked it, she had him return the box to its place in the vault. "How long has this been here?"

He glanced at the file in his hand. "It looks like it was opened almost fifteen years ago."

She grabbed the file before he could stop her, staring at the signature on the bottom of the first page.

Jeffrey Parker Deveraux.

Fifteen years ago. The summer he'd wiped her mother and older sisters from the face of the earth. Except this box told another story. Damn him! Shoving the papers back at the manager, she strode out through the moneyed opulence of the bank and toward heavy glass doors a security guard reached out to open. "Thanks."

His smile turned into shock an instant later. Elena followed the direction of his gaze to find an amazingly beautiful man with blue wings leaning nonchalantly against a lamppost directly outside. The stream of traffic had disappeared from this side of the street, but the other side was so full, it was as if the entire population of New York had decided to walk by.

She stepped out onto the sidewalk. "Illium."

"At your service." He waved his hand at the low-slung Ferrari behind him. It was fire-engine red. Of course.

She raised an eyebrow. "How do you fit the wings inside?"

"Alas, I can only watch." He threw her the keys.

Catching them reflexively, she scowled. "Whose million-dollar car is that and what did he do to you?"

"Dmitri's. And just because."

It almost made her laugh and that, she couldn't have predicted. "The map?"

His eyes—a vivid, shimmering gold, startling against black hair dipped in blue—shifted to the car. "In the glove box."

Not that she wouldn't enjoy needling Dmitri by taking his prized possession out for a run, but . . . "I need a vehicle that won't stand out."

"There's an underground garage two blocks east. Pull into

it and switch." He stepped away from the post, flared out his wings.

"Showing off?"

"*Oui, oui.*" A smile full of pure male charm.

"Is the hair real?"

A nod. "So are the eyes. In case you were wondering." Another teasing smile.

She saw a single feather drift to the curb. "You'll cause a riot if you don't pick that up."

He followed her gaze. "I'll take it and drop it from the sky. Someone will find magic."

Snorting, but oddly touched by the idea, she unlocked the car and got in. Across the street, camera phones continued to snap at insane speed. She rolled her eyes. "Fly off before they mug you."

"I may look pretty, Elena, but I'm rather dangerous." The finest hint of a British accent whispered through.

"That," she said, "I never doubted." Starting the engine, she pulled out and away, aware of him taking off behind her. He might be dangerous but he was no archangel. And what the hell had Raphael been thinking, sending her such a—

He'd known, she realized.

He'd known why Jeffrey had summoned her, why he'd finally deigned to speak to a daughter he considered worse than the lowest street trash.

Not only had he known, he'd accurately predicted her reaction.

And he'd provided her with the most perfect revenge possible. She started to grin. Jeffrey Deveraux's unwanted daughter was considered important enough for an angelic escort so flamboyant, she'd be surprised if there was anyone in the state who hadn't already heard about it.

Her phone rang on cue.

She was at a stoplight, so she answered. "Sara, you have big ears."

"And you're keeping company with what I hear is an angel straight out of wet-dream territory."

"They're all good-looking." But that wasn't enough. Not for her.

"But most don't have wings of blue touched with silver."

"TV?"

"Camera-phone images. Don't usually see angels walking the streets." A whispered sigh. "I've had reports of this one being in the city, but no close-up pictures till now. He's some kind of pretty. I could just take a bite out of that firm—"

Elena started laughing. "Down, girl, you're married, remember?"

"Mmm, talk about taking a bite out of something. Deacon—"

"Too-much-info alert!" The light changed. "I'll call you back in a few minutes."

She was about to turn into the garage when a blue feather fluttered into her lap. Her lips twitched but it was too late to glance up by then. Nosing the car into the darkness of the garage, she brought it to a halt near the still figure of the vampire who'd driven her to Raphael's. He was wearing sunglasses in spite of the underground gloom. She supposed if she had eyes like his, she would, too.

Getting out, she undid her ponytail and quickly braided Illium's feather into her hair just above her ear. "If Bluebell isn't careful," the vamp murmured, "he'll lose his feathers all over again."

Ponytail redone, she retrieved the map and nodded at the old-model sedan behind him. "Keys?" She threw him the ones for the Ferrari.

"In the ignition." Sliding the keys into a pocket, he straightened from his leaning position against the passenger-side door. "Raphael wants you to check in every ten minutes."

"Tell the boss I'll call him when I have something to report, Snakey."

He pushed the sunglasses to the top of his head, giving her the full impact of those eerie eyes. "I prefer Venom."

She raised an eyebrow. "You're not serious."

"It's better than a pansy-assed name like Illium. What the

hell does that mean anyway?" A sharp smile that flashed fang.

Deliberate, very deliberate, she thought. Despite his flawlessly modern speech, Venom was far too old to make mistakes. "Are you?"

"What?"

"Venomous?"

Another savage smile. He touched the tip of one fang with his tongue and when he drew it away, she saw a pearl of golden liquid. "Try me and see."

"Maybe later, after I've survived Michaela."

He laughed, a rich masculine sound that caused a woman stepping off the elevator at the other end of the garage to drop her purse and stare openmouthed. Venom didn't seem to notice, his eyes fixed on Elena. Reaching up, he slid the sunglasses back over his eyes. "No one survives the High Priestess of Byzantium."

Goose bumps crawled over her flesh at the ancience implied by that title. Not responding, she opened the door to the sedan and got in—after cranking down all four windows. As she drove away, she saw Venom head for the woman by the elevator.

29

She'd been driving for ten minutes when she realized she'd forgotten to call Sara back. Spotting an unoccupied loading zone, she pulled off and dialed.

Her friend picked up on the first ring. "Rumor mill's going crazy. They're saying the blue angel flew away with you in his arms."

"Angels don't sully themselves carrying mortals." Except when they wanted said mortal somewhere pronto. "Anything else I should know about?"

"Missing girls—fifteen in the past week." Her voice was pure Guild Director. "Get the bastard, Ellie."

"I will." *Fifteen?* Where the hell were the other seven bodies? "Any timelines?"

"You don't have this already?"

"No." So either the angels didn't know everything, or they were keeping her in the dark. Her hand tightened on the phone. "Give it to me."

"Not much to give. One bunch disappeared two days ago—looks like the same night. And the second lot was last night, maybe very early morning."

"Thanks, Sara. Kiss Zoe for me."

"You okay?" Concern in every word. "I swear, Ellie. You give the word and we'll find a way to pull you out."

She knew they would. The Guild had survived centuries because it was built on a backbone of absolute loyalty. "I'm fine. I have to get this guy."

"Fine. But if it gets too hairy, remember we've got your back."

"I know." Her throat grew thick. Sara knew. Because her next comment was designed to make Elena grin.

"You know how spooky Ashwini is. She called an hour ago to tell me she has a secret stash of handheld grenade launchers she thought I might want to know about. My response was, 'What the fuck?'"

"As usual with Ash," Elena said, laughing.

"But you know," Sara continued, "the damn things would come in handy against you-know-whats. Just one word, Ellie. That's all we need."

"Thanks, Sara." She hung up before she could give in to the urge to say too much. Then, taking a deep breath, she restarted the engine and continued on toward Archangel Tower. Unsurprisingly, Michaela had spent most of her time either at her estate or around the Tower, with the occasional stop at a high-end department store. Elena was waiting to turn off the main avenue, intending to circle around, when it whispered past.

The bite of acid laced with blood.

Screeching to a halt, she got out, ignoring the swearing cabbie behind her, and did a very careful three-hundred-and-sixty-degree turn. *There.* Jumping back into the car, she double-parked and stepped out. Now that she had the scent, she'd be far more effective on foot.

Rich, dark, chocolate. Sinful. Seductive.

She halted, sniffed. "Dmitri." The vampire had either passed this way or was in the vicinity. With most vampires, it wouldn't have mattered—she could separate out the scents. But Dmitri's presence was too strong, and when added to the fact that Uram's trail was older . . . "Shit." Pulling out her phone, she called Raphael.

"Elena."

Her blood fired from the inside out at the sound of that voice—sex and ice, pain and pleasure. "Dmitri's scent is messing up my trace."

"You've found signs of Uram?"

"Yes. Can you get Dmitri out of here?"

A pause. "He's already leaving."

"Thanks." She ended the call. Much longer and that voice of his would creep into her soul and take up residence. Instead, she cleared her head, centered herself, and began scanning again.

Dmitri's scent was fading at a phenomenal rate. Unless he could run very fast, he'd had access to a vehicle. She didn't particularly care. All that mattered was that she'd lost— No, there it was. She turned left, moving at a light jog.

She was five blocks over when something made her glance up. The previously bright sky was turning a dull gray, heavy with clouds. But she caught a flash of blue, one that disappeared in the next instant. Illium. Bodyguard duty? Shrugging it off, she came to a standstill in the midst of an area that seemed mostly residential, though she could see a grocer's tucked discreetly between two apartment buildings.

Foot traffic was lighter than in the crush of shops she'd left behind, but steady. She attracted a few nervous stares and it was then that she realized she had one of her long, thin throwing knives in hand.

"Ma'am." A shaky voice.

She didn't turn. "Officer, I'm on a hunt. My Guild card is in the left back pocket." Hunters had carry permits for all sorts of weapons. And she never went anywhere without them.

"Ah—"

She showed him her empty left hand. "I'm going to reach for it. Okay?" Acid on the wind. Thick, dark blood. Damn, damn! She needed to be chasing that, not pandering to some baby cop who didn't know enough about hunters to be out on the streets. What the hell were they teaching them in the Police Academy these days?

A cry from the woman in front of her and then a flash of blue swept down the street. Elena glanced at the cop, saw him staring up dumbfounded, and ran. She knew he wouldn't come after her. He'd had that look on his face. *Angelstruck.* Approximately five percent of the population was born susceptible to the phenomenon. She'd heard they'd discovered medication to combat the effect, but that most people didn't want to be "cured."

"When I see an angel, I see perfection," one man had said in a recent documentary. "For the fragment of time I spend caught up in their magic, real life ceases to exist and heaven is in my grasp. Why would I give that up?"

For a small, painful instant, Elena had envied the angelstruck. She'd lost her innocence, her belief in a heavenly caretaker, eighteen long years ago. Then the camera had cut to an image of the speaker as he was angelstruck and she'd come close to throwing up. Pure adoration, worshipful and blind. A devotion that turned angels into gods.

No, thanks.

Ten minutes later, the scent was an ache in her throat, a layer of fur on her tongue. She looked around and found herself in one of the moneyed areas of the city, somewhere east of Central Park. Very, very moneyed, she realized, looking at the elegant size of the buildings. No huge apartment complexes here. A moment's pause and she had it—the locus. Leaving it to Raphael to smooth things over if anyone spotted her, she climbed over the locked wrought-iron gate to land in front of a freestanding town house. Seeing a very narrow pathway to the right-hand side, she walked down and around to the back.

"A private park." Amazing. She hadn't known anything like this existed in Manhattan. The rectangular patch of lush green was bordered on every side by similar town houses, all vaguely European in design. Frowning, she touched the wall nearest her and felt no sense of age or time. Fake, she thought, disappointed. Some developer had bought up an undoubtedly pricey piece of land, created an English-type garden complex, and probably made megabucks.

Angels had money to burn.

And the scent, it was so powerful here . . . but not fresh. "He was here, but he's gone."

"Are you sure?"

She jumped, knife hand raised, and found Raphael standing behind her. "Where the hell—glamour?"

He didn't answer her question. "Where was he?"

"In the house, I think," she answered, trying to quieten her racing heartbeat. Also trying not to stab Raphael through the heart for doing that to her. "I thought you didn't show off in public."

"No one's watching." His eyes went to her hair. "They're too busy admiring Illium's acrobatics."

She ignored the possessive darkness crawling to life in his eyes. "We need to get inside the house." Walking around him, she was about to head up to the back door when his hand clenched on her upper arm.

She stilled, ready to throw him off, when she realized he was only interested in removing the blue feather from her hair. "Oh, for God's sake," she muttered. "Happy now?"

He crushed the feather in his fist. "No, Elena. I'm not." His hand opened and glittering blue dust floated to earth.

She decided not to ask him how he'd done that. "You mind a little breaking and entering?"

"Venom tells me there are no heartbeats inside."

Her stomach curled. "Death? Does he smell death?"

"Yes." Releasing her arm, he took the lead.

Elena looked around the side of the house and to the street, spying Venom standing unmoving on this side of the closed—but likely no longer locked—gate. He looked like a bodyguard-cum-driver. Normal for a ritzy neighborhood like this. Satisfied he'd keep them from being interrupted, she followed Raphael to the door. "Wait," she said when he put a hand on the doorknob. "We might set off an alarm, attract attention."

"It's been taken care of."

She thought of how fast some vampires could move. "Venom?"

A slight nod. "He's adept at such things."

"Why am I not surprised?" she muttered, swallowing her gorge at the scent that whispered out from the house. "Oh, God."

Raphael pushed the door fully open. "Come, Elena." He held out his hand.

She stared at it. "I'm a hunter." But she curled her fingers around his. Some nightmares were too vicious to face alone.

They stepped over the threshold together, Raphael's wings fitting easily through the door. "Built for an angel," she said, staring out at the open-plan design. There were no dividing walls in the entire first floor. The carpet in the living area was a Rorschach painting in red on white.

It should have been a violent explosion of color, but instead it was an odd sort of formless gray, the curtains drawn, the inside of the apartment dull with a heavy kind of shade that seemed to muffle sound . . . amplify everything else.

Decay. Acid. Sex.

The tastes mingled on her tongue, threatening to turn her stomach. "He had sex with them."

Raphael looked at the bodies strung up from the rafters, his eyes blue flame. "Are you certain?"

"I can smell it." While vampires were the only ones she could track by scent, her sense of smell was far better than that of a normal human's. And, it appeared, even an archangel's.

"No blood."

She stared at the stains on the carpet. "What do you call that?" She wouldn't look up again, she told herself, wouldn't reinforce the pieces of horror burned into her mind from a single fleeting glimpse.

Hanging limbs waving in the air-conditioned breeze, faces

frozen in a rictus of terror. Pale skin torn open, lips colored blue, hair used as a noose.

Raphael's hand tightened on hers, pulling her back from the edge of the beckoning abyss. "He didn't take their blood. The wounds are brutal but there are no signs of feeding."

She already knew there would be no medical examiner to verify the findings. If they were to have any chance of finding and stopping Uram, she had to look, had to make sure. It was her job. "Cut them down." Her voice was hoarse. "I need to see the wounds up close."

He released her hand. "Your knife."

She put it flat in the palm of his hand, watched him walk to the vermilion explosion of the living room, his wings held out and slightly flared so they didn't trail on the floor. Then he pushed off with a single powerful beat of his wings. It generated wind.

The bodies swung.

Elena ran out the door and into the garden, where she proceeded to lose everything she'd eaten for the second time that day. Her stomach cramped painfully even after it was all gone, and when the nozzle of a hose was handed to her, she grabbed it like a lifeline, washing out her mouth and drenching her face before guzzling the plastic-tasting water as if it was nectar. "Thanks." She dropped the hose and looked up.

Venom smiled, slow, mocking. "Big, tough hunter, scared at the sight of a little blood." He turned off the tap. "My illusions are shattered."

"Poor baby," she said, wiping a hand down her face.

He showed her teeth, bright white against that exotic skin. "Feeling better?" Insincerity dripped from every word.

"Bite me." Turning her back, she forced herself to take the steps that would return her to the abattoir.

"Oh, I intend to." A drawl full of innuendo. "Everywhere."

She threw a knife in his direction without looking, had the satisfaction of hearing him swear as he caught it by the wrong end and sliced open his palm. Strength restored, she walked over the threshold.

Raphael was in the living area, laying the last of the bodies on the carpet. He held the woman gently, cradled against him. As he placed her on her back at the end of the line of similarly positioned bodies, Elena swallowed and walked toward him. "Sorry about that." She didn't explain, couldn't tell him the truth. Not about this.

He looked up. "Don't be. It's a gift to feel horror."

It made her wonder. "Do you?"

"Too little." An ancient darkness swept over his face. "I've seen such evil, even the loss of so much innocence barely touches me."

The inhumanity of it made her heart twist. "Tell me," she said, kneeling, "tell me the horrors you've seen so I can forget this one."

"No. You already have too many nightmares in your head." He met her gaze. "Go, track Uram. This can wait."

Knowing he was right, she walked outside and spent the next ten minutes trying to find Uram's exit route. It was with frustration churning in her gut that she returned to the house. "He flew from here."

Raphael nodded to the bodies. "Then we need to examine the fallen, see if they can tell us anything."

She gave a jerky nod and went to kneel by the first body. "She was cut open by a dull blade from neck to navel." The girl's internal organs were no longer in her body. "Did you find the rest of her?"

"Yes. There is a . . . collection in the corner behind you."

Bile burned in her throat, but she gritted her teeth and kept going. "No bite marks, no signs he tore into her with anything but a knife." As she moved on to the next body, she realized she hadn't looked at the girl's face. And that was a mistake. Uram could've taken the blood from her mouth. She'd once seen a body that had been sucked dry from a kiss.

Stomach tight enough to hurt, she went to touch the face, stopped. "I need gloves."

"Tell me what you need to see." Raphael's wings filled her vision as he appeared on the other side of the body.

"Don't be stupid," she muttered, pushing off his hand as he reached out to touch the corpse, forgetting he'd carried it down. "She could've been infected with a human virus, or Uram might've infected her like you were worried he'd infected the survivor."

Blue, blue eyes met hers. "I'm immortal, Elena." A soft reminder that smashed into her with the force of a ball-peen hammer. Of course he was immortal. How could she have forgotten?

"The mouth," she said, looking away from that face that could belong to no mortal, no matter how blessed. "Open her mouth."

He did so with clean efficiency. Thankfully, rigor had passed, so he didn't have to break the dead girl's jaw, though she knew it would've been child's play for him to do so. Retrieving a slender torch from the side pocket of her cargos, she shined it inside the woman's mouth. "No bites."

They went through the other bodies with methodical precision. Each had been shredded by a knife, some more mercifully than others. The first victim had been alive at the time of her disembowelment, the last dead. "No bite marks. Doesn't mean he didn't suck up the blood from the wounds." Or the entrails.

"Taking blood with the fangs is part of the pleasure."

"Then he definitely didn't feed." Just tortured.

"One of the bloodborn wouldn't be able to resist feeding."

The pieces clicked. "He did this first, the bodies in the warehouse second." The air-conditioning had kept these bodies from decaying, but now that she was looking, she saw a number of signs that this had happened at least a day, more likely two days, past—the color of the dried blood on the walls, the lack of rigor, the bruises that had bloomed on the girls' bodies as blood followed gravity.

All hunters were required to take a course in the general details of death—they were often the first people to find a vampire's kill. Now, pressing against the bruises, she saw no change in the discoloration—the skin didn't pale, then fill back with blood. Livor mortis was fixed. "These girls were practice."

"Yet you followed his scent here."

30

She rocked back on her heels, staring at the single blood-stain that didn't fit the timeline—the one on the carpet. It was too fresh. "You're right. The bastard came back to admire his handiwork!"

"I'll put watchers in place." He rose to his feet after her, his fingertips dusted with blood, his clothing stained where the bodies had brushed up against him. It made her remember the last time she'd seen him, a bloody fist, the panicked beat of a pulsing heart.

Somehow, it no longer seemed horrific. Not after this. Uram had played with his victims—like a cat with a mouse it doesn't want to eat but simply torment. Say what you would about the Archangel of New York—pitiless, hard, certainly lethal—he didn't torture for the sake of it. Everything Raphael did had a purpose. Even if that purpose was to scare people so badly that no one would dare betray him again.

She spoke as he walked to the kitchen area to wash his hands. "I don't think he'll come back—he returned after the warehouse kills, maybe to gloat, maybe to rest, but look at this." She pointed her foot at a bowl that had rolled under a table. "He threw this—probably after finding the blood he'd saved didn't satisfy him."

"This was his funhouse, but he's realized he prefers live playthings."

"Yes, he's going to want fresh meat." The words sounded cold but she had to stay on that level. If she allowed herself to feel . . .

Raphael nodded. "Do you think he'll rise to feed again tonight?"

"Even if he's continuously in bloodlust"—and that was a nightmare she didn't want to contemplate—"I'd say it's unlikely, given the way he glutted himself at the warehouse."

That was when rain thundered to earth outside, as if some great faucet had been turned.

"Shit!" She swiveled to the door. "Shit! Shit! Shit!"

Raphael just watched her have a fit, then calmly asked, "I thought you said Uram flew?"

"Scent markers like the ones that led me here are now all gone! He's been erased from the entire city." She gave a little scream. "Rain's the one thing that messes up the trail this bad—vampires who have any idea of what they're doing run to the wettest places on this earth." She wanted to kill the rain gods, settled for kicking the stone of the counter. "Fuck! That hurt!"

Raphael nodded at the doorway. "Take care of it."

She didn't have to turn around to know Dmitri had arrived. His scent wrapped around her like a damn coat. "Turn it off, vampire, or I swear to God, I'll stake you with your own leg."

"I'm not doing anything, Elena."

She glanced over, saw the tight lines of strain on his face, and knew he wasn't messing with her. "Double-shit. I'm wired, too much adrenaline, I'm going to crash soon." Her ability always spiked before a crash. "Might as well give in to it and catch a few hours' shut-eye." She hadn't slept much more than an hour or two last night, that damn chair had been so uncomfortable. "I won't be able to get anything now until Uram moves again."

Until he killed again.

"Are you keeping an eye on Michaela?" she asked Raphael. "She might be our best bet for catching him."

"She's an archangel," Raphael reminded her. "To augment her resources with my own would be to say I consider her weak."

"She's refusing?" Elena shook her head. "Then I hope to God she has good men and you have good spies." Pissed at the arrogance of angels, at the rain, at the whole fucking universe, she strode out without a backward look. Venom was at the gate. Damn man looked good wet. "I need a car."

To her surprise, he dropped keys into her palm and pointed across the road to the sedan she'd left double-parked somewhere. "Thanks."

"You're welcome."

She decided the vamp was playing with her, couldn't be bothered to snipe at him. Pushing through the gate, she walked toward the car.

Go to my home, Elena. I'll meet you there.

She opened the door and got in, brushing rain from her face, tasting the freshness of it on her tongue. But no, that was Raphael. He was waiting for an answer. "You know what, Archangel? I think it's time I took you up on your offer."

Which particular offer?

"The one about fucking me into oblivion." She had to forget—the blood, the death, the viscera of evil sprayed on the walls of that innocuous-looking town house.

A better man wouldn't take advantage of you in your current emotional state.

"Good thing you're not a man."

Yes.

Her thighs clenched at the eroticism implicit in that single word. Sticking the key in the ignition, she started the car and pulled out. The scent of rain, of the sea, faded from her mind. Raphael had left. But she could still taste him on her tongue, as if he'd exuded some exotic pheromone that rewired her body to scent angel, not vampire.

Not that she cared.

The hanging bodies, the shadows on the wall—

No, there had been no shadows. Not today.

Her hands clenched on the steering wheel as she came to a stop at a red light, her vision hazed by rain, by memories. "Stuff it back," she ordered herself. "Don't remember."

But it was too late. A single, terrifying shadow took shape on the wall of her mind, swaying in the breeze from the open windows.

Her mother had always liked fresh air.

Someone honked and she realized the light had turned green. Mentally thanking the other driver for snapping her awake, she focused every part of herself on driving. The rain should've made it hell but the streets were eerily quiet. As if the gathering darkness was a malevolent force that had captured the population, taking them to earth, to death.

And that quickly, she was back in the huge entranceway to the Big House, the house Jeffrey had bought after . . . *After.* Such a Big House for a family of four. Above her was a mezzanine floor with a lovely white railing, so strong, metal not wood. Elegant, old, the perfect home for a man who planned to be mayor.

"Mom, I'm home!"

Quiet. So quiet.

Panic in her throat, pain in her eyes, blood in her mouth. She'd bitten her tongue. In fear. In terror. But no, there was no trace of vampire.

"Mom?" A tremulous question.

Looking at the huge hallway, she'd wondered why her mother had left one high-heeled shoe in the middle of the tile. Maybe she'd forgotten. Marguerite was different. Beautiful, wild, artistic. Sometimes she forgot the days of the week, or wore two different shoes, but that was okay. Elena didn't care.

The shoe fooled her. Made her step inside.

A crash of noise and memory shattered under the heart-thudding reality of the present. She slammed the car to a shuddering halt, sickeningly aware that something had just ricocheted off her windshield. "Jesus." Unclipping her belt, she opened the door and got out. Had she hit someone?

The wind tore at her hair as the rain pelted down with bruising force. The storm had come out of nowhere, a freak blip on the radar of nature. Fighting against the wind, she walked around to the front of the car, eerily conscious that there was absolutely no one else on this stretch of road. Maybe people had decided to wait out the rain. Blinking water from her eyes, she figured it'd be a long wait.

There was a leaf on her windscreen, stuck to one of the still-running wipers. A solid branch lay a few feet in front of the car. Relief whispered through her, but she checked under and behind the vehicle to be sure. Nothing. Just a branch thrown by the wind. Getting out of the rain, she slammed the door shut and turned on the heater, chilled to the bone. Freezing from the inside out.

Wiping her face with an open palm, she drove the rest of the way to Raphael's with a steely focus on the here and now. The ghosts kept whispering in her ear but she refused to listen. If she didn't listen, they wouldn't be able to touch her, wouldn't be able to drag her back into the nightmare.

She was pulling up in front of the house when her cell phone rang. It had been in her pocket and was drenched, but seemed to function fine when she turned off the engine and flipped it open. She recognized the incoming number. "Ransom?"

"Who else?" Jazz in the background, the singer's voice smoky and low. "I've been hearing things, Ellie."

"I can't tell—" she began.

"No," he interrupted. "I'm hearing things I think you need to know."

"Go on." Ransom had contacts the rest of them didn't, having grown up on the streets. Most people who got out lost their street cred. He hadn't—being a hunter was considered an even better position in the hierarchy of the streets than being a gangbanger.

"There's been a lot of vamp and angel activity over the past few days. They're everywhere."

"Okay." That wasn't news. Raphael had his people looking for signs of Uram or his victims.

"Whispers of girls disappearing."

"Uh-huh."

"Should I be warning the pros?" His voice was tight.

She knew some of those streetwalkers and high-end call girls were his friends. "Let me think." She considered everything she'd picked up about the victims. "I think, for once, they're safe."

"You sure?"

"Yeah. The targets all looked . . . innocent."

"Virgins?"

Elena realized she hadn't thought to check. A mistake she'd rectify as soon as possible. "Yeah, probably. But still, it wouldn't hurt to tell your friends to look out for each other."

"Thanks." He blew out a breath. "That's not why I called, though. Word is, there's a hit out on you."

She froze. "*What?*"

"Yeah, it gets better." Anger vibrated through the wires. "Apparently an archangel wants you dead. What the hell did you do to him?"

Her forehead furrowed. "Not him. Her."

"Ah. I wouldn't worry about it, then." Pure snark. "According to the gossip, your head's wanted on a silver platter— literally, by the way—"

"Gee, thanks for clearing that up."

"—but the hunt's not authorized to begin yet."

Michaela, the bitch, was playing mind games. "Appreciate the warning."

"So what are you going to do? Get the hell out of Dodge or kill an archangel?"

"I do love your confidence in me."

A snort. "Hell, no. I just know I'm in your last will and testament."

"I'm too valuable alive right now."

"And when the job is done?"

The car door was pulled open from the outside, wings filling her vision. "Then I'll reconsider my options. Talk to you later." She closed the phone before he could say anything else, and looked up into eyes so blue they shouldn't have been possible. "Michaela really wants me dead."

Raphael's expression remained unchanged. "I don't let anyone break my toys."

It should've pissed her off, but she smiled. "Wow, I feel all mushy inside."

"Who were you speaking with?"

"Possessive much?"

He cupped her cheek, his hand wet, his hold uncompromising. "I don't share my toys either."

"Watch it," she murmured, twisting in her seat until her feet touched the sodden earth outside. "I might decide to be irritated. I have a question."

Silence.

"Were they virgins?"

"How did you know?"

"Evil is predictable." A lie. Because sometimes evil was an insidious thief that crept in and stole what you most treasured, leaving only echoes against a wall.

A thin shadow, swinging almost gently. Like on a swing.

Raphael rubbed his thumb over her lower lip. "I see nightmares in your eyes again."

"And I see sex in yours."

He rose, tugging her out of the car and trapping her with her back to the opening. Behind him, his wings flared out, gleaming with rain wetness. There was an edge to that sensual mouth, a touch of savagery in the way it curved.

Elena leaned forward and put her arms around his neck, letting herself luxuriate in the sheer strength of him. Today, she was going to break all the rules. Forget about sleeping with a vamp, she was going straight to the top and to hell with it. "So, how does an archangel do it?"

A gust of wind buffeted them, stealing away her words. But Raphael had heard. Leaning in, he brushed his lips over hers. "I haven't agreed yet."

She blinked. Then scowled as he drew back. "What, you're playing hard to get now?"

He turned. "Come, Elena. I need you healthy."

Cursing him under her breath, she shut the car door—the interior was already soaked—and walked toward the house, Raphael a quiet presence by her side. But not restful. No, he was quiet like a jaguar was quiet. Lethal danger momentarily contained. She was still scowling when they reached the door.

The butler held it open. "I've prepared the bath, sir." A glance at her, a hint of curiosity. "Madam."

Raphael dismissed Jeeves with a look and the butler melted away into the woodwork. "The bath is on the next floor."

She headed up the stairs, stomping more than stepping. He'd teased her to fever pitch, but now, today, when she actually needed the release, he was playing with her. Exactly as you did with a toy, she realized. Fine, if he wanted it that way, she'd focus on work. "Were you able to confirm if he had sex with the women?"

"Yes, but only at the town house. The warehouse victims were all untouched in that way—that's why we believe the others were also virgin before he took them." He was at her back, following close enough that his breath whispered over her nape as they reached the top. "Down the hall, third door to your left."

"Much obliged," she said sarcastically, noticing that there was nothing but air beyond the railing to her right—as if the core of the house was one huge, open space.

"Does it mean something—the sexual contact?"

"Could be. But there were no marks on the bodies aside from the death wounds, so that part may have been consensual." Archangels were charismatic, sexy, quite unbelievably compelling. Uram may have turned into a monster, but outside, he probably appeared just as attractive as the Archangel of New York. No, she thought immediately, Raphael was in a league of his own.

"Or it was after death."

She was too tired to be disgusted. "Possible." Reaching the third door, she put her hand on the doorknob. "He may have sublimated the feeding urge with sex for a small amount of time. But only blood's going to satisfy him now." Her hand tightened. "More women are going to die because I lost the scent."

"But less than if you'd never been born," he said, tone matter-of-fact. "I've lived centuries, Elena. Two or three hundred deaths is a small price to pay to stop one of the blood-born."

Two or three hundred?!

"I won't let it get that far." She pushed open the door—and stepped into a fantasy. Her breath rushed out of her as she stood there, staring.

Flames leaped in the fireplace to her left, the golden glow surrounded by dark stone that shimmered with hidden threads of silver. In front of the fireplace was a huge white rug that looked so fluffy and comfortable she wanted to roll around on it—naked. Talk about pure indulgence.

On the opposite side of the room was a door that seemed to open into the bath. She could see the edge of white porcelain fittings, a counter made of the same marble as the fireplace. Inside, she knew a hot bath awaited, a bath her cold bones desperately needed. But still she stood there.

Because between the fireplace and the temptation of the bath was a bed. A bed bigger than any she'd ever seen. One that could've accommodated ten people without any of them touching the other. It sat high off the floor but there was no headboard or backboard, just a smooth expanse of bed covered by lush midnight-blue sheets that promised to stroke across her skin in an exotically delicious caress. The pillows sat on the opposite end to the door, but could as easily have been on this side.

"Why"—she coughed to clear her throat—"why so big?"

Hands on her hips, pushing her forward. "Wings, Elena." A rustling snap as Raphael extended his wings to their full length, then the click of the door locking behind them.

She was alone with the Archangel of New York. In front of a bed made to accommodate wings.

31

Her body chose that moment to shiver.

Raphael's chuckle was husky, male in a way that said he knew he had her. "Bath first, I think."

"I thought you were playing hard to get."

He stroked a finger down her throat, making her shiver again for a far different reason. "I just want to set the ground rules before we do this."

She forced her feet forward, toward the bathroom. "I know the rules. Don't expect anything but a dance between the sheets, don't go all calf-eyed, yadda yadda." The words were flippant but she felt a tug in the region of her heart. No, she told herself, utterly horrified. Elena P. Deveraux would never be stupid enough to give her heart to an archangel. "Is that about— holy shit!" She stepped into the bathroom. "It's bigger than the bedroom!"

Not quite but close. The "bath" was almost the size of a small swimming pool, the steam curling off it pure, sensual temptation. A shower stood to her right, but it had no glass walls, the area defined only by an expanse of gold-flecked tile. A lightbulb went off in her head. "Wings," she whispered. "It's all to accommodate those beautiful wings."

"I'm glad they meet with your approval." The sound of something wet hitting the cool white of the tile had her glancing back.

Raphael's shirt was on the floor, his chest threatening to make her drool. Stop it, she told herself. But it was hard not to stare at the most beautiful male body she had ever seen. "What're you doing?" Her voice came out husky.

He raised an eyebrow. "Taking a bath."

"What about the rules?" She found her fingers were at the bottom of her T-shirt, ready to pull the sodden material over her head.

He kicked off his boots, watching her peel off the T-shirt to reveal the very circumspect sports bra she wore underneath. "We can discuss those in the bath." His voice held the promise of sex, and when she looked down, she realized why. The rain had turned her black bra into a second skin, the soft material delineating her nipples with perfect clarity.

"Fine with me." Unable to look at him and think at the same time, she turned her back and got rid of her boots and socks, before peeling off the bra. Her fingers were on the waistband of her cargo pants when she felt his body heat behind her. A second later, he was tugging the tie off her hair. Surprisingly, he was careful, so it didn't hurt. The wet strands hit her bare back a few moments after that.

Lips on her neck. Hot. Sinful.

She shivered again, goose bumps rising across her flesh. "No cheating."

Big, warm hands stroked up her damp torso to cup her breasts. She jerked at the bold move, moaned. "Enough. I'm cold." Though he was doing a great job of heating her up from the inside out.

More kisses along her neck.

She put her hands over his, and tipped her head to the side to give him better access. He trailed his tongue down, chasing a droplet of water that fell from her hair, down her nape, and along one shoulder, before drawing back. As she straightened, his thumbs hooked into the sides of her pants.

"Nuh-uh," she said, pulling away. "Rules first."

"Yes, the rules are very important."

She waited for him to move around her. He didn't. Her lips curved. And she decided that since she was living dangerously, she might as well go all the way. Undoing her pants, she pushed them and her panties down in a single push, before stepping out of the garments and kicking them aside. That done, she glanced over her shoulder.

The archangel's eyes held cobalt lightning. Alive. Vivid in a way that proclaimed his immortality. Her breath caught but she knew that if she planned to tangle with this particular male, she had to stand her ground. Throwing him a wicked smile, she walked up the steps built into the side of the bath and into the water.

"Ooooooh." Liquid heat. Pure heaven. She ducked under, came up pushing hair out of her eyes.

He was where she'd left him, watching her with those impossible eyes. But this time, she wasn't mesmerized. Not when she had his naked body there for her delectation. The archangel was built like a fantasy, his chest sculptured with the honed muscles of a man who had to be able to carry his own body weight—and more—in flight.

Her gaze caressed the lines of his chest, his abdomen, skated down. She sucked in a breath, forced her eyes back up. "Come here."

He raised an eyebrow, but then, to her absolute astonishment, obeyed the order. As he entered the bath, she found herself gauging the powerful muscle of his thighs—what would it be like to have all that strength around her as he buried himself inside her? Her stomach clenched. Never had she craved a man with such hunger, never had she been more aware of her own femininity. Raphael could snap her like a twig. And for a woman who had been hunter-born, that wasn't a threat . . . but the darkest of temptations.

Her hand fisted under the water as she remembered how he'd made her cut herself. She hadn't forgotten, had no romantic fantasies that he'd change, become more human. No, Raphael was the Archangel of New York and she had to be ready to take that man to her bed. The water lapped at her breasts as he settled on the opposite side, his wings folded to his back, his hair beginning to curl from the steam.

"Why the delay?" she asked, having seen the blatant evidence of his arousal.

"When you've lived as long as I have," he said, eyes heavy-lidded but definitely on her, "you learn to appreciate new sensations. They are rare in an immortal's life."

She found she'd moved toward him. He hooked an arm around her waist, pulling her closer until she straddled him as he sat on a ledge below the waterline, her legs wrapped around his waist.

He settled her firmly against him.

Sucking in a breath, she said, "Sex isn't new to you," and rocked her heat over the exquisite hardness of him. Good didn't begin to describe how it felt. How he felt.

"No. But you are."

"Never had a hunter before?" She grinned, nibbling on his lower lip.

But he didn't smile. "I've never had Elena before." The words were husky, his eyes so intent she felt owned.

Draping her arms around his neck, she leaned back so she could look into his face. "And I've never had Raphael."

At that moment, it felt as if something changed in the air, in her soul.

Then Raphael's hands spread on her lower back and the feeling dissipated. Nothing, she thought, it had been nothing but an overactive imagination. She was tired, frustrated, so damn greedy for this immortal who'd made no secret of the fact that, lust or not, he might yet kill her.

"The rules," Raphael said, catching her gaze, holding it.

She pressed closer, continuing to rub her heat along his aroused length. Today, she needed the pleasure Raphael could provide. And if there was a little sensual cruelty mixed in with the pleasure, so be it. "Yeah?"

He stilled her movements with those powerful hands of his. "Until this ends, I'll be your only lover."

Her muscles tightened at the absolute possession in that statement. "Until what ends?"

"This hunger."

The problem was, she was afraid this fury would never end, that she'd go to her grave craving the Archangel of New York. "Only if you meet a condition of mine."

He didn't like that, his bones sharp against skin gone taut. "Tell me."

"No vamp, human, or angel honeys for you either." She dug her nails into his shoulders. "I won't share you." She might be a toy, but she was a toy with claws.

His expression thawed, those cobalt eyes holding a distinct gleam of satisfaction. "Deal."

She'd expected to have to fight him. "I mean it. Not one lover. I'll cut off the hands they used to touch you, dump their bodies where no one will ever find them."

He seemed amused by her gruesome threat. "And me? What would you do to me? Shoot me again?"

"I'm not feeling guilty for that." But she did. Just an eensy bit. "Does it hurt?"

He laughed, and the open pleasure in it was a caress. "Ah, Elena, you are a contradiction. No, it doesn't hurt. It's healed."

She wanted to be a tough-ass, but that smile of his was doing things to her, melting her from the inside out. "So, what turns on an archangel?"

"A naked hunter is a good start." He pulled her harder against his cock, holding her in place when she would've wiggled. "My wings," he told her, kissing her neck, finding that sensitive little spot just above her collarbone.

It made her soften, return the favor. "Wings?" She nipped at the tendons of his neck, feeling languorous heat crawl up her body—she'd thought she wanted a short, hard fuck to screw up her brains enough that she could come down from the adrenaline buzz, but now that she was in his arms, a slow descent into sensual oblivion sounded far better.

When he didn't answer, she decided to do some exploring of her own. Moving one hand, she stroked firmly along the top edge of his right wing. He went tense against her, the waiting kind of tense, the kind that told her she'd either done something very good or something very bad. Since he was still pulsing hot and hard under her, she decided to go for good and repeated the act. This time, he shuddered.

"They're sexually sensitive?" Eyes narrowed, she thrust a hand into his hair and tugged him up from her neck. "The Bitch Queen was brushing her wings against yours."

He let her hold him, though they both knew he could've broken free in a second. "Only in certain situations." One long finger traced circles around her nipples.

She slapped at his hand. "I'm not buying."

He moved his finger to the dip of her elbow, making her shiver. "Is this sensitive in normal situations?"

"Hmph." But she let go of his hair, let him kiss her properly.

When they came up for air, he said, "They're sensitive, yes. But sexual only in a sexual context—which seems to be always with you."

"Guess a thousand years plus teaches a lot about charm," she said against his lips. Perfect lips. Lips she could nibble on for hours. "You've got all sorts of slick going on."

"For a warrior perhaps."

She was too interested in kissing him to answer right away, her entire body focused on his, her skin so sensitive she thought she might explode. "In the bath?"

He shook his head. "I want to see you in my bed."

"Another fallen hunter," she murmured. "Where's the soap?"

He reached along the rim and picked up a near-transparent bar. As he lathered up his hands and began to stroke them over her shoulders, a clean bright scent that echoed his own—water, wind, forest—rose up around her. "Do many fall?" he asked, running his hands down to soap the exposed parts of her breasts.

It made her lower body tighten another notch. "Vampires are sexy," she teased. "Angels are usually too snooty to bother with humans. I figured you lot were too evolved to enjoy getting down and dirty."

He looked up through lashes dark with wet, soapy hands sliding below the waterline to do things to her that were surely illegal. "Then you'll be getting an education tonight."

She moved on his fingers, inciting him to do more. "Yes, please."

The archangel handed over the soap, but kept his other hand where it was, stroking her with patience most men wouldn't learn if they lived to be ten thousand years old. "Come, hunter, it's your turn to educate me."

"Lesson one"—a breathy statement—"always give the hunter what she wants." Holding his gaze as he drove her to an inevitable crescendo, she lathered up her hands, and began to explore that body of his. Muscle and sinew and strength, he was delicious in every single way. "Oh!" Dropping the soap, she clutched at his shoulders with slippery hands as he pinched her clitoris, threatening to throw her over the edge into orgasm. "Stop that," she whispered, and he obeyed . . . only to slide two fingers deep into her.

"Let go," he said, kissing the taut line of her neck. "Let go."

Let go? During sex? She never had, not since the first time. In her innocence, she'd held on so tight, she'd broken her lover's collarbone. But Raphael wasn't human—he wouldn't break, wouldn't call her a freak. And then raw pleasure made the decision for her. The archangel took her lips in a savage kiss, a duel of tongue and lips, even as his fingers jackhammered into her in hard, fast thrusts. She came in an exquisite burst, her body clenching so tight it almost hurt.

In the aftermath, she was aware of Raphael finishing off the soaping. When he told her to lean back and rinse out her hair, she did so with a dreamy smile. She could get used to this, she thought, refusing to think of the future. Because the truth was, her life span was unlikely to be anything close to an ordinary human's. Hunters lived dangerous lives to begin with. And she was tracking a deranged archangel.

"Up."

She rose, kissing Raphael as he followed. A flicker of surprise lit his eyes. "How long can I look forward to such easy compliance?"

"Wait and see." She let him lead her to the shower, where he rinsed off the last bubbles of soap before grabbing a huge sky blue towel. She took it from him and dried herself, wanting to watch him as he did the same with efficient movements that told her he had no idea of what it did to her to watch him. That intrigued her.

Raphael clearly knew how beautiful he was, how he affected mortals. But seeing him like this, she realized that beneath the arrogance was a lack of vanity—it made sense when she thought about it. Strip away the layers of civilization, and he was, at the core, a warrior, his looks simply another tool in his arsenal.

Without warning, he snapped out his wings, showering her in millions of fine droplets. "Hey!" But she was already wrapping the towel around herself and reaching for another with which to pat his wings dry.

He watched her approach. "They'll dry on their own."

"But will it be as much fun?" She glanced meaningfully at his erection, sliding the soft material over his wings with extreme care.

"Hurry up, Elena." That cobalt lightning had returned. "I'm ready to fuck you into oblivion."

Oh, dear God. Dropping the towel, she pulled down his head and kissed the hell out of him. He liked it if his reaction was any indication. Pushing away the towel that clothed her, he lifted her up until she was wrapped around him. Breaking the kiss, he began to walk out of the bathroom. "My turn, hunter."

32

Raphael dropped her lightly on the bed.

"Nice." She sighed at the decadent feel of the sheets against her skin, her eyes locked with those of an archangel. His gaze was so hotly male, so proprietal that she wondered, for a fleeting second, if she'd made a mistake. What if he wanted to keep her? "Did you ever have a slave?" she asked.

His lips curved slightly, but it was an amusement tempered with sensual demand. "Many." He gripped her ankles, spread her legs. "All very eager to serve—in every possible manner."

She tried to kick out but he hauled her closer, face drawn in a way that was intrinsically sexual. "Some of them had spent years learning to drive a man to ecstasy. The vampires had had hundreds of years to practice."

"Bastard." A cutting denunciation, but her stomach was tight with anticipation, her breasts hot.

"However"—he pulled her up to meet his thrust as he buried himself inside her in one powerful stroke—"none of them did I forbid from taking other lovers."

Her back arched as she tried to assimilate the impact of his entry into her body, the extreme fullness, the stretched ecstasy. When she could finally draw breath, she found him in the same position, as if he, too, was fighting for control. "You don't strike me as the sharing type." Her voice was raw.

"No. If one went to another man"—he began to pull out with slow deliberation—"there were dozens ready to take her place. It mattered little to me."

She was almost beyond thought now, her entire being focused on the point where their bodies joined. What reason remained collapsed under the heady, seductive force of his words.

"If you take another lover, Elena"—he thrust back in, making her gasp—"what I do to him will become a nightmare etched in human memory." And then there were no more words, only movement—the slick motion of body against body, the thrust and parry of male and female, the lush, erotic explosion into ecstasy.

The last thing Elena remembered was thinking that maybe she'd underestimated the force of their combined hunger.

She woke to the realization that she was sleeping on something warm, soft, and silky. Spreading her fingers, she found herself petting—"Oh!" She jerked upright, horrified. A heavy male arm pushed her back down.

"Your wings," she whispered, stroking her hand down the splendor of one.

"They're strong." A lazy masculine statement, full of . . . something.

She was about to turn and look at him when she saw the state of her body. "Oh, no, you didn't!" She glittered from head to toe, angel dust in her pores, on her eyelashes, in her mouth. *The special blend.*

He caressed his hand over her hip, along the dip of her waist, over her breast. "It was . . . not on purpose."

Was that embarrassment she heard in his voice? Frowning, she licked some of the glittery stuff off her lips. It made her body all warm and tingly—as if she wasn't already burning up from the inside out. "Is this like—um—being a little quick off the mark?"

He squeezed the arm he had around her midsection. "Any complaints?"

She smiled, realizing she was right—the archangel had lost control. "Hell, no." Twisting in his arms, she wiggled up to look into his face. Her smile faded. "You look . . . different." Nothing she could explain, nothing she could touch. But . . .

His expression grew shadowed. "You've made me a little more human."

Flashes of memory. Raphael bleeding out from a gunshot wound. "What does that mean?"

"I don't know." His kiss was a fever and he was inside her before she knew it, their coupling fast, furious, and utterly magnificent.

Much, much later, as they faced the promise of a new day, she tried to wash off the angel dust, with only marginal success. Her skin continued to shine but it wasn't as noticeable. And thankfully, the stuff didn't, in fact, glow in the dark. "If someone tastes this," she said to Raphael as he watched her dress from his relaxed position by the fireplace, "will they want to jump my bones?"

"Yes." Those eyes gleamed. "So don't let them taste."

She stilled at the menace in his command. "Don't go around killing people on my account, Raphael."

"You made your choice."

To sleep with an archangel.

"I think the sexual high is starting to wear off," she muttered, pulling on a new pair of cargos in dark khaki, and a black T-shirt. She threw on a black sweater as well. It was early morning and still dark outside, the temperature having dropped along with the rain. "I mean it, Raphael, you go around killing innocent people, I'll hunt you." She didn't bother to hide her weapons—including the special gun—from him as she pulled them out of the overnight bag and concealed them on her body.

His face was expressionless as he watched her, his wings

backlit by the flames, his magnificent body naked but for a pair of black pants. "The honeymoon is over?"

She walked across the carpet to stare up into a face she knew she'd see in her dreams the rest of her life. "Nope." Fisting her hands on his naked chest, she waited for him to lower his head, and then took a kiss. "Here's a tip—you want to call me your toy, go ahead. Just don't expect me to be one."

A hand on her nape, a warning grip. "Don't attempt to manage me, little hunter. I'm not—"

The rest of his words disappeared in a crash of white noise.

Come here, little hunter. Taste.

"Elena." The sharp word pulled her back to the here and now.

"Fine." She cleared her throat. "Glad we sorted that out. The rain's stopped—"

"What do you see?"

She met his eyes, shook her head. "I'm not ready to tell you." Might never be.

He didn't threaten to take it from her by force. "It's still drizzling lightly. That should help keep him in Stupor."

"Yeah." Drawing back, she folded her arms. "I didn't think about that. They don't like the cold, do they?" It was a rhetorical question. "Especially after a glut."

"But then again, Uram isn't a vampire."

She blew out a frustrated breath. "Then what the hell is he? Tell me!"

"He is an Angel of Blood." He walked to the window, but she knew he saw things far more sinister than the predawn gloom. "A true abomination, a thing that should never have existed."

The anger that emanated from him was an almost physical force. "Is he the first?"

"He's the first archangel to become bloodborn in my memory. But Lijuan says there have been others."

Elena's mind filled with the images she'd found of the oldest of the archangels. Lijuan was the only one of the Cadre who showed even the first signs of age. It did nothing to detract from her exotic beauty—her face, her bones, her pale, pale eyes. And yet, there was something subtly *wrong* about Lijuan. As if she didn't belong in this world anymore.

"The first archangel you know of," she murmured, thinking that through. "What about ordinary angels?"

"Very good, Elena." He didn't turn from the window, as remote as he'd been on that rooftop what felt like weeks ago. "Those others were easily contained. Most were young males with little of the intellect Uram seems to have retained after his transition."

"How many?" She stared at the back of his head as if she could force him to speak. "One a year?"

He met her eyes in the window's dusky reflection as she came to stand behind him. "No."

Biting back her frustration, she moved around to lean against the glass so they were face-to-face. "You're obviously very good at covering the tracks of the bloodborn—humans don't even have legends about this."

"In most cases, the victims alone learned the truth—and they did so minutes before their deaths."

"That makes me feel extra special." She found herself tracing the delicate gold edging of a feather near his biceps. "Tell me—these bloodborn, is it a madness they're born with?"

A sweep of sinfully rich lashes against skin she'd kissed not so long ago. "We all carry the potential to become bloodborn."

Startled at the straight answer, she dropped her hand. "What, no warnings about too much knowledge?"

"You already know too much." A smile that hinted at age, at ruthlessness, at things better left unimagined. "It's good you've come to my bed. No one will dare touch my lover."

"Too bad immortals have such fleeting interests." The cold of the glass at her back was beginning to seep into her bones, but she didn't move. "Since I already know so much, tell me why an angel turns vampire."

His face closed over. "You're still human."

She barely restrained the urge to kick him. "I'm also a hunter tracking an archangel. You pulled me into this. Give me the tools I need to fight."

"Your job is to find Uram. It's your ability we need."

We. The Cadre of Ten.

"How am I supposed to do that job if you insist on hobbling me?" It took extreme effort to keep her temper. "The more I know about the target, the better I am at predicting his movements!"

He traced a finger over her cheek. "Do you know why Illium lost his feathers?"

"Because you were in a bad mood?" She blew out a frustrated breath. "Stop trying to change the subject."

"Because," Raphael said, ignoring her order, "he bespoke our darkest truth to a human." The way he said that, the language, made it impossible to ignore his age, his immortality.

Captured despite herself, she asked, "What happened to the mortal?"

"We took her memories." He cupped her cheek. "And Illium was forbidden from speaking to her ever again."

"Did he love her?"

"Perhaps." His face said that that didn't matter. "He watched over her for the rest of her days, knowing she no longer knew him. Is that love?"

"Don't you know?"

"I've seen love defined a thousand ways over the centuries. There is no constant." He stared at her, his own face expressionless. "If Illium loved his mortal, then he was a fool. She's been dust for centuries."

"Heartless," she whispered, sensing the warmth of the rising sun at her back. How long had they stood here that the fading edge of night had turned to dawn? "Couldn't you have allowed him a lifetime with the woman he loved?"

"No." Sharp, clean lines, a face without mercy. "For if one mortal knows, soon another will. You have little concept of secrecy."

Elena saw in his absolute statement, her future. "Not my memories," she reminded him. "Hunt me to ground if it comes to that, but don't you dare take my memories."

"You'd rather die?"

"Yes."

"So be it."

Her blood fired at the finality of those three short words, knowing he'd spoken them as a vow. "You do realize that to kill me, you'll have to catch me."

His smile held the cool arrogance of a man who knew exactly how dangerous he was. "It'll break the ennui of age."

She snorted and glanced outside. "Rain's stopped. I'll go out, see if I can pick up a trail in case Uram didn't spend the night in Stupor."

"Eat first." He moved back. "We never stopped running search patterns—if he'd killed again, I would've heard by now."

Feeling jittery but knowing she'd do better with some nourishment, she agreed. "I'll grab something quick."

"Will you begin your search at Michaela's?"

"Might as well. If he is up and around, he'll probably come by to visit her. There's—" Something rang in a familiar pattern. "Damn, where did I put it?"

"Here." Raphael picked her cell phone out of the clothing she'd thrown over the small bag that held her stuff. "Catch."

"Thanks." One glance at the caller display was enough to make her stomach churn. "Hello, Jeffrey." She wondered what her father would say if she told him she was standing in a room with a half-naked archangel. Probably ask her to strike a deal while said archangel was befuddled with sex.

Looking at the profile of Raphael's highly intelligent face as he switched on a laptop she hadn't noticed until then, she felt her lips curve in a tight grin. "What is it?" The urge to hang up was a pounding need in her blood, but she'd gnaw off her own arm before she allowed Jeffrey to beat her into sniveling cowardice.

"You need to come to my office."

Something in his tone cut through the complex, turbulent layers of her anger. "Is someone there?"

"*Now*, Elieanora." He hung up.

"I need to get to my father's brownstone."

Turning from the laptop, Raphael raised an eyebrow. "I thought you'd said what you needed to say to your father yesterday?"

She didn't bother to ask how he knew—it wasn't as if she and Jeffrey had made any attempt to keep the volume down. "Something's wrong. Is the car still out front?"

He paused and she realized he was probably talking to the vampires mind-to-mind. "Dmitri will drive you."

"Fine." She began to stride out. "If this is one of Jeffrey's power games— Damn it, no, I'm not going to drop everything just because he tells me to." She pulled out the phone and called him back. "I'm on a hunt," she said as soon as he picked up. "I don't have time to come play happy families."

"Then perhaps you'll find the time to come clean up the mess your friend left behind."

Her heart chilled. "What are you talking about?"

"I'm fairly sure she was still alive when he split her open and skinned off the flesh to display her broken rib cage."

33

Raphael flew her to her father's, landing on the street with a smooth grace that would've stunned onlookers, had anybody been watching. But it was too early for anyone but the birds, especially in this exclusive area.

The scent hit her the second they landed. The by-now familiar bite of acid tinged with the thick richness of fresh blood. "Uram," she said to Raphael as they started up the steps. "He knows I'm tracking him."

Raphael scanned the street. "Either he stripped the mind of someone who knew about your involvement, or he saw you on the hunt."

"Glamour." Lips pursed tight, she pushed through the door her father had told her he'd leave open. "Jeffrey's in the study. He said the body's in the upstairs apartment." An apartment she'd always assumed was used as an extension of her father's office.

They went straight up. It was as she was about to push open the door that she remembered Geraldine. Pale skin, perfect suit, vampire scent laced into her perfume. "Hell." She walked through.

There was no one in the living room. Crossing the carpet only after making certain she wouldn't be trampling evidence that could lead to Uram, she followed the scent to the doorway of what proved to be a bedroom. The woman lay exactly as Jeffrey had described. It was as if someone had started to perform an autopsy and been interrupted midway. Her chest was cracked open to display her insides, flaps of skin hanging off her rib cage.

But that wasn't what held Elena frozen on the doorstep.

It wasn't Geraldine. This woman had skin dusted with the gold of a tropical clime and hair a pale, pale blonde. Fine bones, a length that would equal height on the short side of average, lips that had smiled easily in life. Her fists clenched. "It was definitely Uram." A truth forced out through gritted teeth. "I'll follow the scent."

She was about to push past Raphael when he caught her arm. "Don't take foolish chances because you're angry at your father."

"I'm not angry." Her emotions were a chaotic stew she couldn't understand. "She looks like my mother," she blurted out. A faded copy, a pale imitation. But nothing like the wintery elegance of Jeffrey's new wife, Gwendolyn.

"She was his mistress."

"You knew?" Of course he'd known—the Cadre of Ten wouldn't trust anyone it hadn't investigated inside out. "Never mind. My father isn't the issue—Uram's starting to hunt me and mine. He's baiting us."

Releasing her, Raphael walked into the room. "Your father said she was warm to the touch when he arrived?"

She nodded in a jerky motion, feeling as if everything in her body was out of sync. "He checked for a pulse." God alone knew why. "Means Uram hasn't been up and around long. Probably a couple of hours at most."

"I don't believe he took blood from her. There are no marks but the ones that caused her death."

"He's probably still glutted." She couldn't believe she sounded so normal when she was on the verge of screaming.

Jeffrey had forbidden her and Beth from even talking about Marguerite after her death, yet he'd kept this woman, this *shadow* of her mother, with him. But Jeffrey's hypocrisy wasn't the fault of this poor, brutalized stranger—she deserved to have her killer brought to whatever justice the Cadre meted out to its own.

"Glutted," she repeated, forcefully corralling her skittering thoughts, "but not stupid." Uram was beginning to act more like a thinking being. "Most vamps caught in bloodlust don't reach that stage until at least three or four months after the bloodlust first sets in. The only one who's known to have survived that long after turning was—" The name stuck in her throat, a vicious, cutting evil.

"Slater Patalis," Raphael completed for her. "Venom's arrived to complete the cleanup. I'll fly above. I've asked Dmitri to stay out of range."

"Good." She turned away, unable to look at the woman on the bed. "What about my father?"

"He knows only that his lover was killed by a rogue vampire. That's a rumor it's to our advantage to spread."

Venom's scent curled up the stairs as they headed down. "The woman has family," the vampire said. "No one in the city, however."

Elena had a sudden, choking thought. "Did she have children?" A brother or a sister she'd never known about?

It was Raphael who answered. "No. I'm certain."

She gave a jerky nod at the firm answer, and he turned back to Venom. "Her body can't be found."

"Of course. I'll ensure there's a paper trail leading out of the city." The vampire began to climb up. "Jason has returned."

Having reached the hallway, Elena fought the urge to go to her father's study, knowing it would only end in another shouting match. "Who's Jason?" she asked instead, focusing on filtering out Venom's scent and drawing a bead on Uram's.

"One of the Seven."

The Angel of Blood had gone out the back door, she thought, heading that way. "Why are you getting rid of the body? She was torn up, but it looks like classic vampire over-kill."

"Uram may have left traces on her."

She pulled open the back door, felt a stickiness on her palm, and looked down. Rust stained her skin. Dried blood. "He's taunting us." She rubbed her palm clean against her pants, wanting to wash it off, but not enough to chance losing the scent. It was fresh, *clean*, vivid in the clarity of the day after a rainstorm. That was a bonus—with so much having been washed away, the new scents were richer, more intense.

Blood drops a few feet from the door. She didn't want to consider where they'd come from, not when taking souvenirs was Uram's thing. Which reminded her—"Michaela?"

"I've warned her."

Almost able to *see* Uram's scent in the ozone-lashed air, she began running, barely aware of the wind generated by Raphael's wings as he rose to the sky. A group of early commuters got out of her way as she almost sprinted out of the alley behind the building and into the busier street on the other side, but no one looked skyward. Glamour, she thought. It made her skin creep to think Uram could've been watching her at any time since the hunt began.

Another drop of blood, this one buried into the asphalt by the pounding of feet rushing this way and that as the city woke. She noted it but kept running, dodging well-dressed businessmen and shopping-cart-pushing homeless with equal ease. More blood, this drop large enough to have people circling it with wary looks. She wondered if anyone had called the cops. It being New York, she expected not.

Raphael would need to send a cleanup crew here, too. Mentally tagging the spot, she continued to follow the scent, excitement lacing her blood like the most powerful of drugs. Her ability infused every inch of her skin, every element of her being.

This was who she was. Hunter-born.

She felt like she was swimming through acid burned in sunlight by the time she found herself in front of a building that looked surprisingly familiar. Where was she? She blinked awake out of the almost trancelike state she'd fallen into and read the sign.

THE NEW CHILDREN'S MUSEUM
ENDOWED BY DEVERAUX ENTERPRISES

Her blood chilled, horror flooding her mouth, until she read the fine print and realized the museum was closed due to refurbishment. Thank God. If some child had gone inside . . .

Is he in the building?

It was tempting to wrap the scent of rain, of Raphael, around herself, but she resisted, tugging on the echoes of Uram's trail instead. "Either that or we just missed him." Wondering if Uram had broken in, she checked the door and found it locked. Her brow furrowed as she concentrated. "The scent's not that strong by the door."

She took several steps back and turned in a slow circle. There! Squeezing around the side of the building, she made her way to the back, fear, anger, and the thrill of the hunt thrumming in her blood. The parking lot was empty but that wasn't what held her interest. A small door at the back lay open, swinging gently to and fro in the light breeze.

Heart in her throat, she followed the scent and entered. She didn't have to go far.

Geraldine lay in a crumpled heap by the doorway, as if she'd been dumped in a hurry. Sensing life, Elena went down on her haunches and—"Oh, Jesus!" Geraldine's throat was slashed, but she was conscious, her eyes full of terror. Elena didn't know how the hell she was still alive.

"Hold on." She fumbled with her cell phone. "I'm calling an ambulance."

"Don't." Raphael's shadow filled the doorway, blocking all light. "I'll have Illium take her to a healer. He's almost here."

She met his eyes, knew she didn't have time to argue.

"Fine." Her tone asked for a promise the other woman wouldn't be harmed.

"We'll have to remove her memories." Unsaid were the words, *if she lives.*

Geraldine coughed as Raphael gathered her up in his arms. "V-vam—" It was more air than sound, her hand clamped tight around her neck, but Elena understood. Not an accusation—a request. Before she could say anything, however, Raphael was gone.

Elena drew in the scents around her and realized this was as far inside as Uram had come. Stepping back out into the parking lot, she circled out from the museum, trying to find another marker. Nothing. The bastard had dumped Geraldine and flown when Elena and Raphael had gotten too close. She was back at the museum by the time Raphael returned. "Your cleanup crew will have to work overtime today."

"It's necessary."

"Fly me to Michaela's."

"You sound very sure he'll head that way."

"Geraldine was wearing a diamond ring when I met her yesterday. It was missing today, and from the white band of skin on her finger, I don't think she ever took it off."

"It'll be easier if I carry you." Seeing the sense in that, she nodded and Raphael picked her up, one arm around her back, the other under her knees. Glamour spread like water across her skin.

"Did you do it?" she asked as he rose, holding on tight and keeping her eyes closed against the mind-bending sight of her bones disappearing into thin air. "Start the process of turning Geraldine into a vampire?"

"No."

"Why not? She probably won't survive otherwise. And she'd be happy to be one. A win-win situation." Wind laced with the whispered promise of more rain whipped through her hair, stroked her cheeks.

"You're asking for forbidden knowledge again."

"You put me in the path of a monster—not just me, but

people even peripherally related to me—" Panic hit her. "Sara, my sister!"

"We've alerted everyone close to you that they might be targeted by a vampire."

She gripped him harder. "Won't do much good against an archangel, will it?"

"No. The only thing that'll stop him is death."

"How will you kill him?"

"Rip out his heart and shove my power through the hole in his torso, tearing him apart from the inside out."

She swallowed at the graphic description. "Can he do the same to you?"

"He is an archangel."

In other words, yes. Fear clawed at her heart, fear for a being who'd lived more lifetimes than she could imagine. "Why can an archangel only be killed by another archangel?"

"As we age, we gain power—including the power to end the life of an immortal." And perhaps, Raphael thought, recalling Lijuan's coy hints, the power to give life, too. But not a life that was anything close to what life should be. "It's one of the prerequisites of being in the Cadre of Ten. We must be able to destroy each other if the need arises."

"And that's not too much information?"

"You would've guessed." Her intelligence was strong, stubborn, relentless. In all his centuries of living, he'd never met a warrior who challenged him as she did. "The female we found, who is she?"

"Geraldine, my father's secretary."

"Your father employs a lover of vampires?"

"What, you didn't know?" She snorted. "I thought you knew every minute detail of my history."

"Assistants weren't of much interest."

"Yeah, well, Jeffrey doesn't know about her extracurricular activities."

"Illium said he's seen her at Erotique. She dances." Erotique was a by-invitation-only club that catered to upscale vampires who wanted to relax in the company of humans who'd been tutored as to what was acceptable and what was not.

"I've heard the dancers of Erotique described as the geishas of the West."

Raphael caught the edge in that question, wondered at it. "An apt comparison."

Her nails dug into his neck. "More like they know how to pander to men who can't be bothered to make an effort."

"Both male and female vampires frequent Erotique." He paused. "It holds less allure for angels."

Those nails withdrew slightly. "Those dancers—they make good money?"

Raphael made contact with Illium and found the answer. "Yes."

"So what was Geraldine doing moonlighting as Jeffrey's assistant? I guess we'll take out the thumbscrews if she lives."

"Unnecessary. In all probability she was a spy for a competitor with fangs."

"Why was Bluebell at Erotique anyway?"

"He has a fascination with mortals." Illium's Flaw had caused Illium's Fall. It was a lesson taught to all young angels.

"What if he falls in love again? What then?"

"As long as he keeps our secrets, he may love his mortal."

"Except that she'll die in a few decades, while he'll live for centuries."

"Yes." He knew she was no longer talking about Illium. "Immortality has its price."

Her arms tightened around him. "It's too high, far as I'm concerned. Bowing and scraping to a master? Hell, no." Her tone was acerbic. "Maybe that's why you guys Make so many morons into vamps. They're the only ones stupid enough to apply."

He squeezed her. "So now you insult the Cadre of Ten."

"You know Mr. Ebose. You know who I retrieved for him. Come on, seriously—what was his qualification for immortality aside from abject idiocy?"

"That, you cannot know."

"I already know too many secrets—what's one more?"

He dipped with the air currents, making her hold on tighter. "We've arrived."

She sighed, but then he felt the brush of lips against his jaw. "Being with you is an exercise in frustration."

He landed in the woods that separated his home from Michaela's, shed the glamour, met the vivid silver of her eyes. "I've set guards on Sara, Ransom, your father, your siblings, and their families."

Shadows moved across her face, darkening those eyes to storm readiness. "Thanks."

"Do you consider Harrison an idiot, too?" he asked, referring to her brother-in-law. "He is a vampire after all."

Her eyes narrowed. "I have one question—I need to know."

"Beth," he said, watching that expressive face. For a hunter, her shields were surprisingly weak, as if she somehow still saw innocence in the world.

Then she will kill you. She will make you mortal.

Was it not worth the loss of a little immortality to have that strange mix of innocence and strength close to him? "Harrison knew when he was Made that there was no guarantee we'd accept his wife."

"Is it possible?" she asked. "However you choose the Candidates, is it possible Beth could be one?"

"Why does it matter to you?" he asked. "They treat you like so much trash."

Her hand fisted. "Yeah, well, just call me a glutton for punishment." She shrugged. "It doesn't matter that she drives me insane half the time. She's my sister."

"As Ariel and Mirabelle were your sisters?"

34

Her entire body stilled. "I don't talk about that."

He knew the facts, but hearing the odd brittleness in her voice, realized they told him nothing. "Beth isn't suitable," he said, instead of fencing with her.

"Are you sure?"

"Yes." He'd made it a point to find out . . . because he'd known Elena would want to know.

"Aw, shit." She rubbed a hand over her face. "He's a moron but he loves her."

"He loves immortality more," Raphael said with centuries of experience. "Did he not, he would've waited until she, too, was accepted."

Elena looked at him, an inscrutable expression on her face. "Do you believe in anything good anymore?"

"If we're able to kill Uram, then perhaps I'll believe that evil does not always win." Perhaps. He'd seen too much malice done to believe in the fairy tales that comforted humans through their firefly life spans.

Shaking her head, Elena began walking toward Michaela's home. "I'm starving."

"You ran a long distance." He sent a message to Montgomery to prepare food fit for a hunter.

"What happens if you don't eat?"

Another question no one had thought to ask him for over a thousand years. "I fade."

"Get weak?" She crouched, touched the earth, and brought her fingers up to her nose. "I thought I scented something but it's gone."

He waited until she was up again before answering. "No, I literally fade, become a ghost. Food anchors our physical form."

"Then why don't other angels starve themselves—you know, to get the invisibility thing happening?"

"Fading doesn't incur invisibility, just washes us out. Since lack of food also leaches power, being faded is not a good thing."

"So if I want to make an angel vulnerable, I should starve him?"

"Only if you plan to contain him for the next fifty years." He watched shock, then consternation fill her face. "Starvation is a relative concept. Unlike a vampire, an angel will not easily fade."

"Vamps don't fade, they shrivel," she muttered, and he had the sense that she was remembering something. "The older they are, the more they shrivel." She stopped at the edge of Michaela's lawn and looked up at the archangel's window. "Same concept, though, I guess."

"Yes." Following her gaze, he remembered how she'd looked up from that very spot yesterday. "Do you scent him?"

"Yes." She bit her lower lip and glanced back the way they'd come, before returning her attention to the window. "Something's wrong."

"It's too quiet. Where are the guards?" He scanned the area, looking for Uram's distinctive wings. "He can't have reached here much ahead of us. Geraldine's memories have him dumping her when he sensed pursuit."

She shot him a narrow-eyed look. "What was he planning to do—make her into art, shock the people who found her?"

"Yes."

"Figures. Can you do a flyover?"

He gathered his wings, gave an upward push, and was airborne. It was a freedom he'd always taken for granted . . . until he saw the hunger for flight in a hunter's eyes. *No overt signs,* he told her, the mental link effortless by now.

"I'm going in."

That was unusual, how very easily she spoke to him. He knew Elena thought she was only speaking out loud, that he was taking the words from her mind, but that wasn't quite true—she instinctively knew how to arrow her thoughts so they didn't get lost in the jumble of an active mind. She could also block him when she wanted. It hurt her, but she could do it. The arrogance in him wasn't exactly pleased by that, but the archangel found it intriguing.

Catching a downward draft, he winged down to land behind her. "You will not go in alone." No mortal could hope to win against Uram.

She didn't argue, the look in her eyes—focused, hunterborn—saying that at this moment, she saw him only as another tool. With a sharp nod, she closed the distance to the house, but, rather than going around the front, she jimmied open the sliding doors on one side. "I'm drowning in his scent," she whispered. "He's here."

Raphael put a hand on her back. "I'll go first."

"This is no time to pull macho crap."

"It could be a trap. You're mortal." Stepping through the doorway, he scanned the room—the library. "Come."

She followed on quiet feet. "Scent's deeper inside."

He opened the doors to the library and stepped out. Riker was staked to the wall in front of him, a wooden chair leg embedded in his throat. The vampire was still alive but unconscious—likely from the blow to his head that dripped blood down his temples.

"Jesus," Elena whispered. "He's having a very bad week. Do we leave him?"

"He won't heal until the stake's removed."

"Then let's go. I can only deal with one psychopath at a time." She nodded left.

He began walking that way, not particularly surprised when he found another one of the guards impaled on a savagely compelling sculpture from Michaela's years with Charisemnon. The vampire's head hung at the wrong angle for life. "He's dead."

"Broken neck?"

"Decapitation"—he showed her how the head was barely attached by a few tendons—"coupled with removal of the heart. It wasn't planned, though. This was just to get him out of the way." He put a foot on the stair.

"No." Elena pointed in the other direction. "Deeper inside."

A scream shattered the air.

He stopped her from running. "That's what Uram wants." Pushing her behind him, he headed toward the sound. Uram was a master of strategy—he'd obviously figured out that Elena was the linchpin. Take her out and he could evade the Cadre for years—there were other hunter-born, but none as gifted as Elena. And if Uram wasn't executed within half a century of his devolution, he might gain enough power to rule. And the world would drown in blood.

Elena tugged on his wing. He glanced over his shoulder, about to warn her not to distract him. It could prove fatal, even for an immortal. She was pointing up. He nodded. *I know.* Michaela's home had high ceilings, as was the case with the homes of most angels. Her living room, like his, was basically the central core of the house, the upper floors arranged around the edges. Uram wouldn't be waiting below, he'd be waiting above.

That left Raphael at a disadvantage. This house had been remodeled from a human dwelling, rather than being designed for angelic inhabitants. There were no high windows he could use to fly straight through to the living area. He'd have to walk in the door. Elena tugged again, until he bent his ear to her lips.

"Let me go in, distract him. You come in straight after— he won't have time to kill me."

Had anyone outlined this scenario to him before he met Elena, his answer would've been instant. Yes, send in the hunter, distract the bloodborn. And if the hunter died, it was a small price to pay to win this war. But now he knew her, now he'd taken her, now she belonged to him.

Her eyes narrowed, as if she could read his thoughts.

"Go in low," he said, knowing he'd startled her. "He'll aim for head-height. Roll."

She nodded. "He's definitely in there. The scent's crawled into my blood it's so thick, so heavy." Then she was moving toward the doorway.

The next few instants went at inhuman speed. Elena rolling inside, chunks shearing off the doorway, a howl of rage, and then Raphael was in the room, looking up at Uram as the other archangel fired bolts of pure energy at Raphael's hunter.

He launched himself upward, gathering his own energy. This, too, was why he'd been asked to lead the hunt. Of the Cadre, only four could create the energy bolts. It was a gift that came with time—but only if the imprint for it was already there. And unlike with the room of Quiet, this energy didn't have to come from within. As he rose, he drew power from electrical sources, shorting out the lamp burning below.

He threw the first bolt at Uram before the other archangel realized he was there. It hit midchest, throwing Uram against the wall. But Uram wasn't an archangel for nothing. Stopping himself from crashing through the wood, he threw back a ball of red-hot flame. Raphael dodged it, knowing that if it hit his wings, he'd go down. Angelfire was one of the few things that could truly damage an immortal.

Angelfire and a hunter's gun, he corrected. *Elena, did I see you arm yourself with that little pistol you used to unman me?*

Another exchange of blue and red, huge holes in the wall,

dust floating to the earth in serene quiet. As they fought, he watched Uram, tried to see the monster. But the archangel looked as he always had, his new fangs hidden from sight as he focused on repelling Raphael's blows, attacking with his own.

A passing fireball singed Raphael's wing. Shrugging off the shrieking nerve endings, he returned fire, catching the tip of the other angel's left wing. Teeth bared, Uram howled and the monster emerged, red fire in his eyes, fangs lengthening past his lips . . . and a dervish of flame in his hands.

The blood had made him stronger.

That was the draw, the temptation, the insanity. After the Scourge took hold, blood increased an angel's power to the nth degree. But by then, no matter how they appeared, they were so insane that it mattered little. However, Raphael was no green boy to allow himself to be cornered. He dropped at the last instant, and the wave of angelfire hit the wall where he'd been moments ago, decimating everything in its path to expose the outside world, even as he shot upward with a bolt of his own.

Something fired, the sound a loud crack. Uram tipped to the side, faltering, and Raphael saw the tear at the bottom of his wing. He struck out at the vulnerable spot and hit, causing considerable damage. But Uram was already moving. Dodging Raphael's second strike, he flew out the hole created by their battle.

Raphael went after him, knowing he could take him while the bloodborn angel was injured. He'd just swept out into daylight when a body slammed into him. He began to spiral down, managing a soft landing only by dint of years of experience—and put the body on a relatively clear section of the floor.

Michaela.

The female archangel was missing her heart, a glowing red fireball where the organ should've been. Not stopping to think, he thrust in a hand covered with blue fire and pulled out the red, throwing it at a wall and dissipating its destructive force. Michaela's heart began to regenerate in front of his eyes.

"Elena!"

"I'm here." She touched his arm, staring horrified at the mess of Michaela's chest. "Wha—"

Leaving Michaela where she was, he wrapped an arm around Elena's waist and flew up. "Track him."

Understanding at once, she hung on tight and gave an alert nod. When he reached the opening Uram had used to escape, she pointed up, then toward Manhattan. Raphael knew he was fast, but Uram now had a head start. Raphael was also carrying another and though the other angel was injured, so was he. But they were close, so close . . . until they hit the stretch of the Hudson above the Lincoln Tunnel.

The waters of the river churned below, but Elena could find no hint of Uram's scent in the air. Raphael took them down low enough that he could feel a fine spray on his face, but she shook her head. "He knows about water." Sheer frustration. "Either he dived in, or he skimmed so close to the surface that the moisture masked his scent."

Raphael fought the urge to expend power in a useless fit of fury. Instead, he did several wide sweeps along and around the length of river where they'd lost the trail. "Nothing," Elena said. "Fuck."

Silently echoing the sentiment, he flew them back to Michaela's home through a sky pregnant with clouds, sending Dmitri a command to blanket both sides of the river with searchers. The chances of that search bearing fruit were incredibly low—Uram had to maintain glamour only for the undoubtedly short time it would take him to find a hiding place. For an archangel—even an injured one—that was child's play.

Michaela was still where he'd left her, but her heart was now a beating, pulsing reality in her ravaged chest. Her eyes were open, filled with a kind of horror he'd never expected to see. Michaela was too old, had experienced too much, to know true fear.

"He's mad," she said when he crouched down beside her and took her hand. Bubbles of blood foamed out of her mouth. "There's nothing left of the man he once was."

Raphael saw Elena step out, knew his hunter was giving them privacy. Michaela would kill her as soon as talk to her and she felt compassion. So human, was Elena. "He'll return for you." Killing another angel was a vicious rite of passage, a compulsion the bloodborn didn't seem to be able to fight. And once they fixated on someone, they never shifted their interest.

"He said"—Michaela coughed, her heart still visible through the closing gap that was her chest—"that I was the last thing tying him to this existence, that once I was dead, he'd be free to Rise. Rise to what?"

"Death, endless death," Raphael said, continuing to hold her hand. Michaela was a cobra, but she was a cobra who was needed. If they lost her, the Cadre of Ten would be dangerously unbalanced. There was one who could possibly step into Uram's shoes, but no second. "Where were you?"

"He took my heart once before he went after my guards, then again, and left me unconscious on the roof. I'd almost healed enough to fly when"—another cough, but the blood was gone—"he put the fire inside. He didn't have time to spread it."

They both knew if he had, she'd have died an agonizing, and complete, death.

"Go," she said, her eye skating to his wing. "You're injured. You need to heal before he does."

Nodding, he rose, aware she'd be functional in another few minutes. "I saw one guard in the hall, Riker staked by the library. Where are the others?"

"All dead," she told him, lifting her left hand. A bloody diamond glittered on her ring finger. "On the roof."

"I'll arrange extra protection."

She didn't argue with him this time. "No invitation to your home?" She was starting to revive, burying her terror as immortals learned to do very early on.

He met her gaze. "You must remain a tempting target."

Fear skittered in the backs of her eyes. "He won't return tonight."

"No—he's too badly injured. Get the house repaired while he's down." He looked up at the huge hole where the wall had been. "At least as much as you can. I'll send you some of my angelic guards as well."

Michaela sat up, not bothering to cover her bare chest. It was a weapon, her body, one she wasn't hesitant about using. But that wasn't what she was concerned about right then. "Won't that lessen my status as a tempting target?" In that moment, she was an archangel, knowing only that Uram had to die.

"He's arrogant enough not to worry about even other arch-angels, you know that better than anyone."

She looked up, a spark of true pain in her eyes. "I did love him. As much as an archangel can love."

He said nothing, leaving her to consider what immortality had made her as he went to find Elena. She was waiting for him outside, on the edge of the lawn where the woods began. Her eyes immediately shot to his wing. "He damaged you." Anger whiplashed through the air.

"I damaged him worse."

"Bastard got away." She kicked at the leaves as they walked. "How's Her Royal Bitchiness?"

"Alive."

"Pity." The word was caustic, but he remembered the com-passion.

He gripped her upper arm. "Don't ever feel sorry for Mi-chaela. She'll use that vulnerability to destroy you."

"Yet you saved her life."

He slid his hand down to her elbow, then off. "She's neces-sary. Impossible as it may seem, Michaela is more human than Charisemnon and Lijuan."

She said nothing as they emerged into his yard and entered the house. Montgomery was waiting. His distress at Raphael's injuries broke through his usual reserve. "Sire? The healer?"

"That won't be necessary." When the vampire continued to wring his hands, Raphael put a hand on his shoulder. "Be easy. It will heal by nightfall."

Montgomery relaxed. "Should I bring up the meal? It's close to noon."

"Yes." He turned to Elena as the other man moved down the corridor. "It seems we'll share a second bath." Geraldine and Michaela had both left their mark on him, not to mention the scarlet stain of his own injuries.

She winced, touching the cuts on her cheeks—from the flying debris. "Just a quick shower for me. If I soak, my skin might peel off." A glance at her bloody clothes, a result of being carried by Raphael. "Damn, I don't think I packed any more spares."

About to reply, Raphael heard the sound of approaching wings, a rustle that announced another angel—one who wanted to be heard. When he looked up, it was to find Jason in his sights. The angel bowed his head in respect, his black hair pulled back in a queue. "Sire, we have a problem."

35

Elena couldn't help staring at the new angel. His face . . . she'd never seen anything like it. The entire left-hand side was covered in an exotic tattoo composed of fine dots and swirling curves, the ink pure black against his glowing brown skin. There was a hint of Polynesia in that skin, that tattoo, but the sharpness of his facial features hinted at part of her own ancestry. Old Europe mixed with the exotic winds of the Pacific—it was one hell of a sexy combination.

"Jason," Raphael said in greeting.

"You're injured." The new angel's eyes went to Raphael's wing. "This can wait." He shifted slightly, the rustle of his wings alerting Elena to the fact that she hadn't truly seen them. Frowning, she squinted into the dimness of the hall—the stained glass dull without sunlight—but still saw nothing aside from an indistinct shadow.

She had to ask. "Where are your wings?"

Jason gave her an inscrutable look, then flared out a wing in silence. It was a deep, sooty black. The wing didn't reflect light but seemed to absorb it, the edges fading into the spreading gloom. "Wow," she said. "Guess you make one hell of a night scout."

Jason glanced from her to Raphael. "The report can wait, but it's important you hear it."

"I'll join you in an hour."

"Sire, if early evening would suit, I'd like to fly out to check on something else."

"Contact me when you return."

With a short nod, Jason left. Elena didn't say anything until after both she and Raphael had cleaned up and were tucking into the food Jeeves had brought up. But first things first. "Your butler laundered my clothes," she said from her cross-legged position on the bed. The cargos and T-shirt from yesterday had been waiting for her, washed *and* ironed.

Raphael raised an eyebrow in front of her, having chosen to sit on the bed, too, one leg on the mattress, the other foot-first on the floor beside it, his injured wing draped gently across the sheets to promote optimal healing. To her pleasure—and she was too achy and frustrated to lie to herself about how he made her feel—he'd asked her to spread a special ointment on the injured section. She knew full well it was a measure of how their relationship had changed that he'd kept her with him while he was injured. No Dmitri tying her to a chair this time. "I highly doubt that," he said now. "Montgomery runs the house—he'd never sully himself washing clothes."

"You know what I mean, Archangel. He's like the house-work fairy—only better!"

"Somehow, the idea of Montgomery as a fairy doesn't have the same effect on me as it appears to have on you."

"Give it time." She bit into her everything-and-more sandwich. "So, Jason's your spy. Or should I say, spymaster?"

"Very good, Guild Hunter." He ate the other half of the sandwich in about three bites. "Though some would say his face makes him too distinctive."

"That tattoo—it had to have hurt." She winced, having been too chicken to get inked herself. Ransom had tried to talk her into one when he'd gotten the band around his arm. Watching the blood being blotted off his skin hadn't inspired her to follow suit . "How long do you think it took?"

"Exactly ten years," Raphael said, watching her with those eyes that seemed to see straight through to her soul.

She shook her head as she finished off the sandwich. "Crazy comes in all forms, I guess."

Raphael held up an apple. "A bite?"

"Tempting me, Archangel?"

"Ah, but you've already fallen, hunter." He used a sharp knife to cut into the fruit and put a slice to her lips, watching her bite off the end with concentrated interest. "Your mouth fascinates me."

The languid heat in her body, ever present around Raphael, seemed to grow, spread, until it was in every part of her, a living, demanding beat. Swallowing her bite of apple, she crawled around the food to kneel in front of him. When he raised the rest of the slice to her lips, she bit down, holding on to his wrist.

Eyes locked, the living warmth of him against her fingertips, it was more erotic than a kiss from another man. Her lips brushed his fingers.

Something hot and male spread across his face, a look that told her very well where he wanted her to put her lips. But what he said was, "Another slice?"

She shook her head with regret. "You have to heal and I need to start running the trace again." Uram couldn't have gone far. Most likely he'd been forced to return to one of his earlier hiding places. Which meant there was a high chance it was in the circuit they'd already mapped out. "This could be our best shot."

Raphael put down the knife and the rest of the apple, tracing her lips with his finger. "Did you hear what Michaela said?"

"That he's all monster?" She shrugged, even as lust snaked around her like a heady perfume. "No surprise after what we saw at that warehouse."

"Would you hunt me, Elena? If I became bloodborn?"

Her heart froze in her chest. "Yes," she said. "But you'll never become a monster." Yet she remembered the knife cutting into her hand, remembered, too, that vampire in Times Square.

A humorless smile. "That's hope, not knowledge." He shook his head. "We're all as susceptible to the lure of power. The blood makes him stronger, harder to defeat."

Cupping his face in her hands, she looked into eyes that had seen thousands of sunrises before she was even a glimmer in the scheme of the universe. "But you have an advantage," she whispered. "You're a little bit human now."

Angel of Blood

They thought he was down.

That was their mistake.

Agony shot through his wing and chest as remnants of Raphael's blue fire attempted to take hold and burrow. Gritting his teeth, he left his hiding place and flew a short distance to a normally inviting public area that had turned murky in the cloudy weather, full of shadowy corners that made it the perfect hunting ground. The glamour served him well, and he tore out the throats of two vagrants before they ever knew they were stalked.

Their blood raced through him like lightning, pushing out the blue fire until it dissipated harmlessly in the air. No longer fighting off an attack, his body focused on repairing torn muscle and cartilage. By the time he bent his head over the fifth throat—the soft, delicate flesh of a young female, his preferred kind of sustenance—he was ready to fly again . . . at least enough to take the mortal hunter out of the equation. Once she was dead, no one would be able to find him.

He smiled and wiped the blood from his mouth with a clean white handkerchief. Yes, warm was best. For a tempting moment, he considered taking another, but knew he didn't have the time. He had to hit before he was expected, while Raphael's defenses were down and the hunter thought herself safe.

After that, he would sink his fangs into Michaela's heart, drink her blood straight from the source. And he'd keep her, he decided. The urge to tear her apart was overwhelming, but he'd fight it. Why kill that which could provide so much exquisite power? Mortals were too weak, but an archangel . . . Ah, he could drink from Michaela for eternity. She'd heal every time.

He wondered if Michaela had told Raphael he'd already fed from her once. He licked his lips. She'd been sweet. Powerful. Piquant. And now she carried a little bit of him within. Yes, an archangel would make the most perfect of refreshments. He'd build her a pretty cage, so she could watch as he played with his other pets—so she'd know that she was the lucky one, the one he'd chosen to sustain him for eons.

But first, he had to break the hunter's neck.

36

Raphael walked out onto the third-floor balcony, Elena's words still vivid in his mind. *You're a little bit human now.*

Lijuan had warned him to kill Elena for that very reason. His reaction to being shot, the pain, the blood, had strengthened his belief that this hunter was dangerous to him. But what if, with the danger, came something else, an immunity to the madness of power, of age? After all, he'd wakened from the Quiet much sooner than he should have.

As he waited for Jason to arrive, he considered who he'd been when he first met Elena. He'd torn into her mind, terrorizing her without the least care. Could he do so again? Yes, he thought, having no illusions as to his natural goodness. He was fully capable of doing the same again. But whether he'd choose to do it . . . there lay the true question.

Jason entered the balcony from above, landing in a neat way that made him the most perfect of spies. "I expected to see Illium here."

"He's keeping watch over Elena." Raphael would've preferred to give her a vampiric driver as well, but another vampire that close would hamper her ability to pick up Uram's trail. So she was driving herself, with Illium flying above. Raphael was housebound by his angelfire-scored wing—it was healing at a rapid pace, and he could still fly, but to do so would strain the injury and he needed to be in top condition for when Uram rose again.

Elena had been gone for most of the day, calling him with updates as she cleared one section of Manhattan after another. It was strange to realize that despite having a myriad of other matters on his plate, he . . . missed her. She'd become important to him, this mortal with the spirit of a warrior. "Now, tell me."

"It's as you thought," Jason said. "Lijuan wakes the dead."

Raphael felt the biting freshness of the water-tinged breeze coming off the river, and wondered if Lijuan would be as she was if she hadn't killed the human who'd threatened to make her a little bit mortal. "Are you certain?"

"I saw her raise them."

"Do they live?" He turned to face the other angel.

Deep revulsion whispered in the depths of Jason's eyes. "I wouldn't call it life, but there is some spark within, some glimmer of the person they once were."

This was worse than anything Raphael had thought. "Not puppets as we believed?"

"They are that, but they're also more. Abominations that walk, see, hear but never talk. Their silence is drowned out by the screams in their eyes. They know what they are."

Even an archangel's soul could feel the chill hand of horror. "How long can she maintain them?"

"Of the reborn I saw, the oldest was a year old. He was starting to become senile, that spark long gone." A pause, and then the usually temperate angel said, "It's a mercy when that part of their soul dies."

"And Lijuan has complete control over these reborn?"

"Yes. For now, she plays with them as one would with a new toy. But there may come a time when she turns them into an army."

That cold hand closed around his heart. For if the reborn marched on the living, civilization would fall as terror overtook the world. "Those she wakes—are they the newly dead?"

"No," was the disturbing answer. "Those are easier, but she's begun on the older dead—even those that have . . . rotted. She's somehow able to clothe them in flesh." Jason paused.

"What is it?"

"It's rumored their new flesh comes from consuming the bodies of the more recently dead, the ones Lijuan does not wish to reawaken, and I know they must then drink blood to survive." Jason's voice dropped even lower. "There are also whispers that she gains something from the rebirths, somehow absorbs power."

A bloodborn of another sort, Raphael thought, knowing that no hunter had been born—human, vampire, or angel—who could destroy Lijuan should that prove true. "Have your men maintain watch." Jason was the perfect spy, but as Elena had guessed, he was an even better spymaster. "We must know if she begins large-scale rebirths." The Cadre of Ten could do little while Lijuan played in her own lands. More, most of the members would choose to do little. They each had their own games, their own perversions. Raphael couldn't judge them—he'd countenance no interference in his domain, either.

Elena saw a fragment of humanity in him. But was he human enough to save himself from becoming another Lijuan? "Go. Rest. We'll talk more later."

Jason dropped off the balcony before rising in a steep climb, his wings visible until he rose up above the cloud layer. It was why the angel much preferred the night.

Dmitri.

Sire. The response was close. The vampire entered the balcony a few moments later, having just returned from their healers. "Venom reports that the cleanup at and around Jeffrey Deveraux's office, as well as at the museum, was completed earlier this afternoon. Geraldine is dead."

Raphael's first thought was of Elena—she'd be saddened

at the death, though the woman had been all but a stranger. "What of the survivor we found at the warehouse?"

"I was able to trace her identity. Her name is Holly Chang, age twenty-three." Dmitri folded his hands behind his back. "She doesn't carry the mutant variant of the toxin, but she does carry something."

Raphael remembered his conversation with Elena. "Does she need to die?"

"Not at this stage. She's not contagious—and we need to discover the truth of whatever it is Uram did to her."

"Is she human still?"

Dmitri paused, frowned. "No one is certain what she is—she needs blood, but not as much as a vampire, and she does gain some energy from food. She may be the result of an aborted attempt at conversion."

"Without the proper procedure and with the mutant strain in Uram's blood, it should have been impossible."

"The healers and doctors think she may simply have been unlucky enough to be one of those who are easily Made—but now that she's been partially transformed, an attempt at full conversion may kill her." There was a long-buried edge in Dmitri's voice. Like Holly Chang, Dmitri had been Made against his will.

All because Isis had known Raphael's weakness—that he had a heart. More, she'd known that Dmitri was the descendant of a mortal Raphael had once called friend. So she'd stolen Dmitri's mortality . . . and made Raphael watch. That had been almost a thousand years ago. And Raphael had thought his heart dead for most of them.

Before Elena began to matter.

"Be easy, Dmitri," he said now. "We won't abuse her, but we must monitor her progress." If she carried the taint of the bloodborn, she had to die.

Dmitri nodded. "I've got her under twenty-four-hour watch." Another pause. "If I may, sire."

"Since when do you ask for permission?"

The vampire's smile didn't reach his eyes. "Elena makes

you vulnerable. I don't know how, but she does." His eyes went to the injured wing. "You're healing at a slower rate."

"Perhaps an immortal needs a vulnerability," Raphael said, thinking once more of Lijuan's "evolution."

"I—" A cell phone rang.

Raphael nodded at Dmitri to go ahead and answer, readying himself to take off. Dmitri's raised hand stopped him. "It's the Guild Director."

Raphael took the phone. "Director."

"I don't know what the hell you've got Ellie into but I have a feeling it has to do with the girls disappearing around town." Her dislike of him was a taut thread that vibrated with pure anger.

"Elena is lucky to have you for a friend."

"If anything happens to her, I don't care who you are, I'll shoot you myself." Worry mingled with the violent anger to turn her voice harsh.

Had it been anyone but Sara making the threat, Raphael would've meted out swift punishment—perceived weakness in an archangel could lead to death for millions. But he'd never been a hypocrite. He'd done unconscionable things in the Quiet, crossed an inviolable line when he forced this woman to betray one of her deepest loyalties. The scales were not close to even. "Do you have something to share, Director?"

"Five bodies were just found in Battery Park, all drained of blood. They were hidden very well."

Uram had acted fast to replenish his energy. "Have the authorities been alerted?"

"Sorry, couldn't stop it," Sara said, telling him she had her finger very much on the pulse of the city. "But the bodies are in transit in morgue vans—I'm guessing you have to make them disappear. Don't kill the attendants when you do it."

"That won't be necessary." Sometime after his two-hundredth birthday, Venom had gained the power to entrance humans, much as a cobra did its prey—something Raphael was sure Elena would be aghast to discover. The vampire used it rarely as Neha would *not* be pleased to realize she'd lost so valuable an asset. However, it would come in useful today—none of Uram's victims could be allowed to be put under the microscope. Holly might be the only survivor, but that didn't mean Uram wasn't forcing the others to drink his toxic blood . . . or worse. "Thank you for the information."

"Don't thank me. Just keep Ellie safe from whatever monster you've let loose."

Yes, Uram was a monster. *With a monster's strength.* Raphael's heart suddenly sped to a killing beat, though the air was still, the winds silent. "Give Dmitri the details." Handing back the phone, he took off from the balcony. His wing ached but he pushed onward, attempting to contact Illium as he flew.

A dull silence was his only answer—not the blankness of death, but something close. He got a little more when he tried Elena. Pain and nausea and anger.

He arrowed a thought toward Dmitri. *Forget the bodies for now. Find Elena.*

I'm contacting my men.

Jason. The black-winged angel was a master at coordinating the wings of angels under Raphael's command. *Locate Illium. He's down.*

I'm on my way. I'll brief the wings en route.

Raphael flew harder, cursing his own stupidity. Uram didn't need to rest to heal, not when he could hasten the process through blood. Another advantage of the bloodborn, another thing that made them feel as if they'd made the right choice. At this point, Uram would believe himself sane—he'd begun to think, to make decisions, but his personality was warped on the deepest level, his brain swimming in the toxin.

The worst thing, Raphael thought as he pushed himself to reach Elena, was that such devolution didn't happen overnight. Uram's servants had to have known but, unlike Raphael's powerful Seven, the other archangel had kept no one strong nearby. No one but Michaela. Raphael's mouth twisted—he was sure the woman who'd once been called the Queen of Constantinople had helped her lover evade the protocols set in place to prevent exactly this type of thing. Perhaps she'd wanted Uram dead, but more likely, she'd wanted to see what would happen, ascertain if the rest of the Cadre was lying to her.

He reached the part of Manhattan directly across from Castle Point, the spot where Elena had last checked in. "I have a good feeling about this," she'd said. "The scent's been diffused by the moisture in the air, but I'm going to keep circling until I hit a stronger concentration."

"I'll send more angels your way."

"No, don't pull them off the grid searches yet. This could be a trick. I'll get Illium to contact you if I think I have a bead on him."

Elena had obviously been far closer to the Angel of Blood than she'd believed.

As he flew over the area, looking for her car, his eyes—sharp, like a raptor's—found Illium instead. The angel's blue wings stood out even as he lay half-submerged beneath a pier. Diving, Raphael ignored the onlookers who'd begun to gather on the pier as well as the rescue boat powering Illium's way. Several humans had actually jumped in and were helping to keep Illium's face out of the water, though they'd been unable to lift him given the weight of his waterlogged wings. They scattered at Raphael's approach.

Scooping the unconscious angel out of the water, he rose to the sound of camera shutters and cries of wonder mixed with sorrow. Illium had become well-known in the city since his arrival from duties at the Refuge, his blue wings distinctive, his personality infectious. They thought him dead, forgetting that he was immortal.

Uram *could* have killed Illium, but he'd chosen the faster option and disabled, clearing the way to his real target. *Illium, wake.* Raphael held position high above the cloud layer, Illium's shattered body cradled in his arms. The other angel's wings were torn, his bones broken from the high-velocity impact with the water. Bruises and cuts marked his skin where he'd probably hit something in the river. He'd lost an eye.

It would all heal. That didn't mean it wouldn't hurt. But his flamboyance aside, Illium was a soldier, a fighter. Which was why Raphael didn't let him rest. Rather, he focused his mental abilities and slapped the angel awake from within his very mind. Illium came to with a gasp. But no scream.

A single perfect eye opened. "Bastard was waiting in the clouds," he whispered, not wasting time with unnecessary apologies. "Glamour. Ellie . . ." He shuddered, fighting his body's need to go into a healing sleep. "I think she saw me go down. C-c-close. He looked healed . . . but was weak." The last word was almost soundless as his body literally kicked him into the deep comalike state from which no one and nothing would be able to wake him for at least a week.

Though he was far younger than Raphael, he might just be old enough to enter *anshara* itself. It would allow him to heal much quicker, dampening the agony and rebuilding his body before he woke. Otherwise, once the coma broke, he'd be in as much pain as any other being. With so many broken bones, it would be excruciating.

Raphael knew that too well. His mother's last words to him had been said as he lay bleeding on the ground, his wings shredded so badly he'd had no chance to slow his descent. He'd hit the earth at a velocity that would've torn a mortal to pieces. His body hadn't survived too well either. He'd lost pieces. Young as he'd been, it had taken years for everything to fully re-form. Those in *anshara* healed exponentially faster. But there was no magic cure.

Not unless you were a bloodborn angel bloated with toxin.

Jason's black wings appeared through the clouds. He held out his arms, face drawn. "I'll take him."

Raphael handed over Illium's body. "The rest of the wing?"

"I told them to search for the hunter."

"Get Illium to a healer." He dove back down to the pier, pulling glamour around himself before he came into view. What Illium had fought to tell him was very important. If Uram hadn't healed on all levels, then he wouldn't have been able to fly far with Elena's body weighing him down.

Live, Elena, he said, willing her to fight, to break out of the darkness that cloaked her mind in a suffocating prison. *Live. I have not given you permission to die.*

Nothing. Silence. Such silence as he'd never before known.

Live, Elena. A warrior does not lie down for the enemy. Live!

37

"Be quiet," Elena murmured, pulled out of blissful sleep by an arrogant voice that insisted she get up. "I wanna sleep."

"You dare give me orders, mortal?" Ice-cold water splashed across her face, snapping her awake to a nightmare.

At first, she couldn't quite assimilate what it was that she was seeing. Her mind simply refused to put the pieces together. And there were *so many* pieces. Torn, distorted, impossible pieces. Her stomach twisted, the nausea from the head injury she'd sustained when Uram smashed her face into the dash, merging with the horror of the here and now.

She fought it, refusing to reward the monster with her terror. But it was hard. They'd all been wrong—Sara, Ransom, even Raphael. Uram hadn't taken fifteen victims. He'd taken others, people who wouldn't be missed. Rotting limbs, a gleaming rib cage, evidence of his vicious madness littered the room. A room without light, without air. A cell. A crypt. A—

Snap out of it!

It was her hunter sense, the thing that had marked her from birth.

Swallowing her panic, she focused, and realized the room wasn't, in fact, pitch-dark. Uram had blacked out the windows but some light—too sharp, too white to be natural, which meant she'd been out long enough for night to fall—seeped in around the edges. It was that light that had allowed her to see the sickening truth of the room. Torn bodies thrown about like so much garbage. But not all were in pieces. Against the opposite wall, chains locked around his wrists, she saw the withered body of someone who'd once been human.

Then that dried-out husk blinked and she realized he was still alive. "Jesus!" It came out before she could stop herself.

The monster in front of her, the thing that wore the shell of an archangel, followed her gaze. "I see you've made Robert's acquaintance. He was a loyal one, followed me across the oceans without complaint. Did you not, Bobby?"

Elena watched the cruel humor on Uram's face and realized she'd never understood true evil until this moment. Robert was a vampire, that much was clear. No human that desiccated would still be alive—it looked as if the vampire had lost every ounce of moisture in him but for his large, glistening eyes. Eyes that pleaded with her for deliverance.

Uram turned back to her, his own eyes—a vivid, *beautiful* green—dancing with laughter. "He thought he was special because I took him with me. Unfortunately, I forgot about him for a while." That power-filled gaze became angry, tinged with red. The sparkling green was suddenly putrid.

Elena stayed very, very still in the corner where he'd dumped her, wondering if he'd thought to take her weapons. She couldn't feel anything on her body but maybe he'd missed one or two—like the ice pick–thin knife in her hair, or the flat blade that slid into a sheath built into her shoe. She flexed her toes and felt the reassuring firmness of her boots. Ransom had given her the boots as a gag gift—she'd never loved the idiot more than she did at that moment.

Uram's eyes bored into her. "But my loyal Bobby did come in useful"—back to Robert—"didn't you? He made a most appreciative audience for my little games."

Elena saw the way the vampire's hands curled in the chains, the way his wasted body flinched, and felt her fury ignite. Uram had to know what he was doing—vampires were almost immortal, but they needed blood to truly survive. By not allowing him to feed, he'd effectively caused Robert's body to eat itself. The vampire would never actually die, not of starvation. But his every breath had to be agony by now. And if this went on much longer . . .

Elenas thoughts filled with the one and only case of vampiric starvation she'd ever encountered. It had been in a textbook she'd studied during her final year at Guild Academy. That vampire—S. Matheson—had been caught in a family feud involving his sire. Someone had locked him in a concrete coffin and buried him in the foundations of a building under construction.

He'd been found ten years later.

Alive.

If you could call it that. The contractor who'd unwittingly smashed open the coffin thought he'd found a skeleton, and called the authorities. The M.E. was excited by the prospect of mummified remains. He arrived at the site with a small crime scene crew and they began shooting photos, taking measurements as the workmen watched. Then one of the crime scene techs cut her finger while turning the head of the skeleton and before she knew it, she'd lost the finger, the bone sliced clean in half by one razor-sharp fang.

The paramedics had been called. S. Matheson's body had regenerated under the constant flow of transfusions. But his brain had undergone some kind of an irreversible metamorphosis. S. Matheson didn't speak, didn't do anything but smile like a fool and wait for someone to come too close. Three doctors lost parts of their bodies to the flesh eater before S. Matheson disappeared without a trace. The general consensus was that the angels had taken care of him. Not good for business to have a vampire who ate people.

Robert hadn't reached that stage yet. There was still something in those eyes, something that felt and understood humanity. She watched as Uram stalked to the vampire, blocking Elena's view of his actions. Then Robert made an awful sound, and she barely stopped herself from screaming at Uram. Instead, she took the opportunity to slide her foot closer. Closer.

Uram turned, a slight smile on his lips. "What do you think of my work?"

She'd girded herself, knowing he'd done something monstrous. But nothing could've prepared her for the sight that met her—pity choked her throat, sent rage rocketing through her. Uram had taken Robert's eyes. Now, holding her gaze, Uram took the slippery orbs to his mouth, as if about to bite in. She didn't blink.

"You're a strong one." Chuckling, he threw the orbs to the floor, crushing them beneath the heel of his boot. "No nutrition."

Dismissing a Robert who seemed to have stopped moving, he wiped his hands fastidiously on a handkerchief and came toward her. "You are very quiet, hunter. No heroics to save the poor vampire?" A raised brow that was incongruously regal.

"He's only another bloodsucker," she said, sick to her stomach. "I was hoping he'd keep you distracted long enough that I could escape."

He smiled and the chill that crept up her spine felt like the crawling of a thousand spidery fingers. Then, still without speaking, he crouched down, put his hand on her ankle. Smiled wider. And twisted. The snap of the bone sent pain shrieking through her, so hot and vicious that she screamed.

Raphael!

She felt her vision blur as the smothering wings of unconsciousness closed around her once more. But something caught her mind before it could spiral down into darkness. *Tell me where you are, Elena.*

Sweat curled down the sides of her face, stuck her T-shirt to her back. But she held on to that voice, Raphael's voice, and clawed her way back to full consciousness. Uram was still crouched in front of her, watching her with the well-pleased expression of someone who'd cornered his prey. "You smell like acid," she whispered. "Jagged, bright, distinctive."

His expression changed, became curious in an almost childish way. But it was the most distorted version of a child's curiosity she'd ever seen. "What about Bobby?" Another smile even as his eyes turned red again. "He wants to know."

She swallowed. *Water,* she said inside her mind, hoping like hell that Raphael was listening. *I can smell water.* "Bobby," she whispered. "Bobby smells like dust and earth and death." *And there's a noise.* She concentrated. *Cutting, chopping, a steady rhythm. I should know what it is.*

Uram stroked a strand of hair off her face. She waited for him to snap her neck, but he drew back his hand a moment later. Even as relief whispered through her, she realized he was feeding on her terror, torturing her with uncertainty. The bastard was keeping her live for his pleasure . . . or was he?

"Why am I alive?" she asked him.

Be quiet, Elena.

Oh, shush. I'm cranky when I'm hurt.

Uram smiled again, his hand squeezing her ankle. The pain almost threw her into the void, but he knew exactly when to relax the pressure. "Because you're his weakness. It made more sense not to kill you once I thought about it."

It's a trap. Don't you dare let him hurt you.

I will deal with Uram. Your task is to remain alive.

The order almost made her smile, even in the depths of nightmare. "I'm a toy, nothing more."

"Of course." Releasing her ankle, Uram waved off her words.

His ready agreement shook her more than she liked. But hey, given her current projected life span, she figured she had the right to love idiotically. *Love.* Oh, hell. "If I'm so forget-table, what's my value as a hostage?"

"Because, hunter," he said with no hint of fang, as smooth as a vampire who'd been around for a few hundred years, "Raphael is possessive about his toys."

Icicles grew in her heart at the certainty in that tone. "You sound very sure."

"In the time of beauty, of kings and queens, we were in the same court for a century." He tilted his head. "You did not know?"

"Toy, remember." She gave him a close-lipped smile, figuring her real feelings would do for now. "He doesn't talk to me much."

"Raphael has never been a talker, not like Charisemnon." He made a moue of distaste. "That one talks forever and says nothing. I've wished a thousand times that I could crush his voice box. Perhaps I'll get the chance now." He frowned, pushing aside the femur near his foot. "The smell in here is atrocious." Anger filmed his eyes.

She decided not to point out that he'd caused the problem. "You were telling me about Raphael's toys," she said, sensing that topic would keep her alive longer than if he became enraged by the charnel house odor of the place.

His attention returned to her, and, for the first time, she noticed the strange striations on his skin, fine lines of white that ran down his face. It was almost as if she were seeing blood vessels, but they were the wrong color—filled with something other than blood.

"We had our pick of slaves at court," he told her, his voice so deep and true that she could understand how so many had once fallen under his spell. And might yet again if he wasn't stopped. "They were there for our pleasure and we used them at will."

Her throat tightened at the sheer disregard in his voice. "Humans?"

"Too weak for the most part, not lovely enough. No, our slaves were the vampires—then, as now, it was their duty to worship us."

That wasn't quite what it said in the Contract, but Elena played along. "So your slaves were the ones you Made?"

"No, that would have been tedious. They were traded. Oh, you feel sorry for them." He laughed and it wasn't an ugly sound. "They begged to come to our beds. There were fights in the harems if one was chosen over the other."

She expected he was telling the truth. "A win-win situation."

"There were favorites—"

She was only half listening, trying with all her might to figure out where they were. That whipping, cutting sound had faded into silence, but she could hear something else. Cars. Near a road and water. Uram's injured wing looked fine, but from the way it dragged on the floor, she had a feeling it wasn't yet fully functional. So they had to be close to where he'd attacked Illium. God, she hoped the blue-winged angel was okay—the way he'd hit the water would've torn a human apart.

Can't be sure, but I think we're on the banks of the Hudson, close to where Illium went down, she thought to Raphael, hoping like hell that he was somehow blocking Uram from intruding into her mind, *in a room with blackened windows. The smell! It's disgusting in here. Look for an abandoned building, warehouse, boathouse—or the neighbors would've called the authorities by now.*

Unless, she thought, these corpses were the neighbors. But if that were the case, someone would've reported at least one of them missing. She was focusing so hard that she made a mistake. Her eyes wandered. A hard squeeze of her ankle and suddenly pain was all she was, every one of her nerve endings on fire. This time, she couldn't fight the rising blackness, couldn't hold on to the world.

If you die, Guild Hunter, I will make you a vampire.

She scowled inwardly and fought, fought so damn hard. *I don't want to drink blood. And you can't Make me if I'm dead.* It felt like swimming through syrup, but finally, she broke back through the surface of consciousness . . . to promptly lean over and expel the contents of her stomach in a bilious flood. When she finished, wiping her mouth with the back of her hand and raising her head with deliberate slowness, she found that Uram hadn't changed position.

"You weren't paying attention," he said in the most reasonable of tones.

She caught something with her peripheral vision. "I'm sorry. It hurts." *I can see a hard hat. The walls aren't finished. Look for construction.* And that pile—her weapons! Almost within touching distance.

"I do hope Raphael gets here soon." A disappointed frown. "You're not going to last much longer."

"Are you certain he'll come?"

"Oh, yes. The slaves? He used to fight with us if we put a bruise on the one he'd claimed as his." Uram obviously found that amusing. "Can you imagine? He cared."

The line between monster and not was suddenly far clearer than she'd ever believed. Raphael had somehow remained on one side, Uram on the other. "That was a long time ago," she replied. "He's changed."

Uram paused, as if thinking. "Yes. Maybe he won't come. Maybe I'll leave you here." His eyes laughed. "Perhaps I'll tie you to Bobby, let him feed. What do you say, Bobby?" he called out.

The withered thing on the other side of the room seemed to whisper a response. Elena didn't hear it but Uram apparently did. It made him laugh so hard that he rocked back on his heels. "I'm delighted to see that you haven't lost your sense of humor," he said, chuckling. "I think for that alone, I'll give you what you want. I'll put you to the mortal's breast and let you suckle like a babe."

The horrifying image made Elena's anger turn cold, hard, dangerous. She had no problem with feeding a dying vampire— hell, she was a human being, not a sadistic freak like Uram. But she sure as hell wasn't going to be tortured to death by a mind Uram had already broken. Using the archangel's momentary lapse in concentration, she went to reach for the knife in her boot. Her ankle screamed at the small movement but that wasn't what stopped her.

The scent of wind, of rain, of the sea. *Where are you in the room?*

*Opposite the windows, with Uram in front of me. There's
a vampire—starved—on the wall across and to the left of me,
next to the window. His name is Robert.*

His life matters little. He enjoys torturing children.

Then the wall was just gone, sheared away as if by some
violent wind. She saw the crackling edge of blue flame ring
the hole, heard Uram's shout of triumph. Rising to his feet,
the archangel stared at her. "You've served your purpose,
brought him here though he's injured—easy prey." He drew
back a hand and she saw the red fire in it.

If it touched her, she'd die between one heartbeat and the
next.

So she smirked. "If you're that confident, kill me afterward. Unless you don't think you'll be around for it."

He kicked at her shattered ankle, and the pain exploded
over her until her mind simply shut down.

Raphael hit Uram in the back with a bolt of pure energy
as the bloodborn angel, lost in his madness, went to kick Elena a second time. The hit had the intended effect. Screaming
in rage, Uram turned, throwing the red angelfire in his hand
at Raphael and a second bolt at the ceiling, destroying it to
rise into the open air.

Raphael knew Elena was under the rubble, could still feel
the essence of her life though her mind was cloaked in blackness. *Live,* he ordered again, as he rose to fight an evil that
couldn't be allowed to run unchecked. He was aware of people screaming and running below as fireballs smashed into
nearby buildings, bringing things crashing to earth. A car
screeched to a halt, then another, then another, all the drivers
looking skyward.

Raphael flew under a bolt, returned the volley, and had the
satisfaction of singeing Uram. Bleeding from a cut on his
face, the other archangel threw back a firestorm generated by
the life energy of stolen blood, and intensified by the toxin

that had become fused into his very cells. Once an angel turned to blood, there was no going back.

"After you are dust," Uram taunted, flying at Raphael with hands blazing fire, "the city will be mine!"

Raphael evaded the attack but knew he'd moved a fraction too slow even before he felt the agony of angelfire crawling over his wings.

38

He shot upward, into the clouds, higher than angels were meant to go, until his head ached and the fire died for lack of oxygen. Then he plummeted, using his momentum to launch angelfire at Uram's body. The Angel of Blood dodged all bolts but one, taking the hit on his thigh.

Raphael could feel his wings straining as the wounds—both new and old—started to hurt. It wasn't disabling, not yet. But it would be soon. Uram had gotten enough angelfire onto him that pieces of it had stuck. Those pieces would continue to eat through his flesh until they were dug out. He had less than ten minutes before his wings weakened to the point that he couldn't fly. Then he felt a tendon snap and remembered.

He was a little bit human now.

So be it. He'd rather die a little human, he thought with strange clarity, than become a monster. *Elena! Live!* He continued to send that order even as his own strength waned and more and more of Uram's bolts seared his skin, his wings. *You must live.* She had to survive. Her spirit burned too bright to be so easily snuffed out.

And he realized . . . that fragile, mortal life wasn't just im-

portant to him. It was *more* important than his own. *Wake,
Guild Hunter!*

He finally got close enough to Uram to chance another
blow, but his power reserves were running low. Below him,
the city was a spreading darkness as they both sucked power
from the electricity grid, from anything they could. Cars
stalled and died, batteries went flat, pylons overloaded. Still
Raphael kept pulling. But he knew his body was going to give
out long before the available power did.

He hit Uram's wing and it wasn't enough. The Angel of
Blood had glutted himself on his kills and, even weakened,
his wing healed faster than an ordinary angel's, faster than
even an archangel's. Uram laughed and created another ball
of angelfire. But this one he shot toward the half-destroyed
apartment.

Elena!

Raphael intercepted the blast, taking the hit on his shoulder. Pain seared through his body as the fire touched bone
and began eating its way through. Blinking away the sweat
falling into his eyes, he kept fighting, hovering above the
apartment so Uram couldn't destroy it.

"You fool," Uram taunted. "You'd give up immortality for
a mere woman?"

Raphael answered by staying where he was, deflecting the
angelfire Uram shot his way with unrelenting force. He could
sense his men coming closer. He warned them to stay out of
range. Only an archangel could withstand angelfire for longer
than a few seconds. Then one of Uram's bolts hit his unin-
jured shoulder.

The fire had already eaten through one side to expose the
whiteness of bone. His load-bearing muscles were failing one
by one. But he kept fighting, hitting Uram several times,
vaguely aware that Manhattan was now completely without
power, pitch-black under his feet. Farther out, in Queens, in
the Bronx, lights continued to go out in a slow, dark, wave.

More power lay beyond those areas, but his body was
close to giving out. Filling it with as much energy as he could

contain, until the glow of it blazed from his skin, he readied himself for a final, suicidal clash. If he could make contact with Uram's body, he might be able to burn them both up. A high price to pay, but an archangel turned Angel of Blood could tear the world apart, end civilization itself.

Throwing back just enough angelfire to keep Uram from coming closer, but not enough to drain himself, he watched for a gap in his opponent's defenses, for a single mistake. But when his chance came, it wasn't because Uram made a mistake. No, it came because of a hunter too stubborn to surrender to evil.

Gunshots fired from the open side of the torn apartment building, ripping through the bloodborn angel's wings.

Uram screamed and began to spiral down, shooting angelfire as he fell. Raphael flew toward the tumbling archangel, leading with his hands. As one hand impacted on Uram's chest, he held on to to the bloodborn angel with his other and thrust. His hand went through Uram's rib cage to hit his heart.

"Good-bye, old friend," he said, knowing that nothing of the angel he'd once known remained in this monster. Then he released a final, shocking blast of angelfire. It spread through Uram's body like a fever—the dying archangel's grabbing hands threatened to take Raphael down with him. But Raphael had to live. Because if he didn't, Elena would die.

He wrenched back an instant before Uram exploded in a burst of pure white light, lighting up the whole of Manhattan in a single second-long blast. Then it was over and Uram was not only dead, but erased from the cosmos. Not even dust remained.

Bleeding from wounds that continued to worsen as the angelfire dug in ever deeper, Raphael should have landed. Instead, he beat his barely functional wings upward.

One of Uram's last, desperate bolts had hit the building. Raphael knew Elena had to have been on the very edge of the eight-story structure when she'd shot up at Uram. That edge was now gone, but he could feel Elena's life, feel her dying flame. *Elena, answer me.*

Quiet, peaceful, a hush of sound. Then, *Stay a little human, won't you, Raphael?*

A request that was almost not a sound at all. But it was enough. He followed the mental thread to discover her broken body on the narrow ledge provided by a precariously hanging neon sign. Her back was shattered, her legs twisted in a way that was nothing natural. But she smiled when she saw him. And her hand still held the gun that had saved more lives than anyone would ever know.

He dared not touch her, afraid he'd cause her to slip over the ledge. "You are not to die."

A slow blink. "Bossy." It was a sound bubbled through with blood. *The voice isn't working so good.*

I hear you.

Tell me the secret now, won't you? How do you Make vampires?

He could hear the teasing even in that fading whisper. *Our bodies produce a toxin that needs to be purged at regular intervals. The older we are, the longer the intervals.*

Uram waited too long.

Yes. We build up an immunity, but only to a point. After that, the toxin begins to bond with our very cells, mutating in the process. However, that base immunity meant an archangel always had a certain level in his blood. Enough. It would be just enough.

The only way to purge the buildup before it goes critical is by transfer to a living human. Angelic history told of a time when they'd given in to despair at the loss of so many mortal lives, and tried to purge it into animals. The resulting carnage had been such that even Lijuan would not talk of it. *We know we get something back from the transfer, something that keeps the toxin stable, but even after all these millennia, we know not what.*

But . . . A pause, as if she was gathering her strength, determined to have her curiosity satisfied. *The tests? Compatibility?*

He'd answer every question, betray every secret, if it would hold her here. *Only some are born with the ability to survive the toxin, to use it as fuel for the transition from mortal to vampire. The others die.* And despite their cruelty, despite the lack of compassion engendered by age, no immortal wanted to bear the stain of that much slaughter. To promise life and give only death was a step too far into the abyss. *Before the tests, perhaps one in ten made it through.*

Ah . . . Not even a whisper now.

His canines elongated, and a strange, beautiful, golden taste filled his mouth as he felt a tear slide down his face. He was an archangel. He had not cried in over a thousand years. *So now you know—that's why so many morons get Made.*

Weak laughter in his head. *I guess a dying woman can be stupid if she wants. I'm crazy about you, Archangel. You scare the shit out of me at times, but I want to dance with you anyway.*

His heart stopped beating when her voice faded, and he leaned forward, his mouth overwhelmed by the taste of beauty, of life. "I won't let you die. I had your blood tested. You're compatible."

Her lashes struggled to open, failed. But her mental voice, though weak, was adamant. *I don't want to be a vampire. Bloodsucking's not my thing.*

"You must live." And then he kissed her, feeding that golden taste, that intoxicating blend, into her mouth. *You must live.*

That was when the sign gave away, tearing loose from the building and plunging to the ground in a shattering crash. Elena didn't fall alone, gathered as she was in Raphael's arms, his mouth fused with hers. They fell together, his wings close to destroyed, his soul melded to that of a mortal.

If this is death, Guild Hunter, he thought to his mortal as angelfire scored through his bones and touched his heart, *then I will see you on the other side.*

Sara stared upward, tears rolling down her cheeks. The Archangel of New York was falling, and in his arms, he carried a body that streamed bright near white hair. "Ellie, no, you can't fucking do this," she whispered, so angry she could hardly form words. She'd run down here with a crossbow the second things had started turning to shit, knowing Ellie would need her. Ransom had turned up minutes later, gun in hand. But the fight had taken place too far above for either of them to help.

And now Raphael fell and there was nothing they could do.

It was like she was seeing things in slow motion, watching as her best friend lay broken in an archangel's arms, those magnificent wings shredded beyond redemption. There was no time to prepare a soft landing, the wreckage below them full of jagged shards that would tear and destroy—shattered brick, torn-off pipe, even a broken chopper, its blades bent by the avalanche of debris. Sharp edges. Everywhere she looked, the edges were too sharp. Too deadly.

Sara sobbed in Ransom's rigid hold, crying for both of them because she knew Ransom would choose anger rather than the pain of loss. Her eyes blurred, and for a second, she thought she was imagining the wings filling her vision. They surrounded Raphael, soft, dark shadows in the pitch blackness of the night that had fallen over Manhattan.

"They're rising!" She jerked at Ransom's coat, stared. "They're rising!" Raphael and Elena were lost in the mass of wings but Sara didn't care. All that mattered was that they hadn't fallen to earth, hadn't fractured into a thousand pieces as she watched, helpless. "Ellie's alive."

Ransom didn't dispute her claim, though they both knew Ellie's broken body spoke of injuries that could never be repaired. He just held her and let her pretend everything was okay. At least for a moment longer.

One week later, Sara slammed down the phone in her office and stared across at Ransom while Deacon stood by her side, a solid, immovable presence. Her husband. Her rock. "They're refusing to release any information on either Raphael or Ellie."

Ransom's mouth tensed. "Why?"

"Angels don't have to give reasons." Sara's mouth twisted, sorrow so deep and true inside of her that she didn't know how she moved. "That night, we all got a vivid lesson in the fact that archangels can die. Might be Raphael's gone and we're dealing with new management."

"They have no right to keep her from us!" Losing the cool he'd retained till then, Ransom brought a fisted hand down on the chair arm. "We're her family." He froze. "Did they give Ellie up to that bastard?"

Sara shook her head. "Jeffrey's been completely stonewalled. At least my calls get answered."

"Who does the answering?"

"Dmitri."

Ransom got up and began to pace, as if unable to sit still. "He's a vampire."

"I don't know what the hell is going on." It certainly seemed as if the vampire, not another angel, was in charge. Deacon had used his sources—and he knew some very unusual people—to come up with the same answer. Dmitri was running the show, in effect, running Manhattan.

"This is probably useless information," she continued, "but the latest word is that another one of the archangels, Michaela, left the city soon after Uram was killed." Everyone knew which archangel had died—it was the biggest news story of the millennium, even with the angels refusing to offer even a crumb of information.

"Three archangels in one city?" Ransom shook his head. "That's not coincidence. Deacon?"

"You're right. But that just raises more questions, answers none."

Trust Deacon to cut to the heart of it. So apparently calm. But she sensed his fury in the rigidity of his muscles. Her husband chose his friends with care—Ellie was definitely one of them. Touching him lightly on the thigh even as he put one big hand on her shoulder, she said, "There are rumors Archangel Tower's closed itself off even from other angels."

Ransom thrust a hand through his unbound hair, hair that Elena had taken such delight in teasing him over. Now it lay uncared for around his shoulders. "I think you're right—it sounds like Raphael's dead and they're scrambling to find a replacement."

Still at her desk, Sara stared out into the lights of a city that remained half black. So many of the power relays and wires had been destroyed in the archangel-to-archangel fight that the repair job was going to take months. "But why won't they give us Ellie?" That, Sara couldn't understand. "She's mortal. She's not theirs." *Sara* would take care of her best friend, with all the honor and love in her heart.

Ransom turned to shoot her a probing look. "You in shape?"

She understood in a split second. "Good enough to sneak into the damn Tower."

"You'll go in wired," Deacon said, proving once again that she'd seriously lucked out in the marriage stakes. "Both of you. Anything goes wrong, I'll be waiting with an extraction team. Who's here right now?"

Sara thought rapidly. "Kenji's in the Cellars. So is Rose. Just downtime, so they can come out."

"Call them up. I'll get the wire kit."

An hour later, she found herself crouching beside Ransom in the gardens around the heavily guarded Tower. Incoming and outgoing traffic in the area surrounding it was now so restricted that no one had managed to get this close since the night the city went dark. Sara saw a possible entry point, signaled the information to Ransom, and moved. They were inside the unlit expanse of the ground floor a few seconds later.

"I expected you days ago," a smooth voice said from somewhere on the other side of the room. Soft light filled the lobby, as if a switch had been thrown.

Sara recognized that voice at once. "Dmitri."

A small nod. "At your service." His gaze shifted. "Ransom, I presume."

"Cut the crap." Ransom lifted a crossbow loaded with

some *very* illegal control chip–embedded bolts, Sara's current weapon of choice.

"I wouldn't," Dmitri said evenly. "You'd be overwhelmed by my men within seconds, and I'd be in a much worse mood."

Putting her hand on Ransom's arm, Sara met Dmitri's eyes. "We've got no fight with you—we just want to know about Ellie."

The vampire straightened. "Follow me. Leave the crossbows on the floor. You're safe here."

Maybe it was stupid but they decided to trust him, both of them. The vampire got into an elevator. As they went to enter, Sara realized Ellie would probably haunt her if she put herself in harm's way and deprived Zoe of a mother, Deacon of a wife. But Ellie was family, too. Jaw set, she got into the elevator.

The wire—actually a high-tech transmitter nestled inside her ear, with backups in her wristwatch and collar—vibrated just a fraction. Enough to tell her that Deacon had her, that he was with her. The tightness in her stomach loosened. *You can be mad with us later, Ellie. After we know you're okay. We love you too much not to do this.*

Dmitri said nothing as they shot skyward, exiting the elevator on a floor that gleamed black in every direction. Still silent, their guide led them into a small room and closed the door, enclosing them in darkness but for the glittering spread of the city outside. Even at half strength, Manhattan shone diamond bright. "What I tell you tonight can't leave this room. Do you understand?"

Ransom bristled but let Sara answer. "All we care about is what you've done with Ellie." Sara couldn't say "body." Until she saw Ellie dead with her own eyes, she couldn't—*wouldn't*—believe.

"You're her family." Dmitri's eyes met hers. "Chosen, not born."

"Yes." Sara saw a depth of understanding in the vampire's gaze that she hadn't expected. The old ones—and Dmitri was very old—seemed to forget they'd once been human, with human dreams and fears. "We need to see her." Even then, part of her, a stubborn, irrational part, hoped for a miracle.

"You can't," Dmitri said, then raised a hand when Ransom snapped out a curse. "But this I can tell you—she lives. Perhaps not as she would've wished, but she lives."

Sara was so relieved, she almost didn't hear the last sentence. Ransom was the first to understand. "Aw, Jesus. Ellie's going to be *so* pissed if you've turned her into a vamp."

Dmitri raised an eyebrow. "You won't castigate us for taking the choice from her?"

Sara answered for both of them. "We're selfish. We want her to live." Her throat was so thick with emotion, she had to concentrate to form the next word. "When . . . ?"

"The recovery will be slow. Her back was broken, most of her bones shattered," the vampire said with a blunt honesty that was far easier to hear than vague platitudes. "There are those who would use that vulnerability to harm her. Until she can defend herself, we protect her."

"Even from us?" Ransom asked, pain held so fiercely to his heart that Sara hurt for him. "That what Ellie wants?"

"She's in a coma," Dmitri told them. "I'm making the decision and I'd rather be too cautious than chance her life."

Sara sucked in a breath but nodded. "I'd do the same. If I pack a bag of her things, will you have it taken to her? For when she wakes." Because Ellie would wake. She was too damn stubborn not to.

Dmitri inclined his head in acquiescence. "Elena is lucky to have such a family."

After making sure the hunters—*all* of them—had left Tower territory, Dmitri returned to the room where they'd held the meeting and walked out onto the high balcony. There was a rustle of feathers and then Jason emerged from the shadows that had cloaked him till then. "You lied."

"A simple misdirection," Dmitri responded, staring out at

the lights of a city still shaken by the death of an archangel. "They're not ready for the truth."

"What will you tell them when she doesn't appear within the next few months?"

"Nothing." His hands clenched on the railing. "Raphael will have healed by then."

A gust of wind swept across the balcony, bringing with it the familiar scents of a city that had been nothing much more than a few ramshackle buildings when Raphael first claimed it as his territory.

"I've never seen an archangel that badly injured," Jason said. "The angelfire ate through his bones far faster than it should have."

Dmitri thought back to the gunshot wound Raphael had sustained from Elena's gun. "He's changed." But whether that change would prove fatal, they'd have to wait and see.

"Some of the Cadre are starting to turn covetous eyes toward Raphael's domain."

Dmitri set his jaw. "We will hold it for him. Until it is certain."

39

Three months later, when Raphael walked in to take his place at a meeting of the Cadre, the gasps of surprise were genuine. Even immortals, it seemed, had written him off. He slid into his chair and placed his hands loosely on the arms. "I hear you're debating how to divide my territory."

Neha was the first to recover. "No, of course not. We were speaking of Uram's successor."

He smiled, let the lie pass. "Of course."

"You did well in halting him," Elijah said.

Charisemnon nodded. "Pity it came to such a public end. For a while, the mortals speculated that he was the cause of the disappearances in your region—how did you turn the tide?"

"I have good men around me." It had apparently been Venom's idea to frame Robert "Bobby" Syles. He'd made the perfect fall guy—and given his sickening predilection toward children, no one had felt any guilt in blackening his name. A few judicial hints, some rumors of Bobby's depraved leanings, and proof of his having entered the United States was all it had taken.

The world, humans, vampires, and angels alike, didn't want

to believe that an archangel had turned murderous. A battle between two archangels was something they could accept— most thought it had been a fight for control of the area, were happy with that understanding. To see Uram as a killer would've been too much, a fundamental shift in the fabric of the universe as they understood it.

Charisemnon humphed while Titus nodded. It was Favashi who spoke next. "We are glad to see you, Raphael."

He thought she might truly mean it. So he gave a small nod. She smiled, her face beautiful in a way that had made kingdoms fall. But he felt nothing, his heart given to a mortal. "So, you are discussing successors?"

"More accurately," Astaad pointed out, "the lack of them. There is one, as we all know, who may soon become an archangel. But he isn't yet."

"And Uram's territory needs guidance now." Michaela's gaze met Raphael's across the circle, a malicious delight in it that he understood too well. But all she said was, "I can undertake some of the work, but I have enough to handle in my own lands."

"Very magnanimous of you, Michaela," Neha murmured with an elegant trace of sarcasm. "Does your landlust know no end?"

Michaela's eyes flashed. "And I suppose you have no interest in it?"

So it began, the rounds of propositions and rebuttals, alliances and oppositions. Only Raphael and Lijuan, sitting next to him, took no part. Instead, Lijuan touched his arm with pale, delicate fingers. "Did you and Uram speak much before he died?"

"No. He was beyond speech."

"A pity." She moved her hand back to the arm of her own chair. "I would've liked to learn more about the subtle effects of long-term exposure to the toxin."

Raphael raised an eyebrow. "Surely you're not considering it?"

A soft laugh hidden in the sounds of the argument going on around them. "No, I value my sanity."

Raphael wondered if Lijuan could truly be called sane anymore. Jason had managed to gain more details of the other archangel's court—half her "courtiers" were the reborn, creatures who followed her commands with unswerving obedience. "I'm happy to hear that. Ending the life of an angel as powerful as Uram was difficult enough. I dare not think about what it would be to have you turn bloodborn."

Lijuan's eyes sparked with eerily girlish mischief. "Oh, such flattery will go to my head." She leaned back in her seat. "I was curious only because Uram seemed to have better control over his impulses than the young ones who turn. Is it not possible that he was right, that if we could traverse the problematic period, we might come out of it with enormous power on the other side?"

"The problematic period, as you put it," he said, watching the byplay between Neha and Titus, sweet poison against granite will, "turns us into killers without compare. Our most recent investigations indicate that, counting his servants, Uram killed close to two hundred people in less than ten days."

"But he was thinking."

"Only of more death." Raphael kept his tone temperate through sheer force of will. That Lijuan was considering this even on a peripheral level was a very bad sign. "Had we given him a year, he would've torn apart thousands, glutting himself each time. That is what makes an angel bloodborn, the inability to stop, to fight the lust for blood and power."

"I killed the last one, did you know? The one the humans call the father of all vampires." She laughed at the idea. "He was highly intelligent, evaded me for years, even ruled a sector."

"He bled the sector dry," Raphael reminded her. "He had no control over his instinct to kill—a puppet of his own desire. Is that what you would call power?"

Lijuan gave him an inscrutable look, a look filled with things such as he'd never seen and never wished to see. "You are a clever one, Raphael. Have no fear, I will not turn. It holds little interest for me now. As you well know."

He didn't apologize. "Only stupidity excuses ignorance."

That made Lijuan giggle again. "Now you are being cruel to the others."

He wondered over that. If the others truly didn't know about Lijuan's evolution, then they were going to get an extremely unpleasant surprise one of these days. "I believe they've reached a consensus."

The others had split Uram's territory to their satisfaction, rearranging the boundaries of their own lands to satisfy their landlust. Raphael let them do so. His territory was already one of the largest, and even more important, one of the most productive and profitable. He had no desire to haggle over land Uram had beaten into submission. Weakness had never interested Raphael.

No, he was drawn to warriors.

Michaela smiled at him again as the meeting ended, lingering behind with Elijah. "It's a pity, is it not, Raphael," she said after the room cleared of all but the three of them, "that your hunter died?"

He didn't say a word, just watched her.

Her smile widened. "She'd outlived her usefulness in any case." She flicked her hand, brushing aside Elena's life as one would a fly. "I was rather disappointed I didn't get to hunt her, but it's as well—I'll be very busy now that I have part of Uram's land to govern along with my own."

Elijah looked at Raphael. "You liked the hunter?"

It was Michaela who answered. "Oh, he was quite possessive over the mortal. He warned me off from hurting her." A deeply vicious smile. "But now she is dead and you must court me. Perhaps I will accept you."

Raphael raised an eyebrow. "You're not the only female angel."

"But I am the most beautiful." Giving him another smile edged with broken glass, she swept out.

Elijah stared after her. "I'm very glad I never dipped in that particular pond."

"You surprise me," Raphael said. "I thought I was the only one."

"I had been with Hannah for over a century by the time Michaela found me." He shrugged. "I'm not her type in any case, as the mortals say."

"Everyone is her type. And no one." The only person Michaela cared about was herself. "Do you think she ever attempted to seduce Lijuan?"

Elijah choked on his laugh. "Careful, old friend. You will give me a heart attack."

Raphael didn't return the laugh. "What is it you want to say, Eli?"

The other archangel's laughter faded. "Lijuan. She raises the dead."

"We can't yet say if the power is good or evil." Though Raphael knew what he believed. "She's the oldest of us all—we have no template to judge her evolution."

"True. But, Raphael"—Elijah paused, sighed—"you're old enough to know that the powers we achieve with age are tied intrinsically to who we are. That Lijuan should manifest an ability associated with death, it tells us a great deal about her."

"What about you?" Raphael asked, keeping secret his own newfound gift. "What has age brought you?"

Elijah's smile was inscrutable. "But those are the secrets we keep." He rose as Raphael did. "The hunter, you truly cared for her?"

"Yes."

The other archangel put his hand on Raphael's shoulder. "Then, I'm sorry." His sympathy seemed honest. "Mortals . . . they burn so bright, but their light goes out too quickly."

"Yes."

* * *

Illium was waiting for him at the Tower. "Sire." As with Dmitri and Venom, it was a title of respect, not truth.

Elena would've questioned him about that had she been here. And she would've worried about her "Bluebell." "How is your healing progressing?"

Flaring out the wing that had borne the worst damage, Illium winced. "It's almost complete." He looked at Raphael's healed body, a body that had been eaten through with an incredible amount of angelfire. "The difference between angel and archangel."

"Is age and experience." Raphael went closer, looked at the wing . . . and laughed for the first time since the night he'd fallen with Elena. "Now I understand your expression."

Illium snorted. "I look like a damned duck." His words weren't far off the mark. The feathers that had grown over the injured section were soft, white, and delicately . . . fluffy. "I hope to hell these baby feathers fall off and get replaced by real ones. They will, won't they?" He sounded worried.

"Do they impede flight?" Having spoken to the healers and medics himself, he knew Illium had been permitted short bursts of flight.

"No. But they're not as efficient." He stared down, swallowed. "Please tell me this is only a stage of healing. I've never had this happen before."

Raphael wondered what Elena would've done in this situation. Probably taken every opportunity to tease. His heart clenched. "They'll shed within the month," he said. "You lost so much of your wing when you hit the pier, including several layers of skin and muscle, that you're effectively regrowing it from the inside out, instead of just replacing your feathers."

Relief whispered through Illium's eyes as he dropped his wing. "Without *anshara* I'd still be lying in bed, unable even to move."

Raphael's mind drifted back to those months when his own body had lain broken. The field had been isolated, his mental abilities young. Only the birds and Caliane had known he was there. "Yes."

"Sire . . . you've yet to punish me for losing Elena that day." Illium's features were drawn, his normally ebullient personality buried beneath the formal words. "I deserve to be censured. I am one of the Seven, one of your most experienced men, and I let her be taken."

Raphael shook his head. "It was no fault of yours." He was the one who'd made the fatal mistake. "I should've known Uram could hasten his recovery through blood."

"Elena," Illium began, then stopped. "No, questions are useless here. Just know that your Seven stand behind you."

Raphael watched the other angel leave via the balcony, then, after a moment's pause, did the same himself. The wind lifted him up, his repaired body still aching but otherwise fine. He'd be back to total strength within a few weeks. Until then, his Seven would ensure his territory remained safe from covetous eyes.

Lijuan and Michaela, likely Charisemnon and Astaad, too, would never understand that kind of loyalty. Perhaps only Elijah and, in this matter, Titus, had any hope of comprehending what the Seven had given him. Dmitri was the oldest, Venom the youngest, but together, the three vampires and four angels had been with him for a remarkable number of centuries, their allegiance unwavering—but that didn't mean they were ciphers. No, his Seven had all fought with him at one time or another, arguing against his decisions even to the point of putting their lives on the line.

Charisemnon had cautioned him about Dmitri more than once. "That vampire has ideas above his station," the archangel had said. "If you're not careful, he'll take your Tower for his own."

And yet Dmitri had held off all challengers for the three months that Raphael lay in a healing coma. The first month, he'd gone so deep that he'd descended below *anshara*. Had Dmitri—or any of the six others—wanted to end his immortal life, they could've struck a deal with another archangel and betrayed his place of rest. Instead, they had protected him; more than that, they had protected his heart.

The young children playing in the New Jersey park looked up with open mouths as he flew over them. Their awe turned into screams of delight as he landed on the grassy verge that surrounded the playground equipment. He watched as mothers, and a few fathers, tried to contain their children's excitement, afraid of giving offense to an archangel. Fear whispered in their eyes and he knew it would always be so. To rule, he could not appear weak.

Small hands touched his wing. He glanced down to see a tiny child with tightly curled black hair and skin that spoke of distant lands of sunshine and warmth. As he bent to lift the child in his arms, he heard a woman's cry of panic. But the child looked at him with innocent eyes. "Angel," he said.

"Yes." Raphael felt the warm beat of the boy's humanity and it gave him solace. "Where is your mother?"

The boy pointed to a terrified-looking young female. Walking across, Raphael handed over her child. "Your son has courage. He'll grow up into a strong man."

The woman's panic disappeared under a wave of burgeoning pride.

As Raphael walked through the children, several others dared pat his wings. And when their tiny, soft hands came away shimmering with angel dust, they laughed in innocent joy. Sara raised an eyebrow when he reached her. "Showing off, Archangel?" Her hands squeezed the handles of the baby carriage in which a small girl-child slept, peaceful, unaware of monsters and blood.

"Uram never walked among humans," he said instead of answering.

She began to push the carriage along a narrow path powdered with the barest layer of snow, the first caress of winter. No one interrupted them, though four intrepid children dared follow a few feet behind—until their parents called them back. In Sara's carriage, her child raised fisted hands, fighting dream battles. It was fitting, he thought. After all, Zoe Elena bore the name of a warrior.

"Did Dmitri lie?" she asked after several minutes of silence. "Is Ellie dead?"

"No," he said, "Elena lives."

Sara's hands tightened until her bones pushed white against skin the color of smooth, dark honey. "It doesn't take this long for the transition from human to vampire. Once you do whatever it is you do, most vamps are up and functioning—well, walking around at least—within a couple of months at most."

Raphael chose his words carefully. "Most vampires don't start off with broken backs."

Sara nodded jerkily. "Yeah, you're right. I'm just—I miss her, damn it!"

Zoe woke at the sound of her mother's distress, her forehead beginning to crinkle with angry lines.

"Sleep, little one," Raphael said, "sleep."

The child smiled, her lashes closing to create half-moon crescents against plump cheeks.

"What did you do?" Sara asked, shooting him a suspicious look.

Raphael shook his head. "Nothing. Children have always liked my voice." Once, at the dawn of his existence, he'd guarded the nursery, guarded their most precious treasures. Angelic births were rare, so rare. It was logical, their healers and learned ones said. A race of immortals didn't need a very high replacement rate. But being immortal didn't shield one from the need to create a child.

Sara's face softened. "I can see that. When you spoke to her . . . it was different from how you usually sound."

He shrugged, sensing the world begin to sigh with the coming of night. "Sara, Elena wouldn't want you worrying."

"Then why the hell won't she even give me a call?" Sara demanded. "We all know something's wrong! Look, if she's paralyzed"—she swallowed—"it doesn't matter to us! Tell her to stop being a prideful bitch and give me a call." A sob caught in her throat but she refused to shed it. Another warrior. Kin to his own.

"She cannot speak to you," he told her. "She sleeps."

Sara's eyes were wild with grief when she looked at him. "She's still in a coma?"

"In a sense." He stopped, held her gaze. "Trust me to care for her."

"You're an archangel," she said, as if that explained everything. "Don't you dare keep Ellie alive on machines. She'd hate that."

"Do you think I don't know that?" Stepping back, he flared out his wings. "Trust me."

The Guild Director shook her head. "Not until I see Elena with my own eyes."

"I'm sorry, Sara, but no."

"I'm her best friend, her sister in every sense of the word bar one." She reached down to tuck Zoe's blanket more firmly before turning her head. "What right do you have to keep her from me?"

"She's mine, too." He tensed his muscles in readiness for flight. "Take care of yourself and those you call your own, Director. Elena will not be happy if she wakes to find you a worn shadow of yourself."

Then he flew, and the silence was so huge, it crushed him. *Wake up, Elena.*

Still, she slept.

40

Wake up, Elena.

Elena frowned, batting away the sound. Every time she tried to sleep, he told her to wake. Dratted man. Didn't he know she needed to rest?

Elena, Sara has set her hunters on me.

As if he had anything to worry about from even the toughest vampire hunter.

She's threatening to tell the media I'm doing unnatural things with your body.

A smile in her mind, in her soul. The archangel had a sense of humor. Who knew?

Ellie?

He never called her Ellie, she thought, yawning. The first thing she saw when she blinked open her eyes was blue. Endless, fathomless, brilliant blue. Raphael's eyes. And that quickly, she remembered. The blood, the pain, the shattered bones. "Damn it, Raphael. If I have to drink blood, I'm going to suck your gorgeous body dry." Her voice was husky, her anger absolute.

The archangel smiled and it held such fierce joy that she

wanted to grab on to him and never let go. "You're very welcome to suck any part of my body you wish."

She wouldn't laugh, wouldn't surrender to the hunger she saw in those immortal eyes. "I told you I didn't want to be a vampire."

He fed her chips of ice, cooling her parched throat. "Are you not at least a little glad to be alive?"

She was a lot glad. Being with Raphael . . . oh, well, how bad could blood taste? But—"I'm not doing any vampire lackey stuff."

"Fine."

"I'm only drinking your blood."

That made his smile widen. "Fine."

"That means you're stuck with me." She jutted out her chin. "Try to throw me off for some bimbo and we'll see who's immortal."

"Fine."

"I expect—" That was when she felt the weird lumps under her back. "Whoever made this bed did a shit job. It's all lumpy."

Blue, blue eyes laughed at her. "Really?"

"Hey, it's not fun—" Her words ended on a choked breath as she turned her head and saw what she was lying on. Wings. Such beautiful wings. A rich, evocative black that swept gracefully outward in subtle increments of indigo, deepest blue, and dawn until the primaries were a vivid, shimmering white gold. Midnight wings. Incredible wings. And she was squashing them. "Oh, my God! I'm crushing an angel. Let me up!"

Raphael helped her rise when she held out her hand. The tube stuck into her arm hindered her movement. "What?"

"To keep you alive."

"How long?" she asked, shifting to look over her shoulder. His answer was lost in the rush of white noise that crashed across her brain. Because she hadn't been squashing anyone . . . but herself. "I have wings."

"A warrior's wings." He brushed his finger over one edge

and the sensation rocketed through her entire body. "Wings like blades."

"Oh," she said when she could speak again, "I guess I really am dead then." That made sense. She'd always wanted wings and now she had them. Ergo, she was dead and in heaven. She turned. "You look just like Raphael." He smelled of the sea, a clean, fresh bite that made her body sing.

He kissed her.

And he tasted far too real, far too earthy, to be a figment of her imagination. When he drew back, she was stunned to see the emotion in his eyes. It was shocking enough to make her forget the magic of the wings at her back. "Raphael?"

That blue glittered fever bright, the skin pulled taut over his cheekbones. "I'm very angry at you, Elena."

"So what else is new?" she quipped, but found herself stroking the arch of his wing.

"I am immortal and you tried to save my life by endangering your own?"

"Stupid, huh?" Leaning close, she rubbed her nose over his. Stress-touches, she thought stupidly, they were called stress-touches, the little things that lovers did to anchor each other, the things that were their secret language. Her and Raphael's language had barely begun, but it held a promise so raw, so rich, her heart twisted inside her chest, almost afraid of the fury of it. "I couldn't let you be hurt. You belong to me." Such an arrogant thing to say to an archangel.

He closed his eyes, dropping his forehead against hers. "You'll be the death of me, Elena."

She smiled. "You need a little excitement in that boring old life of yours."

Those eyes opened, blinding in their intensity. "Yes. So you will not die. I've made certain of it."

She was half convinced she'd imagined the wings, but the beautiful sweep of midnight hadn't disappeared when she checked out of the corner of her eye. "How the hell did you attach prosthetic wings to my back in the course of a . . ." She paused. "Okay, no soreness from the wounds so, what, it's been a week? No, longer." She frowned, trying to reorder splintered pieces of memory. "I had broken bones . . . my back?"

The archangel smiled again, his forehead still touching hers, his wings arching over to shadow them in their own private world. "The wings aren't prosthetic and you've been asleep for a year."

Elena swallowed. Blinked. Tried to breathe. "Angels Make vampires, not other angels."

"There is one—how would you put it—loophole."

"Loophole? More like a giant cavern if I have wings." She held on to him, the only solid thing in a shifting universe.

"No, it is the tiniest of holes, barely a pinprick. You're the first angel to have been Made in all the years of my existence."

"Lucky me," she whispered, brushing her fingers along his nape and drinking in his sigh of pleasure. This moment, it felt frozen out of time. Here, she was simply a woman, and he was simply a man. But like all moments, it had to pass. "What are the requirements?"

"Nothing we've ever been able to manipulate, though angels have tried for millennia." Those incredible, unearthly eyes held her prisoner. "The one and only time an archangel can Make another angel is when our bodies produce a substance known as ambrosia."

A snapshot of memory—the golden, melting heat of his kiss, the delicate sweetness, the lush sensuality, the taste that was an erotic sensation and whispered caress in one. "The mythical food of the gods?"

"Every myth holds a grain of truth."

She couldn't help it, she kissed him again. And the taste of him rushed over her in a tumultuous wave. He was the one who broke the kiss.

You were very badly injured, Elena.

The aches inside her were a testament to that truth. That didn't mean she had to like it. "Tell me about ambrosia then." A bad-tempered command.

"Ambrosia," he said against her mouth, "is produced instinctively at a single point in an archangel's life."

Images of his shredded wings, the living burn of angelfire. "Near death?" She touched him, checking, exploring, convincing herself he was alive.

"We've all been near death more than once." He shook his head. "No one has ever been able to pinpoint the trigger."

"But?"

"But it is legend that ambrosia only rises when—"

She held her breath.

"—an archangel loves true."

The world stopped. The air particles seemed to still above her, the molecules suspended as she stared at the magnificence of the man who held her in his arms. "Maybe I was just biologically compatible." It came out a ragged whisper.

"Perhaps." The possession of lips against her neck. "We have eternity to discover the truth. And in that eternity, you will be mine."

She thrust her hands into his hair, feeling heat spread through her body in a rolling wave. But she couldn't surrender. Not until they got one thing straight. "Fine—so long as you don't think that gives you the right to rule my life."

He came over her as she lay back down. "Why not?"

She blinked at the cool arrogance of that question, and realized that her existence had just become a whole lot more interesting. Forget about hunting an archangel, she was about to learn how to dance with one without losing herself in the process. Exhilaration spiked through her bloodstream. "This is going to be some ride, Archangel."

Epilogue

Elena had had visions of flying in through Sara's window and startling the heck out of her best friend, but that was before she realized that while she might be awake, actual movement was a whole other story. Which was why she was still in bed when a blindfolded Sara was shown into her room at the Refuge.

Raphael had moved her to the angelic stronghold soon after his own recovery, but had managed to keep her hidden. Only the Seven and trusted healing and medical personnel knew about her. However, he hadn't even tried to argue when she asked to see Sara.

Her friend folded her arms and gritted her teeth as she was led across the carpet by Dmitri, who seemed to take perverse pleasure in wrapping his scent around Elena while she was too weak to defend herself. To everyone's surprise, she'd come through the transformation with both her hunter abilities *and* weaknesses intact.

She and Raphael were continuing to "discuss" her status as Guild Hunter.

The lush caress of liquid satin across her skin, tempting

and inviting. Rubbing her arms, Elena scowled at Dmitri and was about to speak when Sara blew out a breath. "I don't know what your boss thinks he's going to achieve by abducting me. We're not going to end the strike."

Strike? That explained Raphael's cheery mood this morning. If the hunters were refusing to do their job, vampires had to be reneging on their Contracts left, right, and center. "Now my head's really swollen."

Sara froze, then scrabbled to pull off her blindfold as Dmitri slipped out of the room, closing the door behind himself—but not before encasing Elena in another decadent wave of scent. She was still getting her breath back when Sara's blindfold dropped to the floor.

Her friend's eyes went wide. Then she turned sheet white under the exotic beauty of her skin.

"Christ, Sara, don't faint!" Elena yelled, reaching out as if to catch her.

Sara braced her weight against a chair. "I'm hallucinating. Or that fish they fed me on the plane was laced with LSD."

"Sara, if you don't come and hug me, I'll shoot you." That gun Sara had put under her pillow had saved not only her own life, but Raphael's as well. "It's me, you idiot!"

Sara swallowed, then rushed to the bed. Their arms wrapped around each other so tight that breathing became optional. Elena didn't care. Blubbering, they started to talk at the same time, laughing and crying.

"Thought you were—"

"—Raphael said—"

"I said, no way in hell—"

"Damn straight—"

"—and Ransom was ready to come up—"

"—woke up and I had wings!"

They both stopped, stared at each other, giggled, then drew back.

"Holy crap, you have wings." Sara took the cup of coffee on Elena's bedside table and chugged it. "Is that what I think it is?"

Destiny's Rose glittered from its position on her bedside table. "Raphael's being stubborn."

Choking, Sara put down the empty coffee cup and thumped her fist on her chest a few times before saying, "Now, explain to me why you have wings."

"I don't know if I can. I'm learning as I go here—but what the heck is this about a strike?"

Sara grinned. "Got me here, didn't it?" Her smirk was very satisfied. "They've been keeping you from us, Ellie, telling us you were alive but nothing more. We thought you'd been paralyzed—" Her breath hitched and suddenly her hurt was a living, breathing entity between them. "Couldn't you have called me, Ellie? A *year*. Didn't you trust me?"

Elena squeezed her friend's hands. "I woke up exactly twenty-four hours ago. The first person I asked to see was you. But don't tell Ransom, or he'll get jealous."

"You were in a coma for a year?" Sara's mouth dropped open. "How come you're mobile? Are you? Your muscles—"

"Yes," she said before Sara's fears could take root all over again. "I don't know. They said something about healers and exercise but I'm sorta stuck on the wings."

Sara shook her head, reached out to touch, then snapped back her hand. "Angels don't like it when—"

Elena grabbed her friend's hand, put it on the sleek feathers that were her own. "I'm still me."

Sara's hand whispered over her wing, and though the sensation was nothing like when Raphael touched her, it *was* a kind of intimacy—the kind between friends. "Ransom still with Nyree?"

Sara nodded, laughter in her eyes as she dropped her hand back down to the sheets. "I don't think he can believe it himself. So, you have wings."

"Yes."

"Angels don't Make other angels."

"Then what am I? Chopped liver?" A disturbing tendril of thought wormed its way into her brain. She'd said she was still the same, but was she really? Could she share everything with Sara now when to do so might be to expose the secrets of an entire race? Later, she told herself, she'd think about that later. "So, do you like my wings? Aren't they the most exquisite things you've ever seen?"

Sara started laughing. "Vanity, thy name is Elena."

"Thank you very much," she said on a wave of determination. Losing Sara's friendship wasn't an option. And if she had to fight an archangel to keep it, so be it. "Now, tell me all the goss."

Outside, on the jagged rocks that guarded the Refuge, Raphael stood shoulder to shoulder with Dmitri. "A human sits in the Refuge," he said, his hair whipped back by the wind. "It breaks one of our deepest taboos."

"She has no idea of the location—you can wipe her mind to ensure she can't betray what little she does know." Practical words from the leader of his Seven.

"Yes." But he wouldn't and that was the change that was his. "Or I could trust Elena's word on Sara's sense of honor."

Dmitri nodded, and when he next spoke, his tone was quiet. "Elena will change us."

"She already has." As wild and relentless as these fierce mountain winds, his hunter would never simply accept the way of things. And for a race of immortals, that might be the rudest of awakenings. Anticipation hummed in his blood.

"Jason's returned," Dmitri said, pulling him back to the present.

"When?"

"Two days ago. Some of Lijuan's reborn managed to injure him, but he'll recover within the week."

Raphael nodded, knowing that more changes were afoot than the Making of an angel. "So it begins."

Turn the page for a sneak peak at the second novel in the Guild Hunter series, *Archangel's Kiss*

1

Elena gripped the balcony railing and stared down at the gorge that fell away with jagged promise beneath. From here, the rocks looked like sharp teeth, ready to bite and tear and rip. She tightened her hold as the icy wind threatened to tumble her into the unforgiving jaws. "A year ago," she murmured, "I didn't know the Refuge existed, and today, here I stand."

A sprawling city of marble and glass spread out in every direction; its elegant lines exquisite under the razor-sharp burn of the sun. Dark-leafed trees provided soothing patches of green on both sides of the gorge that cut a massive divide through the city, while snow-capped mountains ruled the sky-line. There were no roads, no high-rises, nothing to disturb the otherworldly grace of it.

Yet, for all its beauty, there was something alien about this place, a vague sense that darkness lurked beneath the gilded surface. Drawing in a breath laced with the biting freshness of the mountain winds, she looked up . . . at the angels. So many angels. Their wings filled the skies above this city that seemed to have grown out of the rock itself.

The angelstruck, those mortals who were literally en-thralled by the sight of angelic wings, would weep to be in this place filled with the beings they worshipped. But Elena had seen an archangel laugh as he plucked the eyes out of a vampire's skull, as he pretended to eat, then crush the pulpy mass. This, she thought with a shiver, was not her idea of heaven.

A rustle of wings from behind her, a squeeze from the powerful hands on her hips. "You're tiring, Elena. Come inside."

She held her position, though the feel of him—strong, dangerous, uncompromisingly masculine—against the sensitive surface of her wings made her want to shudder in ecstasy. "Do you think you have the right to give me orders now?"

The Archangel of New York, a creature so lethal that part of her feared him even now, lifted the hair off her nape, brushed his lips across her skin. "Of course. You are mine." No hint of humor, nothing but stark possession.

"I don't think you've quite got the hang of this true love thing." He'd fed ambrosia into her mouth, changed her from mortal to immortal, given her wings—*wings!*—all because of love. For her, a hunter, a mortal . . . no longer mortal.

"Be that as it may, it's time you return to bed."

And then she was in his arms, though she had no memory of having released the railing—but she must have, because her hands were filling with blood again, her skin tight. It hurt. Even as she tried to ride out the slow, hot burn, Raphael carried her through the sliding doors and into the magnificent glass room that sat atop a fortress of marble and quartz, as solid and immoveable as the mountains around them.

Fury arced through her bloodstream. "Out of my mind, Raphael!"

Why?

"Because, as I've told you more than once, I'm not your puppet." She grit her teeth as he laid her on the cloud-soft bedding, the pillows lush. But the mattress held firm under her palms when she pulled herself up into a sitting position.

"A lover"—God, she could still barely believe she'd gone and fallen for an archangel—"should be a partner, not a toy to manipulate."

Cobalt eyes in a face that turned humans into slaves, that sweep of night-dark hair framing a face of perfect grace . . . and more than a little cruelty. "You've been awake exactly three days after spending a year in a coma," he told her. "I've lived for more than a thousand years. You're no more my equal now than you were before I Made you immortal."

Anger was a wall of white noise in her ears. She wanted to shoot him as she'd done once before. Her mind cascaded with a waterfall of images on the heels of that thought—the wetly crimson spray of blood, a torn wing, Raphael's eyes glazed with shock. No . . . she wouldn't shoot him again, but he drove her to violence. "Then what am I?"

"Mine."

Was it wrong that sparks sizzled along her spine at hearing that, at seeing the utter possession in his voice, the dark passion on his face? Probably. But she didn't care. The only thing she cared about was the fact that she was now tied to an archangel who thought the ground rules had changed. "Yes," she agreed. "My heart is yours."

A flash of satisfaction in his eyes.

"But nothing else." She locked gazes with him, refusing to back down. "So, I'm a baby immortal. Fine—but I'm also still a hunter. One good enough that you hired me."

Annoyance replaced the passion. "You're an angel."

"With magic angel money?"

"Money is no object."

"Of course not—you're richer than Midas himself," she muttered. "But I'm not going to be your little chew-toy—"

"Chew-toy?" A gleam of amusement.

She ignored him. "Sara says I can walk back into the job anytime I want."

"Your loyalty to the angels now overwhelms your loyalty to the Hunters Guild."

"Michaela, Sara, Michaela, Sara," she murmured in a

mock-thoughtful voice. "Bitch Goddess angel versus my best friend, gee, which side do you think I'll choose?"

"It doesn't matter, does it?" He raised an eyebrow.

She had the feeling he knew something she didn't. "Why not?"

"You can't put any of your plans in action until you can fly."

That shut her up. Glaring at him, she slumped back against the pillows, her wings spread out on the sheets in a slow sweep of midnight shading to indigo and darkest blue before falling into dawn and finally, a brilliant white-gold. Her attempt at a sulk lasted approximately two seconds. Elena and sulking had never gone well together. Even Jeffrey Deveraux, who despised everything about his "abomination" of a daughter, had been unable to lay that sin at her feet.

"Then teach me," she said, straightening. "I'm ready." The ache to fly was a fist in her throat, a ravaging need in her soul.

Raphael's expression didn't change. "You can't even walk to the balcony without help. You're weaker than the fledglings."

She'd seen the smaller wings, smaller bodies, watched over by bigger ones. Not many, but enough.

"The Refuge," she asked, "is it a place of safety for your young?"

"It's everything we need it to be." Those eyes of purest sin shifted toward the door. "Dmitri comes."

She sucked in a breath as she felt the temptation of Dmitri's scent wrap around her in a glide of fur and sex and wanton indulgence. Unfortunately, she hadn't gained immunity to that particular vampiric trick with her transformation. The flip side was also true. "One thing you can't argue with—I can still track vampires by scent." And that made her hunterborn.

"You have the potential to be of real use to us, Elena."

She wondered if Raphael even knew how arrogant he sounded. She didn't think so. Being invincible for more years than she could imagine had made that arrogance part of his nature . . . But no, she thought. He could be hurt. When hell broke and an Angel of Blood tried to destroy New York, Raphael had chosen to die with Elena rather than abandon her broken body on that ledge high above Manhattan.

Her memories were cloudy, but she remembered shredded wings, a bleeding face, hands that had held her protectively as they descended to the adamantine hardness of the city streets below. Her heart clenched. "Tell me something, Raphael?"

He was already turning, heading to the door. "What is it you'd like to know, Guild Hunter?"

She hid her smile at his slip. "What do I call you? Husband? Mate? Boyfriend?"

Stopping with his hand on the doorknob, he shot her an inscrutable look. "You can call me 'Master.' "

Elena stared at the closed door, wondering if he'd been playing with her. She couldn't tell, didn't know him well enough to read his moods, his truths and lies. They'd come together in an agony of pain and fear, pushed by the specter of death into a union that might have been years in the making had Uram not decided to turn bloodborn and tear a murderous path through the world.

Raphael had told her that according to legend, only true love allowed ambrosia to bloom on an archangel's tongue, to turn human to angel, but perhaps her metamorphosis owed nothing to the deepest of emotions and everything to a very rare biological symbiosis? After all, vampires were Made by angels, and biological compatibility played an integral part in that transformation.

"Damn it." She rubbed the heel of one hand over her heart, trying to wipe away the sudden twist of pain.

"You intrigue me."

He'd said that at the start. So perhaps, there was a component of fascination. "Be honest, Elena," she whispered, running her fingers over the magnificent wings that were his gift to her, "you're the one who fell into fascination."

But she would not fall into slavery.

"Master, my ass." She stared at the foreign sky outside the balcony doors and felt her resolve turn iron-hard—no more waiting. Unlike if she'd still been human, the coma hadn't wasted away her muscles. But those muscles had gone through a transformation she couldn't imagine—everything felt weak, new. So while she didn't need rehab, she did need exercise. Especially when it came to her wings. "No time like the present." Lifting herself up into a proper sitting position, she took a deep, calming breath . . . and spread out her wings.

"Christ, that hurts!" Teeth gritted, tears leaking out of the corners of her eyes, she kept stretching the unused, unfamiliar muscles, folding her new-formed wings in slowly before expanding them outward. Three repetitions later and the tears had soaked into her lips until the salt of them was all she could taste, her skin covered by a layer of perspiration that shimmered in the sunlight streaming in through the glass.

That was when Raphael walked back in. She expected an explosion, but he just took a seat in a chair opposite the bed, his eyes never leaving her. As she watched, wary, he hooked one ankle over a knee, and began to tap a heavy white envelope bordered with gilt against the top of his boot.

She held his gaze, did another two stretches. Her back felt like jelly, her stomach muscles so tight they hurt. "What's"—a pause to draw breath—"in the envelope?"

Her wings snapped shut behind her, and she found herself leaning against the headboard. It took her several seconds to realize what he'd done. Something cold unfurled within the core of her soul even as he got up and dropped a towel on the bed, then retook his seat. No fucking way was this going to keep happening.

However, in spite of the turbulent fury of her anger, she wiped off her face and kept her mouth shut. Because he was right—she wasn't his equal, not by a long shot. And the coma had messed her up some. But as of now, she was going to work on those shields she'd started to develop back before becoming an angel. There was a chance that—given the changes in her—she could learn to hold them for longer.

Forcing her rigid shoulder muscles to loosen, she picked up a knife she'd left on the bedside table and began to clean the pristine blade with the edge of the towel. "Feeling better?"

"No." His mouth firmed. "You need to listen to me, Elena. I won't hurt you, but I can't have you acting in ways that bring my control over you in question."

What? "Exactly what kind of relationships do archangels have?" she asked, genuinely curious.

That made him pause for a minute. "I know of only one stable relationship now that Michaela and Uram's is broken."

"And the Bitch Goddess is another archangel, so they *were* equals."

A nod of his head that was more thought than movement. He was so damn beautiful that it made thinking difficult, even when she knew he possessed a vein of ruthlessness that was sewn into the fabric of his very soul. That ruthlessness translated into a furious kind of control in bed, the kind that made a woman scream, her skin too tight across a body that knew only hunger.

"Who are the other two?" she asked, swallowing the spike of gut-deep need. He'd held her since she woke, his embrace strong, powerful, and at times, heartbreakingly tender. But today, her body craved a far darker touch.

"Elijah and Hannah." His eyes glittered, turning to a shade she'd once seen in an artist's studio. *Prussian.* That's what it was called, Prussian blue. Rich. Exotic. Earthy in a way she'd never have believed an angel to be until she found herself taken by the Archangel of New York.

"You will heal, Elena. Then I will teach you how angels dance."

Her mouth dried up at the slumbering heat in that outwardly calm statement. "Elijah?" she prompted, her voice husky, an invitation.

He continued to hold her gaze, his lips at once sensual and without pity. "He and Hannah have been together centuries. Though she's grown in power over time, it is said that she's content to be his helpmeet."

She had to think for a while about that old-fashioned expression. "The wind beneath his wings?"

"If you like." His face was suddenly all hard lines and angles—male beauty in its purest, most merciless form. "You will not fade."

She didn't know if that was an accusation or an order. "No, I won't." Even as she spoke, she was vividly conscious that she'd have to use every ounce of her will to maintain her personality against the incredible strength of Raphael's.

He began tapping that envelope again, the action precise, deliberate. "As of today, you're on a deadline. You need to be on your feet and in the air in just over two months' time."

"Why?" she asked, even as delight bubbled through her bloodstream.

Prussian blue froze into black ice. "Lijuan is giving a ball in your honor."

"We're talking about Zhou Lijuan, the oldest of the archangels?" The bubbles went flat, lifeless. "She's . . . different."

"Yes. She has evolved." A hint of midnight whispered through his tone; shadows so thick they were almost corporeal. "She's no longer wholly of this world."

Her skin prickled, because for an immortal to say that . . . "Why would she hold a ball for me? She doesn't know me from Adam."

"On the contrary, Elena. The entire Cadre of Ten knows who you are—we hired you after all."

The idea of the most powerful body in the world being interested in her made her break out in a cold sweat. It didn't help that Raphael was one of them. She knew what he was capable of, the power he wielded, how easy it would be for him to cross the line into true evil. "Only nine now," she said. "Uram's dead. Unless you found a replacement while I was in a coma?"

"No. Human time means little to us." The casual indifference of an immortal. "As for Lijuan, it's about power—she wants to see my little pet, see my weakness."

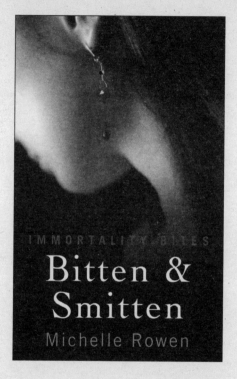